We Never Took a Bad Picture

by Ashley N. Roth

APRIL GLOAMING

-First Edition

Publisher's Cataloguing-in-Publication Data

Roth, Ashley N
We never took a bad picture / written by Ashley N. Roth / designed by Theo Hall
ISBN:978-1-953932-33-4

1. Fiction - General 2. Fiction - Literary 3. Fiction - Family Life: Marriage & Divorce I. Title II. Author

Library of Congress Control Number: 2025930482

"Sweeping elegantly through decades of American life while bursting with intimate, visceral close-ups, *We Never Took a Bad Picture* lays bare one struggling family's heartaches and betrayals, their moments of joy and forgiveness and acceptance, as they attempt to hold on—to make it last in spite of it all. I won't forget Gloria, Artie, or anyone else in this absorbing tale. It belongs on your shelf of Great American Novels."

–Susannah Felts, writer and founder of The Porch

"In *We Never Took a Bad Picture*, Ashley N. Roth has written a beautifully complicated story. But it's a complicated story we all know from our own lives. From the most picture-frame worthy family to those on the obvious brink, all families have a past that can't be forgotten, and there's nothing like living so many years together with unresolved trauma to change the fire of love into the grind of work. Roth's lyricism gives our lives the heft and present-ness it deserves. On a literal level, how Roth organizes her book proves time really is the revelator. We see the beginnings and endings almost simultaneously: nothing is lost over the churn of years. Most important, though, is we also see those glimmering instances that make the day worth it—those true moments of bliss. Those are what we live for, no matter how quickly they might come and go. This book makes that point so apparent. It's a message of love."

–Chet Weise, writer, musician, editor at Third Man Books

As promised, for Pandora.

Part 1

Chapter 1

January 2018

Gloria held her breath, waiting for her husband of nearly fifty-five years to notice silver was the wrong color.

She'd fanned paper samples over the polished wood of their dining table, placing her two favorite shades—Twinkling Thunder and Shimmering Storm—front and center, while the printed pricing options hung off-stage to the right. Artie was at the head of the table, where he only sat for special occasions.

"Which one should we use?" she asked him for the second time.

Artie, sitting with pristine posture, scratched his head as if making an actual decision.

"They all look great. Do you have a favorite?"

Gloria allowed the tiniest bit of air to leak from her mouth.

"I like these." She pointed to the piece of glossy cardstock that convinced her a silver party was a good idea. The paper was the exact shade of the Tin Man's tear-soaked cheek right before he rusted himself stiff.

"Looks good to me." Artie's own trapped breath whooshed out. He hated making decisions.

"Wouldn't it be fun to have a theme for the party? Maybe something like halfway to diamond? These silvers are sort of diamondesque, right?"

Now she was poking the bear. She'd gotten away with the silver palette, but Gloria just had to know if he was that dense, that skilled at blissful ignorance, or simply lying to her face. Gloria sat in the chair to his right.

"Diamond?" Artie asked.

"It's technically too late for gold."

"Oh, yes, the anniversary party."

Gloria's suspicions rose. What on earth did he think these pieces of paper were for? It had been almost six years since he'd agreed to a Golden Anniversary party. She'd stalled, but he never asked why. He wouldn't understand if she told him the truth: gold made her gag. When she brought up the party again last year, he had agreed with a simple nod.

They both knew the significance of silver, the color forever chained to their twenty-fifth anniversary. They both knew what happened that year; they'd tried so hard to forget it.

"Do you like that idea? Halfway to diamond? Or does it automatically fast forward us into being that much older?" Gloria tried to smile, placing two manicured nails on a pair of paper squares. "I like this one for the invitations and this color for the envelopes," she said.

Artie nodded. "Looks great. You know I'm not good for this kind of stuff." His eyes drifted up and met hers. Those eyes were the one thing that hadn't changed in all these years. Such a dark blue they were almost black. The skin around them sagged a little more, changing what had once been sleepy eyes to officially droopy—but they were still the eyes she had fallen in love with over a half a century ago. Only, locking eyes with him now, she didn't feel butterflies. She didn't even feel the tepid comfort they'd secured after a sprawling tapestry of highs and lows. Instead, Gloria's stomach thrashed with the quivering anxieties that should have dissolved ages ago. That's what forever did, right?

"What about this?" Gloria scooted the pricing list in front of him. This was where her husband shone. Facts and figures and making smart financial decisions. This is where he could display some electricity to prove he was still alive.

"How many people are you planning to invite?" His voice finally squeaked with panic. He hated big performances.

"Fifty? A hundred? I want to make it worth it."

Artie slouched slightly.

"That's fine," he said, returning to his monotony. Maybe he had perfected willful stupidity.

Gloria cleared the table, throwing away the samples they no longer needed and sticking a pink Post-It to the top of the ones she'd chosen, stacking them on the kitchen counter beside the Keurig pot. She'd go back to the shop tomorrow, and she and the cashier would pretend Gloria wasn't the strange customer who wandered in every January, pretending not to know what she wanted. She would feign her own naiveté when she imagined a full themed event with the music and clothing and decorations of 1988. She would never actually go that far, but Gloria couldn't help but wonder how Artie would behave if she did, if he would finally wake up.

Gloria took a deep breath. Artie still sat at the dining room table, his arms on the cleared space in front of him. From a normal, sane perspective she didn't *really* want to see what would happen if he shuddered back to life. She hadn't forgotten what it was like before, and she knew she walked on a dormant volcano daily. She wouldn't feed the fire under any normal circumstance, but lately, every time she shut her eyes and thought about her son, he appeared in a more and more gossamer fashion, and sometimes she wasn't sure her fading memory added parts to Teddy that were never there.

"Artie?" Gloria spun around from the kitchen, her right hand still flat over the stack of tiny papers.

Artie looked up.

"What if we called the party Silver Plus Thirty? Instead of Halfway to Diamond?"

Gloria wasn't sure she imagined the darkness clouding his eyes, or if she only wanted something to storm his vacant stare. He coughed slightly, cleared his throat, and said in the same mastered tone, "Let's just go with your first choice. Diamonds sound more like marriage than boring old silver."

Gloria pressed harder into the stack of papers, smashing them into a single brick. She smiled at Artie.

"Denise and Bill are moving back just in time. We couldn't have the party without them."

From the counter, Gloria noticed her husband's shoulders tense.

"Aren't you glad they're coming back? It's been too long," Gloria said.

"I didn't know they were," Artie responded, staring at the empty table.

Funny. Denise had called two days ago, confirming the closing of their new Malibu mansion. In that same conversation, she apologized for telling Artie the news first, when she'd spoken to him a few days prior.

"He didn't tell you?" her best friend had asked.

"You didn't know." Gloria echoed her husband. Artie's neck twitched. She didn't have the energy to dissect his strange behaviors.

"Where do you want to eat for dinner?" Gloria asked instead.

Artie cleared his throat, looking up. It was Sunday. They always ate at the same place on Sundays.

Artie had a love-hate relationship with his workplace traditions. He loved pushing through the automatic doors before the store was open, knowing the exact moment there would be a burst of fake rain showering the produce wet wall. He loved the recorded thunder that played right before the spouts exploded over the romaine, kale, and two types of parsley. Artie appreciated his own attention to detail, the way he rotated the apples so their best sides faced the customers, and the way he arranged the bananas in a visual representation of the ripening process, from bright green to bruised soft black. He enjoyed wiping the damp plastic packages of cut fruit. There was comfort in the smiles of familiar cashiers and even in the quivering of new hires who so desperately wanted to make the best impression. Artie eagerly listened for the symphony of registers beeping after the store was officially open. He strained his ears until they rang, searching for the chorus of genuine *hellos* and *have a good days* singing through the aisles. Artie never tired of hearing a case of paper bags hitting the waxed LVT floor with a muffled thud.

That wasn't entirely true. Even Artie had the occasional bad day where he didn't welcome the sounds and interactions of his daily life. Sometimes, he was simply tired of them. On the bleakest and rarest of days, he hated the mechanical repetition, the carousel of every day being the same.

But he always *needed* the routine, the sameness, even on those days.

Artie thrived inside his grocery castle, marching toward his quiet office space housed behind the dairy cooler and the receiving area, weaving between the gruff talk of back-stock workers, the smell of rotting spoilage, advancing with authority toward the temp and inventory logs his employees were always scrambling to fill out before the health department made their unannounced visits. Artie's mere footsteps sent employees scurrying to find a working pen, rushing to calibrate broken thermometers. That's when he came alive.

At Allen's Market, Artie was the go-to man, the father with all the answers. Every question, every concern, every decision needed his attention. He was the final word. He reigned here, where everything happened exactly as and when it should. Everything was mapped out quarterly, yearly, weekly. Exactly as it was supposed to be. The repetition, the routine—it meant he was doing everything right. It meant he was succeeding.

It also meant Joan Allen continued to do everything right.

She walked into his office on the first work date of the new year with a stack of projections pretending to talk business. This was her routine, as was her spiked coffee and deep conversations disguised as casual office chitchat. If she didn't come in prying and cloaking her whiskey-breath with chewed-up breath mints, Artie might believe the back-stock gossip of Joan coming down with old lady senility.

Joan was the biggest comfort inside Allen's. She still wore outdated suits and shoulder pads. She still soaked her chest with stale Chanel. She still got her hair set at the beauty parlor and asked the stylists for the same unflattering shade of muted auburn. Allen's had evolved and warped under the advances of technology and food trends, but Joan remained a relic, preserved in a time Artie never allowed himself to admit he missed.

"Some things never change." Joan fanned herself with the stack of crisp papers. Her voice was graveled from smoking, even years after she swore she quit.

"Like us." Artie raised his sober cup of coffee to her barbed French Roast.

"I feel like we've changed a lot, Artie." Joan slapped the papers on Artie's desk and sighed. "How can we not when everything around here is in a constant state of makeover. You know there's another reset next week? You know what's worse? It was my idea."

Artie tried to smile. One thing that didn't fit into his routine was Joan's sudden disgust for the very company she had nurtured all the way from handwritten sale signs and wooden barrels filled with bouquets of pantry staples. The new Joan was a bitter pessimist who suddenly sighed a lot. Inside the office, she occasionally embraced the old smiling self who made swift and practical business decisions and praised a collective company effort. But, out there on the sales floor among the squeaky shopping carts and overflowing bulk bins, she sought out the ugliest blemishes. Reasons for why the profit-margin was shriveling. Reasons to justify another sliced labor budget. The old Joan loved challenges and knocking down barriers. This Joan was tired of trying new ways to spruce up a store that people only shopped at now because of dutiful nostalgia. They could go to Ralph's for better prices, Whole Foods for a wider vegan selection, Bristol Farms for some overpriced truffle spread. Their customer base was loyal, but they were literally dying and leaving behind descendants who either weren't raised in the glory days of Allen's Market, or who barely remembered the store that gave every kid a new balloon, a lollipop, and a sticker of a smiling squirrel.

Joan looked at him like she knew what he was thinking, and she probably did. He hoped she didn't hear his brain ponder the sag of her face, wondering whether it was age or simply a heavier pour into her morning cup.

"Is Gloria still insisting you retire?" Joan asked, sucking in her coffee with short, quick sips.

Artie choked on his next sip of tepid, weak coffee. Joan's sharp observations never faltered.

"I'll take that as she is, and you're still pretending to go along with it."

Again, that acute sense.

Just that morning, Gloria had reminded him to talk to Joan and check up on his retirement plan, so Gloria could calculate and budget their next phase of life. He'd promised he would talk to her. Luckily, Joan ensured he kept that promise.

"She does want me to retire."

"What about you? What do you want?"

Artie didn't know how to properly articulate the qualities that tethered him to Allen's. At the grocery store with its merchandising and inventory and COGs and old-fashioned customer service, he reigned king. There was always something to do, always someone who wanted his expertise—employees *and* customers. Even as systems and procedures changed, woven into fancier computers with more intricate algorithms, Allen's allowed him to evolve slowly. Even as the world of food became more convoluted than technology, Allen's staff and customers celebrated him and his stacked layers of expertise—Artie was the aficionado of everything from industry to menu ideas.

Home was different. Sure, he enjoyed filling out Sudoku and reading stacks of murder mysteries and true crime. He liked watching movies and finding favorite shows he could stream in one gulp. But an electrical silence hummed at home, and it was the antithesis to the sycophantic purr of Allen's. At home, the roaring quiet hummed in the kitchen, in the sound current beneath the loud bathroom vent; it hummed in the new plumbing. It only abated during family gatherings, drowned out by boisterous conversation and laughter. It howled louder after everyone had gone home. He tried to drown it out with the TV. He tried having regular conversations with his wife. Nothing worked. Artie heard the silence growling at night; he felt it shiver while he slept.

The hum was old news. The only difference was he no longer could muffle it with children or booze or arguments. In the quiet, sober house, it was loud and insistent, like a neglected ping in a car threatening to leave you stranded on the darkest highway with no signal or call box.

Artie couldn't tell Joan all that, though, and he silently pleaded for her to shut off her natural clairvoyance.

"I like working," he told her. She balanced an empty cup between her nylon knees and smiled with her lips sealed shut. "I like having purpose. I like routine."

Joan stood up, smoothed her skirt, and gave a quick chuckle.

"You can't fool everyone, Artie, pretending to be an everyday workaholic."

She closed the door before he could attempt to decipher her statement.

He plugged in the week's projections, planned for higher comps, and approved the latest "Go Local" marketing plan. He needed Allen's, and Allen's needed him.

⌒⌒⃰⌒⌒

Artie ate reheated canned clam chowder for dinner alone. Gloria wiped around the stove's burners with a fresh Magic Eraser.

"Did you ask Joan?" she asked without looking at him. She rinsed out her Nutrisystem box in the sink before stuffing it into the trash compactor, her finger hovering over the on switch, waiting for him to respond.

"It was too busy today. I'll ask tomorrow," he lied.

Gloria scrubbed harder.

"What about the party?" Artie asked, hoping he sounded excited. "Any word from that meeting space they used for the high school reunion?"

Gloria sat across from him, holding a glass filled with water and a dissolving pink powder.

"It's available." She took a long sip and grimaced.

"Let's talk about that instead."

He wiped his mouth and listened to her decorative and social plans thread together into a single note while he thought about the big produce order that would be arriving around four in the morning. He nodded when she paused and smiled when she looked at him with an expression he could paint in his sleep.

"Can you believe it'll only be a week before Denise and Bill are back?" Gloria stared past him, holding her drained diet drink. Artie turned his attention to the texture of the wall.

It was a funny sensation having someone recognize all the thoughts you weren't supposed to have. He had fifty-five years of wedded bliss to thank for that. Even funnier, after fifty-five years, she still maintained her poker face, pretending she couldn't scoop them right from his head.

Make-believe was the secret to marital immortality. He should know—the Joyces had perfected pretending.

Chapter 2

1958

Denise burst from her narrow closet, transformed. Gloria clapped and cheered. Her best friend had captured Marilyn's strut and stolen Jayne's voluptuous pout. Denise's golden hair cascaded over one eye in rippling waves. She gripped both hips, holding her skirt in place, although the back was clipped with a clothespin.

"How do I look?" Denise twirled over the smooth yellow carpet.

"Like a movie star," Gloria said, trying not to slouch.

Denise ignored the compliment, sighing as she leaned against her open window. Dust danced around her like snowflakes, the sun a celestial glow venerating Denise into a pin-up saint.

"Now, it's your turn." Denise pointed at Gloria, shimmying her hips.

"I don't know. I won't look like you."

Denise laughed, tilting her head back to reveal a perfect Grace Kelly jawline. From the chipped painted ledge of the windowsill, Denise picked up a pack of pastel cigarettes. She lit the cigarette like Lauren Bacall, blowing tiny smoke rings.

"You aren't supposed to look like me, silly. You're supposed to look like *them!*" Denise smashed her unfinished cigarette into the windowsill, singing the furled edges of peeling white paint. She fell to the ground, digging into her pile of strewn laundry. Tossing aside nude pantyhose and wadded skirts, she unearthed a stack of crinkled movie magazines. Denise held one up, its pages read and reread so much they'd turned transparent.

Gloria had discovered her future best friend in Mrs. Walters' 6th grade classroom, her desk scooted to the outskirts of the seating arrangement. The kids talked to everyone but Denise, and Gloria knew it was because they didn't know how to talk to someone who was going to be *someone*. Denise knew it, too. Unfortunately, for Denise's starstruck dreams, she wasn't about to be found in the bleached center of nowhere: Lakewood, California. It wasn't a beach city. It wasn't Hollywood. It was crisp sidewalks and identical box houses. It was a big neighborhood park with a bunch of dead grass overrun with lizards. It was only home to the Lakewood Mall, where not a single talent scout went to go shopping. Gloria couldn't wait until they were old enough to ride the bus—or even cars—to more exciting places. She knew her best friend would take her along the ride to fame.

"Look!" Denise jabbed her finger into the faces of Jane Russell, Diana Dors, and Elizabeth Taylor. Denise's bright blue eyes danced over Gloria's brown hair, brown eyes, skin that turned brown if she got too much sun.

"This is who you are going to look like."

Denise's delicate finger grazed over Sophia Loren's perfect olive neck like a gun holding the actress hostage. Her fingernail slid over Sophia's raised, arched eyebrows and faint cleft in her chin, over the cat-like eyes and curled lips.

"You are going to be her." Denise closed her eyes and pinched her fingers into lobster claws, like the seance they'd seen on *I Love Lucy*. Gloria held her breath, while Denise opened her eyes and dunked her fingers into thick pancake makeup and rosy cream bliss. She plucked open a plastic tube of lipstick, gliding a deep red over Gloria's parted lips. Gloria sucked in the saliva that threatened to dribble out. Denise slid a pencil over Gloria's dark, thick eyebrows.

"We can't create an arch like this," Denise murmured, chewing the sides of her own starlet red lips. From the makeup arsenal, she produced a shiny pair of metal tweezers. With scientific precision, Denise yanked out rows of tiny hairs, their black roots popping from hot, red skin. Gloria stayed still, allowing the heated pain to smolder out. It reminded her of her mom slapping her across the face, her fingers covered in gaudy costume rings that felt like brass knuckles on the side of Gloria's cheeks. Gloria's cheek stung for hours, and she had traced the soft pink welt for over a week. She would purposely douse it in rubbing alcohol, enjoying how the cool sizzled beneath her skin.

"You really took that like a champ," Denise said. "I bawled like a big baby the first time Mom plucked me."

Gloria was disappointed the pain faded so quickly.

Denise dusted her with more powders and spritzed her neck with Chanel perfume. She shoved a pink cashmere sweater and white miniskirt into Gloria's hands, helping her wiggle from the mangy things she'd come over in.

"Go look." Denise nudged Gloria to the mirror, her hands over her eyes even though Gloria squeezed them shut. The hands flapped from her eyes like fluttering wings.

Gloria didn't recognize herself. Her cheekbones had been chiseled with layers of plum and bronze blush. Her lips had a shape. Denise had padded both their bras and hips with the stuffing her mother used for quilting. Gloria had never had a shape before. Her legs had never glistened like they did in the perfect tan panty hose from Sears.

But the most stunning transformation was her hair. Normally, it hung from her head like limp molasses. Now, it was full and buoyant, frozen stiff with hairspray. In the shifting sunlight, it shimmered shades of honey and chestnut.

"Teach me how to do that," Gloria whispered, her mouth hanging open.

"It's so easy!" Denise flipped her head upside down and pulled up swaths of her own blonde hair, digging into each tail backward with a white plastic comb. She sprayed the tangled mess with enough hairspray to make them both cough before smoothing the whole head of hair like she was calming a large dog. Afterward, her hair was big, round, and as perfectly tousled as Ann Margaret's. Gloria memorized each step: brush backward, spray until you cough, brush, and smooth, and spray some more.

Wearing their new looks, they splayed across Denise's bed and practiced kissing on their arm, reapplying their lipstick after each imaginary necking. Denise confessed she'd kissed a couple of the boys at school but only with quick and closed lips.

"I didn't want to look like I didn't know what I was doing," she said before tickling her arm with her tongue and instructing Gloria to do the same. "We have to be prepared for high school. We have to know how to kiss boys."

Denise always had it mapped out. Gloria was the complete opposite. She never knew what she should do next—especially when it came to boys. It was easy for Denise. She was beautiful, while Gloria had to force her chin out to create a jawline line and be conscious to hide her buck teeth behind her big lips. Denise already bled once a month. Gloria's puberty arrived by sprouting dark hairs along her lip. Gloria's mother said it was the Italian in her that made her hairy, so Gloria couldn't hate it. Those dark hairs were all she had of the father she'd only met once.

Denise was oblivious to their differences. Since their friendship began, she lumped them together as one. The daughters of a legendary war, she liked to say. They were baby boomers, children of the celebrated soldiers who fought the nation's most celebrated war. Their fathers had seen men shredded by shrapnel, had watched historic stone crumble under a blaring ambush. Their fathers witnessed men choke on mustard gas, turned away as their comrades' legs dissolved under gangrene. Denise was obsessed with the heroism of soldier fathers, always including Gloria's ghost father when she praised her own. Gloria didn't know how to interrupt Denise's diatribe with the actual truth—what was the point? They both knew the facts. Denise's dad came out and wiped his personal massacre clean, spreading a white picket fence and manicured lawns over the ugly memories. He bought a three-bedroom yellow house that came with lemon and avocado trees on a street where matching houses with matching trees were bought with the same government money. Gloria's father never bought one of those houses. He couldn't shake the memories, the accusations of loving Mussolini, the echo of the word Wop. There wasn't enough drink on American soil to erase the bad dreams—and, still, Gloria's mother outdrank him every night. She probably still did. Who knows why her father had to run off to some rural unknown to find himself in the glorified frontier while her mother worked doubles at the diner to pay for his absence? Gloria never outwardly asked these things. She let her friend ramble on about how great all the men of the era were, the fathers who fought for their country. Just like she let her ramble on now, demonstrating on her own arm what the perfect kiss should look like.

"Now, you," Denise said. Gloria wiggled her tongue over the hair on her arms and tried not to laugh.

Denise's mom broke into their lesson by announcing a lunch of tuna melt sandwiches and salty chips that burned the lips made raw from all the imaginary kisses. She poured sun tea into beveled highball glasses, pouring something slightly different into her own.

"Don't forget to wash your own plates," Mrs. Duffy said, walking out the screen to their backyard where she sat on a yellow folding chair, drinking her mystery drink and smoking three cigarettes in a row. Gloria had been enamored with Denise's mother almost as quickly as she'd been with her friend. Mr. Duffy was fine; he just wasn't as exciting. He built the cabinets, changed the lightbulbs, mowed the grass, and made the garage smell like tobacco, beer, and mechanical grease. Mrs. Duffy smelled like bouquets of flowers and cookies. Her cheeks were silky, her arms, too—Gloria lived for those hugs hello and goodbye. She always had a rainbow of fruit arranged in a wicker basket on the dining table. Her bananas never browned. Mrs. Duffy had three rotating aprons: a gossamer-like yellow one embroidered with ducks, a scalloped white one that hit her knees, and the red and white gingham one that was Gloria's absolute favorite. The white squares were stained with all the sauces, glazes, batters, and roux she had prepared on the turquoise countertops surrounded by vegetable-themed wallpaper, inside her perfect house on the quiet circular street.

From the kitchen counter, the girls watched Mrs. Duffy finish her drink and light another cigarette. They scarfed their lunch and guzzled their tea, refilling each of their glasses twice. They rinsed off the smears of mayonnaise and tiny flakes of toasted crust. Gloria knew the drill. There was no sense in fully washing them because Mrs. Duffy always trailed behind them with three cycles of rinse, wash, repeat. Gloria's mother let their sink overflow. She never wore aprons.

Gloria and Denise spent the rest of the afternoon imitating the Big Bopper and planning their future weddings. They wrinkled their skirts while reading magazines to learn more about dating and etiquette, taking quizzes to find out if they would make good wives. Gloria scored higher. Their hair fell flat. The winged edges of their eyeliner smudged. Denise had to know—who did Gloria have a bigger crush on, Elvis Presley or Ricky Nelson? She displayed both choices as vinyl sleeve perched on her shoulders. Gloria honestly didn't care about either one. She was a Frank Sinatra girl, but given these two choices, she went with the boy in the yellow sweater who had a shy smile and some amount of vulnerability. Not like Elvis, who looked like he expected everyone to pick him.

"Ricky," Gloria sang, sticking it to that cocky boy who thought he had every girl wrapped around his finger. Gloria danced over to Denise, plucking out the record and sticking it on the portable Dansette, digging the needle into the third groove for "Be-Bop Baby." The teenagers twirled around the room, further rumpling their starlet attire and ruining more of their makeup.

"I'm glad you'd choose Ricky!" Denise shouted over Ricky's dainty crooning. "Because then we wouldn't fight! I would marry Elvis! You would be my maid of honor!"

The record stopped. Denise smiled.

"You want to know something else?"

Gloria nodded.

"I wouldn't even wait until the wedding night to do you know what." Denise spun around, maybe ashamed of her honesty after reading all about how to be a good girl in the magazines. Gloria was glad she was turned around, so her friend couldn't see her blush.

"Do you want to stay for dinner?" Denise asked, still facing the other way. Gloria did want to stay. She could smell garlic and butter and had noticed the colander on the counter, but she also had an urge to walk outside in her outfit while there was still daylight. It was disheveled but still better than anything she had ever worn before.

"I think I should go home tonight. Can I give you these clothes tomorrow?"

Denise spun around, smirking, like she knew all of Gloria's silly impulses.

"Of course. Just bring them to school tomorrow."

Gloria strutted down the stairs, only slouching a little when she passed Mrs. Duffy in the kitchen.

"You aren't staying?" Mrs. Duffy's voice was almost syrupy, always inviting.

"I don't think I should. I've had the last four dinners here. I should probably see what my mother is up to."

Mrs. Duffy's smile was tight, close-lipped.

"Yes, I suppose you should. Do you want me to send you with some of our leftovers from last night?"

Gloria didn't have time to produce phony uncertainty before Mrs. Duffy thrust the green Tupperware containers into her hands.

"It's just a noodle casserole. Nothing too fancy."

"Thank you, Mrs. Duffy," Gloria carried the smooth plastic containers like they were frail fossils of a creature not yet discovered. Mrs. Duffy closed the door behind her, and Gloria took quivering steps over each garden stone. She held her breath. Maybe that was why she heard the noise.

It was a thick, grating whimpering. Gloria set the Tupperware stack on the damp dirt beneath a thorny bush pimpled with tart berries, kneeling beside the plastic tower to see if she could get a look at what was making the awful sound. It was a boy wearing a white t-shirt with topographic sweat stains. Dangling out of one of the shirt's rolled sleeves was a scrawny arm that ended with a fist slamming into the brick side of Denise's neighboring house over and over again. Blood ran from his knuckles and down his arms like freeway lines. Gloria still held her breath. The boy continued to pound into the stoic brick, into the powdery mortar that held it in place. She leaned forward, as if she would find a reason for why he was doing this, and a twig snapped beneath her knee, snagging Denise's nylons. A tiny, stitched ladder crawled up her thigh. Denise was going to kill her.

The boy turned around, his face round and doughy and splotchy. Searing sunlight shone over his scattered freckles, the raw patches of acne, the glistening snot sliding down his lip. He narrowed his eyes and twisted his lips into a limp snarl. Gloria almost laughed. He was completely harmless.

"Who's watching me?" he shouted in several directions, his swollen, bloodied fist shaking at the air. He stalked the yard, stomping with extra force in the sludgy, muddy puddle where an unraveled garden hose lay like an innocuous sunbathing snake.

"You better come out!" the boy screamed, his voice shaking between a struggling baritone and the squeal of a rabbit caught by a tomcat. Gloria wove her fingers into the bushes, thorns piercing the soft underbelly of each finger. She bit the insides of her cheeks until she tasted wet metal. Her eyes closed for only a second, but when she opened them, the boy was gone. Before Gloria could even scan the yard for him, a sharp finger poked the lower slope of her cashmere back.

"What are you doing here?" he growled. Gloria unraveled her fingers from the bush's prickly branches and slowly stood up. When she turned around and faced the boy, she stood at least an inch taller than him.

"Why were you watching me?"

Gloria's throat tightened. The boy's hair was thick and dark, the rose tangerine sunset turned it a smoldering purple.

"I—I was just leaving my friend's house, and I heard a noise," Gloria stammered.

His eyes were dark blue with tiny green specks.

"Who? Her?" He pointed to Denise's house. Gloria nodded, smoothing the sides of her tight skirt. It felt like a whole year ago she and Denise had twirled around her room pretending to be Sweater Girls.

"Why were you punching that wall?" Gloria asked so quietly, she wasn't sure the words had come from her own mouth.

The boy's face went slack, vulnerable, before he balled his hands back up and sneered at the brick house, which now had a pie cooling on its open windowsill.

"I was pissed off at my old man. Well, at her, too." He gritted his teeth.

"Her? Your mother?"

"Yeah. She should know better by now than to try and talk smart to him when he's been drinking. She should know not to bring up all these things that set him off. At least wait until the next day, when all he's got is coffee and some breakfast in him."

Gloria nodded, her hand finding his arm and staying there.

"I understand," she said.

"She should know I can't just stand by and let him start swinging at her." Tears bubbled in the corners of his eyes.

"She should know that he'll take it out worse on me."

Gloria examined his face. The violet smearing under his eye socket, the skin beginning to swell around the tiny cuts on his cheek. His bottom lip jutted out, opalescent, and caked with thick, dried blood.

"She's stupid," he continued. His voice deepened and turned to gravel. "She just needs to wait for him to sober up. Is it that hard to wait until the morning?" He squatted down and began pummeling into the sidewalk beside them. The impact was soft, like the sound of jelly. His knuckles oozed gelatinous gore. He gave his arms a good shake and stood back up.

"I don't even know your name," he said quietly.

"It's Gloria."

"Gloria what?"

"Gloria Accetta. I mean, Gloria Evans."

"Well, which is it?"

"It was Gloria Accetta my whole life. But I've been Gloria Evans for a few years, so I guess I don't really know."

The boy laughed.

"You look a little young to have already gotten hitched."

"My mother just thought I shouldn't have my father's name anymore."

"Is he dead?"

"No, he's just gone."

The boy swelled his chest and made some awkward expression that Gloria knew was a pale imitation of someone like James Dean or Marlon Brando. He lifted a hand to her face, his fingers still damp with fresh blood.

"Can I kiss you?"

Gloria said yes, her eyes on the grass. She dissected each clump of clover, each bent dandelion stem. She traced the milky insides as it drizzled down the hollow stalk to the gummy dirt they both stood on.

He kissed better than her arm. Gloria tried to follow his lead. Salty sweat and mucus dribbled inside their lips. Tacky blood stuck to her chin. When he pulled away from her, he looked older. Not quite Rock Hudson but maybe heading in that direction.

"You have a boyfriend?"

"I don't think I'd be here if I did."

"So, you don't?"

"No, I don't."

"You want to be mine?"

"Your what?"

"My girlfriend. Go steady, you know?"

"Okay."

He kissed her again before she guided him to the bushes and to her Tupperware stash. Together, they dug their dirty fingers into the cold, wet noodles guiding the wiggling pieces into their open mouths. Gloria tried to remember to be ladylike and wipe her mouth after a few bites. He chewed with his mouth open, the cut on his lip splitting wider. Fresh, watery blood surfaced each time.

"You didn't ask my name?" he asked.

"What is it?" she whispered.

"Arthur James Joyce. Get it? My dad loves to read him. James Joyce, I mean. I'm really just Artie."

Gloria grinned a big, goofy grin.

Artie. She fell in love with him while the sun melted into the blurred horizon.

She couldn't wait to tell Denise.

Chapter 3

Gloria had been dying to see Denise and Bill's newest home. She knew it would be stunning, but not even her own wild imagination could have constructed the home she and Artie pulled up to that Friday evening. Their three-year-old Camry glided over the smooth pavement, crawling up a sweeping driveway that spiraled upward like a Victorian staircase. Gloria stared out Artie's window. A clear stretch of the Pacific Ocean popped into view, its water stitched to a thin strip of sand that Gloria just knew belonged to her best friend. She imagined Denise and Bill soaking their bare feet in the warm coastal sand, drinking their morning Keurig cups—probably wearing soft designer robes they'd bought as expats living on the Mediterranean.

"Artie, look at how blue the water is over here." Gloria leaned over him, stretching her neck and scanning for oily streaks or murky patches of dirty water. How wild to think that this was the same ocean she and Artie lived only a few blocks from, the same one that had been condemned for nearly a decade and still wasn't exactly swimmable. Their version of the Pacific smelled like salted trash and oil rigs. Their beach was a ribbon of sand littered with needles, used condoms, and shards of glass from the beers that were technically prohibited.

Gloria was so immersed in comparing oceans and beaches, she hadn't noticed they'd parked. The Buchanans' silver and white fortress towered above them. Up close, it was even more impressive. It was a bizarre and beautiful home. The glass walls revealed a metal skeleton, not the common, concealed wood bones of most homes. Bill wouldn't need the expensive stud finders that beeped to let him know where the sturdy posts were. This mansion's metallic guts were blinding. A few windows were draped with heavy off-white curtains. The others were stark naked. Bill sat behind one of these clear walls, reclining on a gray leather couch in front of a glowing flat screen nearly as big as the metal wall it screwed into. Behind another slat of glass, Denise wore a coral sundress and an even tan, looking closer to thirty than seventy-three. She stood at a marble kitchen counter, holding a white sponge over a surface Gloria knew didn't house a single crumb.

"This is a lot nicer than their last home," Artie finally said, switching out his prescription sunglasses for his normal pair of clear, thin frames.

"We never saw their last home. Remember? You couldn't decide on a time to go. Who can't decide on an ideal time to see the French Riviera?" Gloria hiked her shoulders back, swallowing the old impulse to blurt out every annoyance. Artie remained stoic and serene.

"I mean, their last California home. That one had a lot more character; this one has a lot more..." Artie shook his head and opened the car door.

"Money?" Gloria offered, already out and sliding her black flats over the concrete driveway. How did they get the gravel to feel like it was polished?

The car locked with a staccato beep, and Gloria almost laughed. Nobody around here wanted their car, her old scarf, his suede jacket with the elbows rubbed raw.

Denise stood at the front of the house, waving. The silver door beside her flung open.

"I've been watching you both from the window for forever, wondering if you'd ever get up here." Her voice was sturdy, her laughter still dulcet.

Gloria tried to walk up the stairs with ease, hoping she could suck enough of her stomach so Denise wouldn't think she'd let herself go. But she also knew there was no denying the contrast of how time had treated the two of them. Denise's cheeks were smooth and tugged back with the help of an expensive surgeon. Her eyes had been lifted. Her makeup was contoured and highlighted, her teeth bleached snow white. She'd always been meticulous about her looks, never letting a few pounds slip on. She probably had a mini gym in this house, reserved her sugar for a glass of night wine or a spoonful during the holidays. She probably did yoga with the sunrise. As if reading her thoughts, Denise led them in and pushed a pink yoga mat off a tiny chrome bench by the door to make space for Gloria's dated Kate Spade purse.

"Do you want something to drink? Wine, beer?" She looked at Artie, "Coke, water?"

"You have Coke?" Artie asked, his hands in his pockets.

"A few. Still makes a good mixer." Denise's laugh was different this time.

"I'll just have water," Gloria said, feeling suddenly very aware of her feet swelling in her shoes and wondering if this was even a house where she should wear shoes inside. She looked at Artie's gray New Balances, the laces tightly wound. Denise skipped over the faux marble floor in bare feet, her nails freshly pedicured and painted the same coral as her sheer dress. She danced them into the kitchen where Bill stood holding a highball glass. His face was comforting, aged, his neatly combed hair a wet sterling. He was the only authentic thing in this postmodern funhouse.

"I'm having two glasses of wine tonight. Maybe more. We haven't seen you two in so long; this is more than a celebration." Denise lifted a large, filled wine glass up to the art deco light fixture, setting it down to pour a hissing can of Coke into a glass for Artie.

"I was just telling Artie how upset I was that we never made it to visit you out there."

Denise smiled, the skin around her eyes frozen from Botox.

"You didn't miss anything. It was a place mostly filled with boring old people." Denise half-smirked. "Which I guess is supposed to be us now."

"Us, too." Artie sipped his virgin Coke, his eyes locked on Bill's murky cocktail. "We were even looking at communities designed for old people. Thank God we decided against it. I'm just not ready to give up and die. I don't want to hear ambulances coming up the road and wondering which of your neighbors died simply from being old."

"Isn't that the truth?" Denise lapped up a taste of wine. "That's why I love it here. First off, there are no neighbors, no clique to join or hate. And when we do go into the areas where there are more people, everyone is young and fashionable and just living."

"I don't think these communities are as grim as Artie is making them out to be. It's building community, helping each other—and they seem to know the kinds of things we need to keep our brains and bodies moving. They have craft classes, exercise bikes, board games, a pool!" Gloria stared at her lap, embarrassed by how old and boring she knew she sounded.

"God, Gloria, I would ask when you turned ancient—but you've always been that way." Denise's expression teetered between pity and affection. She smiled wider to show she didn't mean anything by it.

"You want a pool, Gloria? We've got one. I've got some fancy exercise machines you can use, too."

So, she was right about the gym room.

"I think it sounds all right. Being around your people," Bill spoke up after taking a hard gulp of his drink.

"But, Bill, those aren't our people. And they shouldn't be theirs either. Why don't you two move up to Malibu?"

"It's too far from work," Artie quickly interjected.

Denise poured another heavy glass of wine.

"Shouldn't you be retired by now?"

Gloria stiffened, trying to be subtle when she turned along with Bill and Denise to wait for Artie's response. He was seemingly mesmerized by the carbonation dancing in his glass of Coca-Cola.

"Soon," he said so quietly, the word had to crawl into their tilted ears.

"You know you can't wait forever," Bill said, holding his glass with both hands. The tips of his fingers were still yellowed by years of smoking, even though there wasn't a smidge of cigarette smoke in the house, and Gloria hadn't seen an ashtray.

"I won't wait forever."

"I mean it. We can all pretend by living wherever that we aren't getting older, but time's a bitch, and she keeps trucking along no matter how many facelifts or secluded beachfront properties you get. Enjoy your life before it's gone."

Bill sucked down the rest of his drink, burping with his mouth closed before he slammed the glass on the marble counter.

⌒☙⌒

The four friends forced years of conversation into hours, all of them piled onto the gray couch whose cushions hissed each time Denise's bare thighs peeled from its surface. She waltzed to the kitchen to refill everyone's drink. Gloria had graduated to lemon water with crushed ice, while Artie nursed a second Coke, swallowing belches when the group burst out into a chorus of mismatched laughter. They laughed over high school memories, like the time Bill and Artie had gotten their friend to dress up like a girl and tricked their other friend to ask him to prom. The duped friend had even leaned in for a passionate kiss before noticing the scruff under layers of pancake makeup they'd borrowed from Gloria. The trickster had gone missing in Viet Nam and the tricked died in a car crash at twenty-two, but they didn't bring that up. Not here. It was unspoken that they would keep their memories locked in a bubble where it was fun to skip class, drive fast, smoke cigarettes, and learn every Buddy Holly song on guitar.

The reminiscing slid into all the funny things their kids had done over the years. Remember when Autumn was sprayed by a skunk in the shed when she was four? Between loud wails and cold baths of tomato juice, she cried out that he was fuzzy, and she'd only wanted to give him a kiss. Remember when Deirdre and Keith ruined a perfect lawn when they tried to burrow to China, only getting far enough to puncture their sewage line and spew scatological fumes down a suburban street that had never smelled anything so terrible? The four of them laughed so hard, remembering the kids pinching their nose and gagging and wondering why Bugs Bunny had never run into this problem. Mascara bled down Gloria and Denise's faces. Bill choked on his own chuckles. The muscles in Artie's gut ached from his own laughter.

"Maybe I will have just a small glass of wine," Gloria chirped at the first quiet space between stories. Artie wondered if he should remind her about her heart medication—but they were all acting so young and boisterous, heart medication didn't exist here. Health problems weren't the only realities held at bay. There was a gulp of air each of them took before telling another funny memory, and Artie couldn't help but wonder if that was them reining in whatever Teddy story they wanted to tell. Fortunately, Teddy's hijinks were few and far between.

"I'm going to have a smoke—join me, Artie?" Bill stood up, wheezing from their hours of shared laughter. Artie didn't bother to tell him he'd quit ten years ago, about the time they flew over the Atlantic.

Bill led him to the metal porch, standing beside a single white orchid planted in a silver pot. Moonlight sparkled in the flower's wide petals.

"It sure is nice to see you two again," Bill took long drags from his Marlboro Red, the folds in his neck pinched tighter with each inhale.

"It's been too long," Artie said.

"You know you two could buy a place close by, and it would almost be like those early days again, only with nicer things and an ocean in our backyards instead of some pain-in-the-ass fruit trees."

"Denise said the same thing."

"Well, why not, guy? Why keep doing the same thing you've been doing for years when you could be living in paradise? We ain't gettin' any younger." Bill suddenly looked more weathered. The Bill he met in high school over-doused in his dad's cologne and left the car grease stains on his pants because he thought it attracted more girls. Bill perfected the pristine pomade swoop of the hair before anyone else in their group. That same hair was now brushed all over his head, the spotted, pink scalp showing through the thin layer of dark gray hair. Denise had paid good money to preserve herself. Bill was too manly to resort to such tactics and too stubborn to lay off the smokes and booze. Time wasn't on his side, and if Artie would take a good look at himself in the mirror, see the splattering of his own age spots, the silvery strands of his own thinning hair, the pink spot on the back of his own head, the sagging of his own skin—he would know time wasn't his friend either. The memories they were cracking up over in the living room were nearly half a century old, and they felt like they'd only happened yesterday. Another fifty years would sprint by like it was nothing—and Artie knew even thinking he'd be around to see the next thirty was highly unlikely.

"What do you think the average life expectancy is?" Artie heard himself blurting out. A flock of seagulls screeched in the pause before Bill's response.

"I suppose it's still somewhere around seventy-five, eighty. But I saw a guy on the news who was something like one-hundred-twenty. He was still taking shots of whiskey in his coffee every morning."

Artie had seen the same news story. The guy was one-hundred-fifteen, and he looked like hell.

With the husbands on the porch, Gloria and Denise were free to explode in a gust of secrets and inner thoughts only they could share with each other. That's what they used to do when the men stepped away. But this time, they sat quietly. Gloria wondered whether they'd reached a level in their friendship where they were clairvoyant mind readers. Only Denise didn't look like she was reading minds. She looked stiff and wooden when moments before, she'd been the epitome of animated. Denise twitched under Gloria's scrutiny.

"You're looking at me in such a strange way." Denise forced a limp laugh.

"You're acting strange."

"I guess it's been a long time. We've never had a strange moment before."

Gloria stared at her glass, the way the pond of wine flickered yellow and green and gold. There were so many conversations that hadn't fit over the phone.

"No, we haven't," Gloria muttered. Denise squeezed in beside her.

"We came just in time, right? For the party? I'm glad you decided to have it this year. We can plan the whole thing together. What are you thinking? Something super swanky and ritzy and overpriced? Something simple?"

Gloria looked up from her glass, setting it on the clear coffee table. This was like old times.

"There is sort of a theme, I suppose. I've been calling it Silver plus Thirty."

"Oh?" Denise's arms folded over her. "Silver? Weren't you going to have a golden anniversary party?"

"Yes, but I hate gold. The silver invitations were so much prettier. I thought about renaming it something like halfway to diamond, since it's technically a fifty-five-year anniversary now—but Silver Plus Thirty seemed a little more original. What do you think? Maybe we could even theme it from that year?"

"Your silver year?" Denise's voice was low and dark, a sort of purr and growl. "1988? You want to theme it *1988*?"

"I guess the 80s were an ugly style time."

"Gloria, it isn't that. You can't theme your party that year. It's weird—and—it's a little morbid. Did you tell Artie this party theme idea?"

"I told him I liked the silver invitations better."

Denise sighed and rubbed her temples. Her skin stretched over tiny blue veins.

"Oh, Gloria. You know you can't do that. I'm hoping it's the little bit of wine making you think that's a good idea. I wouldn't give it any hokey theme—and definitely not a resurrection of *that* year. I wonder if that's why we moved back, so I could be your voice of reason."

Before Gloria could explain herself, the husbands walked in, and everything went back to normal.

They cooled down the night with updates on the kids. Autumn was shacked up with a guy ten years her junior who was as full of as many fame-seeking fantasies as she was. They were currently living in Stockholm, hosting bonfire art events, paying for their elaborate meals and well-decorated flat with his parent's hefty inheritance. Autumn had won $10,000 for a poem a few years back. That probably helped. She swore she'd fly out for the anniversary party, though.

Deirdre—Dee Dee—and Keith led somewhat normal lives. Dee Dee wrote about fashion and subtle plastic surgery for *Vogue*. Keith worked at the same lighting company as Bill, giving presentations on eco-friendly electricity and creating watts that mimicked the Prozac-effects of unadulterated sunlight. His children were in sports and gymnastics, attending schools in the Palisades. He saw them every other weekend now. Dee Dee was planning a fatherless pregnancy.

"But there has to be a father," Gloria, egged on by her first sip of wine in years, said.

"Not according to her. And I don't mean she's planning on some one-night stand—she's declared herself done with men and their disappointments. Unfortunately, her clock is still ticking, but she's a modern, independent woman who's placing her bets on expensive sperm from a fine gene pool filled with wealth, good looks, and a lineage of fancy college. Trust me, Gloria, I don't get it either." Denise waved off the whole scenario with her hand, which Gloria realized was the one feature she couldn't immortalize. The skin on her hands was just as thin as Gloria's, with the same arthritic tilt of her knuckles.

"What about Veronica? And little Edie? I've seen her photos on Facebook. She is adorable, and what a great personality!"

Gloria sighed. "I guess they're okay. Veronica is still running that vegan bakery in Portland. She's been with the same boyfriend for years, so much better than the ass who gave us Edie. Luckily, he backed off after the restraining order and stopped pretending he wanted to be a father."

Denise nodded, leaning back against the cushions, and setting her empty glass on the clear top of the coffee table, her eyes sinking with sleep. Gloria elbowed Artie a little sharper than she'd intended, motioning with her head toward the front door.

"We should probably be going," he chirped on cue.

The friends exchanged long hugs and promised to make visits a more regular, routine event.

"Don't forget to start looking for houses out here!" Bill shouted from the open front door. Denise waved from behind him.

Chapter 4

1950

Artie failed his father first.

Clyde Arthur Joyce worked hard, his fingers often slick with grease and dirt, the tips calloused and yellowed from chain-smoking filterless Lucky Strikes. Artie's father had floated from a shaky military jet to the sticky sands of Normandy to win the second World War. He had witnessed men shredded by shrapnel and saw others rot while still alive. He returned to the sunny suburbs as a common hero who wore a gray jumper with his name sewn into the top pocket. Clyde slid through mud and guts for the good of his country and then slid through sewage and copper pipes for the good of the homes inside of Los Angeles County.

Artie's old man knew the underbelly of nearly every house from Long Beach to Pasadena. He first carried his arsenal of tools throughout Lakewood, Downey, and Norwalk to a chorus of coos from happy housewives and the accolades of satisfied husbands, which ferried him all the way up to Glendale and then to fancy movie-star mansions in the Hollywood Hills. Clyde was proud of what he did, everything from unclogging debris from sinks and bathtubs, to screwing in a new matte pipe piece, to quieting a leaky commode. He wanted his oldest son to be as proud and invested as he was and to continue this simple, humble legacy. Artie bounced unbuckled in the truck's front seat for miles and miles all over Southern California as a small child. Clyde let him hold all the fancy screws and wrenches normal people didn't have in their house; these were special tools—reserved for the men who fixed other people's stuff.

"The rest of the world just needs a plain old flathead and Philips, maybe a wrench. And that's fine because we don't want them to know how to fix all their own problems, or we won't have any to fix, and we won't have any money to pay for ourselves." Clyde broke down reality to five-year-old Artie, who sat on his hands so he wouldn't want to suck on his thumb. The week before, Clyde had poured vinegar and stinging hot sauce all over his tiny fingers. It still hurt when Artie wiped his eyes.

When they reached the last house on the day's list, Clyde gave Artie a single important task: hold the basin wrench and hand it to his father when he called or motioned for it. Clyde slipped under the house, his dirty legs thrashing while he dug through the home's bowels. Artie clung to the basin wrench with both of his small hands, his tongue sticking out while he dutifully watched his father. Long, strong legs and black boots kicked at the blades, knocking over a dandelion. A thick boot heel smashed an unsuspecting bee who buzzed while he died. Artie had to get a closer look, to examine the filmy wings flapping in rigor mortis. He had to know if the bee died with his stinger still attached. Artie never heard the pipe pop and burst. He didn't notice the thick sewage exploding over his father's screaming face. It wasn't until the slimy hands grabbed his neck that he knew he had done something wrong. His senses returned with a vengeance. He felt the stinging slaps of leather on his bared behind that night. He smelled the sour breath of belched whiskey and canned meat. He tasted the week-old resin of the hot sauce left on his puckered thumbs. A voice older than he was, living inside his head, swore to never be like Clyde.

Artie failed his mother next.

His perfect, beautiful mother. The very same mother who spread butter over the entire surface of his toast, who shaved the bland, dry crust and fed it to the crows outside. His mother who warmed a thick slice of banana bread for when he came home from school. The mother who cut rhubarbs into slivers and folded the pieces into a mound of shiny, soft strawberries, pouring the whole glittering mixture into a buttery cavity and holding his hands while she asked for his patience. She never failed him. When she woke him up in the morning, she peeled back the covers and gently cracked open the blinds one by one to save his eyes from an unforgiving sun. Dorothy, his wonderful mother, only thought of him— sometimes of the other children, too, but always him. He was where her sun set. He was her world.

Every day, she stuck two pieces of hard butterscotch candy inside his metal lunchbox, tucking a note into the handle of his thermos. Dorothy Joyce peeled his fruit before he ate it. She diluted rubbing alcohol with a warm, wet washcloth before placing it over his scraped and bleeding knee, telling him how proud of him she was for slaying the imaginary bad guys.

"You're tougher than Hopalong Cassidy," she said with genuine awe.

When she kissed him goodnight, she always smelled like roses and powder. Artie sometimes wondered how to capture that essence and suck it inside of himself. Maybe if these wild thoughts were ever possible, she could have been kept safe. If he could have buried her inside of his heart, he could have paid her back for all she'd done for him. He wasn't strong enough, though. His gangly arms were made of soft, knobby muscles. His voice was still tinted with baby. She still had to protect him.

Clyde liked to drink. He cracked open a beer as soon as he walked through the door, his heavy day-end sigh the same pitch as the hiss of the bottle cap breaking loose. Clyde drank this beer by himself on the back porch, rolling cigarettes and swatting away the flies who swooned over his plumber's stench. He popped open his second beer at the dinner table, while Dorothy set out hand-washed placemats and a plastic pitcher of iced tea with lemon slices. He drank his third as dinner was set on the table. Artie's mother hung a cross in every room, and Clyde was raised under the fear of God, so he finished his third beer before he said grace. He spit when he prayed. Artie smelled the beer souring inside his father's empty stomach. Safely bent in prayer, he blanched and made sure to nod with enthusiasm at each word of thanks. Clyde sipped his fourth beer with his first bite of dinner. He slurped his pea soup and belched while picking burnt bacon from his teeth. He dropped one fork and then another, each one swiftly replaced by his wife. Artie's tired mother rushed to rinse off the dirtied fork, pulling a fresh gleaming utensil from the drawer that got stuck each time it was yanked open. Clyde cleaned his plate before Dorothy had taken a single bite or a sip of her tea. Clyde had a fifth beer with his heaping pile of seconds.

"You not going to eat your momma's cookin'?" He nearly shouted at Artie, Glenn, and Maura. The kids responded by shoveling potatoes into their cheeks, chewing quickly before swallowing bites much too big for their tiny throats. They drank their tea quickly before Clyde could see them choke. Clyde skinned his plate clean for a second time and then went outside for his sixth beer, which he also washed down with straight whiskey. Dorothy dumped her own untouched dinner into the trash. She turned her back from her children, washing the same plate over and over. She pretended to sneeze.

Artie, Glenn, and Maura played quietly with a boxed Bingo set, whispering the letters and numbers. Their hands shook setting down the plastic chips on their boards. Dorothy continued to wash dishes. Clyde continued to drink. Night after night after night.

The breaking point came the night the three siblings, who always kept their voices barely above a whisper to not disturb their dad, were almost shouting while playing Traffic Jam. The sky, split between burnt orange and bleeding pink, hid behind the curtains Dorothy rushed to close once Clyde's voice started to boom louder, the obscenities Artie and his siblings pretended not to hear getting louder, too. They wheeled their plastic car pieces over the looped road on the unfolded board, forcing out squeals of fun when they landed on the spot they wanted.

"You're the one who drinks every single night! You are the one who came home with some floozy's perfume on your neck!"

That couldn't be the same mother who spoke so softly even when chastising them. Their mother didn't paddle their bottoms with spoons like the other mothers. Now, she was screaming, the cords in her neck fanned out. Her cheeks flushed purple as their father pummeled his fist into them. Artie and his siblings fixed their stares to the board, their fingers hovering over their own car piece. All of them forgot whose turn it was. They began talking loud gibberish, trying to time their cacophonous nonsense to the loud punches of their father's sharp knuckles slamming into their mother's delicate bones. They didn't stop talking, not even long enough to breathe, not until his fist was off their mother's wet face, off the kitchen wall, off the row of painted portraits of each kid as a smiling, stupid baby.

This became nighttime routine. They forgot how it was when Clyde was safely drunk on the porch, bellowing out Hank Williams, drinking from a bottle and spitting into the yard. That was a cherished memory— back when their mother only angrily scrubbed their dinner plates and washed her face before crying herself to sleep. Now, she cried openly, mucus-beaded wails from the kitchen while holding frozen hunks of meat to her eye. Her children cuddled on the couch with her when he didn't come home, all of them too big to fit on her lap. Dorothy smoothed the hair on all three of their heads like they were infants. She baked bread pudding for dinner and warmed hot chocolate on the stove. They drank the cocoa under the whirling ceiling fan because it was never cold enough in California for hot cocoa. They twirled around the room to the sounds of Glenn Miller.

"Let's play a game!" their mother begged after they were all out of breath from dancing. It was already 10 o'clock, and they all had school in the morning. Artie said yes before Glenn or Maura could say no—he hated school.

They brought out a stack of games from the closet, each of the boxes white and weak at the seams from overuse. Their mother slid Yahtzee from the top. Maura complained that Artie was the only one who had luck shaking dice in a little red cup.

"And he's so loud about it. The shaking *and* the winning," she grumbled, scanning her own pitiful pile for even a pair of matching die, chewing on a tiny pencil. Artie rolled a large straight on his first try. Their mother rolled a Yahtzee.

"You're lucky, too!" Maura touched each one of the scattered dice, each face a slash of dots, a diagonal three. Dorothy etched her fifty points on the score paper before flashing her children a wide, charming smile they knew she had perfected.

"It sure looks like I am." Dorothy bit her lip and shoved her cup into Glenn's fanned hands. It took her youngest child two shakes to get four sixes.

They played three games of Yahtzee and ate ice cream straight from the carton with four bent spoons. She promised to excuse them all from school in the morning. Artie's mother rolled four Yahtzees total. Artie only got two.

1959

Artie's plan to save his mother took years. He plotted during boring classes or when sneaking cigarettes outside after school. His imagination was still young enough to think he could conjure a commanding voice that would shake his mother's useless porcelain knick-knacks off the tiny wooden shelves and startle his father. In reality, he trembled when he thought of his father's fist, the dark glaze that swallowed his eyes after a certain number of drinks, the vituperative venom he spat when he was done. His father had always had those grated edges, but they used to be quiet like a sleeping snake. His nighttime drinks turned into the stick that provoked him to strike.

"But not my mom," Artie told himself in the bathroom mirror, in the reflective windows he passed, in the side mirror of his father's parked work truck. He had to look away from the house, wandering his eyes over other people's front porches, over their clipped grass, over Denise Duffy's bedroom window. Artie often found himself looking at that window because Denise often forgot to close her drapes and often liked to unhook her bra right in front of the window. This day was the same, her window wide open and naked. She danced around and posed dramatically with a girl Artie had never seen before, both wearing their hair in big blue curlers. The other girl had skinny knees and a slouch someone hadn't beat out of her yet. Mid-dance, the girl froze at the window. Artie froze—afraid they would find him out there gawking. They didn't.

Artie stayed still, studying this new girl. She was no Denise. His lifelong crush was Betty Grable incarnate—doll-like features, an early-developed womanly build, who recognized the crude jokes teenage boys told each other that they all thought were secret. She even laughed at some of these jokes. Denise's friend didn't look like she laughed at those jokes—and her nose was a little big, her jaw a little small. Still, there was *something*. She had big brown eyes he could see all the way from his own yard. Something in those ordinary eyes filled him with the courage he'd been trying to muster for too long. He marched into his house and looked his dad right in the face when he took his first swing.

"You're not going to hurt my mom anymore." Artie's voice didn't come out as powerful or booming as he'd imagined. Nothing on the walls or shelves even quivered. His father laughed. A rotting cackle.

But he didn't hit Artie's mother. He hit Artie instead.

His father pelted him with tight boxer fists until white flickered behind Artie's closed, swelling eyes. Clyde pummeled his cheeks until they went numb. The family ring Clyde wore on his finger landed against the soft cartilage of Artie's nose. It popped and snapped, a thick goo sliding from his wounds and into his mouth. A salty metallic pudding. His ears rang between his mother's screams. Her hands yanked him from the assail. She clawed his father's face, drawing blood. Clyde became an enraged monster and dragged his hands over the shelves of Dorothy's prized porcelain people, shattering them into splintered, glittering shards. Maura and Glenn watched from the hallway. Artie knew they were holding their breath, waiting to turn invisible. He used to be where they were.

Clyde panted, his forehead threaded with swollen veins and thick with sweat. He closed his eyes and mumbled something that sounded like a prayer before slumping outside to drink the rest of his nearly empty bottle. Artie walked out the front door, to the side of the house, where he pounded his fists against the bricks until the skin spilt between his bloodless knuckles. He was railing the bricks when he felt eyes on the back of his head. He hoped it was Dorothy, so she could see how angry he was and how hard he tried. Or he hoped it was Clyde, who could bear witness to his son's true violence, cut from his own cloth and willing to kill his father if he could.

It was the girl. The one who'd been up in Denise's room. Her hair stiff, flaked with dried hairspray. The outside of her colorless lips painted with pale pink lipstick. Her tight wool skirt made her crouch pigeon-toed behind the bushes. She never saw him sneak behind her.

Chapter 5

March 2018

To the droves of shoppers filling their squeaky shopping carts, Allen's Market looked the same as it did all the other days they came to get five pounds of red potatoes, two jars of spaghetti sauce, and salami sliced as thin as they wanted. To everyone working at the store, it was pure chaos. Artie tasted the anxiety as he walked in and saluted the cashiers, patting the dairy stocker on his back. The poor guy nearly leapt a mile in the air.

"Didn't mean to startle you," Artie apologized. His employee simply nodded, continuing to fill holes on the yogurt shelf.

Inside his office, Artie sipped his watered-down coffee and shuffled through his emails. There it was—the impetus for all the frenetic energy in a single red-flagged message. What was the big deal? Change was all part of the business—and that's all the e-mail said: there would be an all-store meeting to discuss some big changes. They'd had millions of these meetings. They'd had heightened store gossip before, too—although those rumors failed to create the sort of static currently hissing in every corner and crevice inside Allen's Market.

After Artie flushed his deleted e-mails, he decided on a much-needed morale walk. Maybe he'd open some of those overpriced cookies that weren't really moving and leave them in the breakroom for the team members. Maybe he'd do a fun gift card raffle at tonight's meeting. He had barely risen from his ergometric office chair when a new e-mail from Joan glittered across his computer screen.

Meet me in the office at 9. It's important.

Important didn't mean anything special, Artie thought, closing his inbox. Joan might want him to give one of his seasoned speeches on company change. She always loved his comforting rhetoric. He knew how to target solace. He'd tell the new long-haired receiver it would be okay; he would still have a check to count on that would pay for the house he shared with his bandmates. They could still blast their awful music and chain-smoke on the porch. Artie knew how to sincerely ensure their oldest hire she wasn't going anywhere. She could keep her gym membership and early-riser water aerobics. There would still be a place for her to stash her trendy diet bars, and he and Joan would continue to ignore the fact that she was eating food they didn't sell at Allen's.

Important could mean something else, but Artie wasn't going to feed those suspicions. He knew how to reinvent and go with the flow—he'd been doing it with Allen's since 1963.

He was seventeen when they hired him to bag groceries. His father woke him up early on a Saturday morning, knowing he'd snuck in late the night before. Clyde also knew he'd been drinking, even though he didn't tell his son what he knew. He simply told him to get up, comb his hair flat against his head, and tuck in his shirt. He told him he had a job interview.

"Look respectable for once," Clyde said before closing Artie's bedroom door to give him exactly twenty-five minutes to look like a hardworking young man who needed a job, not a scruffy teenager who only cared about playful rebellion and winning fights.

Clyde seemed to drive slower down Lakewood Blvd that day, dragging out the surprise job for as long as he could. A week earlier, Clyde had asked Artie to officially join the family business.

"You're my first son. Your name deserves to be on the truck," Clyde had beamed for the first time ever. But Artie hated even going with his dad on jobs—he always had. He hated thinking about what lived under people's houses. He hated the smell of sewage and septic tanks. Artie tried to say all these things as nicely as he could, but Clyde took the blow to heart. The morning Clyde drove Artie to the small grocery store down the street from the flagship McDonald's was the first time Artie's father had acknowledged his existence since he'd refused his labor lineage.

"Where are we going?" Artie had asked his dad, watching the rows of shops and square houses blur together behind the car window.

"You need a job. You don't want the one I had for you, but you need a job. Don't worry—you won't get too dirty doing this one."

Clyde pulled into the parking lot, telling Artie to stand up straighter, even as he walked with his own signature slouch. Artie stood by the oranges, then advertised with handwritten signs and big plastic numbers. He inhaled the citrus perfume while his dad haggled his future. Clyde had done some plumbing work for the new store, and in turn, they would hire his son no questions asked. It was George Allen who first shook his hand and offered him a schedule that would tie up all his weekends and some of his school nights.

"You know what they say about idle time?" George said with a wink. His wife Joan was behind the register, weaving friendly conversation with swift work. She whittled down line after line of customers who promised to come back soon. Artie didn't want to give up his time with his girlfriend or the guys or the movie nights or the drives down to the beach to get loaded. He didn't want to work as hard as these old men wanted him to.

"Can you start today?" George asked, waving in code to his wife who marched up with a crisp, folded apron.

Artie knew he didn't have a choice. Clyde was already out the door, an unlit cigarette clenched in his teeth.

That seventeen-year-old feared change, just like Artie's current team feared it. For Artie, those changes became beneficial. They became promotions, shared office space with George and Joan. Entire days where he never saw the sales floor—or daylight—working nine hours in front of schedules, invoices, catalogues, all while smoking two packs a day and drinking a gallon of coffee with the Allens. He brought children, a granddaughter, and a great-granddaughter into the back of the store, where they ate from free inventory and played with merchandising strips. Artie's life grew parallel to his growth within the company. They were intertwined. When Allen's changed, Artie changed.

Technology swept away some of their competitors and even some of his colleagues. But Artie always rode the waves. He plugged in the company's first Xerox and sent the first fax. He committed to learning and mastering word processors. When they became relics, he brought one home for Veronica to play with. He willingly went back to Apple computers and adopted their new moniker with ease. When smartphones were clunky, glitchy things, he was still the first in line to buy one. It made him accessible, always available to answer questions. It was survival. Those that feared technology faded into oblivion. That's why he embraced social media as an old man and was the one who penned every company Tweet. He used slang and acronyms appropriately, never sounding cheesy.

This was how he survived the world of business and the world in general. He knew the importance of a filtered photo and sharing cute videos of his great-granddaughter. He wasn't like his aging coterie—*he* was still relevant. They wanted him to slow down, to take up golfing and crosswords full time, to find solace in hours at the park listening to the cacophony of tone-deaf birds and snorting geese. He wasn't opposed to occasional leisure, to occasional relaxation—but he wasn't ready to succumb to full-time atrophy.

Gloria, on the other hand, was more than ready. She craved their sedentary season. She seemed to think they could reclaim love and passion in shared inertia. Artie was different. Her current livelihood was wrapped up in organizing a lifetime of family photos, perfecting sugar-free desserts while starving herself for the big party in July. Artie simply couldn't measure his life's worth through a stupid party—or whatever was supposed to happen afterward.

Artie strolled into Joan's office with an ease earned after years of workplace companionship. She'd added extra pizazz to her coffee today; the wafting vodka stung his eyes. Joan didn't notice him at first. She paced the front of her desk. A welter of loose papers covered her desk calendar. Pens were strewn over the clutter like outstretched fingers. He coughed, and she looked up, her eyeliner and taupe shadow smeared into a murky gray.

"Joan?"

"I was going to come find you instead of sending that email. I've been prepping what I'm going to say—almost like showroom prep, or trying to seduce a new vendor. Except, I still don't know what to say." Joan picked up her green mug, sloshing it into her open mouth. She swallowed and winced. "I've never had to prep any of our conversations, Artie. You know that. You've always let me be unedited and unprepared."

"Then just say what you need to say."

Artie hoped he sounded built for change, even as he sensed the space between them curdling for the first time in fifty-five years. Pulpy jitters leaked into his body, and he suddenly felt like every other frantic member of the Allen's team.

"Artie, I'm selling it. This whole thing. I need to. We're sinking." Joan wiped her eyes and turned away. "Blame it on the internet or bigger grocery stores—but we just don't matter anymore. Nobody cares about some old-fashioned store that isn't even trying to be that old-fashioned anymore."

Joan looked past him. Inky make-up snaked into her face's many crevices.

"I don't want a second mortgage." Her voice was hoarse. "I don't want to downsize or get rid of my home elevator I never use. I don't want a more efficient car or cheaper clothing. I don't want to do my hair less, and I like fancy massages. I enjoy my excessive lifestyle. I've built it from the ground up. I know it's selfish, but, Artie, I'm old. I deserve to be selfish now."

Artie found the chair closest to him and slid into it.

"Selling?" was all he could say.

"Oh, Artie, it's not that bad. They're a big company with a lot of money and they're giving us a fat check. They'll keep old employees. We'll be the only ones set free, and free is the right word. We're getting out before it all collapses around us and we have nothing."

"You're selling to *them?*" The infamous mega-conglomerate had been hounding Joan for years. "They already own everything."

"They won't own us, just Allen's. You'll still get your pension. Aren't you planning to retire, anyway?"

Joan grabbed his hand. Hers was cold and threaded with spindly, algae-colored veins. Her wedding ring, thirty years expired, spun around her thin, crooked finger.

"Aren't you retiring?" she asked in a near whisper.

Was he? He'd said he was. Before, he imagined it would have been like holding the gritty lip of a swimming pool—even if he went through with it. Sure, he'd be kicking his legs and tasting chlorine, but there'd be something solid he could still grab on to: Allen's. Nearly every single memory burrowed into his brain was strung between work shifts, between climbing a single company's ladder. The new product waiting for him on a palette after his hotel honeymoon. The family babies hoisted on his shoulders and paraded around the logs of cheeses and meats, finding those babies sneaking behind the bakery to taste a freshly iced cake. The first cashier to ask him to close the door, her crossed legs glistening with skin-toned pantyhose. His father popping in between jobs and taking him out for a mustard-soaked pastrami sandwich. Allen's heartfelt sympathy cards for Artie's biggest losses. The going away party with vanilla sheet cake, the welcome back party with red velvet cupcakes. His livelihood would become an empty socket. What was he going to hold onto now?

"It won't matter for us," Joan kept saying. She'd started to cry, sticky mascara stuck to the lines on her face.

Gloria didn't notice anything was wrong with Artie at first. He came home a little earlier—six pm, the time most people walked in the door. He kicked off his black sneakers at the door and poured himself three glasses of ice-clogged water. Each one drank in fewer than three deep gulps. It was a slightly strange way to walk through the door, but Gloria was consumed with figuring out a dinner that could fluff up the same boring things she'd been eating for weeks. She resigned herself to eating another tiny boxed dinner sent by Nutrisystem, breaking the dry brownie into crumbs she would try to savor. She was going to ask Artie what he wanted, but he was downing another glass of ice water like it were an oversized shot of tequila, which convinced her tonight would be a lovely evening to cheat on her diet.

"Let's go out to that new seafood place," she said. Artie pushed his glass under the ice dispenser. Ice gurgled behind the new chrome refrigerator before it spat into his glass.

"Sure," he said, the agreement almost mechanical, almost like it was connected to the ice crusher, the thick black cord plugged into the wall.

Gloria rushed to find a forgiving shawl. Artie combed his hair and put on tighter, shinier shoes without saying a word.

Artie remained taciturn throughout the entire congested strip of Ocean Blvd. He flicked on the oldies station when they reached the Villa Riviera, immediately turning down the Ronettes to a muted hum. Gloria had always loved that song—in the 60s and when it resurfaced in *Dirty Dancing* and she could twirl Veronica around the freshly mopped kitchen floor, her granddaughter singing, "Baby, baby, baby." Her granddaughter liked to be held.

The restaurant was wedged at the sandy hem of Long Beach. From their table, it was impossible to tell the water had once been condemned for its mix of spilled oil, polluted sludge, and other hard-to-pronounce contaminants. From where they sat, this slice of sea looked like Denise's ocean. Simply seeing her friend again was causing their lives to mirror each other like old times.

Artie fastened his plastic bib with the metal clamps first. Gloria would normally comment on how ridiculous the bibs were, before acquiescing to save her velvet top—but Artie still hadn't said a word, and she didn't want to spoil this dinner.

They chose their lobster first. Claws handcuffed in plastic, their frantic antennae eyes tapping the glass making futile final pleas to stay alive. Gloria ignored them. Insects of the ocean, with soft meat for brains. The crabs, too. Gloria ordered a pile of Dungeness legs for them to share. When the bent claws arrived clouded in steam, with the tiny metal bowl of melted butter, Gloria cleared her throat and asked Artie what was wrong.

"Wrong?"

"You haven't said a word. Even less than usual."

Artie stuck his tiny fork into the broken leg, ripping out a shredded piece of meat. He let it dangle before submerging it into the pond of melted butter.

"Joan is selling Allen's. I'm being let go," he said, pushing the pink and white meat farther into the silver bowl.

Gloria knew better than to let Artie see her smile. She lifted her black cloth napkin to her face, pretending to chew the bite she had never taken.

"So," she chewed slower on the nothingness, "does that mean you'll be retiring for sure?"

Artie sighed, grabbing his glass of water with both hands, gazing at the trays of drinks being delivered. She knew he wanted something sugary, effervescent if he couldn't have something designed to get him drunk. But he was on strict orders from the doctor to watch his blood sugar, and the latter hadn't been an option in nearly thirty years.

"Yes, I guess it means I will."

Gloria wiped the clean corners of her mouth, her smile growing wider behind the napkin. She saw long cruise ships on clear international water, with buffets and rooms full of board games with other relaxed strangers. She saw a home in the country outskirts of Portland, close enough to Veronica and Edie, far enough to have horses and baby sheep, maybe some soft chicks for Edie to cuddle with and take photos of beside scraggly bales of hay. She saw Autumn realizing parties had worn out their welcome, or at least saw her wanting to create a poetry retreat in a room they would save for her. Gloria envisioned a wall of family portraits, with the *entire* family. She painted a future of crafts, cold movie theaters, quiet nights of reading from their own Kindles on opposite sides of a room full of plants they bought to feel alive—a stretch of shared leisure before an earned expiration. Their well-deserved season of healing.

"I know you wanted to leave on your terms, but really it couldn't have come at a better time," Gloria said.

Artie waved over the waiter.

"I'll have a Coke. The biggest size you've got."

"But, Artie—"

"I know, I know. The blood sugar, right? Don't want to get diabetes now that I'm retired, is that it?"

Gloria didn't want to argue. Maybe it was a celebration. Maybe she should indulge, too.

"And I'll have the crème brûlée, please."

She hoped the waiter couldn't see the soft parts of her spilling over her elastic waistband. She'd be back on her diet tomorrow.

❧👁❧

Visits with Bill and Denise became the revised Saturday routine. Gloria and Artie woke up a little earlier to get to the cleaners right when they opened and scooted grocery shopping to Sunday afternoon. They erased the diner from their weekend schedule and plopped it into Wednesday nights. These were temporary shifts because soon, all nights would be free. Artie and Gloria both acknowledged this, each of them inflecting different words. Gloria lifted up "soon" with enthusiasm. Artie felt the weight of "all."

Gloria flickered through the radio stations on their drive up. When Artie was alone, he listened to ball games, or occasionally to the Beach Boys CD Veronica had sent to him from Santa last Christmas. Gloria skidded through NPR, hard rock, and willowy country before landing on a station playing the soothing "Sleep Walk."

"Remember this song?" Gloria asked, humming along.

Artie nodded. The song's churning instruments fell into the sluice of California traffic. Even when the song switched to an old Supremes hit, and then to a song by the Kinks, Artie still heard the haunting voiceless song—all the way up the smooth driveway, and even when they walked through the heavy chrome doors where Denise asked if he wanted something to drink.

These new Saturday nights had a rigid agenda. First, surrender to whatever trend diet Denise swore would keep her forever young. Now, she was avoiding carbs—except for her two fat glasses of white wine. Their flimsy dinner made the wine hit faster—watery zucchini noodles, cashews soaked in some cheese-like yeast, asparagus sauteed in water and dry herbs. Artie, of course, didn't truly know how the wine hit. He politely turned it down, always asking for water with extra ice or occasionally one of those sparkling water things posing as a no-calorie fruity soda. Bill threw down beers with the same quickness he'd done all throughout the 60s and 70s. Retirement gave him a case of the "fuck-its." His words exactly. He didn't care if he got drunk. Gloria sipped her own modest glass of wine, leaving behind a smear of nude lipstick after each dainty pull. She'd spread out her medication, leaving a couple off for Saturday. She swore the palpitations were worth it.

After the threadbare feast and the others properly buzzed, they sank into Denise and Bill's squishy sofa. Sometimes they rattled dice for Yahtzee, other times they picked apart language with a Scrabble game they'd had since 1976. The letters yellowed and brittle, the board weak at the seams. Mostly, they talked. Denise tiptoed into the kitchen, returning with a half-full glass and winking at Artie. He forced a smile back. Bill kept losing track of the conversation, going outside for cigarette after cigarette. Gloria simply smiled. Artie rolled through the night as expected. He cracked jokes. He complained about work. He drank another glass of water, this time with a squirt of lemon at Denise's slurred insistence. They swam through memories. They laughed at things from twenty, thirty, forty, fifty years ago.

"Do you remember that time Autumn ran away?" Denise sat on the armrest, her skirt riding up her unaged thighs.

"Which time?" Gloria and Artie said, a few beats from being in sync.

"The time she ran away right after Teddy was born. She had her little stick with the basket, her little clothes rolled into balls and falling out into the street. Remember the cops had to bring her home? Remember how mad she was when they acted like she was actually going to go to jail?" Tears streaked down Denise's pinched face. Mascara bled into her powder, her subtle, gold highlighter. Her lips, smooth with collagen, looked like they might pop. Bill chuckled. Of course, they all remembered Autumn with her limp, scraggly stick and dirty socks spilling into the sticky asphalt. Of course, they all remembered Teddy—even if none of them were supposed to. Artie avoided looking at Gloria, hoping she wouldn't notice how nonchalantly Teddy's ghost had entered the room.

"Joan sold Allen's. I'm getting fired—uh, I mean 'let go'," Artie blurted out. The laughter dried up.

"So, guess you really will retire?" Bill grinned, his tobacco-tanned cheeks folding like an accordion. Artie didn't have to look at Gloria to know she was beaming.

"I was going to all along."

"Yeah right," Denise slid from the armrest into the crook of the sofa. "You would never leave that place, and nobody understands it. Who doesn't want to live like this?" Her long, bare arm dragged over the room of crystal knick-knacks, polished aluminum, and empty glasses.

Artie took another sip of water and nodded. It wouldn't be like *this*. It wouldn't be sterile and woven between fantasy vacations and Botox. It would be the senior life of the ordinary. Apple pie domestic waiting for the end. It would be the life he'd been trying to escape with work. He never knew how to be a full member of the house—and God knows, he tried.

There was Gloria's birthday when Autumn was four, and Artie had the wild idea to bake his wife a cake. The girl sucked her fingers and pointed to the cabinets when he couldn't find the sugar. He mixed up baking powder and baking soda. He stirred the thick batter with a butter knife and poured too much milk in the frosting. The cake was served in a bowl— a wet, sticky mound drowning in sugary pink syrup. Autumn had sung to her mom with Artie. Gloria had looked happy, sure, but Artie knew he'd messed it up. It was her home, her life. He only knew how to destroy it.

Bill patted him on the shoulder, releasing the snag of ancient nostalgia.

"You'll love retirement. Allen's is the past. Who needs it?"

Artie toasted with his glass of lemon seeds and ice cubes, tilting his head for effect.

"Who needs it?" the four friends said, tapping their glasses together.

Artie needed Allen's. He needed deliveries and bottom lines and crisp-faced boxes. He needed the questions, the respect. He needed purpose. He needed place. He needed a reason to wake up in the morning.

"I have so many plans for us when he retires," Gloria sang to her friends, never once looking in Artie's direction, Denise and Bill wanting to hear them all.

Chapter 6

1963

Lying next to her best friend of seven years, on the eve of what was supposed to be the best day of her life, Gloria confessed *it* still hadn't come. They squeezed closer together, the quilts pulled over their heads, and started to whisper.

"Does it really matter?" Denise cupped Gloria's ear, her breath humid and hot. Gloria nodded.

"It does matter. What if I'm already, *you know*?"

"So what? You're getting married tomorrow, aren't you?"

Whispering, they retraced the steps to figure out how it could have happened. They landed on a dusky evening two months earlier, which Gloria couldn't help recall in a breathy, dreamy tone. She painted an image of glowing headlights and a fictitious scent of rose and honeysuckle, because that smelled better than the Steinbrau and rubbery hot dogs his breath had reeked of when he'd nuzzled her neck. He promised things like Vegas and parties on a covered porch. He designed imaginary jewelry with his tongue, promising pearls and diamonds and whatever rare gem she would decide was her favorite. He promised a garden, a driveway, a blender that matched the kitchen walls.

"Just imagine it." He chewed on her ear, and she giggled. "The world will be ours."

Gloria kept some of the details to herself. Her hair loosening from its mound of Aquanet, the way he ran a single finger down her throat and along the buttons of her blouse, how he dipped a whole hand under the waistline of her miniskirt and let it hover over her. It was when he did that and she pulled him close enough to her that he had asked, "Are you ready?"

She had also pulled him close enough to feel *it*. Gloria had liked that, too. She'd felt like a queen or a movie star—like all those silly dress-up games in Denise's closet because she had made it happen. They'd been at this spot before, all the high school kids had. All the girls let the boys go just far enough and then they'd push them off, so their dates could finish themselves off to avoid the infamous pain reserved for teenage boys. Why hadn't she pushed him off that time? Gloria didn't ask or answer that question aloud because she knew the answer, and it made her just like the awful women she'd heard about at her grandma's church ever since she was in diapers.

Gloria finished the story by simply saying he had asked, and she had said yes.

"Was that wrong?"

"No, no. I'm just surprised. You have always been such a goody-goody." Denise giggled.

"So, I'm not anymore?"

"No, no. It's not that. You're just—you just surprised me. I'm not thinking anything bad of you."

Gloria didn't believe her. Not even Denise had let a boy go *all* the way.

"Did it hurt?" Denise asked.

Gloria couldn't remember. She just remembered feeling immediately shy after and covering herself with her hands and asking him to look away.

Denise wiggled out from under the lasagna of quilts Gloria's granny had covered them in.

"That must be when it happened. But that wasn't that long ago, and you'll be married tomorrow, so I wouldn't even worry about it."

Moonlight oozed in through the curtains, turning everything eerie and white.

"Yes, it must be."

She didn't tell her friend about the times after or how Artie had joked about not wanting any surprise babies.

"It'll be okay tomorrow." Denise yawned, rolling to face the window. "You'll be a normal virginal bride."

Gloria rolled the other way and shut her eyes as tight as she could, waiting for morning.

❧ ✦ ❧

Tomorrow arrived with Gloria's grandmother cooking breakfast and Gloria fighting to pretend the smell of batter and bacon didn't turn her stomach. She sat at the circular dining table watching her grandma set each place with the white placemats she usually reserved for the holidays.

"This is just as special as any occasion," she said, shaking the dust from them before setting the mats down.

Gloria sat between Denise and her mother, both women wearing fluffy robes and pink sponge curlers just like Gloria. Her mother smoked cigarettes and guzzled two cups of black coffee. She was probably relieved that her motherly duties would end in a few hours. Denise gushed over how amazing the room smelled. Gloria had to swallow the bile in her own throat.

"Come watch me." Grandma Stella waved Gloria over. "You'll have to do this starting tomorrow. Artie will want breakfast, and he'll want it to taste like a wife made it."

Gloria pushed her lips together, watching Grandma Stella ladle out each dollop of pancake batter and flip over each slimy strip of bacon. She had to look away when the yolk congealed on the fried egg, praying her grandmother hadn't noticed.

"I hope I'll remember all of that."

"And it's okay if you don't." Grandma Stella's eyes watered as she held Gloria's face with both hands. "I'm so happy for you."

Gloria sat back down, feeling her mother's eyes dousing her in a stare Gloria hated.

"You worried about the wedding night?" She didn't have to look to know a sneer was on her mother's face. She knew what it sounded like.

"I'm terrified," Gloria lied.

"It gets better," her mother sighed. Gloria kept her eyes on flickering flames beneath the skillet.

"Your favorite." Grandma Stella sat down a yellow plate filled with a towering stack of beautiful golden pancakes and a carafe of syrup.

Gloria smiled and chewed each bite at least twenty times, crossing her fingers under the table each time she was brave enough to swallow. She promised herself she could puke in the shower as soon as all the plates were clean. Her grandma had to believe she was still a good girl who was ready to be a good wife.

❦

At half past two, Gloria walked up the carpeted aisle inside the tiny white church. Artie stood at the altar, his hands clasped in front of him. Gloria took her time with each step, her fingers throbbing from the pricks of the bouquet's thorns. It was a pleasant distraction from the queasiness that finally subsided when she found herself directly in front of Artie. They were almost there.

They whispered and stuttered their vows, each of their hands trembling when they slid the ring over the other's finger. They took posed, strained photos in front of a tall white cake. Artie sliced a small spongy square. Gloria dutifully opened her mouth. After, they ducked under a veil of pelted rice and drove away in a car fastened with a tin can bustle. JUST MARRIED scrawled in shaky cursive over the back window. Gloria kneeled on the passenger seat, watching their families stand in rice-made snowbank, waving wildly. Gloria waved back.

Once they were around the corner, Artie pressed hard on the gas. Gloria braced herself with the headrest and the passenger door.

"Easy." She laughed.

"Well, we're married," he said in a flat voice she'd never heard before. He lit a cigarette and shook the stiff pomade from his hair.

"Finally." Gloria coughed out another phony laugh.

"Can we stop and get some drinks before the hotel?"

"Sure."

Artie came out of the convenience store with two six-packs of Budweiser and a bottle of cheap champagne. He carried them up the gray steps to their hotel room. Gloria held her wedding train, clutching it to her front like it was an injured animal. She waited at the door, hearing the first can pop open.

"Artie?" she called.

"What?" he called back.

"Aren't you supposed to carry me in?"

He sighed but came to the door and hoisted her up and over the threshold.

"Sorry, I've never done this before." He smiled, touching her arm.

They each sat on the edge of the sinking mattress. She waited for him to smoke three cigarettes and drink another beer. She sipped the champagne he'd popped for her over the bathroom sink.

"A toast," he said, after opening his third beer, and finally scooting close to her. She raised the tiny plastic cup of flat bubbles.

"A toast to us and our lives." His smile was lopsided. Gloria touched her cup to his beer can. He took the cup from her hand and set it on the TV next to his empty can. When he came back to the bed, he started to kiss her neck and grope at the buttons running down her laced back. His fingers crawled over her. She swallowed another urge to vomit. She closed her eyes. She waited for it to be like how it had been in the car. Her dress oozed into a crinoline puddle on the stained carpet. His pants flung beside it. His mouth was hot and astringent and yeasty. Gloria lay on her back while he clambered over her. He finished in less than a minute, kissing her cheek before turning on the TV and falling asleep after two more beers. Gloria dumped the rest of her champagne into the sink. She washed her face with cold cream, wiping it off with a scratchy motel washcloth. She leaned over the toilet and forced her finger down her throat.

Gloria lied at her first doctor's appointment after the blue vials at home confirmed what she'd known all along. When they asked about her last menses, she blurted out the first date she could think of: her wedding a month before. Waiting for the doctor to calculate her due date, she fabricated a whole alternate life. Her wedding dress delicately removed, her hands held by his and being told how much he cherished her, and how much he looked forward to spending a whole lifetime with her. She imagined herself frying him an egg during their first breakfast together, the whites curled and golden at the edges, the yolk shiny and firm. She imagined a magical wedding night baby, conceived in wedlock.

"Your baby is due May 13th."

None of that was true. A baby was already inside her when she walked down that aisle; she knew it. Her first wifely breakfast was gritty, bitter coffee and eggs with leaking yolks and blasted, burnt whites. Her first dinner was even worse. A bleeding, gummy meatloaf Artie blatantly spat into the trash. Their first home was nothing like she'd dreamt, a tiny apartment with yellowed walls and cabinets made of peeling laminate. It was also two blocks from Artie's parents. His mother sent over a replacement dinner of buttery biscuits and a firm meatloaf swaddled in tinfoil.

"Do you think we'll have a house when the baby comes?" Gloria asked the evening after the doctor's appointment. She wore a pastel pink apron Denise's mother had gifted her, along with a Betty Crocker picture cookbook. Gloria spooned out a chunk of shortening and cut it into the flour mixture she'd beaten by hand.

Artie sat on the only chair they owned, a wooden rocker with splintered legs his parents had found in their garage. A nub of smoldering cigarette clenched between his teeth while he etched in his crossword guesses in pencil.

"Sure, we'll have a house. This is just a starter place, and then we'll have a starter home. We've only been married a month!"

"But now we know there's a baby coming, and this place smells bad. And we don't have a place for the nursery." Gloria folded parsley into the dough.

Artie set down his crossword, smashing his cigarette into the ashtray, and waltzed over to Gloria. She dropped dumplings into the soup with a cereal spoon. He'd promised real kitchenware whenever he got his first raise at the store. Artie kissed her neck and rubbed her wrists with his calloused fingers.

"I'll talk to the boss tomorrow and see about a promotion, but Gloria, I've only been there a few weeks. I mean, I could ask for more hours or see about a different department."

Gloria focused on the dumplings bouncing between the peas and shredded bits of chicken. No, he hadn't been there long, and it would be silly to ask now.

"It's okay. I'll try to be more patient."

Artie kissed her again, and she forced a big, wide smile.

"I know we'll get a house eventually. I just thought marriage came with a house—and a serving spoon." She laughed, waving the steaming silver spoon between them.

"That's because you're thinking of our parents. Of course, they have houses and a whole kitchen full of fancy spoons. They've been married for years!"

He went back to the crossword, and she decided it wasn't worth reminding him her mother had never been married or that she'd spent her childhood shuffled between apartments, cars, her grandmother's crowded attic. Her mother was never much for cooking and stirred everything with common silverware. It wasn't worth explaining, not even to her husband.

Chapter 7

April 2018

Allen's started handing out severance packages on April 12th. Joan and Artie stood side by side, promising supervisors, stockers, and tired cashiers that something better was on the horizon.

"Good luck, and thank you for all you gave to the company."

Artie felt sick each time he said it, knowing it was probably a lie. Joan smiled beside him, smears of lipstick on her teeth and her mouth a miasma of minty mouthwash and astringent booze burps. They shuffled through the stack of crisp envelopes while the replacement staff punched in their employee numbers on the touchscreen time clock behind them. The last check slipped into the hand of a woman Artie had hired himself over twenty years ago, back when her hunch was a youthful and sloppy slouch, not a permanent, hardened skin shell. Her eyes watered when he wished her good luck.

Artie turned to Joan, expecting some sort of shared celebration, like when they cut the ribbon on a new store or special renovation.

"Don't you feel like we should be doing more than just handing out envelopes?" Artie asked.

Joan laughed.

"What did you have in mind? Should we have made a performance out of it? A ball?"

He hadn't imagined anything that extravagant. Although, he had half-imagined champagne and his fantasy-self taking a few measured sips. He could taste the burning, dancing bubbles in his throat. Just the thought sent a rush of heat through him he hadn't felt in years. He'd forgotten the thrill of taboo adrenaline. He hadn't forgotten that it was that exact sensation that always propelled him into stupid, painful, exhilarating decisions. Even so, he suddenly missed it so much. The pang was a palpable throb in his chest.

"I don't know—but doesn't it seem like the whole thing didn't really matter that much if it can all be over with a piece of paper?"

Joan patted his arm. "Maybe it didn't mean that much to anyone other than us. And that's perfectly fine by me."

Artie smiled at his boss, while his imagination shifted from celebratory bubbly to his own body stretched over a cold metal strip. His daydream flickered and saw him collapsing at his desk, a perfectly timed expiration before the world ripped out the last bits of meaning from under him. His mental movie followed a fat life insurance policy delivered to Gloria, who decided to take the retirement cruise they'd been planning and transform it into a girls' trip to soothe their many shades of so-called bereavement. There would still be plenty left over for Gloria to buy a bunch of stuff she didn't need, to placate the resentment he knew she would feel.

Of course, nothing he imagined happened. He continued to stand beside Joan wearing a loose smile she probably knew was fake. There wasn't a ribbon or celebratory cocktails. There wasn't a cinematic heart attack. Joan shuffled back to her office, her tiny shoulders pinched to her ears. Artie walked back to his own office and sat in front of the blank computer. His time and duties were quickly dissolving. He opened and closed his desk drawers, finding an old brittle invoice wedged behind a broken stapler. It was from the year 2000, and yet it looked like an old pirate scroll. If he stumbled on an invoice from his earliest days in this office, it would be mummified dust. He reorganized the top skinny drawer, throwing away any pens with nibbled caps. Then he sat some more. Artie never realized how entombed his office was. He couldn't make out any of the machines or wires or squeaky shopping-cart wheels. It was simply coagulated silence, and it was going to drive him insane.

April 12th. He'd missed Autumn's birthday. He scrolled through his phone and found her most recent number, not thinking about time zones or anything sensible like that. The phone dialed before screeching the number was no good. He tried three different variations of the number, getting more screeches and one person who spoke quickly in a language he didn't understand. He logged into Facebook through his phone and sent her a message with an animated birthday candle performing a glitchy dance.

Then he sat again in the quiet, wondering what he was supposed to do.

Gloria hovered over the dining table where all the old photo albums lay like loose bricks. The first step was getting the albums out of the closet. She'd been thinking about that first step ever since that Saturday Teddy's name had resurfaced into the universe and the world hadn't imploded. It was almost as if remembering him was completely normal and innocuous. Even so, she was going through the other albums first. One step at a time.

She left the living room TV on low volume for comforting white noise. She could barely hear the roundtable of famous women arguing over current events as she peeled back another vintage plastic sheath. Gloria tugged another snapshot from its sticky skin, exposing a new precious memory to scalding sunlight and starving bacteria.

Gloria churned every family picture through the same painstaking process. She held them by their edges, the gelatin ridges examined, another forgotten face or moment dissected. The newest one she balanced gingerly across her fingers was from Artie's birthday party in 1971, a moment snared in time with a mustard-yellow veneer and the look of the times: limp, shaggy hair, a fat mustache, a shirt strategically unbuttoned to reveal a few curls of dark chest hair. Gloria tried to remember the entire day, not just the moment captured: Artie's mouth a pursed zero as he blew out twenty-six candles. Behind him, a map of yellow wallpaper with the soft bumps nobody ever noticed. She remembered the tantrum Artie threw when he tried to paste the wallpaper up himself.

The cake in the picture was slathered with thick, whipped white frosting, but Gloria couldn't recall the cake's flavor. Spongy angel food? Dense chocolate? Maybe it was gooey fruit slid between sheets of yellow cake—that had been Artie's mother's favorite. Gloria hated that cake. She always gagged on the mushy, bloated strawberries that reminded her of phlegm. That disgusting dessert was most likely the exact cake in the picture. In fact, Dorothy Joyce had probably insisted she be the one to make Artie's cake, shooing Gloria from her own kitchen and taking over. Gloria pressed her hands to the table, forcing her mouth to regurgitate a forty-year-old taste from her mouth.

It didn't have to be Dorothy's cake.

Gloria held the picture in her own hands, in her house, and Dorothy was dead. Gloria could decide the cake was chocolate and that she had made it, that she had lit every single tiny waxy candle and sang to Artie the loudest. It was her memory, her family album—she could even say she had sung in perfect pitch, and everyone would have to believe her. Gloria took the pen from her notebook where she was drawing out storyboards of photo montages. On the back of Artie's birthday picture, she wrote: Artie's 26th. Chocolate cake made by Gloria. Then, she took the picture and added it to the stack designated to all the Artie moments from the 70s.

Organizing photographs and scribbling out visual design was the first bit of party planning Gloria had gotten to really do since booking the venue back in January. She'd starved off nearly twenty pounds with a version of Denise's Paleo, slathering her vegetables in cold-pressed avocado oil, the same oil her thick strips of fatty bacon crackled in. Gloria didn't think she'd easily tire of steak and eggs, but looking at all the photos from the carb-loving past was making her realize how much she missed pasta and soft, fresh bread. She marveled over a blurry casserole from the next page in the album when a photo slipped free and landed in her lap.

Teddy.

He was five and wearing that bright red hat she'd bought to match his Tee-ball uniform. He'd loved the hat as much as he hated the ball flying toward him. In the photo, he stood in short grass and smiled big enough to reveal his first lost tooth. Gloria's chest throbbed. Simply looking at him now, she was yanked into that moment and could feel his tiny fingers, the thick cotton of his striped shirt, the squishiness of his knees when she pressed a Band-Aid into an imaginary injury. He loved Band-Aids.

Gloria sat down.

One step at a time.

Artie flung his jacket over the photos Gloria had left fanned across the middle couch cushion. Gloria opened her mouth and pointed, but she was still struggling with the fact that they were even there, that she hadn't just put them back in the closet. She thought about getting up to hang his coat and shoving the pictures back into the sagging box they came from, but she'd been trying to do that for hours even before Artie came home. He was oblivious to her paralysis.

He putted around the kitchen before making his way to the bathroom for his usual post-work decompression. Gloria had to use the time wisely; she had to force her legs to move and her hands to scoop up the pictures. She'd already spent the day losing herself in the moments she'd promised to forget. After the first Teddy photograph, she'd become gluttonous—digging straight into *his* box, trying to snare everything she saw before knowing she'd have to bury it again. The way he barely cried when he was born and when he was placed in her arms instantly began pecking at her chest and neck. A little boy who held her hand even when the kids at school made fun of him. He begged her to sleep in his bed, and she obliged almost as a reflex, sometimes waking up on purpose just to hear the sibilant whistling of his childish snores.

The gargling flush from the hallway yanked her back to the present, to a house that had forgotten Teddy had ever lived here. Gloria stammered over the photos, the pile now fanned out and displaced chronologically. Her fingers were independent from her brain, filing them back into a rigid timeline and forcing them to stand on top of each other. The bathroom door opened, the loud fan clicking into silence. Gloria threw the jacket back onto the couch and turned around.

"What's for dinner?" Artie asked in a voice that wasn't his own. "Or should I say, what diet are we doing tonight?" That was more like him. Making everything into a joke.

"Five types of vegetables. It's more of a lifestyle switch than diet." She tried to sound carefree. Artie didn't notice either way.

"Lifestyle. Diet. All the same," he grumbled, tearing a paper towel from the roll sitting in the middle of the table Gloria hadn't had a chance to wipe off.

"We have napkins," she said.

"I thought you left this here on purpose," he balled the paper towel up and held it between two fists.

"I guess it doesn't matter."

Gloria brought out the roasted beets and fennel, realizing on scent alone that she'd used too much lemon. The asparagus, seared in herbed water, was black and wrinkled. Only the cauliflower steak, dripping with an infused coconut oil, looked like the blog post. The salad, which on its own contained at least five vegetables and made her first answer a lie, was soaked in oil-free vinegar dressing that stung Gloria's eyes as soon as she opened the bottle.

Artie ate dutifully, cleaning off his plate and salad bowl and going in for seconds. Gloria picked at hers. She tried Denise's advice of imagining herself squeezing into that silver dress she'd purposefully bought three sizes too small. When they were finished, Gloria still had several leaves of romaine and half a shriveled beet that she pushed down the garbage disposal. When she turned it on, the metal teeth gnashed her leftovers into pulp, quieting the sound of Artie gently pulling open the fridge. Gloria knew he thought he was being stealthy when he went into the other room to unwrap an ice cream bar and snap open a Dr. Pepper. She let him believe he was sneaky. Gloria drank three glasses of water in a row—another trick of Denise's to create the illusion of satiation. She swallowed her night pills and imagined they were Werther's hard candies.

She went back into the living room to suggest the night's movie. Artie sat on top of his jacket. He sat on top of Teddy's photos. Gloria's throat spasmed, and all she could do was point and gurgle, "Teddy. Teddy."

"What?" Artie's voice had a mean snap to it.

"You're sitting on Teddy's photos."

Artie didn't get up, looking paralyzed himself.

The phone rang. Nobody ever called the landline. Gloria kept pointing.

"Get the phone." Artie still sat, his hands outstretched on either side of him.

Gloria's hand strangled the phone until the ringing stopped. She closed her eyes, refusing to look at the Caller ID box, not wanting to confirm any of her worst fears.

When she opened her eyes, Artie, his jacket, and the spread of photographs were all gone. The only thing left was a voicemail that she knew had to be bad news.

Chapter 8

1963

Artie resented the lies that tumbled out of his mouth on his first day as a husband. He couldn't help but place the blame on Gloria who should've told him she didn't know what she was doing. On her first morning as a real wife, she poured him sludgy coffee. She scooped slimy eggs onto a plate, serving it with burnt toast she scraped with butter. He lied when he kissed her hand and said it was the best food he'd ever eaten because she made it.

In hindsight, Artie should have expected Gloria to be a clumsy wife. He shouldn't have taken every stumble so seriously. She would grow into the role, just like she grew into a girlfriend from the awkward girl who fed him cold food from Mrs. Duffy's Tupperware. She hadn't even known how to wait for him between classes, wiping the sweat off her hands before she held his. He taught her to kiss with her tongue and how to be like the other girlfriends. He gave her the reassurance to unbutton her shirt in the backseat of his car but still wear white to their wedding. All women probably failed as wives at first. Even his own mother must have.

Artie was impatient, though. Her weaknesses continued. Her earliest pancakes bled raw batter. She could never time the grills or the little blue gas flames, creating stacks of burnt bread she slathered with oily margarine. She even tried scrambling eggs for simplicity but still ended up with soggy yellow mounds. Artie became a half-and-half drinker to balance out the thick, gritty cups of Folgers and started choosing a banana for breakfast. Somehow, Gloria even messed that up—buying bananas that were too bright or ones that were already too soft and bruised the next day.

They ate mushy spaghetti on top of an overturned box they pretended was a dining room table. Gloria confessed she'd never made banana bread after Artie told her the bananas would be perfect for that task. His stomach clenched with nostalgia. His body ached to see his mother's cooling baked goods perched on the cleanest of windowsills. The windows of their tiny apartment were always caked with film and dust, the screens woven with wings abandoned by frantic flies and wasps. When they opened a window, they always found a grave of mutilated insects. When he'd opened his childhood windows, he had only seen squirrels and birds. That was home. This was hell.

Artie had several honest conversations within himself. Was he being a perfect husband, leaving his dirty laundry in a pile rather than tossing it into the paper bag Gloria insisted was a hamper? Was he taking her out or bringing home flowers? Was he pretending to be excited about the new baby? Was he making enough money at the grocery store, ringing up leaky bottles of milk and stacking wobbly apples so they wouldn't fall, rather than stepping up to the lucrative world of plumbing? These wealthier men, his dad's colleagues and competitors, came to Allen's Market and handed him hard-earned cash from their wet, blackened fingers.

"You still have dreams about singing songs and hitting home runs?" they sneered to the boy they remembered, counting back the change he gave them to make sure it was right.

Artie and Gloria ate dinner with his parents on Sundays. He tried not to openly savor each golden bite of scalloped potatoes, the juicy kernels in his creamed corn, the warm muffins his mother wrapped in a towel so they could take them home, like she knew how much his palate was suffering.

Clyde and Artie smoked together on the back porch. It was strange being out there, in his father's space. Crickets and burping toads studded the dark night's quiet. This was man territory, but that was Artie's territory now, too. His dad passed him a bottle of scotch from underneath the rickety wooden chair he was sitting in. Artie made sure not to grimace when he took his first swig. His dad smiled wider than Artie had ever seen. It must've been the smile that caused Artie to blurt out every regret he'd been feeling the last few months. He regurgitated old childish dreams of becoming a baseball star or singing at the Grand Ole Opry Clyde listened to on the radio. He complained about the nothingness he felt working at Allen's.

"I feel like I've decided my whole life already, and none of it was what I imagined. I'm barely out of being a kid, and everything is already mapped out. It's like now all that's left is waiting to die."

Clyde cackled so hard he choked on his own drink.

"What did you really think was going to happen in your life? That you'd really become rich and famous? Or did you think you could just race cars and get drunk with your friends for forever? What did you think— you'd trade in ol' Gloria for that neighbor girl when she finally realized you were alive? And that she'd forget she was Gloria's best friend? Oh, boy, son, you made me laugh so hard my belly is hurting. I never dreamed up such a fantasy. I knew what life was: work, marry, kids, provide. I never thought it was supposed to mean anything."

Artie yanked the bottle from his dad's calloused hands and took the biggest gulp of booze he'd ever taken. It burned his throat.

Clyde grabbed the bottle and tucked it back under his chair, pushing Artie back inside the house. He went to the porch a second time alone while Artie sat on the couch, watching his wife and mother sip matching martinis in curdled quiet.

"I just told your mother," Gloria said softly.

"Told?"

"The baby," his mother said. Her tone was different, sharper than he'd heard. She stood up and went to the kitchen, washing the same clean glass over and over again.

～ ♕ ～

On their way home, Artie noticed a change in Gloria. She glared out the window. She smoked like she enjoyed it, shooting out her exhales like darts. Maybe she'd noticed how different their lives were, too.

"You know, my mom would love to share her cooking tips. She's been doing it for years, and really loves it. It would be no problem."

Gloria's head whipped to face him, her full lips pulled up around her teeth.

"Why would she need to show me her tips? Why didn't you tell her we were having a baby?" Gloria's voice and shoulders sagged, and she resumed staring out the window. "I don't need any help."

"It might be a fun way for you to bond. She could do the things with you that your mom doesn't like to do."

Gloria pressed herself against the car door. He knew it was the wrong thing to say, but he didn't try to fix it. Just like she didn't protest or squirm when he drove her to his mother's the next Sunday and left her there for hours. She came home with a crisp copy of the *Joy of Cooking*, her arms white with flour. Her next meatloaf was firm on the outside, moist and tender on the inside. Her morning waffles fluffy with gold, crisp edges. She baked a pile of soft biscuits flaked with chives and full of butter.

When Artie came home with his first good promotion, there was a loaf of banana bread steaming from the windowsill, the thick wood and metal screen wiped clean and smelling faintly of lemon and vinegar. He'd barely noticed because his head had been swimming with the new cashier they'd hired—a girl who sucked on a red lollipop during her break and played with the buttons on her sweater when she asked what time he got off.

Chapter 9

May 2018

Gloria never understood why Veronica chose the waterlogged Pacific Northwest. She remembered the day Veronica packed up her gray Hyundai Accent—its bumper held in place with yellow duct tape—to run away before that nutjob could discover she was pregnant and suddenly want her back. Northeast Portland's rain-streaked doll houses were close to Powell's and were as far as Veronica could go where she had at least a few friends and could afford the community college. Nobody could have predicted Veronica would meet Ethan only a month later, asking for the same chocolate croissant in a hip vegan bakery—a starter kit version of the place Veronica and Ethan would eventually open themselves. A story they still swore they didn't make up.

Gloria shivered inside her rental car. Rain glazed the windshield, blurring the darkening sky. The city was gray, blue, and other shades of overcast, causing the tiny coffee stands to pop in their varying colors, even if they were an ugly beige. Gloria had an uncharacteristic impulse to drive through for a latte—maybe pick one up for Ethan and Veronica. But they were probably tired of their local coffees, just like she was tired of whatever new juice bar filled the vacant spot in the closest strip mall. Besides, coffee would be such a pathetic gift. She knew what Veronica was going through, knew it the instant Ethan told them Veronica was in the hospital, that she would be okay. The baby was receiving around the clock NICU care. He lied and said he was hopeful. Through text, Ethan told them the baby didn't make it. Only the day before he had sent them photos of their newest great-grandchild, a red and wrinkly worm threaded with wires and tentacle tubing coming from his tiny nostrils and pink puckered mouth. Gloria made herself forget that baby's face, as she pulled up to Veronica and Ethan's wet gravel driveway practicing her strongest expression.

She walked up to the door, pinching her sweater tighter around her. Edie's pink tricycle was tipped next to a flooded flowerbed. Water pooled in the grooves of the fat rubber tires. Gloria knocked three times.

Ethan gave Gloria the official tour. It had been a while since she'd been to Portland, and they'd moved houses last year. He led her into Edie's room, mumbling as he interpreted each piece of artwork taped to the pink walls. Gloria could barely hear him, straining her ears as he pointed to a tiny turtle shaped from tinfoil and covered with flecks of glitter. Normally, she would simply ask him to repeat himself, but she wasn't going to push him. Gloria knew all too well the mechanical workings of grief. Dinner still had to be made for a small child who didn't fully comprehend loss and death. You still had to remember how brown they liked their toast, how many globs of strawberry jelly to smear into the melted butter. You still had to show awe for their school-made crafts. Autumn had been an adult when her brother died, but Veronica had been only a little older than Edie.

"How are you?" Gloria instantly regretted blurting out anything. She bent over to pick up a plastic banana and a stuffed frog.

"I'm—okay," Ethan shoved his fists into his pockets and dug his heels into the floor. Through the holes in his jeans, his knees clenched. He kept his eyes locked on hers. They were dry as bone. Gloria knew that song and dance. She suspected the tips of his fingers were chewed to rags and yellowed from smoking too many cigarettes. He'd probably had a few extra beers the last several nights and tried to scrub the residue from his tongue before she got there. He'd probably do the same tonight. Gloria could also predict Veronica's coping—the gluttony of excessive baking and mothering. Attempting the stiffest meringues, the most avantgarde pie fillings, perfecting cookie crusts, digging into her creations after everyone was in bed, eating them straight from the pan while she stood barefoot in the kitchen, falling asleep with sticky sugary substances scaled over the soles of her feet. There was probably a bottle of warm wine hidden somewhere in the bedroom.

Gloria embraced Ethan, holding on as tight as she could, her own breathing caught in her chest. When she felt like she might faint, she pulled away and asked him, "Where is Veronica?"

Veronica didn't want to talk. She only wanted to watch movies. *Beaches, Terms of Endearment, Turner and Hooch, Steel Magnolias, Ghost.* She had a stack of old VHS tapes but found the movies streaming. The VHS tower was simply a grounding tool, like a charged crystal.

Gloria sat on the couch—a bright yellow thing Veronica had proudly found online and in what she called "perfect" condition. The cushions shriveled beneath them, and Gloria had to sit on two bed pillows just to pretend she was comfortable. Her granddaughter watched the first movie from the opposite side of the couch, nibbling the edges of her fingers and stretching the wrists of the thermal shirt she was wearing. Gloria recognized the ribbed arms as something she used to see poking out from Veronica's band t-shirts back in high school when she went through a long phase of trying to look as strange as possible. Veronica still had a unique style. Her hair was a faded teal, and her arms were scribbled with permanent woodland creatures, cats, vintage artifacts, and poetic verse. Gloria had finally gotten used to them.

Glowing in the reflection of Bette Midler and Barbara Hershey's immortalized friendship, Veronica was snared in time. She was four, five, six, sucking her thumb and begging Gloria to rub her back with her long red acrylic nails. Her hair wrapped up in pink sponge curlers and wearing a Barbie nightgown or one of her plastic costume dresses. They had watched these same movies then, Veronica interrupting the whole time to ask what and why things were happening. Was she going to die? Why did she die? Do moms die? Her quivering voice echoed so loudly in Gloria's mind she wondered if her granddaughter was still asking those questions. When she looked at her, though, she was curled up, her hands disappeared into the thermal sleeves, biting her lip, trembling.

"Veronica?" Her own voice sounded like a helpless child. Her granddaughter looked at her and straightened her face.

"It's such a sad movie," she said, a sagging smile stretched over her face.

"You've always loved this movie."

"I remember how scared I was everyone was going to die. Mom, especially."

Gloria twitched inside. Sometimes she forgot Autumn was really the mother, that she was the grandmother.

"I remember," Gloria said. She didn't mean for it to come out so flat. Veronica scooted a little closer, her knuckles peeking out from the sleeves. They were shiny with the tears Veronica thought she was hiding.

"Do you ever talk to her?" Veronica had been asking where her mom was almost since she was born. Gloria never had a good answer.

"We tried to call her for her birthday, but you know those European numbers. Sent her something on Messenger."

"Yeah, I did, too. She didn't answer, but she also didn't see it."

Veronica stared ahead. On the screen, the newly orphaned girl collected her cat and got in the car, watching the house she had to leave behind. Veronica began to sob. This was the part that always got her as a child, too. The finality, the little girl leaving everything behind. Veronica slid closer, close enough for Gloria to notice it had been a few days since she'd showered, brushed her teeth, or eaten much other than a sip of coffee or some swigs at night. Maybe that's why she'd sat so far away. She thought Gloria would judge her, the way she'd judged her high school outfits. *My love bug,* she thought as loud as she could, *I understand.*

"Did you want to be a mom?" Veronica whimpered.

"It was the only thing I ever wanted to be. Remember how you said singer, vet, all those other things? I only wanted to be a mom. It's a little sad, isn't it?"

"It's beautiful. You were a good mom, Grandma."

Veronica switched to the next movie, clasping her hands together and side-smiling to Gloria.

"This one was our favorite."

Steel Magnolias. They'd worn out every VHS they'd ever had of the movie. It was always their's—never hers and Autumn's, or hers and Artie's. Teddy never lived long enough to see it. Gloria used to pretend he was watching it with them. He would have loved it.

"Grandma?"

"Yes?"

"Does the hurt ever get better?"

"Yes," Gloria lied.

Veronica scooted closer, her cheek squished against her grandmother's knee like it had been years ago. She asked about the party, and Gloria gave wispy responses. It was coming quickly, two months away—and all she'd done was starve herself into a new dress and gather photographs she knew her husband would hate seeing on display. She didn't tell Veronica any of that—simply described the decorations and design, and how Denise was taking over, and promised they would have vegan options. Veronica didn't mention her pain anymore, just watched the movies until her breathing turned cloudlike and Gloria knew she was asleep. In the darkness, the TV glowing and muted, Veronica's question tumbled around. Does the hurt ever get better? She realized she didn't know which hurt Veronica was referring to. Teddy? All the babies before him? How much did Veronica even know? How much did Gloria still remember?

In the darkness, she untangled her own stories. She narrated each painful loss—periods she didn't want, heartbeats turned apparition, the nightmare she couldn't erase from her mind. Veronica began snoring. Gloria talked about Teddy. Her chest cleaved when she reminisced about the day he was born, how he had clung to her with sticky salamander fingers the moment the midwife set him on her chest. She told the quiet room how Autumn had recoiled with disgust when her parents set her up with a pile of pillows and laid the swaddled baby into her wriggling lap.

"I don't want him," Autumn had said, looking both of her parents in the eyes.

"You don't have to hold him," Artie reached over to scoop up Teddy, who only blinked at the ceiling. When Artie picked him up, the hours-old infant squirmed, his shriveled hands reaching for his older sister.

"Oh, look, he loves you." Gloria's heart had swelled until it hurt.

"Well, I don't love him," Autumn had marched away from her parents and the baby, slamming her door with all her might after glaring at them all for one hard minute.

Gloria had forgotten that memory, and she told her sleeping granddaughter so. She spun atonement into Veronica's dreams, telling the blank television screen that she had forgiven her daughter.

It was only herself she still had resentment for, for harboring those moments that made her love one of her children just a little less.

She resented Artie, too. Oh, it felt good to tell that to the darkness. She turned the TV off and blurted out a list of the first transgressions that shimmied to the surface. There were so many. Gloria could pick the scab off each one and hate Artie just a little more, just enough to give herself the courage to put whatever pictures she wanted up at the party. She didn't need permission. She didn't need to keep up her end of the bargain.

"You forgot to ask if I wanted to be a wife," Gloria whispered to her sleeping granddaughter. "It was the only other thing I wanted."

It was Gloria's turn to weep, but nobody was awake to hear it.

Over the next few days, Veronica helped Gloria sort through more pictures and offered to make the desserts. Her cheeks glowed and she ate a salad, a piece of toast. She still cried and wanted to watch old movies at night. During one of the brighter parts of the day, holding a photograph of Gloria and Artie on their wedding day, she came up with an idea.

"Let's recreate this wedding dress! Grandpa can wear a tux—it'll be so cute!"

It was pointless to bring up the silver dress she'd already bought. Veronica hadn't been this alive the entire time she'd been here.

Veronica's friend, Abby, came over one night with a pink box of Voodoo Doughnuts and a six-pack of fruity craft beer. The whole night was comical—a girl with a green mullet and taffeta mini-dress measuring her in Veronica's bedroom. Maybe it was due to the first beer she'd had in years, but she wasn't ashamed when Abby mumbled the numbers she found when the ends of the measuring tape touched. They rubbed through a stack of white lace and tulle, and Abby sketched out the neckline and satin buttons that went all the way down the back. She erased and drew again until they all agreed it was perfect. The whole night reminded Gloria of sleepovers with Denise half a century ago—nights with hot rollers and lipstick stains on their pillowcases, with soft, spongy strawberry shortcake Mrs. Duffy carried to them on a glossy yellow tray. Veronica said it reminded her of her own sleepovers, the ones at Gloria's house where her friends stuck stick-on earrings to each other's ears and ate mint chip ice cream right out of the box.

Only instead of a parent or grandparent bringing the treats, it was Edie. She clung to Ethan lately, giving Veronica space to not have to mother on demand. She carried in boxes of cookies and popsicles. The boxes sweated under her soft arms.

They showed Edie the drawing of the dress Grandma Gloria would wear, even if only during a portion of the party. She said she wanted one just like it. Abby loved the idea and drew a duplicate for her.

For the fifth night in a row, Artie ate take-out on his back deck, the day's heat stuck in the lawn chair's colorful plastic. Warmth crept through his jeans and gently singed his bare forearms. He loved it. He thought about Gloria stuck in the dreariest place and would have felt sympathy if he wasn't enjoying the crumbs of his Caesar salad croutons spilling over the torrid concrete. Jumpy birds and skittish khaki lizards crept along the hem of the deck.

He had debated grilling a burger or a fat, greasy sausage, but he couldn't shake how social grilling felt and how lonely it would be to get the charcoals to the perfect glowing red without any witnesses. He considered calling up to Portland to see how they were all doing, but then he knew they would ask about the party, and Gloria might get the guts to ask him what happened to the photos. She most likely wouldn't, but he didn't want to risk it. So, he ordered expensive food packaged in flimsy Styrofoam and compostable cardboard. He ordered tuna melts and pastrami and fried rice and potato salad. He bought overpriced tiny bags of potato chips and a bottle of full-sugar, full-caffeine Coke. He sat on the deck until the sunshine bled from the sky and was siphoned from the plastic lawn chair, the metal dining set, the closed grill they bought from Lowe's last summer.

It was peaceful. It was dull. It was decompression from a job that was now creating busy work for him. Organize old filing cabinets. Upload digital accounts to some new cloud. The office staff whittled further. Joan even asked if he would think about retiring earlier before laughing so hard she spat coffee all over her hands.

"I'm half-kidding. It's just, we're really flailing here. But I know you'd go down with the ship—I just want to tell you I might get us all off before it sinks into whatever these guys have planned for it."

When she walked away, he noticed how frail she'd become. The curve of her shoulder, her arms swimming in a cream-colored blouse, her narrow neck branched with veins like twigs. She'd once been something fierce and strong, a Katherine Hepburn type, and now she was wilting. She never forced an answer to her rhetorical request.

Artie scooted the crumbs with the edge of his shoes over to the patient birds. The sky swirled shades of sherbet. Warmth still stuck to the dry gusts of wind. Once upon a night like this it would've been the perfect night for an ice-cold beer, one submerged in a plastic cooler filled with clanking ice. Even though he knew there wasn't another person there, Artie couldn't help but look over his shoulder to see if anyone heard his thoughts.

Yes, he told no one, *I'm still human. I still want things that are bad for me. I still want things I want.*

He hung into his old anger for a moment, just for old times' sake. Then he went inside the house, closed the glass over the screen, and drank his second real Coke of the week while watching the cowboy movies Gloria had hated ever since they got married.

Chapter 10

1964

Autumn Catherine Joyce was born April 11th, 1964, a month earlier than the doctors predicted, although Gloria knew her daughter was perfectly punctual. Gloria labored alone, save for the doctor who spoke to his nurse and showed her the baby wailing like a rabbit snatched by a neighborhood cat. Artie passed out cigars in the waiting room down the hallway. When they let him in to see Gloria, his flask was empty, and he slurred when he congratulated Gloria on all her hard work.

A nurse wheeled Gloria to meet her new baby hours after they'd been ripped apart. Autumn lay in a plastic crib with her eyes squeezed shut, swaddled in a scratchy hospital blanket.

"Give her this," the nurse instructed, handing Gloria a glass bottle filled with chalky formula.

"I wanted to nurse her."

The nurse's face scrunched, and then she shrugged.

"Suit yourself." This was the zenith of modern living, of multifunctioning appliances and domestic convenience. Gloria knew she was an anomaly, but she wanted everything inherent to motherhood. She'd waited so long.

The nurses tried again to convince her it was best to mix the sour formula with tepid water. They told her coddling was bad for the baby. They needed to be fed and then plopped into a mechanical swing or bouncer, so that Gloria could be a good wife and tend to all the things that would make her husband happy. Gloria wasn't worried about him.

She was worried about her baby—and the baby's immediate resistance to Gloria's mothering. Autumn blinked at her with thick eyelashes and amber eyes, a freckling of white baby acne on her fat cheeks. Gloria hummed lullabies and pulled her baby to her bare chest. Autumn's lips puckered, opening like a fish before she clamped down with stiff, wet gums. Gloria kept trying. She tried until her nipples cracked and bled and crusted with yeast and infection. She tried in the hospital every thirty minutes until she was sent home. She tried from the corner of their stuffy apartment sitting on an old, tattered rocking chair, forgetting Artie's dinner. She tried and tried and tried. Autumn either refused or bit like a rabid dog, even shaking her head the way dogs did with trespassing squirrels.

Gloria eventually gave in to the canisters of sour powder fortified with all the nutrients her baby didn't want from her. She packed the canisters in four paper bags when they moved into their first starter home, a faded yellow house with a broken, unpainted fence and sputtering faucets. Denise showed Gloria her engagement ring, while Bill and Artie carried in the few boxes they had and hoisted the scraggly rocking chair over their shoulders. Gloria shoved the formula into the back corner of her new pantry. It was more than Autumn could finish, but Gloria knew there would be more babies.

Gloria lived like a machine for Autumn's first year of life. She gulped for air between washing diapers, wiping spit up from the carpet, boiling rubber nipples, and making the bed with snug, tight corners. She sang in a whisper to Autumn, watching the stars fade into dusky dawn before exploding into bright sunshine. Autumn hated sleeping.

Denise came over almost daily with groceries and frilly dresses with matching bows that crinkled in Gloria's hands.

"When are you going to have one? Maybe you could have a girl, and then they can be just like us. But if you wait too long, they'll be too far apart." Gloria squeezed her free hands between her naked knees. Denise held Autumn on her lap, decorating the baby's cheeks with pale-pink lip prints.

"We're barely married!" Denise blew a dainty raspberry into Autumn's squishy arm.

"So are we."

"You're different. You couldn't wait to be a mother. I can. Plus, Bill just started this completely useless job, but they have amazing business trips that I get to go on, too. We're going to Miami next month. I couldn't do that with a baby."

"It's not a vacation. It's a business trip. You wouldn't have to go."

Denise laughed lightly before folding her face into strict seriousness.

"No, I would absolutely have to go. Men don't become husbands instantly. That's what my mother told me. She said you have to make them want it—and make them be it. Speaking of which, does Artie ever work 'late?' My mother said that's the first thing they do when they don't know how to be husbands."

Gloria didn't like what her friend was implying. She especially didn't like it because he had been suddenly later than usual. It had to be a coincidence.

"Artie comes home every day," Gloria finally responded, thankful she hadn't had to lie to her best friend. Denise opened her mouth then shook her head.

"I'm glad," Denise said, handing her Autumn. The baby reached for her mother with arachnid fingers, her wet pink gums gnashing together between slobbery nonsense. Gloria held her tightly, pressing their faces together.

"Let's go outside for lunch. It's such a perfect day."

The sun toasted the top of their heads while they ate egg salad sandwiches. Gloria wondered if Denise remembered her own mother doing the exact same thing.

Artie wanted a big family. He crawled beside Gloria every night, begging her for another baby. They never came. Her cycles were sometimes postponed, erupting at the most inconvenient times. In the cold aisles of the grocery store while Autumn screamed from the cart. When Artie reached for her legs under the sheet, yanking his hand back and running into the bathroom to rinse blood from the crooks between his fingers. One time it was five days behind schedule, spurting out while she rinsed Autumn's soiled diapers. She'd been convinced this time would be an actual baby, hating that every time she'd put her hands over her middle it had still been hollow.

Then, there *were* pregnancies. Partial babies that lived in the mixed vials of pregnancy tests or in the speckles of bright red that stained her sheets, that clouded the toilet water. She had tense conversations with Artie in their kitchen, while Autumn dragged a toy dog between her legs with a leash made of unravelling yarn.

"What if something's wrong with me?" she asked with an extra wide smile so Autumn wouldn't be suspicious.

They kept trying. Artie kept trying. He woke up earlier on his days off. He brewed coffee and brought Gloria her mug first. He mowed the lawn. He sat cross-legged on the floor with Autumn doing clunky puzzles, building block towers, tending to fabric baby dolls even though he'd never given a bottle or changed a diaper in his life. He slept with his arms around his wife. He praised her hair, her cooking. He kissed her hello and goodbye every single day. They tried every night after he would read Autumn her bedtime story. There were more blue vials, more missed cycles, more bloodletting that she knew was more than just a late period. She flushed with her eyes closed.

Then, one finally stuck.

Artie restricted her to the lawn chairs, the sofa, the bed. Denise came over to lift anything that would break whatever magic had finally happened.

"You're still not going to do this with me."

Denise shook her head.

"I will eventually."

"What if you end up like me, and it's a lot harder than you think?" Gloria placed her hands on her stomach. The swell was so slight only she noticed it. Sometimes, when she laid her hands over her middle, she swore she felt a pulse.

"I'm happy being Autumn's fun Auntie, and this baby's, when they come."

"He."

"What?"

"When *he* comes."

"You know already?"

"No, but I know."

Autumn blew bubbles beside them.

"I don't want a new baby," she said, not looking at them.

"This is the first I've heard of this!" Gloria laughed, before reeling it in to a gentle chuckle.

"I just want it to be Mommy, Daddy, and me. Babies make my Mommy sick and sad." Autumn tipped over the bubble jar and smeared her bare foot in the suds.

"Sibling rivalry already." Denise shooed the words away. Autumn walked out to the grass and began yanking the blades one by one before ripping each one in half.

"I'm sure that's normal." Gloria squinted through the sun.

"I'm sure it is."

"Does Bill want you to wait?"

Denise lit up a Virginia Slim, taking slow and measured inhales.

"You just won't let it go." Denise blew out a string of smoke.

"Well, does he?"

Denise sighed. "Since it's you, I'll tell you the truth. No, he wants babies as bad as you want me to have them. But I'm not ready to give everything up yet. I know I'm supposed to, but I'm just not ready."

"How do you manage that?"

Denise smiled wide and leaned forward, one hand on her knees, the other on the arm of Gloria's blue lawn chair.

"He doesn't know how it all works, not really. And I have a calendar with codes he'll never figure out. You can time it—when you want to have them and when you don't. What do you think they did when women died having babies?"

Gloria didn't know how to answer a statement she found so accidentally unforgiveable.

The placidity was deceiving. Gloria was tired of lounging and watching dust curdle on the wall trim. She was tired of eating her mother-in-law's cooking. She only took on the mildest of tasks. Washing the silverware, folding the laundry, taking a duster to the windows, buttering toast.

"I'm fine," Gloria insisted at Artie's panicked face. "I won't break. This will be just like Autumn."

Her stomach grew enough for others to notice now. Especially Autumn, who scowled at Gloria's middle every chance she got. She tried to crawl on her mother's lap but was scolded—gently by Gloria and then irrationally by her father, whose voice was louder than either of them had ever heard. He later apologized to them both.

Gloria was thinking about the look of heartbreak on her daughter's face while she cracked eggs into a mixing bowl and whirled in a small stream of milk. The eggs were still striated with white when she felt a sharp cramp. Her slippers dug into the linoleum, and she froze.

Autumn waltzed into the kitchen, mid-sentence, demanding to know why her Mommy wasn't answering her.

"Not now," Gloria said each word slowly and so quietly, she wasn't sure Autumn heard her.

"What's wrong?" Autumn whispered, too.

The cramping collapsed into clenching. She wanted to throw up.

"Go get Daddy," Gloria said, lowering herself to the floor.

Artie came in still wearing his bathrobe, his hair wet and white soap dripping from his chest. He bent over and picked her up. Gloria tried to tell him not to, but the force of being lifted from the ground broke the spell.

She felt the stickiness between her legs, the trickle of viscous water. She closed her eyes.

When she opened them, a jellied pink thing shivered on their kitchen floor. Autumn cried. Gloria turned away, still squeezing her legs together. Artie used a napkin and spatula to scoop it into a box they buried in the backyard.

Artie waited a few weeks before caressing Gloria's arm while she pretended to be asleep. His hands roamed over her body. They felt like centipedes. Goosebumps scattered over her shoulders. All she could see were fleshy baby bird eyes and a mouth sealed shut. She hugged herself tight.

"I'm not ready," she said to the depth of her pillow. He rolled over.

She wasn't ready the next time or the time after that. Denise showed her how to track the time on the calendar, so she could decide when she could be ready.

"I just can't go through that again," she told her friend after they mixed Manhattans on the kitchen counter. Gloria couldn't stop thinking about how close they were to where her baby had been born and died.

Gloria's calendar hung inside the pantry. She looked at it every morning for the day and the day after. When Artie approached her on the wrong days, she invented headaches and cramps or made sure to go to bed much earlier than he did.

He stopped asking.

He stayed longer at work every night eventually. Sometimes, even later than the store was opened. Artie said he had extra responsibilities, and she chose to believe him. When he came home, smelling sour and faintly of a scent she recognized as her own and yet it wasn't her own, she couldn't think up anything plausible and cried herself to sleep, scooting as far to the edge of the bed as she could.

In the morning, she brushed Autumn's hair and clipped in pink barrettes that Autumn yanked out immediately afterward.

"You'll be my only baby, my favorite baby. It'll be just us forever and ever." Gloria tuned her promises to upbeat songs evoking the raspy timbre of Ronnie Spector.

Autumn held her mother's cheeks with both hands and stared into Gloria's eyes, unblinking, her brow folded sternly.

"Do you promise? Do you mean it?"

Gloria sang back to her, "I do. I do. I do."

Autumn snuggled up next to her chest, her ear on Gloria's heartbeat.

"I don't want a brother or sister. I like to play by myself."

"I know, baby."

"I just want it to be us, Mommy."

"I know."

Autumn wove their fingers together, making their pinkies interlock the tightest.

Nearly three years later, Teddy broke the promise Gloria made to her daughter.

Chapter 11

June 2018

Gloria's phone shimmied across the spotless kitchen counter. She didn't need to see Denise's name or her ageless Bitmoji to know the call came from her best friend. They'd had the same phone routine since they were teenagers, minus a temporary twenty-year lapse when time differences became too confusing. Now, with Denise and Bill back in the states, they were back on schedule. Fridays, 4ish.

"Hi, Denise." Gloria placed the call on speaker.

"It's only a month away," Denise sang. Gloria and Artie's actual anniversary was July 13th, 1963. The party was set for July 20th.

"Yup," Gloria tried to sound excited. She thought about the venue, how she and Denise had nearly collapsed in their shared reaction to the beautiful antique stone building. Denise and Gloria had gushed over the marble fountain, the slick dance floor, the antique postcards hanging in the bathroom, the lightbulbs framing every mirror. Together, they pointed to the Queen Mary's partial view through the window. The stone walls were the perfect mosaiced amphitheater to arrange their curated photo montage. Denise had loved the idea of honoring their long marriage via projected and framed photographs.

"You don't sound like a woman who is about to show the world what a successful marriage looks like. You know I found all those girls from school?"

"School?"

"Oh my God, Gloria, where is your head? I found all the girls we went to school with, and guess what, they're all living miserable lives. They probably won't show, but don't you just love the idea of showing them how you two made it?"

Gloria tried to laugh.

"There's something else I've been thinking about." Gloria chewed her words slowly, like her mouth was full of bubblegum.

"Add it to the list!"

"Someone needs to talk about the pictures with Artie. He won't want to be surprised."

Gloria heard the panic in her own voice. The silence that followed made it worse. Denise knew Teddy was a sensitive subject for Artie, even if she didn't know every detail of their agreement.

Finally, Denise sighed.

"Do you want me to do it?"

"Would you?"

"Gloria, I'm your best friend! Remember, Maid of Honor? I'm just continuing my duties fiftiesh years later." Denise sighed for the second time. "I hate that it's been that long. I suddenly feel so old."

"You're the best."

Just like the old days when she wondered whether they should go bowling or watch the boys get drunk at the park, Denise ended the call by asking if they should keep their lunch date for Saturday—or swap it for Sunday brunch instead.

Gloria told Denise to decide.

The next Friday Denise called at 4:23.

"Have you talked to him yet?"

"Well, hello to you, too! Not yet. It's delicate—I have to find the right time."

"We don't have much time for the right time."

Denise ignored her, telling her about how she had scanned in nearly every photo and digitized all their old home video footage—8mm, every size of VHS camcorder tape known to the industry. She promised it would be Oscar-worthy.

"That all sounds wonderful, but Denise, he isn't going to care what quality they are if he feels like I've blindsided him."

Even through the phone, Gloria sensed Denise's expression changing. Pinched and serious, possibly even swallowing judgement. Maybe she thought Gloria was doing just that—intentionally jostling something out of Artie. Denise used to say Gloria didn't realize she was pushing his buttons, that her just being her seemed to do that too often.

"You're not blindsiding him," Denise finally said with strained inflection. "You two just see it differently."

That phrase. They'd heard it at hippy couples' retreats, on the soft couches across from a procession of therapists. They just saw things differently. A common marital ailment for which there was no cure.

"I don't know if there is a way to see *this* differently. He's erased our child. Everyone at the party would think the same thing—they would think I want to erase him. I can't handle the thought of everyone walking around saying, 'Where's Teddy? They forgot about Teddy.'"

There was a pause where Denise held her breath. She was a master at thinking before speaking.

"Nobody would judge you, Gloria, either way."

What she meant to say was nobody would question Teddy's absence. After his funeral, there had been a steady stream of deliveries: food, flowers, sentimental cards. Condolences flooded their home—arriving from a safe distance. Friendships and social scenes dissolved further by promotions, recitals, healthy family vacations to Big Bear. All that was left was the core: Artie's family, Denise and Bill, and Joan Allen. The core didn't bring up Teddy. Just like they didn't bring up how they thought Artie was going to drink himself to death or blow his brains out, or how they noticed Gloria said less and less. Nobody talked about what happened to the Joyces. Nobody dared talked about how uncomfortable they were to be around—so quiet and still and strained. Holiday circles shrank. Casual get-togethers disappeared. The Buchanans moved overseas. Nobody wondered where Teddy was. They knew where he was. They'd been to the funeral, watching the glossy bed lowered into the ground.

"I don't understand it," Gloria said, trying to rub the image of Teddy's casket out of her eyes.

"Everyone grieves differently. That being said, I told you I'd talk to him, and I will. I just want you to think about why he's avoiding it. It isn't simply to forget Teddy. Everyone suffers differently—maybe he does, too?"

Gloria pretended to agree it was possible Artie could suffer quietly.

Artie knew Joan was avoiding him. Her office was locked, nobody had run the coffee pot, and when he walked over the office, he couldn't sniff out any remnants of the same musky perfume she'd been wearing since 1963.

The warehouse guys smoked Camels outside. None of them had seen Joan.

He decided to pursue the old-fashioned route and pick up the phone. She answered on the third ring, her voice thick from a pharmaceutical sleep.

"I knew you'd call," she laughed, then coughed.

"I've been trying to find you for weeks. Everyone just says you're 'out.'"

"Because I am out."

"Clearly."

"Listen, Artie, I've been telling you we're collapsing for months now. I've been trying to wait for this retirement, but you haven't given me a clear date. We're going under, remember? I'm giving up. I don't care about this business anymore, about keeping it afloat for someone else. Hell, I've probably got ten years max to live. Maybe I want to go see some places before I die."

"You've seen a lot of places."

"Never been on an African safari."

"So, you've been avoiding me because you're just not coming in anymore? Or you don't know how to tell me I'm fired?"

"You'd never be fired." Something curdled on the other side of the phone. Dainty, heartbreaking sobs. The beautiful crying he'd seen in so many girls and women, the crying that hollowed him out and made him weak, while also empowering him as their savior. Ladies' crying used to get him into trouble.

"Can I come over?"

"You can do whatever you want."

Artie scrambled for his wallet and keys, forgetting to lock the office behind him. He drove like he'd done as a teenager, weaving between chugging semis and other generic sedans like his, slamming on the brake at each red light and skidding through the green. He didn't notice when his phone slid from the seat to the floorboard. When it rang, he mistook the buzzing for a fly. He rolled down the window. The roaring wind of his car going faster and faster drowned out the feeble pulses of his phone alerting him to a new voicemail.

It was from Denise.

Artie leapt out of the car, forgetting to do his normal patting of his pockets to check for his phone and wallet. Joan opened the door in a silky robe printed in some sort of paisley mosaic. Beneath the robe she wore a skinny-strapped tank top and drawstring shorts. Her legs were bare. Artie noticed she didn't have a bra. He welcomed this brazen comfort. Their intimacy wasn't tainted with sex. It was just unadulterated friendship. Besides, they were old—she was even older than him. They were past all that.

"You actually came over." Joan smiled wider than he'd ever seen. She was someone who smirked, a tight professional note of approval. Everyone told her to smile more. She told them to fuck off. She told them successful women couldn't smile. Wives, mothers—they got to do the smiling. Not middle-aged widows with businesses to run.

"Why wouldn't I?" Artie wiped the clean soles of his shoes on both of her welcome mats. When he stepped inside her Laguna Beach home, he noticed the lights were all turned off—something that almost didn't matter because her house was a honeycomb of open glass. Just like Denise and Bill's. All rich people lived in crystal caves.

"Couldn't you figure out what I was saying, though? Why would you make me tell you in person that I need you to leave? I need you to retire. Then I can just fully hand it over to them, cash my check, and stop playing this game of the company's just changing and not dying. It is dying. You know that, right?"

"Isn't that what I'm doing? Retiring? God, you sound just like Gloria."

"I need you to do it much sooner. I'm holding up Allen's like it's a house of cards. It's killing me, and I can't do it myself. I can't force you into retirement. Just like these young bigwigs can't force me, but they want me to leave, too." Joan spun around, gliding over her shiny marble floor. Artie heard the soft pads of her feet hitting the gleaming floor, knowing she had any hint of callous scrubbed off twice a month.

She led him to the chrome kitchen, where two filled glasses sat side by side on the center island.

"Joan—you know I can't drink."

"It's a special occasion." She stared at him, her eyes wide and suddenly looking like a child who wasn't sure what the right way to behave was. Joan picked up both glasses.

Artie's mouth wetted. She'd probably poured the swankiest Scotch, the stuff he'd barely known in his time as an active drinker. For a sliver of a second, he considered that it might not be a big deal if he had one drink. A sip wouldn't just flick on some switch. He'd never been physically dependent. It was always a choice to self-medicate. A choice to quench his demons, to rouse them, to drown them.

Maybe it could be a choice to just have one.

He was different now, wasn't he?

Joan stepped toward him with her offering, the glass shimmering, sweating. The closer she got to him, the more complex her face became. Bright violet eyes and pale, naked eyelashes that reached the line of her tattooed eyebrows. Full lips feathered with smoker's wrinkles. Teeth too white to be real. An expression on her face he couldn't remember ever seeing before, a face in a different language. She was so close; they were nearly touching. He could feel the drink's ice cubes through his shirt. He held his breath.

"Do you remember when you came into my office right after George died? You just knew you were next in line. Do you remember how cocky you were back then? You burst through my door like all the gallant swashbucklers you'd seen at the show. Like you were the Errol Flynn of the grocery store." Joan cradled the glass, the underbelly of her fingers dripping with condensation.

Artie had forgotten that day until now. His boss dead of a random heart attack. The boss's widow sat behind the desk refusing to cry in the building. He had wanted to console her but also to confirm his competence to step up to the highest rung—right beside her. He'd glimpsed one of her rare smiles.

"Artie, Jesus, you take this so seriously. Sure, sure—have a promotion," she'd said, closing the door before pouring them both a drink. After she'd poured the fourth, she'd sat on the desk and her skirt had scooted above her knees. Artie was used to a barrage of hints from every woman who worked here, every woman he saw at the bar, every woman who cooed and told him he "looked just like young Elvis." He wasn't accustomed to seeing it from Joan. She was pinched and sharp and all-business. The boss's shrew wife—the now dead boss.

She'd tilted forward, her blouse opening enough for him to see the edges of her bra—he was surprised she wore provocative lace. Artie was always flooded with testosterone back then and he was cocky, sickeningly confident—pinning down any woman at any time was the only strength he believed himself to truly possess. His work success was merely due to him being loyal to a growing company because he didn't know how to do anything else, and he didn't want to be roped into the family business. This strength—this sexual prowess—was the only bond he shared with his father. It was his only skill. He didn't think twice about grabbing Joan's thigh and kissing her hard on her open mouth. She didn't think twice about slapping him.

"I'm not one of your office whores. I was faithful to my husband."

Artie had hidden in the crevices and corners of Allen's for weeks. Joan found him at his desk, giving him the papers to sign for his new position and hike in pay.

Why, years later, was Joan bringing it up while urging him to shuck his sobriety for one drink before he went through with his official retirement? She passed the drink into his hands, the tips of her fingers skating over his.

"I found your audacity disgusting back then—especially when you kissed me. I was ready to kick you out, fire you in cold blood." Joan grabbed her drink from the counter, holding it to her chest. "Then I woke up with a hangover and thought about your family, your loyalty to my husband—I gave you the benefit of the doubt that you were just another oversexed man. I wondered if I'd given some sort of signal. Women always blame themselves."

She took a dainty sip, smaller than he'd ever seen her drink.

"Something happened that day, though, didn't it?" Joan looked at him. "We built this amazing dynamic at work—that day didn't ruin us. I watched you use that same ploy with other women and found each conquest more disgusting than the last—but then, I found out you were human. I found out I wasn't perfect. George wasn't perfect. Gloria isn't perfect. None of us are. We are all like those gross human yahoos in *Gulliver's Travels*. Did you ever read that part? With the horses?"

Artie nodded even though he wasn't sure if he had. He held the drink with both hands, sniffing up its essences and counting the little pulses scampering beneath his skin.

"What am I even trying to say, right? Why even bring that up now? To bury some weird, uncomfortable incident from almost forty years ago? It's not that. I'm confessing." Joan set her drink down on a marble side table.

Joan reached back for her drink and took a second heartier sip—the gulp she was known for. She inched closer, enough to where their bellies grazed each other. Close enough for Artie to wonder if she could feel his old man paunch.

"I'm drunk enough to tell you I'm shamelessly in love with you. I hated the kind of guy you were, and then I found myself thinking about that kiss and wishing I could have taken it further without it leaving a mark on me. And now I'm old, a retiree, and nobody cares in this world who an old lady wants to fuck." Joan laid her head on his chest. "Although I haven't been with anyone but George, because nobody was you. I hate whatever witchcraft charm you have, but I had to tell you." She tilted her head up, her eyes glassy. "I'm in love with you," she said again.

The drink suddenly made sense. He was being drugged. He knew why she was doing it, so they could blame the alcohol later. It was such an easy scapegoat. Most people relapse. He could take the drink, the simple excuse. But he had promised, and he was trying so hard to keep just one promise in his life.

Joan was quiet, her face dampening his shirt. He wasn't prepared to remember what had simmered between them, even before George died. He'd always respected how Joan was immune to his cliché flirtations, how later they became inside jokes. Joan whimpered and he knew she was embarrassed, that she might fire him tomorrow to save face. She was proud. But she was also vulnerable right now, shivering and waiting for him to reject her. Joan was the one person who always got the real him.

His hands on her back weren't the feeble hands of a man whose mind seemed to only teeter between death, party planning, and executing retirement. No, the man holding her was strong and unworried. He didn't care about the consequences. Joan wasn't a typical conquest. She wasn't going to ask him to leave his wife or when he would call again. The man who decided to kiss her wasn't a pathetic old man. He wasn't even Artie.

Afterward, he helped her rinse out the glasses, including the drink he left untouched. They circled July 10th on the calendar and labeled it ARTIE'S LAST DAY. They swore to forget what happened. In another time and place, something might have come from it.

Artie walked out of Joan's door, whistling a Left Banke song he hadn't thought about in years.

It took less than five miles of bumper-to-bumper traffic for Artie to realize what had happened. Remorse and regret sluiced through him, watering his eyes and transforming the thread of red brake lights into one blurry line. The hard rubber of the steering wheel grated his palms, which were suddenly slippery with sweat. What had he done?

Joan. *Joan.* A woman he'd known nearly as long as Gloria. The quiet, ambitious wife to the man who served Artie promotion after promotion. The hardened widow who kept profits high. Artie's friend and confidant, a safe platonic outlet—the safest woman to be around for a man trying to keep his word. It wasn't just about drinking. He couldn't ride out fidelity, not even at the end of the line. He wasn't the young man he pretended to be back at Joan's house. He was an old man. A pitiful old man swooned by someone finally wanting him, and just like that, he'd broken yet another vow. Right now, when he was so close to ending things as a good man, a man who kept his promises.

Rows of cars inched onto the slope of the freeway's entrance. Artie swerved with them, braking harder than he meant to as he slid into the flow of traffic. He wasn't thinking about how late he would get home. He barely noticed the blinking lights of cars snaking into his lane. He drove like a ghost. He felt like a ghost. Some repulsive old man Cassanova reliving his slutty youth. Wasn't his sort bound to a certain type? Old lady wasn't usually it.

Maybe he'd made the whole thing up.

It all seemed like some sappy movie they made with aging actors, a boomer rom-com. Like he and Joan had been meant for each other since 1963, coincidentally the same year they were celebrating next month. His fucking wedding anniversary. This wasn't remorse flooding him now. It was something prickly, cold. Artie had to pull over quickly to the tiny gravel shoulder. Was his arm going numb?

Artie tried to press into his pulse through the thin skin of his neck, the smooth underside of his wrist. Each point bleated weaker than the last.

Why had he done it? Classic Artie, trying to find a legitimate reason for each of his mistakes when there was never a good one. He'd played this game before, blaming women's skirts, the way they buttoned their shirts, the magnetism of new perfume. He'd blamed friends and bartenders and hard days at work. God, Joan had tried to get him to drink. That was low, really low. She knew how long it'd been. Artie remembered holding the drink, feeling its cool perspiration, the chimes of swimming ice cubes. He remembered the flimsy justifications ricocheting in his head.

This was different.

We're older—this isn't me 'chasing tail.'

One time. Nobody will ever know.

I've been loyal for so long.

Artie's arm turned flesh and bone again. He found his pulse. He gripped the steering wheel. He was still alive.

Before he could pull back out into to the sludge of slow cars, he had to slow his brain. Memories whipped around so fast he couldn't wrangle a single scrap. Then they slowed, a churning carousel. There he was at thirteen, sitting in the garage with Marty, his best friend since 3rd grade. They had their hands down each other's pants, their eyes squeezed shut and their hands sliding up and down. They'd tried to wink and swagger around girls and just wanted to know what happened if someone else touched it— just to prepare themselves so girls didn't think they were complete dweebs. After they were done, Artie had rubbed his hands with motor oil so Clyde wouldn't smell the sissy on him. Artie didn't like men, he just liked being somewhere else. Years after that day, Marty drove off a cliff near Griffith Park, weeks after asking the prettiest girl in school to marry him, days after she said yes. He'd left a note on his bed at home, saying "He wasn't right and couldn't make himself." Artie had only nodded when he'd heard about that, chanting over and over in his own head: I am right. I am right.

Marty was dead, and Artie had screwed so many women, he'd lost count. Chain of painted nails and lipstick lips. Lines of bare legs. A string of soft laughs, of sugary breath. Each one more intoxicating than any drink. Drinking left him with hangovers—headaches and dry mouth. Women left him charged, made him feel like a cinematic cowboy. At first.

His memories flickered. Gloria, asleep in the rocker with baby Autumn wailing. Then, wiping the blood from her legs, digging a small hole in the backyard. Next. She's smelling each crook of baby Teddy, sleeping on the floor beside his bassinet just to make sure she doesn't lose him. There she is walking through the garage door and screaming at Artie to put the gun down. It was the most life he'd seen in her for almost a year.

He'd held her wrists and pressed her back to the icy garage floor.

"You ruined my life," she'd said with gritted teeth and a glare he hadn't noticed before. Gloria had always adored him to a fault, something that had made him more bitter. The hatred in her eyes was grating, hot. He'd started sobbing. He'd never even really cried. Gloria glared until she patted his back like some recalcitrant child. Her fingers combed his hair. They'd been avoiding each other, but now found each other in a way that had been far too long. He promised her, still naked and sticky with sweat.

"Don't promise me now. You don't know what you're saying."

He kept promising. When he unloaded the gun into a starless night sky. When he poured the last of his beers. When she took the last picture of Teddy off the wall.

The memories dissolved. He sat in cold, crisp reality. He was just an old man pulled over to the side of the 405, consoling himself after a nonexistent heart attack and a very real infidelity. He was a man who failed at everything, even at cardiac arrest. He was a man who would fail at merging back into traffic, who would fail to tell his wife the truth, who would fail at celebrating his lengthy marriage—because what were they there to celebrate? Time? Anyone could survive fifty-five years fogged with cocktails, a stranger's soft thighs, and perennial family vacations.

Bill called Gloria, telling her she needed to sit down.

He tried to spare the details of the crash to Gloria, but she kept asking until he told her every ugly detail. The truck turning too sharply, the blood on the airbags, her head nearly severed by the windshield's thick glass. People standing on the street recording the whole thing with their iPhones. When he ran out of details, he asked, "Do you believe me now? Do you believe she's dead?"

Denise. Dead. The only one she'd ever been truly honest with. It was Denise who she confided in when she noticed Artie's laundry smelling of perfume, when she counted the days since they'd last been intimate in their marriage. It was Denise who gave her a plain cardboard box that they opened together between the plastic patio chairs. A white magic wand. Only Denise would give a gift like that.

"We don't really need them." Denise had winked, her navy mascara never smudging, her false lashes glued right at the seam of her eyelid. The coroner had to be in awe of Denise, even after the accident. Did her makeup stay perfectly in place? When her head sliced through the windshield, did blood stick to her hair? Gloria dug her knuckles into her closed eyes, rubbing them dry and snuffing out those morbid images.

She paced around the kitchen before calling Artie again. The cashier who answered said he'd left the office hours ago. Gloria left another hysterical voicemail before it was full and couldn't handle any more messages. She paced more. She dug into the freezer and found frostbitten fudge pops, unpeeling all four and chewing them with her mouth open to weaken the spoiled taste. Her mouth still tasted of muted, icy cocoa when Artie walked through the door. He rushed to her and hugged her for the first time in at least a decade.

"I'm retiring. I'm done." His tone was gallant, performative—so much so, Gloria looked around to see if they were filming a commercial.

"Denise is dead," she said, still not sure if she was in real life. Her eyes itched when she blinked.

Artie paled.

"What?"

"She was supposed to call you."

"Call me?"

"Before. She was supposed to call you." Gloria shivered. Her eyes burned with new tears.

Artie patted his sides, his face slack and concerned.

"My phone. It's gone." His eyes turned feral as he darted outside. Gloria watched him through the blinds, watched him drag both hands down the sides of his head and neck. She stepped out the front door, shielding her eyes from the sun.

"Did you check under the seat?"

"It—it can't be there." Still, he bent and dug under the seats, standing up with the sleek black phone in his hand. A lopsided, relieved smile on his face.

He had thirty-seven missed calls from Gloria and twenty new messages. From Denise there was one. On speaker phone, they listened to her urgent plea for him to call her, to talk about the party. Her message was cut off mid-sentence, the rest of the thirty seconds filled with static, screeching sounds Gloria would never erase from her ears.

Chapter 12

June 1971

Gloria leaned over the ship's deck, her eyes fastened on a ribbon of dolphins weaving in and out of the translucent sea. She admired the synchronized muscles of their blue, rubbery bodies while blowing out lazy tendrils of cigarette smoke, reaching behind her for the blended strawberry daiquiri she'd been sipping on for the last hour. Her belly was stuffed with fruits and breads and tiny pickles from the ship's upstairs buffet. Her daughter was with Artie's parents, safely landlocked, along with all the bad vacations they'd tried as a family. Sweaty car trips. Arguments in front of legendary landmarks. A camera buried under suntan oil and extra diapers that were never enough. Disembarking was supposed to be paradise. She could sleep in and drink coffee at the same time as her husband. She could wear a different sequin dress every night and finally have somewhere to wear the jewelry Artie gave her out of guilt. She could pretend his arm around her in the morning was sincere and roll over until she was buried in his chest. There, in the sparse dark hairs, she could tell herself she was still madly in love with a man she rarely saw on land.

The boat strolled over the crystalline Mediterranean. A decadent gift courtesy of the Buchanans. Denise begged them to come after Gloria said the offer was too extravagant.

"I know how much you love cruise vacations, and I need a friend on these. Bill pretends we're away for fun, but he always sneaks paperwork. He wears his swim trunks, but I never see him actually get in."

Gloria gave in to her best friend before asking Artie, although she already knew he loved how cruises provided easy lapses in all the stupid choices he'd been making throughout their marriage. Cruises provided a restricted environment, forcing him to be a good man. Denise was right, though. Gloria loved them, too. She liked getting dressed up for him, having something to diet for. It was fun dancing and drinking and choosing two desserts every night. On the early cruises, their foreheads touched while they slurped up spiked slushees, musing over a child that wasn't their responsibility for a few days. They watched the strip of dust and dirt from the water with binoculars. It was so far away.

This cruise hadn't felt like the others. Gloria found herself sticking to deck furniture, striped indents down her thighs and across her shoulder blades. That's why she stood up, peeled herself from the plastic chair, choosing to listen to the roar of salty wind instead of Denise's endless questions about what motherhood was *really* like.

"I just can't do it anymore. He's starting to think there's something wrong. Who knows another couple married for as long as us who hasn't at least had one pregnancy? Plus, maybe I'm ready now. I've traveled—and we have a lot of money, so it should be the right time, right?"

Gloria nodded. The dolphins leapt higher.

"What's the hardest part about Autumn? She always seems so sweet and fun when I see her, but I know she has to be difficult sometimes."

Gloria sighed and spun around, flopping back on to her reclined deck lounger. She crossed her arms over her eyes. The sun sizzled on her arms. What should she say? The demands for cutting off crusts and choosing the *right* spoon every time? The pressure to brush out tangles without inflecting even the slightest pain? What could she say that would be the farthest from all the times Autumn danced around her hollowed stomach, hugging the vacated space, and cheering for a mother that belonged only to her?

"She is sweet and fun." Gloria pushed the swell of love into her voice.

"Does she crawl into bed with you still? I always hear about never getting to sleep."

"No, she doesn't do that."

Gloria sometimes crawled into bed with *her*, on the nights Artie was out later than his usual late. The little girl would roll away from her and press herself to the wall. Gloria found herself snuggled up to a hill of stuffed animals, sometimes for comfort and sometimes for warmth because Autumn had cocooned herself in every blanket.

"Do you think I'll be a decent mother?" Denise asked, but she wasn't looking at Gloria anymore, and Gloria was thankful because she found her brain wandering to the last few days on land, where another girl dared to call the house and ask for her husband. When Gloria had asked to take a message, the girl had giggled and hung up. Instead of lashing out in anger, she had wondered if any of these girls had virulent wombs like hers. She wondered if Artie really did want more children.

Denise picked up the paperback *Love Story* she'd tossed beside her empty drink. She pulled her bare knees up and began reading. Gloria was thankful she could return to the role of being simply another vacation wife who drank bright cocktails, read magazines, and wore big, round sunglasses. Gloria picked up her own book and read the first page, the first sentence over and over again, wondering if anyone, including her best friend, could tell she'd practiced this smile, this face, in the mirror for years now.

Artie sat on Bill's deck, his eyes closed, letting the rush of salted wind whirl in his ears. He was on his third cigarette, and Bill swore he just had a couple more numbers to crunch. Artie wanted to admire his friend's work ethic, but he also needed this fellow dedicated workaholic to be the buffer between him and every woman on the boat who dared to meet his eyes head on.

This was supposed to be his second, third, fourth honeymoon or whatever stupid moniker he and Gloria wanted to give to their pathetic attempts to save their marriage by deserting themselves as far away from real life as possible.

"You about ready, buddy?" Artie called through the open door. Bill bent over a crisp file, fluttering through invoices with an unlit cigarette perched on his ear.

"Just a few more minutes," Bill called without looking up. Artie lit another cigarette before smashing it into the glass ashtray, embers scattering and burning the hairs on his arm.

"Why don't you just meet me at that one bar? The big one," Artie stood up, shoved his hands in his pockets, and walked back into the Buchanans' cabin.

"Sure thing," Bill said. He punched numbers into the clunky desktop calculator. It screeched as it printed numbers on the rolling receipt, as Artie slammed the door as loud as he could.

Bill never looked up.

Five days was too long. Gloria was tired of reading, of lounging, of deciding between raspberry danishes and buttery croissants. She gagged each time Denise snapped open the tanning oil. She was tired of rubbing it into her own atrophying legs and her friend's slouching back. Most of all, Gloria couldn't stomach another conversation about Denise's impending attempts at conception and the normal, successful pregnancy she was sure to have.

"Things are rough between me and Artie," Gloria said, scraping through the silence before Denise could ponder her future nursery's color scheme. Denise rolled over to her stomach, her entire body slick with tanning oil. She squinted, even though the sun glowed behind her.

"Aren't they rough between everyone? Isn't the whole thing just a long rough patch?" Denise bent her elbows, her titled head leaning on her folded arms.

"I don't know about that. For us, it's different. I think there has been too much, and we...we're just having a hard time moving forward." Gloria dug her toes into the plastic weave of the lounge chair. "What I mean to say is, I can't move on. I can't get past it all."

"And what if you don't get past it? People get divorced all the time. It isn't really the end of the world."

"But you just said we're all going through a rough patch?"

Denise flopped back to her back, covering her eyes with her hands.

"I'm just saying do what you want to do."

"I do love him." Gloria's voice was small, trapped. Denise sat up, throwing her legs over the side of her lounge chair. She placed a hand on Gloria's arm.

"I don't think he deserves your love," Denise said in a tone Gloria had never heard before.

"What are you saying?"

"I'm your best friend. I've seen it all. Sometimes, it's hard to see to it all and not say something. I just don't want to see you stuck or regretting not doing something and hating your husband with every fiber of your being. He won't change, none of them do." Denise pulled her hand back and squished it between her thighs.

"Do you ever hate Bill?"

"Oh, Lord, sometimes. Don't look at me like that." Denise shielded her eyes. A faint spray of freckles bloomed over Denise's pale, smooth cheeks. "I'm not talking about myself, though. I'm thinking about my poor mother. She's still waiting for things to get better. I don't want you to become her. Hell, I don't want to become her. I want you to be happy. You deserve to be happy."

Gloria rolled to her side, away from Denise. She couldn't recall if she'd ever told Denise how badly she'd wanted to become Mrs. Duffy. She'd been bedazzled by the aprons, the baked bread, the chipped pieces of pickles swirled into tuna salad. She'd missed the stewing resentment.

"I don't want to leave him. I just want him to want me." Gloria clenched her body together, hating how pathetic she sounded. "The other cruises were like that. It was like we were newly married—even like the time before we were married. I loved having him seem genuinely excited to see me."

Denise laid another hand on Gloria, this time spinning her back so they could face each other.

"No marriage is like that. Nothing is like that. Nothing lasts. You didn't bring the you-know-what with you, did you?" Denise winked. A hot blush burned under Gloria's budding tan.

"I brought mine." Denise stretched like a snake. "I always do. Bill is so busy with work, and like I said when I gave it to you, with that thing, who needs a husband?" Hearty laughter bellowed from Denise.

"It's not the same."

"Okay, okay. You're right. I love the doting and kissing and stupid handholding, too. But, in the meantime, there is something else you can do. And I think it'll be good for you. You could use a good ego boost—and maybe that confidence could give you a little upper hand. You need to realize what you have, so Artie can realize what *he* has."

Denise stood up, yanking Gloria up with both arms.

There wasn't time to change the subject.

Denise dragged Gloria past the day-drinking sunbathers and a croquet game between senior citizens, past the room of board game tournaments. Gloria's shoulder sockets screamed once Denise removed her talons from her arms.

"Bill is probably working in there, but we don't have to be quiet. He won't notice us."

Denise wasn't exaggerating. The two of them strolled directly in front of him, untying their espadrilles, the shoes hitting the wall with a loud thud. He didn't flinch. He sat on the edge of the tightly made bed, the pillows jeweled with mints wrapped in shiny white paper. Manila files fanned around him like peacock feathers. A stack of glossy advertisements sat beside his legs, which stuck out from Bermuda shorts that Gloria knew Denise felt were wasted in this room.

"We go to breakfast, and they come to clean up the room. He takes those files with him there, too. Then, he comes here and tells me to wait, he'll be there soon. I don't even think he knows where *there* is. Nothing can pull him away, and you know what? I have no clue what any of those papers even mean." Denise smiled as she relayed this to Gloria, but she looked straight ahead, not blinking. "It all seems so boring. Aren't some of us here on vacation?"

Denise shook her head, wiggling out of her white crochet cover up and untying the strings of her white bikini. Bill scribbled on a paper while Denise stood still, completely naked, and stared at her husband. Gloria slid sideways into the tiny cabin bathroom, crouching as she stepped out of her own shapeless cotton cover. Denise poked her head into the bathroom.

"I told you, he won't notice you. You don't need to hide in here."

Gloria stayed in the bathroom, tugging off her daisy-printed one piece, the cold cabin air latching onto her bare skin. She draped one arm over her breasts, letting the other swing strategically down her belly button.

"You're so modest," Denise said, coming into the bathroom with a heap of clothes, bangles, and rope necklaces. Gloria felt like she was thirteen again. Denise picked through the pile, hooking out the things she chose for the two of them. A pink mini dress with the midriff open and held together with giant silver rings for Denise. A short black dress woven with sequins so small they looked like fish scales for Gloria.

"This is perfect for you," Denise said.

The dress's long sleeves belled at the ends. Its neckline plunged to the top of Gloria's ribcage. Denise meticulously arranged Gloria's cleavage, insisting she give Gloria a little extra hair teasing and a pair of thick false lashes.

"You have the best tits." Denise held her own in mock despair. "Seriously, you look amazing."

Just as she did all those years ago, Denise spun Gloria in front of the mirror. It was a transformation; the black go-go boots the perfect touch Denise swore they would be. It was a miracle she packed both the white and black pair—like the night was meant to happen, Denise mused dreamily.

Denise sauntered past her husband as he dragged a yellow highlighter across a carbon copy. Gloria scooted behind her friend. Bill whistled.

"Woooowwzzeee. Are we all meeting up tonight? Did I miss something?"

Denise rolled her eyes. "Nope. Just a girls' night. You keep at it."

"You look stunning, Gloria. You both look stunning," he quickly added.

After Denise closed the door behind them, she pinched Gloria's bare thigh. "Consider yourself a miracle. You actually got him to look up."

⚜

The boat's main bar was cool and dark, too early for the masses who were tidying up games and soaking fading sunshine before dinner.

"The perfect time for us." Denise waved both of her tanned arms over the room of empty stools and booths. "We'll sit at the bar—front and center."

Denise ordered them each a shot. She feigned ignorance in the cocktail list, resting both elbows on the smooth bar top when she begged the bartender to decide for them. He presented two glasses of something Cuban and sweet.

"Cuba? Is that where you're from?"

"No, I'm Italian." the bartender wiped the dew from the bar with a rag. "Can I get you anything else?"

After he left, Denise whispered into Gloria's ear. "He isn't supposed to really fraternize with us. Don't worry, either he'll loosen up, or we'll get a lively one."

The second drinks were pink and fizzy. New bartenders arrived, tying their aprons and wiping other areas of the bar with crisp towels. This group smiled more. They poured stronger drinks. Denise convinced two of them to take shots with her. They poured one for Gloria, who sipped to stave off wincing and gagging. A blended fruity drink appeared in front of her, soaking the napkin beneath it.

"This might be more to your liking," one of the bartenders said from behind the drink. It was definitely more palatable than the burning glasses of straight vodka. Gloria pinched the tiny straw to control how much drink went down.

"Your friend is a character," the same bartender said. He stood in the same spot, wiping the same rag over the same puddle of evaporating condensation.

"She is," Gloria said to the cherry bobbing in the froth of her cocktail.

"She is having man trouble?"

Gloria's head snapped up.

"Why do you say that?"

"Women only come to talk to men behind the bar to make their own men jealous." He smiled, baring a strong set of white teeth meant for one of Bill's Colgate advertisements.

"That's funny," Gloria said, smiling before feeling self-conscious about her own imperfect, crooked teeth.

"It is true?"

"I guess you could say that—aren't all of us married ladies always having some sort of man trouble?" Gloria laughed before pressing both of her hands over her mouth. "I didn't mean to say that!"

"You said nothing wrong." The bartender showed off his teeth again in a wide smile that crinkled his gold eyes. There was a syrupy edge to his voice. Everything he said sounded like churned music.

"Where are you from?" Gloria blurted out as he mixed a new drink— which he swore would be weaker than the previous four. Her face warmed. "You have a nice accent," she sputtered.

"Romania," he answered, giving the silver cocktail shaker a boisterous shake.

"Oh, I've never been."

"You don't hear much about it. Other than Dracula's castle in Transylvania, of course," he winked.

Gloria and Florin exchanged names over the next drink. For two more drinks, they talked. She rattled on, mostly, giving one-dimensional descriptions of Artie and Autumn and the dead garden she'd planted in the backyard. He glossed over life as a cruise ship employee. The surface-level conversation was safe and boringly benign—and then, it shifted. Gloria couldn't figure out how they segued into her crying while she blabbed about her absent mother, her failing quest to be the perfect wife, the barrage of bloody miscarriages. Florin listened quietly, resting his coarse palm over her right hand. Her left, married hand, was tucked in her lap, slid between goose-pimpled thighs.

"I don't even know why I want more babies. All for that sliver of when they're first born? For that first moment of eye contact? It doesn't last. Why do I keep trying?" Gloria bit her lip while Florin wiped her tears with the driest part of the bar rag. With their foreheads touching, he talked about his own mother dying and how he didn't miss her because she was the most vicious, violent person he'd ever known. He told her how he loved to be at sea because he hated to be at home. He was afraid of life on land.

Gloria shut her eyes, mostly to stop the room from swaying but also to imagine herself in a world where she flirted for a few years and met the right person. In that world, she had exactly two children, and none of her pregnancies failed. With her eyes closed, she saw herself growing old with a best friend. When she opened her eyes, Denise was slipping from a barstool, refusing the help of the bartenders she'd been entertaining for hours.

"I've hit my limit of ego-boosting," she slurred loudly. Her teased hair stuck in patches to her rosy face.

Gloria had almost reached her own limit, but Florin had gone to the kitchen to sober her up with something greasy and breaded. He'd given her a dinner roll to tide her over. Gloria offered it to Denise, who waved her off, sashaying out from the cold bar. The door swung closed behind her.

Artie shouldn't have told Gloria to have a good time. He should've made plans for them. He should've done more than march around the boat's decks with another bottomless beer he tried to make festive with one of those papery umbrellas taped to the tip of a tiny toothpick. Alone, the only noise the crashing and roaring of an infinite black ocean, all he had time to do was untangle a life of bad choices. He decided to pace out the thoughts around the deck. After the squeak of his sneakers on damp wood became excruciating to him and every person he passed, and after the sky and ocean blended into each other's darkness, Artie came to the decision that he would woo his wife like he'd done successfully on the previous boats. It would be like work, like every other task he put his mind to. He puffed up his chest and took another stroll around the deck, scanning the face of every dark-haired woman. He ignored the beautiful ones, only searching for the familiar face of his wife.

On his second lap, he ran into a different familiar face. Denise stumbled from the ship's main bar, an upscale mahogany room with dark walls and jazz simmering at low volume. The same bar Artie had asked Bill to meet him at hours ago. Artie held Denise up with both hands.

"Where is Gloria?" he asked. Denise smiled, her eyes closed.

Artie peered in the bar's windows and saw a mutated version of his wife. Big, teased hair; sparkly, witchy sleeves; and heavy, Tallulah Bankhead eyelids. This woman couldn't be Gloria, though, because her forehead was bent against the forehead of some strange man. The inherited rage buried inside Artie knew that was his wife—he also knew it wanted to strangle the life out of the man across from her.

"What the hell is going on in there?" Artie released Denise. His fingers folded into two tight fists.

"Oh, nothing for you to get worked up about. It's a familiar story— ignore the wife and then blow up when you see her finally having a good time." Denise leaned against the bar's windows, her eyes still closed and her tongue lapping at the corner of her lips.

"Ignore? We've been doing the whole thing! The dinners. The dancing. You two went off to have some girl time—is this what girl time consists of?"

Denise laughed.

"It's such a stupid, minor incident to what you normally pull. Let her have a little fun and feel pretty and wanted for one night. Trust me, she's too goody-two-shoes to do anything else." Denise's eyes opened and latched onto Artie's. Hers were sagging, bloodshot, and framed by streaks of wet mascara. She wobbled slightly, her stare scattering.

"I think I overdid it." Denise put a finger to her mouth. "I think I might be sick."

Artie folded his anger, holding one of Denise's arms to steady her as she hurled Mai Tais into the choppy water. Between vomiting, she blurted out disjointed laments. Bill's work mattered more than anything. She didn't want her body to be ruined by motherhood. She didn't want to ruin her life. Through the middle opening of her go-go dress, her stomach muscles flexed with each push of bile. Artie knew it wasn't possible for her body to be ruined by anything. The stench of puke was probably the only thing keeping even a mild hard-on at bay. Of course, with Denise, hadn't he always been keeping a hard-on at bay?

Denise straightened up and wiped her forearm over her mouth. She stared at Artie like she could read his mind.

"Remember how you used to watch me through my window?" she asked. Artie refused to nod. How many times had she known he was out there? The first time he'd watched her they were both barely pubescent, and he had merely been intrigued witnessing a girl he wasn't related to changing her clothes. As time passed and they grew older, she morphed into a miraculous night vision, growing the same curves he'd discovered in his dad's stash of dirty magazines. The second miracle was she never closed her curtains. Every night, Artie found the most secluded part of his backyard and watched her sling one frilly slip for another. One of those nights he swore she gave a small, flirty wave like he'd seen pin-up girls do in the movies.

"All the girls at school had some boy or boys watching them. I heard them all talking about how some creepy neighbor boy was peering up at them. They couldn't close the curtains fast enough. That's when I knew something was wrong with me." Denise leaned over to him and lowered her voice. "I never closed my curtains. I loved knowing someone was watching. I even planned out the things I would change from and planned hair and makeup like it was a performance. Isn't that strange?"

"I'm sure the other girls just did what they thought they were supposed to do." Artie chastised himself for not coming up with something better to say.

"You might be right." Denise wagged a finger at him, teetering on her heels. "Or, they didn't really want to close the curtains at all. Maybe they just thought that's what good girls are supposed to say."

Denise swiveled around, staring back into the bar through the window.

"You know there's never any right thing for a girl to do. Look at your wife. Look at Gloria. Hasn't she done everything she's supposed to do? And what has it gotten her?"

Denise spun around again, her hair whipping in the wind. She pointed a finger at Artie, nearly grazing the tip of his nose.

"And haven't you fucked every piece of pussy that's crossed your path? Oh, don't look so shocked. I'm not a good girl, so I don't need to talk like one. My own mother said Carole Lombard was known for swearing like the dirtiest sailor, and wasn't she the pinnacle of glamour?"

"I'm not in the mood for feeling guilty, Denise."

She laughed. Even when she was mocking him and beyond shit-faced, her laugh had a pleasant, melodious cadence.

"Who's trying to get you to feel guilty? I'm only saying how little it matters if Gloria or anyone else does the right thing. It wouldn't even matter if she slept with that charming bartender. Is that better? Do I sound like a lady? Is it better to say sleeping when the whole phrase means anything but?"

"I think you've had too much to drink." Artie hooked his arm under one of Denise's dangling tentacles, walking flush with the edge of the boat in case she got some wild idea to jump overboard.

"Do you think I've made the right choices?" she whispered, her heels digging into the wooden deck and forcing them to stop. She tilted her head up, the moon offering a forgiving light that smudged out the smeared makeup, erasing the vomit crusted to her chin.

"Let's talk again about you watching me. I liked knowing that you were watching me—but you knew that. Don't you remember that one time?"

That one time could mean any number of times, but Artie instantly knew which time she was talking about. They were sixteen, and Denise had performed a clumsy striptease in the window, leaving her tiny bedroom lamp on for ambiance. Artie had sat in the same worn patch of grass, holding his breath and wondering what she would do next. He couldn't have predicted the way her fingers traced her collarbone or the sides of her blooming breasts. Her fingers dancing down the slope of her stomach. Right before she hooked the sides of her white panties, beginning to roll them down, she motioned to him, pantomiming what he was supposed to do. Her hands twisted and turned, demonstrating. He was supposed to reach into his pants and pull—and he did, nearly spewing from his own touch. Artie shivered at the memory. He hadn't felt that excitement since.

That moment was an hour before he and Gloria had a date, two hours before he pinned her to the backseat of his car and didn't wait for her to say no. It was a month before their wedding night. Eight and a half months before Autumn was born.

"It took a long time for me to look at Autumn and not feel wholly responsible. I think that's why I said yes so quickly to Bill's proposal. I think it's why I'm still giving in—but I think he's catching on to my timing thing. Oh, but I know having a baby will ruin everything!" Denise yanked her arm from Artie, beating at her own thighs like a toddler having a tantrum over spilled juice.

"Because you saw what having a baby did to me and Gloria?" Artie whispered, hoping the ocean didn't hear him admit it. Denise laughed again, harder this time.

"A baby didn't do anything to you! Gloria is quite possibly the only woman truly meant to be a mother. What happened to you two had nothing to do with a baby. It had to do more with the fact you were never in love to begin with." Denise inched closer to Artie, wagging her finger at him. "If you were, you would've stopped going to your little spot in the yard."

Artie saw those nights as if they were right in front of him. His cowlick, his pimples drying up while he sat like a transient pervert jacking off beneath the same window where his mother cooled her summer pies. He saw Denise spinning around, peeling a pink slip over a stiff bouffant she'd primped for hours.

"I did fall in love with Bill. Real love. Don't you remember? I stopped coming to the window when I realized he was everything I wanted."

Denise sighed. Her chin puckered and quivered.

"I don't want to ruin what we have with extra responsibility. I only want to travel and enjoy each other. He wants a baby, though. He wants a lot of babies. He seems to think the perfect future is me getting fat with a bunch of kids hanging off of me wondering when their daddy will finally be home from the work he can't seem to ever pull himself away from." Denise glanced upward and locked eyes with Artie. He'd forgotten that look. "I don't want to be my mother."

Denise's eyes glazed over, looking past him. Then, she smiled. She put a finger to her lips and grabbed both of Artie's hands, pulling him into an empty room that had been used earlier for BINGO. With surprising force, she pushed Artie into a chair and leaned onto his thighs. "Do you ever wonder if you and I were supposed to get married?" Denise asked, skipping her fingers up his pants and to the buttons at his waist. "We're the same. We've always been the same."

Artie held his breath. He wanted her to stop talking, so he could focus on controlling himself. She was on the last button, tugging him out of his pants.

"Aren't we supposed to?"

She needed to stop talking.

Then, she was quiet, her mouth filled with the part of him that was no longer in his control. Her head bobbed on his lap, her lips snug around him.

He should've pushed her away and told her she was too drunk. But this was his normal. Believe himself to be a good man before finding himself with another pretty face pressed against his dick and asking for nothing in return. He hoped Gloria was getting hers with that slimy bartender. She deserved it more than he did.

When Denise was finished, she picked up a glass filled with melting ice and swished around before spitting into the crystal-clear goblet.

"Go back to your wife." Denise waved him off.

"I'll take you back to your room," Artie offered, pulling his pants up.

"Just go," she said, turning away from him and burying her face in her hands.

Gloria refused to remove her clothes. She lay on the bed, staring at the smooth ceiling and tracing her life to this moment. Her choice to be Artie's girlfriend, to be his wife, to be a mother—all brought her here. Would Florin have seemed as magical if she'd met him before Artie? Or before the first time she mused on which of her life decisions were horrible mistakes?

Gloria reached under her dress, trying to touch herself the way Denise and all the magazines said was normal—even necessary. But it just felt like her own cold fingers. There wasn't romance or affection with herself.

Gloria closed her eyes and imagined Florin. She imagined his sweet cologne, the way his slight stubble might feel against her skin.

That was the trick. Gloria's hands ceased to be her own hands. They were imaginary promises from a man she'd had a single conversation with. She allowed herself to believe they were real.

A door opening—and then closing—ruined the fantasy.

Artie came over to the bed. He was pale, his hairline damp. He stumbled closer. Gloria was about to roll over when he reached over and held her in place by one arm.

"You look amazing," he said. It didn't sound insincere, but Gloria didn't care.

"I'm sorry for everything," his eyes watered. She wasn't in the mood to hear what her drunk husband had to say.

Artie removed his clothes, and then he pulled the skirt of Gloria's dress above her hips. She closed her eyes. There was Florin. He was opening the door to a house that smelled like cookies and was filled with flowers in every room. There was a baby safely in her arms, swaddled in soft cotton. Florin came home at 5 o'clock every night, and every night she knew there wasn't anyone else.

When Gloria opened her eyes, Artie was still on top of her going through the same mechanical movements he went through when they pretended to work things out.

She waited for him to finish.

⌇

They were home from the cruise for two weeks when Gloria realized how stupid she'd been. She'd lost track and that exact moment between Artie and her had occurred at the worst possible time.

She perched over the toilet, a clump of tissue dabbed between her legs. Each time it was still stark white. She tried to squeeze out blood for two more weeks. The clumps of tissue continued to come back clean.

Even before the doctor confirmed her worst fear, she was already worried about how long she could keep this one safely inside of her.

Part 2

Chapter 13

1972

Theodore Finnigan Joyce was born in water. He was born twenty days before *The Godfather* premiered and four months before Artie was able to convince Gloria *Deep Throat* was really a movie *everyone* was watching.

Teddy swam from between his mother's legs into a plastic inflatable pool they'd set up in the den. Thin blue tarp covered the beige shag carpet and the yellow couch they'd pushed against the window. Teddy floated to the surface of the murky water, instantly pecking his mother's skin, reaching for Gloria in a Kodak moment nobody thought to capture with the camera they'd tossed over the back of a chair. The midwife rinsed mother and baby with fresh, clear water from a white bucket. Even as she did that, Artie caught the woman's signal. He was told to hand her a crocheted blanket to wrap the new baby in. The blanket around his new son was yellow and green, a blanket Gloria had stitched herself years before for a pregnancy nobody could bring themselves to talk about.

Artie followed the woman with the freckled arms and long sand-colored hair into the newly remodeled bathroom, both removing their clothes like reptiles peeled off skin. He was repulsed when she lifted her arms, showing off damp tufts of hair. He hated the feminist look. Artie gagged when he kissed her neck and tasted sweat. Holding his breath, he forced himself to thrust until he was red and raw, until he could forget he was a father of two, a shitty husband, and a man who sent his daughter to his mom's because he couldn't parent alone. He came at the same time as the midwife Gloria had raved about, the same woman who scratched his back with nibbled fingernails. Artie swallowed boozy bile. He'd been celebrating alone since Gloria's water broke on their bedroom floor. The woman squeezed his ass. He felt like he'd popped a blister.

He fumbled and apologized, yanking himself out of the hippy woman, not looking at her when he rinsed the throbbing pain best as he could in the bathroom sink. She knocked over a bottle of Mr. Bubble, stretching her arms and nearly purring as she proclaimed their shared minutes to be some of the best in her life.

Afterward, they'd walked back to the den a safe distance apart. Artie's shoes slid over the tarp. The pads of the midwife's bare feet slapped the blue plastic. Gloria barely glanced up when they came back to the converted birthing room, completely ignorant to the possibility of what had occurred flush against the bathroom tiles she'd chosen last week. She bent over the baby she didn't think she could ever have, nuzzling his head and tracing hearts into his fat cheeks. Artie watched, mesmerized, but also feeling an urge to announce what he'd just done—a horrible part of himself wanting to break the spell. The midwife interrupted his internal demon.

"Do you want to try nursing?" she asked Gloria.

Teddy took little coaxing from his mother, unlike Autumn whose papery newborn claws scratched her way to freedom from the wicker bassinet. Autumn liked to sleep alone. He wondered if his daughter was having fun with her grandparents, knowing she'd rather be anywhere than watching this grotesque display of affection. Gloria laid soft kisses on Teddy's hand while he suckled from her with his eyes closed. Artie went to the kitchen to pour himself another celebratory drink. And another. And another after that.

～❀～

Artie never changed a single diaper. Not for Autumn. Not for Teddy. That stuff came naturally to Gloria, while he waited for the age where he could be an active parent. For Autumn, it worked. She loved to be hoisted on shoulders. She loved to be pushed high enough on a swing to make her belly bubble. She loved to slosh in the muddy banks of creeks, scooping up tadpoles from the polluted water. She loved helping her dad re-home a salamander under a slick stone. In return, he shook up a bubble solution in old plastic bottles and helped tie dandelion strings into princess crowns. He pretended to gobble up mud pies. She was impressed by his magic tricks. Autumn was Daddy's little girl.

Teddy was different. He didn't want to be Artie's anything.

He slurped globs of noodles until he choked, watching Artie. He licked his plate clean.

Teddy, stop crying.

When Teddy was three, he held his breath while tears drizzled down his red cheeks. Artie tried to restrain his sighs, his obvious frustration.

Teddy learned to swallow tears whole. Around his father, he wore the same face Artie wore with his own father. Dead, vacant eyes with each facial muscle frozen in place.

Man up, Teddy.

Sobs swallowed over scraped knees. Hobbling several blocks with one leg twisted and broken. A skinny sissy crying to his mother who blotted his first black eye with a steak Artie would later throw across the living room in an explosive rage.

Teddy, be stronger.

Artie had accidentally dislocated the boy's shoulder when he was in kindergarten.

The apple doesn't fall far from the tree.

Artie hated that idiom. He hated that he loved whiskey, the smell of a stranger's skin, the scraping of thick guitar strings under his finger. He could sing a perfect imitation of Hank Williams that made his father proud.

Artie became just like his old man. Having a drink with the girl who chewed pink bubblegum while ringing up customers. Flirting with the girl who was so nervous she shook while writing Happy Birthday in melted chocolate. Her hands even trembled when she pulled down his zipper. He didn't know if his dad preferred shiny pantyhose or a cold bare leg—he didn't even know which one sold him more. He only knew he was just like Clyde.

Teddy, who liked licking the spoon, building bird feeders, and planting tomatoes in old cans, was nothing like his father or his grandfather. Artie sometimes wished he was.

Six-year-old Teddy puffed up his chest, his mother's hand clasped in both of his.

"I don't want to play baseball," he told Artie, his eyes locked on his mother.

Teddy never liked the sport. The ball spun at him too fast, and now he wanted to do some church choir. Church? Choir? That was worse than any goddamn ball. His wife and son shouldn't have teamed up against him the same night George said they needed to shrink costs by about ten percent. That was also the same night he'd poured his evening drink without any buffering ice cubes. Just like his dad, he'd yelled and dented the wall with his fist. Gloria screamed and lunged for him, leaving bloodied scratches from her fake nails. She'd never attacked him before. He knew at that moment she loved that untainted, sniveling boy more than she wanted to repair the damage Artie had done to them.

Resentment stirred inside him.

Guilt swarmed his insides.

He drank until the walls shook and his mouth shriveled down to his throat. He drank more until he dug in the garage and found his dad's old, busted rifle back in his hands. He wondered about the taste of metal, thinking about when his dad gave him the gun after they'd slept in the forest waiting to kill some deer. Artie couldn't shoot. Those deer had the same thick, showgirl lashes of every girl in the bar who further splintered his marriage. His dad slept in the tent while Artie admired the bucks with the velvety fingers stretched from their heads, their muscles rippling beneath satin skin when they leapt away because he'd stepped on a branch and startled them. He twirled the gun in his fingers like a straw at the soda shop. His fingers were still too weak to pull the trigger.

He slept off a good hangover before promising once again he was going to straighten up. Gloria's hair was still in pink spongey curlers, and she was bent over the tub shaking Comet over the spotless porcelain, nodding when he made his declaration.

He apologized to Teddy. He offered to drop Teddy off to the humble white church for choir. The other children stood like daffodils, glowing in the sun like a pious shepherd painting. Teddy's lip quivered.

"Break a leg," Artie said as gently as he could. Teddy's eyes widened. "It's just an expression."

Teddy hugged his neck so hard that Artie saw little starred explosions. Artie sped away before he witnessed the angelic herd of children swallowing his son.

Artie signed up for guitar lessons. He slipped into the small studio space while Teddy sang with the other choir kids. Artie's guitar teacher was a kid with long stringy hair and dirty blue jeans.

"Show me what you know," the kid demanded, folding his arms with authority. He stood while Artie wobbled on a tiny stool. Artie strummed his three known Buddy Holly songs with gusto before finishing up with "Hey, Good Lookin." He told the teacher it was his father's favorite. Unfortunately, he forgot most of it, and in a panic chose strings and chords that were too high and shrill. His sweating, shaking fingers scrambled over the strings to salvage the song, but he was only able to snap a couple strings. The kid chuckled, saying, "You've got a lot to learn."

Artie sat quietly while the teenager demonstrated chords and solos and other skills he was dying to show off, all the while plotting how to never return to this stool of shame. He could pick up some how-to book or maybe abandon the music thing all together. That night, he sat in his garage drinking a bottle of Coke, his guitar balanced on his knees while he laced silver-plated copper threads through the pickup, stretching them around the tuning peg with such force he was afraid they would snap again. He opened a Coors like a real yank of anything would do the trick, but the guitar was still there, still like a corpse, quiet like every other dead object. What did he expect? He would bounce into some fulfilling rock star life, shake off the cycle of clocking in, mowing the lawn, taking out the trash? That he was meant to have an instinct for melody?

He wanted to hurl the guitar across the garage. He wanted to break it into pieces with his bare hands. He wanted to shoot the hollowed body with the gun he couldn't get rid of. He glared at the thing, and like some sort of cinematic magic, it twisted and turned and became a puzzle of smaller parts that clicked together in a way that made perfect sense. Strings woven with precision, the miniature amphitheater formed by a scooped hole in wood, the function of a smooth neck. He instinctually knew the workings of these things, the pragmatism of parts, of function. Before Gloria knocked on the garage door and said dinner was ready, he'd disassembled and reassembled the guitar six times, all with slight, unique variations in the finished sounds. The melodies weren't songs but single plucked strings with meaty chords he rotated through like an assembly line. His imagination was admittedly bludgeoned out of him years ago, but knowledge of mechanics still flourished within him. The beer remained untouched.

The next morning at breakfast, Gloria buttered his toast, and he announced to his forgiving family they could have a new beginning. Paternity, fidelity, innovation, promises. Nashville.

Chapter 14

1978

Autumn's parents stirred sugar into the first successful sun tea brew of summer before explaining the move to Nashville would be good for her, good for the family. She wanted to spit tea into both their faces but spat it over her mother's garden instead. Neither of them noticed and even if the tea killed off some tomato leaves or sprigs of cilantro, it wouldn't matter, would it? They were going to be a thousand miles away, planting new seeds in some boring hick yard.

Beth tried to make it better the next day when they laid on the warm swath of sand belonging to Redondo Beach.

"Maybe you'll meet some cowboy stud," Beth laughed, squeezing baby oil over each knee.

"Cowboys are disgusting."

"What about some Elvis lookalike? Not gross, fat Elvis but like the cute one in *Jailhouse Rock*."

Everyone said Autumn's dad looked like Elvis, so that suggestion wasn't soothing at all—but Autumn appreciated her friend. Beth had been there since she first taught Autumn how to shave her legs in third grade and how to cultivate the expression that let you get away with stealing candy, and later, swimsuits and halter tops. Beth was the first to feather her hair, go intentionally braless, and let a boy stick his hand down her pants. She taught Autumn to flood her belly with Tab to abate hunger, to scoot food over her plate so it looked like she ate more. Beth was tall with blonde hair; a flat, tan stomach; and round breasts that looked like the girls in the movies. Already at fourteen, Autumn's hung like an old lady. Beth swore Autumn would be thankful.

"Boys want them *big*, they don't care how 'up' they are," Beth said, dusting sparkles around her eyes and trying on her assorted variety of platforms—all while stark naked. Beth celebrated the nude form before it was vogue. From that same room, she poured music into Autumn's ears— new music nobody at school had heard: The Runaways, the Cars, Blondie, the Ramones. She showed her magazines that turned sadomasochism into fashion, blended glitter with gore. It was Bowie glam to a new angrier level. Beth decided to bleach her hair invisible and shove a safety pin through her lip.

"Maybe you're meant to teach the country capital about punk?"

Autumn nodded sadly, envisioning a carousel of rodeos, churches, and spurs on everything. She scratched Beth's bleach-burning scalp with the back of a teasing comb. This was their goodbye.

Her second ceremonious goodbye unfurled on a wet beach towel, next to a surfboard, with gritty sand digging into every crack and crevice good girls didn't expose. Vinny shared a bottle of Boones Farm first, then a more astringent bottle of top shelf vodka he'd swiped from his own parents. They watched the sun slip beneath the ocean, their bodies numb enough to cement their goodbyes into something cliché: an eternal first time. Autumn knew she would never forget the silky feel of his long dark hair; his cold, skinny arms; the way his shoulder blades were like smooth stone wings. She didn't cry when they kissed goodbye, and she promised she would come back to visit, that she would remember how to balance on a surfboard. He promised he'd wait, that "Moonage Daydream" would always be their song. They both knew they would never see each other again.

Inside the house, oblivious to Autumn's transformation, her parents took turns singing old country songs off key. Autumn was already sick of Hank Williams and Patsy Cline, and she hadn't even laid eyes on stupid Nashville.

"You have two boxes to fit your stuff into." Gloria tried to squeeze her whole face into Autumn's bedroom door. Autumn had barricaded her door with bell bottoms, books, and old stuffed animals.

"Two boxes?" Autumn hit her tanned bare legs with open palms. She did it again to feel the sting, to punctuate her frustration with a smack she hoped stung her mother. She'd lived in this house since she was three. Her life couldn't be crammed into two boxes.

"We're all starting fresh. If it's something sentimental that you absolutely can't part with, Grandma and Grandpa will store it—but stuff you actually need has to go in two boxes."

Autumn bit her lip until she broke the skin—it was the only way not to explode and go off on her parents. She wanted to tell them to invest in therapy, splurge on a divorce—anything but uproot them all to save their own selfish selves. Each time she rehearsed the big showdown, though, it came out too vituperative, even if they deserved it. In the only room she'd ever known, Autumn packed and unpacked the same two boxes—stuffing shell necklaces into her platforms, choosing between KISS posters and sneaking her books in with Teddy's toys. He would never beg or complain. He was excited to give his toys to charity. He couldn't wait to get his first cowboy hat.

On July 25th, the moving truck arrived to load up the boxes. Their garage sale was three days before that. Several church charities loaded up the scraps left behind. Autumn's parents let the kids keep the whopping five bucks they made from selling old clothes and toys. When someone bought the hideous green jumpsuit her mom had just given her for her birthday, she made sure to announce the sale, waving her handful of quarters intentionally beneath the glowing sunlight. Of course, her mother didn't notice—she couldn't. She was too wrapped up in this whole fresh start, as if Artie's old flings and their drunken arguments could just be scraped off. It was as bad as wiping mold off a piece of old bread. If it were up to her, Autumn would throw away the bread and the cheating husband.

It didn't shock Autumn when she thought of her dad in that role anymore. How many girls had she met at his work who wouldn't dare look her or her mother in the eye? How many times had she picked up the phone and heard a conversation that shouldn't be happening? How many times had she smashed a pillow to each ear but still heard the detailed accusations and—even worse—the volatile making up between two people who should never be together?

And, now, he was having a midlife crisis where he regretted never pursuing something artistic and meaningful and probably blaming all his bad choices on his initial impulse to latch onto boring, safe, domestic security. And because of his whims, she was going to have to leave sunshine, surfing, good music, avocados. He was literally walking out of a job he'd always had to tinker with nuts and bolts on the periphery of music. He couldn't even come up with a catchy commercial jingle. Nope. All he was going to do was stick a new piece of wood on an old, rotted guitar, stick some keys on a toothless piano, import some dead animal skin for a busted banjo. He was going to hijack a world that didn't want him. It was no better than digging under houses and replacing people's shit-pipes—the very job he'd always scoffed at and pissed his own dad off by doing so. God, her entire family was pathetic.

Artie put his arm around Gloria's shoulders as the moving truck drove away. Autumn knew all the neighbors thought they looked like something out of the movies. Gloria's dewy skin streaked with dirt like it was put there on purpose. Artie's black hair dancing in a sudden cinematic wind burst. Teddy skipped over to them, wrapping his freckled arms around Gloria's legs, rubbing his cheek on them like he was a stray cat. Autumn was probably being accused of being a moody teenager by whomever snooped through the curtains, her arms folded across her chest and her face pinched into a well-deserved scowl.

Their new home was a brick rectangle surrounded by grass, violets, and uneven dirt fifteen miles from downtown Nashville. Her parents were overjoyed because Bill Monroe and Kitty Wells had called the same area home.

Gloria called their new house "ranch-style," a decor she took to heart, painting the house shades of muted earth and decorating every room with brass horses and rusted horseshoes. Autumn didn't tell anyone she was glad her room was farther away from everyone else's. Teddy learned he had allergies in Nashville but kept quiet—his little nose red and peeling at the nostrils. Artie spent most of their first weeks in his new shop. The shop shared space with notable recording companies and was down the street from a seedy stretch of honky-tonks and souvenir shops. He was home every night for dinner: barbecued meats and soupy greens served in green casserole dishes, scooped with wooden spoons sold in a country kitchen pack. Her mother called Denise to gush about how happy they all were. Twice a week, they went to some hippy couples' therapy group and came home speaking in "I feel" statements, and Autumn was pretty sure there was some hallucinogenic bonding happening certain Saturday nights—all in the name of finding their chakras and rekindling their lost love while Autumn wrote another letter to Vinny, even though he hadn't responded to the last three. Beth had responded with hearts and xoxo the first time, the second note was three single sentences with her signature taking up more paper than whatever meaningless news she sent out from the golden state. Autumn cranked her Sony Walkman up as high as it would go, but no amount of wailing Stooges could drown out her parents' Hindu chants cassette and loud declarations of love. Autumn was anxious for school to start, just to find someone to complain to.

The pickings for best friends were slim at her new school. The girls still ironed their hair and wore peasant shirts, and the boys were not the cowboys Beth had imagined for her, although they amped up a fake drawl every time she was around. Autumn scanned the crowd for anyone who looked like they'd heard of glam, punk, or even simple sunshine. She was met with a sea of Crystal Gayle wannabees and men proud of the dead deer rotting in the bed of their pickup truck. All her observations were scribbled in another letter to Beth. Her therapy was writing a long letter to a friend who didn't exist anymore.

Autumn found her first Tennessee friend reading in the last row of their shared English class three weeks into their freshman year. She was tired of hearing the bubblegum laughter of cheerleaders sitting in the front, so she went to the back and sat beside the boy with dark curls who read a book propped behind a Pee Chee folder. The bland athletes on the folder had been hand-decorated into grotesque caricatures that were something between KISS and cameos of legendary actors on Looney Tunes.

"Did you draw those faces?" Autumn asked. The boy kept reading— rather, he kept the book and folder over his face, but Autumn saw his eyes stall and lose focus. She leaned over, poking the folder and causing it to fall to the floor. Behind it was the bright yellow cover of Virginia Woolf's *Mrs. Dalloway*. Autumn expected *Brian's Song* or *The Shining*, the only two books she'd seen any boys read.

"Why are you hiding your book?" Autumn poked. The boy sank into his seat, wearing a glare she knew he had practiced in the mirror before.

"Because I decided to go against the grain and not stick to my usual casual smut or *Sports Illustrated* today."

Autumn continued to stare.

"I don't feel like explaining the lack of masculinity in my reading choices, not even to a girl from California." He raised the yellow folder up higher, leaving only the soft curls of his hair exposed.

She sat in the same seat class after class, watching the boy read other books behind that same folder. *Play as It Lays*, *Home to Harlem*, something hand-bound with a bright red cover. She learned his name was Daniel, the only person in the class who raised their hand when the teacher asked a question. His voice was smooth and confident, sometimes knowing things the teacher didn't know but would scurry to pretend she did. Mrs. Whitman started assigning group work, a skit built on *Great Expectations*. Rehearsals, visuals, all the same boring stuff—but this time Autumn knew wouldn't be boring because when she pulled down the Pee Chee folder and saw Daniel reading *Valley of the Dolls*, she laughed, and he didn't get defensive. She knew he would agree to be her group partner. When she told him she'd walked down Cielo Drive and had read everything Jacqueline Susann had written and seen every part Sharon Tate had ever played, he was impressed and formally introduced himself with a handshake.

"I'm Daniel."

"I know," Autumn replied.

Daniel and Autumn finished the book, sculpted a skit, and turned a ball of tulle into a tattered veil under the bleachers of the football field in three days. Neither of them offered their homes as backup. Autumn did offer him a joint, which he tentatively took and nibbled at. She showed him a true inhale and how to cough without looking like a weirdo. He was a quick learner.

"You aren't gonna make too many friends hanging out with me." Daniel wagged his finger at Autumn who rolled her eyes and said, "Who cares?"

Autumn's parents barely noticed her improved mood between meditations and slapping another horse painting on the den's dusty yellow walls. Teddy, however, worked hard to try and excavate the impetus for her bouncing through the house, for the cheesy smile she couldn't scrub from her face.

"Did Vinny finally write back?" he asked, licking peanut butter from an apple slice.

"Who?" Autumn dug into the green fridge, her hand resting on the old familiar Tab before sliding over to the gallon of milk. She slammed the door shut, crawling her fingers into the cupboard and pulling out Teddy's canister of Nesquik.

"Vinny! That boy you were always talking about. And why are you drinking that? I thought you said chocolate milk will make you fat?" Teddy had too many questions and too good of an eye. Autumn leaned over the wood kitchen island, fake wood really.

"For your information, little squirt, I stopped caring about Vinny ages ago, so I don't care about him writing me back. Second, don't you see the way people eat around here? Nobody is trying to look good for the beach in this place."

Plus, Daniel had said he thought Farrah Fawcett was too skinny. He wasn't going to pinch her sides like Vinny. They had substance: conversations about communes, about protests, about their shared disdain for the guns everyone else was obsessed with. He wasn't worried about fatness, diets, or getting so stoned you became comatose. He was interested when she said she wanted to show him some of her records at her house, and after he asked if her parents would mind, he said he would gladly come learn about what was going on "over the pond" as she liked to say with an over-the-top London accent.

Autumn believed her parents had successfully shunned all negativity and would welcome her new friend with open arms. Nashville had that effect on them. Artie was meeting the legends his father adored, calling back home to list off all the famous names to Grandpa Clyde. He was finding his niche as the handyman of string instruments. The city gulped up his efforts, and he stayed drinking water and Coke. Gloria grew a glow that first year, her hair long and glossy, accenting her newfound love of halter-style dresses that accentuated a perfect collarbone. They made it a whole year like that. A whole year of Autumn being made fun of by rah-rah girls and jocks who called Daniel a sissy, the kids who had parents holding office at the Capitol or on Music Row. For a year, Daniel and Autumn's friendship existed under the bleachers or at the school library. It was in the school library where he'd shown her a book of poetry he'd found inside their school. "It must have been put there on accident," he'd said as his finger had slid over hers. Her parents were warm, welcoming hippies now. They would love him.

Two days before Daniel was coming over to learn about the Ramones and the Sex Pistols, Autumn heard the forgotten, familiar sound of her parents' scathing arguments. Teddy's room was closed. His way of coping was quiet retreat. Autumn's way was to hold her breath. Her lungs filled with stagnant air, her ears swallowed the cause: a woman calling the house and asking for Artie, a woman with a drawl who was dismissive of Gloria, a woman Artie insisted was only a customer, a woman he wouldn't put in her place. Autumn exhaled. Her parents screaming was intelligible, a single thread of shrill venom.

They made up the next day. Artie was on time for dinner, looking like he hadn't slept, his hair wet with grease and his fingernails bitten to the raw pink skin. Gloria held a bottle of celebratory champagne and a tiny carton of rainbow sherbet. She insisted he'd gone long enough, and they were overdue for a celebration. She even poured a splash for Autumn and gave extra sherbet to Teddy in a fancy crystal goblet. Autumn watched her father drink the glass eagerly and pour another. She hated her mother. She hated her father.

She tried to sneak Daniel in the next day to avoid their embarrassing displays of weakness and dysfunction, but her dad came home even earlier and looked Daniel up and down the same way the football players did at school. After she and Daniel listened to records with the door open at her father's insistence, after he declared an instant love of punk rock, after Daniel gave her a stiff, platonic hug at the door, Artie cornered his daughter in the hallway.

"I hope you're only friends," Artie's breath had smelled like saltines and beer, a smell she didn't know could exist out here, too.

Autumn and Daniel pushed their simmering courtship back into hiding, and Autumn wondered if it would ever go beyond reading poems, listening to records, or lapping up vanilla ice cream at Bobby's Dairy Dip. He showed her old battlefields, the club Jimi Hendrix used to play at, and the Woolworth building her own parents had only seen on TV. He showed her rotted, forgotten Victorian homes. He plucked a magnolia flower from a hanging branch, and she blurted out she loved him—and had been in love with him since that first day she'd sat beside him in freshman English.

Daniel's grandmother lived by herself and couldn't hear very well, and in a backroom filled with stacks of Lincoln Logs and porcelain baby dolls, Autumn gave him the virginity she forgot she'd given to Vinny on a beach she could hardly remember. In that room she cried and told him about her father's drinking, the gifts he gave to other women, her mother's refusal to leave him, the way Gloria looked at Teddy and never looked at her. Daniel kissed the top of her sun-bleached hair and held one of her hands while he told her all people were damaged. He held that same hand, in that same room, when he told her his father had gotten a new job in Atlanta, but he would visit in the summer. He promised to write.

Daniel's absence taught Autumn poetry. Without him there to speak through songs and stories, her mind began to knit out her own roundabout way of saying her feelings through poetic strategies like imagery, lofty allusions, and metaphors that even surprised her when she wrote them. She wrote the final drafts in blue pen and sent them to Atlanta. Daniel replied to each one with gushy appreciation and awe through his own illustrious haikus. Autumn read these letters while her father drank and her mother cooked another therapy pie. They stopped their weekly therapy sessions and replaced "I feel" with "When you did." Autumn barricaded herself with the letters. With Daniel, she was an artist, a creator, a person who had a way with words. The letters were her safe place until the letters stopped coming, just like the ones before from other old friends too far away to be real anymore.

Autumn wandered her high school alone. She reverted to her old way of ignoring the world around her and numbing herself. Maybe that's why when one of the hated jocks stepped out from the blur and asked her to prom, she said yes. He prefaced the request with some boring story about their fathers knowing each other, everyone knowing his father, really. Autumn waved him off, muttering, "Yes, yes."

The impending prom date invigorated her parents, redirecting their attention to taking pre-prom photos in front of the brass horse figurines or in front of the green floral sofa. Gloria praised Autumn on her plain pink dress.

"It's such a classic choice." Gloria spritzed her daughter's neck with Chanel. Autumn tried to force a weak smile. She dug through the stack of mail on the kitchen counter before walking out the door with Brett, pulling him away from Artie who wouldn't shut up about baseball and Conway Twitty. Before the door shut behind them, Artie grabbed Autumn's limp hand.

"His dad is big time!"

The prom took place on May 5th, 1981. It was the night Brett told her that nobody had ever said no to him. It was the night Autumn hopped out of a moving car, rolling into a damp ditch. It was the night Brett held both of her wrists with one hand and asked if she was sure she knew who he was. It was the night she came home with dirt and leaves crusted into dried sweat on her arms and neck, a pink welt rising beneath her right eyebrow, sticky mascara smeared all over her splotchy face.

Prom was when Autumn's final virginity was scraped out. It was right before her curfew when a well-loved descendent of country royalty called her a whore right before he spat in her face, after he pinned her down for a "finale." Autumn slept in her room over the summer. After she realized her period was two months late, she lay in bed in the same unwashed t-shirt and baggy corduroy pants staring at the ceiling and willing the world implode.

It took weeks of puking covertly into jars and hiding them in her closet until her parents went to sleep or passed out, whichever came first, to finally sit in the den with them, standing in front of the boxy brown television and mumbling she had to tell them something. She tried to weave together the night's events, dancing around the words rape and sex and picking at a loose cuticle when she muttered that he'd forced her to do something, and now she was sick and late. Her mother asked if she had a reputation. Her father removed his belt. Autumn squeezed her eyes and covered her head. Gloria pulled Artie off, warning him about the baby. They never said what they thought about Brett.

Artie went to have a civil beer-to-beer with Brett's famous father. They talked about sports and the weather, waiting for the bearded men singing Jim Reeves and George Jones covers to sing a little louder before they made actual arrangements. Brett called Sunday afternoon after they went to church, told Autumn they would pay to get rid of it, that they knew a doctor who would keep the procedure quiet. Autumn wrote to Daniel, who never wrote back.

Gloria drove Autumn to the quiet industrial side of town. The streets smelled like tires and rotted fruits. The doctor's office was snuggled between warehouses and abandoned buildings, a location only certain people were privy to, Gloria couldn't help but say. The office had hard blue chairs and a metal table with a year-old *Seventeen* magazine splayed over it, its spine white and worn. Beside the magazine sat a nearly empty box of tissues.

"You don't have to do this," Gloria said so quietly Autumn wasn't sure she'd heard her right.

"You still could, of course—but you can think a little longer."

Autumn had been thinking. She'd been thinking about Daniel, about the blinding California light, about getting a new thesaurus because she was struggling to find the right words for her feelings. The new poems she wrote ended up crossed out or torn to shreds.

"I was your age when I got pregnant with you."

Autumn opened her mouth to say, "But you were married," though a tiny squeak came out instead. It wasn't like she was vying for that life either.

"Your father and I could help you. We could do everything."

Autumn looked at her mother's face, initially feeling pity for a woman whose greatest ambition was motherhood, an ambition her body repeatedly rejected. Gloria twisted the braided belt around her waist until it looked like it would snap. The corners of her mauve lips were pinched and white. Years of bloody unborn things were etched into the whole family's memory, even if Gloria held them front and center. Autumn had hated those babies before they were born, each one supposed to be her replacement, a chance to do better. Little Teddy was practically still sewn inside her mother. She couldn't watch that happen to this one, too—but then, she couldn't stand up when the nurse called her name. Gloria went with her, and Autumn saw the fan of metal instruments that looked like torture tools and began backing away from the papery disposable gown.

"I can't," she told the nurse and her mother, who started to cry.

Gloria told Artie while they sat on the deck drinking spiked iced teas. She waited until he'd had one, but before the second, so he was loose enough to think another baby, this time born from his teenage daughter was a good idea. Autumn told them the next morning when they were hungover that she was dropping out of school. Artie had another civil beer with Brett's famous father, who told Artie he would be sorry.

A gossip smear campaign shredded Artie's business almost immediately. Banjos, slide guitars, and thick acoustic necks were suddenly better preserved and better repaired by their own built community. Another moving van came to the ranch-style house, the boxes held together with sloppy packing tape. Gloria threw away the brass horses. As they drove in reverse, back to Artie's old job and old habits, back to Gloria's preserved domestic veneer, back to the slapping sound of the ocean and smell of smog and traffic, Artie revealed that Daniel had written back to Autumn—he had just thrown them away because he knew what was best.

"You'll understand when that baby is born," he said, swerving into the lane for the 10W.

Chapter 15

July 2018

Artie sat on the couch, eating the soft middle of a burnt toaster waffle, scrolling through Facebook then Instagram. He slid past a filtered image of his great-nephew's cat caught mid-yawn, a sunset, and a cup of creamy coffee before stalling on a photo of him and Gloria from a trip they'd taken to Vegas in 1975. Both smiled widely, their hands touching although there was a noticeable amount of space between them. Gloria was stunning, her hair, dark and shiny, flowed down her back.

He'd forgotten that version of her. He'd forgotten that version of himself, too. His hair long enough for the times but not too long to look like a lazy hippy. The cockiness in his old face was still palpable, pulsing in the pose of a man who'd probably already found the woman in the casino he would pursue after his wife drank enough to be out solid for the night. Time hadn't forgotten that version of Artie. It was painful, his glasses fighting with the glare of the phone and unforgiving time. He wanted to close his eyes, but like every other tragic accident, he couldn't look away. The picture immortalized Gloria's widest smile. He knew she was forcing it. He could see it in the stiffness of her elbows, the way she tilted from him—a microscopic lean only he would notice. Only he, her husband, would know that her beautiful smile—the one strangers always complimented—wasn't real at all.

He stared at the picture until his morning coffee dried on his tongue. His eyes lanced further through the layers in the picture—the prism of emotions in Gloria's eyes, the way his bicep was always flexed to ward off vulnerability. The wall of the Vegas club smeared with fresh white paint. The rigidity of Gloria's ring finger. Artie could smell that day. Taste her musky perfume, the stale clouds of casino cigarette smoke. The photo— really a photo of a photo pressed inside some forgotten photo album pulled out on one of Veronica's yearly visits—was nearly breathing. He was about to toss the phone across the room when he noticed the dots beneath, meaning there were more pictures, more captured memories.

A camping trip with the Buchanans. Christmas 1990, when his hair was barely turning silver and Gloria had stopped feeling a need to pose beside him. A snapshot from last summer when Veronica brought Edie. He and Gloria had stood together then, giving long practiced smiles, their aged arms behind each other's back. How did he look so much older now? Sure, his hair was pure silver and his jaw a little loose, his middle swollen with time—but there was something softer, younger from the year before. Gloria, too. Then he noticed the hearts floating above them and realized it was one of those forgiving filters. He almost laughed. How nice it would be to have a live filter draped like a gentle vellum over everything decaying around him.

Artie was happy to scroll away from these memories and had almost thought about ignoring the caption—but since it was from his granddaughter, he decided to look.

HAPPY ANNIVERSARY TO @GLORIALOVESARTIE and @DodgerBlueArtie. 55 years together! Look at how beautiful they are.

Anniversary.

He'd forgotten.

He blamed the party. He blamed Denise. He blamed the venue for agreeing to postpone the party. Artie wanted to cancel. Wasn't Denise's accident bad enough? Did Gloria really want to see how much worse it could get?

Artie ran his hand through his thin hair and downed the rest of his coffee. He could shower fast, run out and get the biggest bouquet of flowers he could find. Or he could scramble to create a relaxation day at any spa that could squeeze them in. He could see if some overpriced Italian or seafood place would take a last-minute Saturday reservation.

First, he had to wish Gloria a happy anniversary. Maybe that would bring her back. Since Denise died, her usual household locations had been vacant. Her recliner where she played social media games and read on her Kindle. The kitchen where she peeled back the tiny lid of her last bit of Nutrisystem. The dining table where her readers sat, the frames licked with faint dust.

He knew where she was—the same place she'd been since Denise's funeral. In bed. Not *their* bed but the guest bedroom with the fluffier comforter and a heaping stack of soft pillows. The bed wasn't one of her old spots. Gloria had been the type to shoot straight up at dawn since they'd gotten married. Even when the kids were babies, she took the shortest of naps—and kept those limited to slumping on the couch or even sitting in a chair. Since Denise died, she slept and slept. It was like she'd stopped existing except for the sibilant sobbing she stifled until late at night when she thought he was sleeping. He pretended to sleep through her night sobbing and never asked if she was okay. He would do anything to avoid her asking how he felt about Denise.

Artie headed for the guest room, not worrying about showering, or combing his hair, or even tightening the fraying terrycloth belt around his robe.

"Gloria?" He opened the door.

She was barely visible—save for the top of her hair, oily and frazzled. He walked closer, taking tiny measured steps.

"Gloria?"

He slowly peeled back the comforter. She lay curled on her side, her eyes open but looking at the dresser. The skin around her eyes plump and red.

"Happy anniversary. I didn't forget."

Gloria shook her head, yanking the comforter back over her. Artie walked out of the room backward, closing the door.

Artie stood outside the closed bedroom door, straining his ears. All he heard was his own galloping heartbeat. He opened the door and held his breath. She was crying. The raw weeping was overwhelming. It made him dizzy. Artie stumbled a little, bracing himself on the door before closing it behind him, eclipsing the room in dull shade.

Gloria was the Gloria he knew half a century ago. Small and weeping and fragile. A forgotten sensation rippled through him. It ballooned in his chest, in his stomach, clouded his head until he thought he would faint. His growing erection was straining so hard against his pants, it hurt. This was love.

Artie flung the comforter back again and crawled into the bed. He sank into the mattress. Gloria rolled over and buried her face into the part of his chest exposed from the robe. Wetness slicked through the hairs on his chest, down under the robe. She squeezed tighter, pressing her whole self against him.

Gloria looked up at him for the first time in almost a month, but really, for the first time in years. Time melted from her face, and he saw her as she was outside Denise's house, holding the Tupperware with two hands, a thick layer of movie makeup on her face.

"If I could go back in time, I would change everything," his voice cracked. "I hope you know that."

She didn't say anything back, just hugged him tighter. He leaned down to her, inching closer to her face. She stared ahead, blinking slowly.

When their mouths touched, they smashed together awkwardly, like fledgling lovers in the backseat of a car.

He'd forgotten how to touch her. Artie tried to bat away his insecurities, the feeling that his wife was a stranger, had always been a stranger. He tried to stay in the moment. Artie's head spun, one hand was on Gloria's shoulder, the other a lobster claw pushing into his eyes and trying to push out the images of all the times he'd destroyed his marriage. Each moment glared on an unrestrained projector in his mind he could never turn off.

He pulled back and looked at his wife. Let him be washed in her face looking at him with adoration just this once. Let him keep his eyes on her face the whole time. She was never the enemy. Artie—he was the one who ruined it. The one who couldn't make it better. He couldn't fuck his way out of everything. He couldn't fuck his way out of failure. Not even now.

After they were done, she rested her cheek on his chest, and he ignored the urge to pee.

"Artie?"

"Yes?"

"Did you love Denise?"

He didn't know what to say. Was she prodding into something she'd always suspected? Did she mean love like family?

"Denise was the only person who ever truly cared about me," Gloria said. She quivered in his arms. "She was my best friend, and I don't know how to go on without her."

Gloria slipped off him and buried her face in the pillow. Artie couldn't stop seeing the Vegas picture his granddaughter had posted. They had deceived reality with their perfect photo albums, with Gloria's masterful scrapbooking. Knowing how to smile and pose for each captured moment, knowing how to fool the future generations who would muse over how in love they must have been.

❦

Artie didn't know what his last day at work would look like. He'd created so many fantasies of his own death he'd lost count, but imagining his last day at work was impossible. When he tried, the only image he conjured was the Allen's breakroom flooded with flimsy Party City decorations and employees sitting down to eat a piece of free cake. They'd clap halfheartedly for a man they only saw strolling with reps and regional managers, a fixture at the quarterly store meetings they all dreaded going to. The other scene he sketched was ridiculous, his own inside joke. He would waltz in wearing a loud tropical shirt, already holding the Piña Colada that would become part of his retirement signature look. Magically, the cocktail wouldn't affect him—either because his new sedentary future had siphoned out the vibrancy of toxic alcoholism, or because he'd become a little wiser in retirement and learned to sip and stop at one. Both possibilities only existed in this farfetched fantasy. In the same slapstick story, he would tear up his final check because he was diving so far into retirement he didn't need worker bee paychecks—even though all his checks were directly deposited and whatever he was tearing up with that alter ego was merely a statement, one that would also be emailed to him that same day. Even in fantasyland, he was bound to concrete facts and logic and incapable of carefree reverie.

He hadn't ridden an illusion since he was a child. Back then, he'd lain on the grass, closed his eyes, and pretended Lou Gehrig rose from the dead guiding Artie to baseball fame under his healthy, non-diseased tutelage. Artie was hitting a legendary home run when Clyde shook him back to reality and told him only idiots and fags lived in a world of make-believe. Ever since then, he daydreamed with caution.

Today, he allowed himself to dream. It was his last day at Allen's Market. He was parked in the far back row where all employees were instructed to park, and he was ten minutes early.

His head swayed between his own crafted disparate possibilities: one tragically deflated, the other a flamboyant joke. Artie knew today wouldn't be either of those things, and only inside of his black Toyota Camry with the seats that still smelled brand new could he be honest with himself and say he was terrified of this unknown. What if he walked away and nothing happened to the store; it simply functioned like he had never existed? What if he became just an 8x10 photo hanging over the public restrooms: smiling with his apron and managerial bronze name tag? What if that was all his efforts amounted to? What was going to happen to him at home with Gloria, who had just barely started to nibble on half a piece of toast? He wanted to believe this was an opportunity for them to time travel to 1963 and start fresh, but instead, all he could do was laugh out loud, a dry, brittle, bitter laugh.

Even back in 1963, he'd run Gloria with a hard-on Denise had sparked. If he could time travel, he might have broken up with Gloria, pursued

Denise and let her break his heart. In that alternate universe, Gloria could have found a man worthy of her, a man who took Autumn out for ice cream instead of the jewelry store, a man who would have encouraged Teddy to try out for theatre, to understand why his scrawny, emotional son wasn't a natural for rough sports.

He didn't live in that alternate reality and neither did his wife. She was stuck with him and his retirement money that would have to be rationed in between trips to see Veronica, a couple cruises, and weekly dinners out until they died from the heart disease they staved off with rows of medication.

Artie positioned his rearview mirror so he could see his reflection. He practiced the looks of honored humility and controlled nostalgia. He straightened his little bronze name tag, the grooves of his engraved name scraping next to his clipped nails. He smiled and rehearsed how he would say thank you, how he would wave as he walked out the automatic doors. In his mind, he saw Joan waving back—sending him off to a life she could never have and promising with her eyes that she would never ever tell a soul what they had done. He walked out of his car toward the store with aisle signs expected to be revamped next week, in a style the email called "clean retro sentiment."

The grocery store was as cold as it always was, the temperature set to keep produce firm and frozen in time. But today it felt colder, nearly metallic—like the inside of a walk-in freezer. Wendy—an elderly cashier who'd been at Allen's since Artie was hired—stood at the side of her favorite register, dabbing her eyes and smearing indigo mascara. Wendy was one of the few he had an entirely tame history with.

Wendy's shoulders shook. Artie couldn't help but place one soft hand on her back. She looked up at him with shock.

"Artie!"

He pulled his hand back and stuffed it in his pocket.

"You're—you're here?" she said.

"Yup. It's my last day. I wouldn't miss it for the world." Here he slid in one of his honed smiles.

"Oh, oh. Your last day. You should go in the breakroom." She nodded wildly like she suddenly remembered something. "Or maybe the office? You haven't heard anything, right?"

Artie began to feel this had nothing to do with his retirement hurrah.

"What's going on, Wendy?"

"You just need to go in the back. To the offices upstairs maybe."

Artie marched past the registers, into the breakroom. No streamers. No colorful plastic cups or plates. No ranch dip and veggie tray, or whatever else people had for retirement parties. One of the meat department guys stood at the microwave, his bloodied apron flung over his shoulder. He looked at Artie and nodded.

"Congrats, Mr. Joyce. I hear it's your last day. I signed your card," the man said, staring at his wet non-slip shoes and shifting his weight from foot to foot.

"Thank you. I haven't seen the card yet, but I'm sure I'll appreciate whatever you wrote." Artie gave a limp wave as he walked out of the break room, past the rows of blue metal lockers and self-purchased locks. A broken chain of laminated posters reminded employees to update their beneficiaries, to text their mental health number, to join the hiring panel for their next bakery manager. He jogged past all of these, skipping up the back stairs faster than he'd gone in years. Hugging himself to shield off the coldness that penetrated deeper as he walked past the cubicles, past his own desk with the last few things he was going to pack up today. He didn't burst into Joan's office, but stopped in front of it, because instinctually it was all starting to make sense. He and Joan had been woven into each other's fabrics for so long that he could feel what was happening. Two men in crisp gray suits asked if they could go sit down somewhere.

At the glossy conference room table in the squishy black chairs, these strangers told him the front-end supervisor had gone to Joan's house around 10, two hours after she hadn't shown up to work. It had taken him that long because her hours weren't set in stone, her times did change sometimes, and maybe someone had forgotten to leave him a note. The supervisor had gone down there after calling her cell and house and getting no answer.

"Mr. Joyce, I know Ms. Allen wasn't merely your boss or coworker, and that's why we wanted to tell you personally. Gary found her in her car. She was already gone. I'm sorry."

Artie blinked until the men blurred. He wasn't going to cry. Not in front of them. They slid him their business cards although he knew who they were. They were the higher-ups for the company that was swallowing Allen's whole, who were now asking if he could stay on a few months to help ease the transition. The remodel would be both started and finished by then. He wouldn't have to manage figures or orders or any of the numerical paperwork stuff. They just needed him for morale. They needed him on the floor.

"We'll give you an even heftier retirement bonus." This man, young enough to be his grandson, leaned forward in contrived camaraderie.

"Oh, Gary found this, too." The other man, the one who asked fewer questions, handed Artie a purple envelope with his name written in Joan's distinct penmanship.

"Sure, sure. I'll stay for another month. Can I have the rest of the day, please?" Artie heard himself groveling again, eager to keeping climbing the corporate ladder he'd clung to for fifty years.

"Of course, of course. We'll hold a meeting next week, a memorial, really. Could you speak to the store about Ms. Allen? Also, before you go, just do a quick sweep and make sure everyone is okay."

Artie nodded, shaking both their hands before swiveling sharply out of the room. He held his breath the entire way past the cubicles, down the stairs, past the workplace propaganda, past Wendy who was now smiling and ringing up a family of three. On his way out of the automatic sliding doors, he nearly collided with a young girl holding a white cake box.

"Oh, excuse me," she stammered. Artie kept walking.

"Wait!" she yelled behind him. He turned around.

"Are you Arthur Joyce?"

"I've been trying to get ahold of Joan, but I can't reach her. I saw your name tag," she pushed the box into his hands. "This is for you."

Slowly, he lifted the lid. A cake with perfectly designed chocolate frosting, the rim swooping like lace, and on the center of the cake an imposed photo of Artie from 1972, smiling and holding up a glass of champagne at a party Joan threw to celebrate his biggest promotion. Written in dark chocolate cursive were the words: *Enjoy Your Life, It's Yours Now*.

Artie forgot to thank the girl, running to his car hugging the cake box too tightly and holding his breath.

Inside the car, he gently set the cake on the floorboard before letting himself explode into primal wailing, thankful for tinted windows and an insulated, soundproof interior.

Chapter 16

1982

The drive back to California was quiet. Autumn sat beside Teddy in the backseat. She pressed her stomach and wondered if anything was really in there. Teddy held her hand with loose fingers, giving her the out to yank away and pretend they had never touched.

Autumn squeezed him back and folded his fingers tighter around her. When he fell asleep on the seam of Tennessee and Arkansas, she rolled her sweater into a pillow. His cheeks were slick with the same drool her unborn child was about to have. Autumn couldn't sleep. She watched the bland stretches of each state until she saw the first sign for California. There was a painful urge to claw everything with feral fingers.

"We're almost home," Gloria said. Autumn couldn't identify the tone of her mother's words.

They tried to change things up in their home state. They moved closer to the beach. Her parents bought one of the craftsman Carroll Park homes Gloria had always swooned over. She painted the walls of their new home a soft pink and draped yellow curtains over the kitchen window. She hung a Patrick Nagel up over the new white couch. With Teddy, she tore grass from the yard and planted tomatoes and zucchinis in the soft dirt. Teddy planted a small row of sunflowers. He drizzled water over them, asking them to grow. Artie kissed them all goodbye, heading back to Allen's. He had a fancy new title and a bigger office. Allen's was glad to have him back.

Autumn's boxes were opened, her posters and clothes and boots still inside. Her sheets balled on the corner of her naked mattress. The baby—a girl, confirmed by a grainy ultrasound—somersaulted inside of her. Autumn allowed Teddy to feel the movements with tiny, trembling fingers. When she was alone, though, the baby sloshing around inside her body freaked her out. She found herself crawling into Teddy's bed. He rolled to face her; his hand hovered over her like he was afraid to actually touch her. His hesitancy scratched at her heart, but when Autumn opened her mouth, she couldn't tell him she was sorry, that she'd never meant to hate him.

Veronica Elizabeth Joyce was born on her exact due date of March 8th, four days after her Uncle Teddy turned ten. Gloria praised Autumn's easy pregnancy and easy-enough labor. A nurse brought the baby to Autumn, the baby's little fingers and toes made of prickly quills. The nurse watched her squirming, probably thinking she was just another typical selfish teenager mother. Autumn tried to feign cooing and smooshing the baby up close to her, but she passed baby Veronica over the moment someone else wanted to hold her. Fortunately, Gloria and Teddy were the baby-obsessed types. Teddy had practiced swaddling on stuffed animals he hid in his closet and knew how to support a baby's tender neck.

"You're so good with her," Autumn said, after they'd gone back to the house and her parents locked themselves in a bathroom to argue about the same things they'd been arguing about for years.

"Is it weird that I love to help with babies?" Teddy whispered.

"No. It's sweet. I wish I loved to help," Autumn laughed. Teddy laid Veronica in her wicker bassinet before looping his spindly arms around Autumn's neck. His hug hurt.

"I can't breathe," Autumn twisted from his embrace. Then she cried so hard she fell to her knees, her throat burning from the mangled sounds coming out of her mouth. Her chest felt like it would collapse. Her spine became a row of dominoes, waiting for one of the ends to be given the tiniest nudge. Teddy patted her back until her sobbing became dry gags, then little whimpers. She crawled to her bedroom, forgetting she had a newborn who needed bottles and diaper changes every three hours. Teddy slept beside the bassinet in the living room because he didn't forget.

Gloria had always shone in motherhood. Except when Teddy was first born, and Gloria had to mother two small children. Teddy's birth was a stench that lingered in the air of their home. Autumn tasted it in the eggs her mother made, the eggs that were too runny because milk leaked through the front of her nightgown.

"Oh! He's hungry!" she scooped the slimy eggs onto Autumn's plate, forgetting to slice the crust from her toast. Her father wasn't any help because he couldn't do more than pour a bowl of cereal—and even then, he always put too much milk, turning her cornflakes into instant mush. Resentment coiled inside Autumn's belly—empty as it was because she couldn't eat something that squishy. She hated the new baby. Hated him for taking her mother and hated him more when his birth seemed to nudge her father back into late nights closing the store. Her mother slithered through her motherly duties then—packing Autumn's lunch and still packing tiny notes, even though the handwriting was sloppy, rushed. Sometimes she only wrote: Love you!

Autumn was only a child, but she couldn't help but want to get rid of the baby who hypnotized her mother with his greedy milk hunger, his sticky, clingy fingers that Gloria kissed over and over. He tried to touch Autumn with those hands, but she avoided him at all costs.

Her own fledgling motherhood reignited that familiar contempt. Gloria was again consumed with a blind dedication to a new baby, able to click off her entire periphery just like she'd done with Teddy. She caressed the soft skin, massaged ointment into the speckles caused by cradle cap— little flecks of dark, loose skin that Autumn shrank from. Gloria didn't chastise her, and Autumn barely noticed when the wicker bassinet was transferred to her parents' bedroom. Artie barely noticed, too, since he was still burdened with a slew of imaginary around-the-clock grocery tasks, a frail husk they could all see through, right to the dirty bar stools and nightly hotel rooms, or worse, the frilly bedspreads of girls newly living in their first adult spaces—girls probably not much older than Autumn. They could all see through his lies, as they always had, but Gloria was blissfully cushioned between 3am bottle feedings and wiping spit up with soft pink washcloths. Autumn could disappear and nobody would notice.

Teddy hovered near baby Veronica and Gloria but still found time to knock on Autumn's door. She found herself hardening her voice against her will. He rifled through the piles of cassettes tossed in a shoebox, gently asking if she wanted to listen to them. She flipped through an *LA Weekly* she'd snatched outside the liquor store when she went to pick up her first postpartum pack of cigarettes, hoping they would stave off hunger, so she could fit into her old clothes again. Teddy chose *She's So Unusual*, playing it at such a low volume, Cyndi Lauper sounded like a faraway fairy.

After Teddy walked out, she continued to lie in bed, the thin newspaper pages of the magazine sticking to each other and her fingers. The sounds of her own baby muffled, she looked to see who was playing at the Whisky, the Roxy, the Troubadour. Places that were several bus rides away, buses snaking through all the dangerous pockets between suburbia and the pulse of what every other young person was living. Autumn tore through her closet to find a stretchy black miniskirt and a white blazer with pointed, jagged shoulders that could pass for New Wave. She carried her shiny black pumps on the ends of her fingers, tiptoeing down the carpeted steps. From her father's precious garage, she borrowed one of his stashed $50 bills. She'd take the bus the next time. Tonight, she'd let a taxi show her the way.

Autumn swiftly became a fixture of the Sunset Strip. Her adventures turned off time and whatever responsibilities of hers that her family had absorbed. Veronica cut a tooth while she won a table dancing contest, with a prize of two free drinks and an invitation to a rooftop afterparty. Inside the glass mansion with glowing pool and bubbling jacuzzi was a white rug dance floor, a white leather sofa, and parallel rows of white cocaine cut into sharp lines. Autumn found herself kneeling on the rug, her knees sinking into its plush material and snorting fast enough to get it over with and fast enough to go unnoticed. She stood up, sour sludge sluicing down her throat. Effortlessly, she twirled around the room, and another line later, felt compelled to rattle off her life ambitions, her brief stint in Nashville, her parents' horrifying marriage. She forgot, throughout it all, to mention she had a baby who was fifteen months old, who was close to speaking intelligible words. A girl with blood red hair and nearly black lipstick led her to the kitchen where people stirred up shots flavored like birthday cake. A group of scrawny boys with ripped jeans held out their demo tape like it was a tray of steaming crab legs, their hands a fancy serving platter. Girls with neon nails dropped their cigarettes into half-filled champagne glasses. From across the room, a man with teased hair who looked like Judge Reinhold held up a fan of cassettes: OMD, Echo and the Bunnymen, or Soft Cell. Everyone screamed out something different before taking the shot that tasted more like cough syrup than cake.

The parties unraveled like a roll of film, layers of asymmetrical haircuts and danceable synth on Hollywood Boulevard crumbling into goopy black hair dye, burgundy lipstick, and black bell sleeves meant to imitate bat wings. There were nights at the Rainbow surrounded by pretty boys in spandex strutting a glossier pink lip than she could ever pull off. New best friends showed her how to tease her hair and gave her tips for bleach that would keep it from falling out. Luckily, Autumn's stark white rat's nest blended into the Siouxsie Sioux scene, too—and the punks who pierced their own noses, ripped their own fishnets, and sterilized their own needles with Bic lighters because their connect at the medical supply had become quickly unavailable. She used their DIY attitude as an excuse to play it safe and just smoke the stuff instead.

"Everyone smokes it at first," a Nick Rhodes doppelganger said as he demonstrated how to fatten a vein. The days and nights blurred into oblivion.

Autumn was jostled into the lucidity from the floor of an apartment building that used to be some famous hotel in the 20s.

"What day is it?"

Nobody answered.

"What time is it?"

The only answer was the traffic on the streets below. Autumn walked out the door to a hallway lit with flickering fluorescent tubes. She shielded her eyes as she walked down the stairs and onto the sidewalk with bare feet. A tattooed payphone booth beckoned to her. Autumn called her parents collect, begging them in a single gulp of air to let her come home, to come find her.

"Where are you?" Her father's voice was the thinnest it had ever been. In the background, she heard a squeaky child's voice and another man's deep timbre. Was Brett there to take Veronica?

"Who's there?" Autumn nearly screamed into the phone.

"Autumn. Look, we'll come get you. We'll get you help."

"Is Brett back?"

"What?"

"Who is talking back there?"

"Autumn, it's just us. Your mother, Teddy, and your child."

Teddy. *His* voice.

"Autumn, are you okay?" There he was, her grown brother.

How long had she been gone? She'd been sleeping on couches and cars, in bed with bands who were flattered by her fandom. When they asked what she did, she pretended to still write poems, to be crafting the next best screenplay. She'd lost time.

"Autumn?" He still sounded afraid. She could still feel his tiny fingers on hers as they drove back through the patchy nothingness between Tennessee and California.

"Teddy. You sound like a man." Autumn started to cry.

"Dad will come get you. They won't be mad," he began to whisper. "We've just been so worried." Autumn could hear his voice shiver, knew he'd learned to swallow the feminine display of emotions their dad loathed so much.

"I'm on Sunset and Wilcox. I'll walk to Vine, right by the exit."

"You'll wait for him?"

Autumn squeezed her eyes to block out the sun. Her skin brailed from the sudden wash of sunlight. She gagged on exhaust and warmed puddles of puke and piss. A few blocks away, her friends were probably stretching on their makeshift beds of quilts and sleeping bags. They were calling their guy, digging through the garbage bags of clothes, playing a tape warped from loving the songs too much. She belonged with those people. She almost said to forget it, that she hadn't meant to call her family—but Teddy sounded so alone, and she could hear her own daughter speaking in complete sentences, squealing for a mommy she didn't know.

"Okay. I'll wait."

She waited, her hands wedged between her thighs. When her dad pulled up in a black Pontiac she'd never seen before, he beeped a joyous, soft honk. Autumn stood up from the bus stop, suddenly feeling the nakedness of her arms and the concrete warming under her feet, and realized she'd run from the apartment leaving her one bag behind.

"I left my purse," she said quietly.

"We'll get you a new one," Artie reached over, clicking the door unlocked and pushing it open. It closed back on itself. Cars behind Artie honked, wiggling a stern middle finger as they sped past. Autumn stood there, paralyzed. He had to yank up the emergency brake and come around, telling her she was too skinny before he pushed her into the passenger seat and pulled the seatbelt tight around her like a straitjacket he latched into place.

Autumn's room had been converted into a My Little Pony theme, complete with an intricate rainbow mural only her mother could have done. Each seam of the rainbow's colors faded in the same patterned gradient. Each cloud was haloed in a reflected prism.

"You can sleep in here with Veronica." Gloria fluffed up the pillows. She still wouldn't look at Autumn. She'd only caught Gloria scanning her arms for a second before they made eye contact, and she hadn't looked at her since. Veronica sat on the edge of her made bed, hugging a pink Care Bear with both arms, her mouth hanging open. Her long dark hair swept into a tight side ponytail.

"You're my mommy?" she asked in her delicate voice. Autumn nodded, already feeling her arms and legs crawling with invisible bugs.

"Mom, she shouldn't stay in here. Not tonight. Or maybe I can stay in Teddy's room?" Autumn shut her eyes and rubbed her already throbbing temples. How could she explain coming down and dope sick to her mom who thought smoking pot was doing drugs?

Gloria only went to the little girl and hugged her.

"Autumn, maybe tomorrow you can stay in here. You know, she asks about you all the time. Teddy's been promising her you were coming back." Everything her mother said sounded rehearsed. Autumn waved to the little girl before rushing to the bathroom to go through the motions of vomiting, yet nothing but dry skin flaked off her lips.

Teddy kept her cocooned in old quilts on his bed while he slept on a pile of clothes on his floor. He brought her water with crushed ice—from their parents' new fridge—and found a collection of pop tarts, fudgesicles, and Chips Ahoy cookies for her insatiable sweet tooth. He dug under the couch cushions and in the pockets of old jackets for loose change to build a stash of Snickers, Butterfingers, and a bag of Hershey Kisses inside his nightstand sock drawer. Her parents peeked their heads in at night and feigned concern. That's when Veronica came in, too, touching her mother's sticky, cold face and peering into Autumn's eyes.

"You're sick?"

Autumn nodded. Veronica returned with a warm 7UP and a sleeve of stale saltines. Autumn tried to exaggerate their healing powers while forcibly chewing and sipping without cringing.

She preferred being alone with the brother she used to hate. She tried to tell him she was sorry for all the times she tattled on him just to get him in trouble. She was sorry for causing violent fights between their parents. He listened, his face as angelic as it had always been, now wearing smudged eyeliner and his hair flopped in the front in some sort of Devil's Lock, although the curls made it something else, too. Each day he wore a different black band shirt and each day he put on a different cassette. All the tapes he played had been the soundtrack to her former life. Maybe there was something to those supposed connective strings. Maybe she'd funneled the Damned and Sisters of Mercy, pointy boots, and the Avant Garde method of teasing hair in a way that was subculture and not Valley Girl. Between naps, Autumn promised to get herself right, so she could take Teddy to the Scream.

"You wouldn't like the Rainbow. I mean, I love glam metal—but it would probably be too cheesy for you. There are places out there I know you'd love."

Teddy kneeled beside the bed, beside his sister, like he was saying his nightly prayers.

Autumn detoxed quietly. Her parents thought she was avoiding them. Veronica barely noticed her ghost-like mother, who started offering to read her bedtime stories. None of them knew the truth, and Autumn wasn't about to dissect the past several years for them. Besides, that wasn't the family's style. They were better skilled at sweeping things under, describing swaths of life with euphemisms, giving vague over-the-phone updates like *She was having a rough time, but it doesn't matter because she's back. She'll look for work soon.* Autumn heard these from the hallway when she was on her way to the kitchen for toast or to brew stronger coffee. She made sure to spread the Sunday help wanted ads across the dining room table, circling all the jobs she didn't want in bright yellow highlighter. She called the few that seemed bearable, but they must've heard her lack of interest because they all closed the phone calls saying she would hear back if they were interested. They never called back.

Autumn stared at the first page of *Dead Souls*, which Teddy insisted she read, and which she could only think smelled musty. She picked at the little orange price tag on the back jacket. Apparently, Teddy had only paid fifty cents—which explained the moldy speckles on the book's inner spine. He sat on the floor, furiously writing out his speech for his English class. He was using the curriculum's rhetorical strategies to prove how terrible Reagan was.

"I mean, that's the gist," he explained to Autumn, never looking up from his notebook, a lead smear on the side of his left palm. Autumn envied this time in Teddy's life, which was surprising because she had always thought high school to be a snag in her fluid existence. But watching Teddy reminded her of Daniel and his devotion to politics and old, moldy books. She remembered him encouraging her writing. She'd heard his voice when she told the afterparty crowd she was a poet. They never wanted to see her work, just the aloof, artistic role was enough for them. It was cool to be a struggling artist.

"I don't know what I want to do." Autumn interrupted Teddy's writing fury, even though she was mostly only musing aloud.

"Do?"

"Jobs, life. I feel good about making those cookies with Veronica and playing with her ponies, but I don't feel like a mother. I called some of those stores looking for sales associates, but I don't want to do that either. Dad even asked if I wanted to work at his store and the thought of ending up like him, rotting away in the same place, doing the same thing is beyond miserable."

Teddy kept writing, but she could tell he was listening. He pushed hard with the pencil when he reached the end of a sentence.

"But look what happens when I do what I want to do. I can't do that for my whole life, you know?"

Teddy looked up.

"You're young, though," he said.

"Kind of. I'm a mom, so does it really matter? Even if I'm not a good one. Am I even really a mom?"

Teddy got up from the floor, dusting lint from his black pants and sitting on the bed beside his sister.

"You are, but I don't think you were ready to be—and I think that's okay. Mom loves doing that sort of stuff, and Veronica is happy."

"What if I mess Veronica up?"

"You won't because it isn't just you. We're all together, one big, dorky family."

"Do Mom and Dad know you hate Reagan?"

"No, and I would never tell them."

"Do they know we listen to all the same things? Do they know you read books with titles like *Dead Souls*?"

Teddy laughed and shook his head.

"Good. They wouldn't like it. They would probably think it was my fault."

Teddy hugged her tight, his arms still soft like Veronica's. He hugged her like that when she went to work her first shift with her dad at Allen's. He promised her it was only a tiny step before she discovered what she was really supposed to do. In her hand, he slipped a tiny black notebook and on the first page he wrote: For Poems.

Autumn couldn't remember the first time she visited her dad at work. There was a faint memory of hitting the button so the cash register would pop open or being paraded in an empty grocery cart. She wasn't paraded now—in fact, Artie kept his distance after telling her in a low voice that everything she did reflected on him. She rearranged a pile of oranges, ignoring the gawking stares surrounding her. She wondered how much they knew about her—or thought they knew.

Artie stuffed Autumn into the bakery's back-of-house, where she spent her shift giving new life to dried frosting and attempting calligraphy in melted chocolate. She blew on a misshapen "HAPPY" when she saw Artie strolling too close to a woman with flouncy blonde hair and tight light-blue jeans.

"Who is that?" Autumn gestured with her piping bag, squirting pink buttercream onto the cutting board counter.

"That's Artie Joyce, our boss."

"I *know* him. The girl."

"Who knows?"

"Does he know her?"

"I don't even know her."

Autumn watched her father weave though wooden bins of shiny apples, his hand slipping to the woman's hip like it had been there before.

"I think he knows her," Autumn said, more to the cake than her coworker who was breaking apart lumps of frozen bread.

"Oh, he's like that with all the new girls. Everyone says he's always been like that."

Autumn watched from behind the counter for months. Watched her father's hands on different hips, watched those same hands reach for the rolls her mother served with dinner. Watched those hands point fingers at Teddy, install batteries in Veronica's plastic fishing game. Watched those fingers click the knob to turn on the TV. Those were the hands holding onto a beer so cold it made his hands sweat smoke. Those were the hands that haunted her dreams and made her thrash worse than detoxing, keeping Teddy up all night and leading to his first failed test.

She blamed those hands when she called up one of her old friends and asked if she could stay with them. The voice on the other end was slurred and syrupy, tripping over itself when it welcomed her with open arms. Autumn knew what she was getting herself into.

Autumn left a note for her brother with her friend's phone number, begging him in half-cursive not to tell their parents where she was. In a sloppier sentence, she asked him to try and convince Veronica she wasn't all bad.

"You can come up anytime," she wrote last, underlining the woods with a thick black rectangle.

She left with $80 from her dad's garage stash.

Chapter 17

August 2018

Autumn wanted to be angry when she stumbled on the Facebook posts highlighting the latest tragedies in her family's life, but after practicing the breathing exercises recommended by a self-help book she'd bought for $5, she realized it wasn't entirely their fault. How else could they reach her? Maybe they'd tried to reach her. Maybe their letters had gotten lost in the mail. Maybe they went looking for postcards at local gift shops and drug stores and could never find any. Maybe the whole world had turned digital and distant. Maybe they'd forgotten her.

Her own internet had been down for months. Jorgen insisted it was the most frivolous expense, and his galleries weren't producing a steady enough paycheck—not yet. Autumn held no weight in the argument. She didn't expect to get paid ever unless she counted the occasional measly contest prize or the even more meager freelance content. Without internet, the latter would dwindle to nothing. Jorgen ignored that excuse because if that was absolutely necessary, there was always the little digital cafe down the street. Her allowance—fiscal and otherwise—didn't allow for social media excavating although she always checked her email and the Google voice account when she made the trek to the cafe to peruse submissions and pitch ideas. Neither account had a message about Veronica's surgery or Denise's accident. Even worse, Autumn remembered the day she had cut several items from the grocery list to pay for a phone call just to hear their voices, and they had rushed to get off the phone. Piecing together dates and times from the posts, she realized her mother had been more than "unavailable" and her father's exaggerated busyness was a lie. There had been a string of tragedies on the other side of the phone. They just didn't find it necessary to let Autumn know.

Autumn was on her second glass of overpriced Chardonnay while Jorgen was in Stockholm on another business trip that wouldn't be "a proper fit" to accompany him, which was why he finally acquiesced and blessed her with connections to the real world of Facebook and Instagram and Snapchat filters.

"Just for now," he had said before kissing her on the cheek and walking out the door.

Sipping the last drops of her second glass, Autumn wanted to type out a frantic response to her daughter, expressing how much she felt her pain of losing a child—but before she could click submit, she saw how disingenuous her reaction would be, and besides, there was a photo posted of Gloria and Veronica and Edie eating Voodoo Donuts from their signature pink box, and none of them looked like they needed her input. Too little too late, even if she'd only just found out about it.

Instead, she sent a direct message to her mother—allowing it to be as whiny and erratic as every impulse urged her to be. *Why didn't anyone tell me my child lost the baby? I didn't even know she was pregnant. Why didn't anyone call me about Denise? How is Bill? What happened in the accident? Was there a funeral? I'm still here, you know. I'm just far. I still have email and a number. Why doesn't anyone call me?*

Autumn pushed send with a gusto unfortunately lost in the quiet of computer communication. She drank a third and fourth glass of wine, hovering over the message to her mother and willing the little circle to appear—to confirm she had read her cry for help.

The idea of Sweden had instantly charmed Autumn back when she was pushing fifty and wanted to live anywhere beyond crummy Hollywood apartments and the heavily air-conditioned pods of retail. The promise of pursuing whatever artistic talent Jorgen swore he could smell was especially alluring. Jorgen didn't believe in hoarding wealth. He didn't believe money was worth anything, really. He found the sharing mentality of Communism too beautiful for the greedy human soul, and Autumn couldn't agree more.

Veronica was fully grown, so Autumn didn't need to pretend to be a good mother anymore although she still made an illustrious show of introducing her daughter to Jorgen. They seemed to hit it off, with her daughter nearly pushing her on the plane, promising to store whatever sentimental garbage Autumn had gathered over the years. Her parents murmured that maybe a Christmas right outside of Stockholm could be a festive change from the arguments over who wanted mashed potatoes with real butter and who wanted them with soymilk.

Looking back, Autumn knew she had moved too fast, packing Teddy's notebook into her carry-on and wearing the jacket her brother had studded himself even though it looked dated and blotted with irregular sunlight-faded patches. Jorgen pinched the worn seams and furrowed his brow. Autumn knew he was debating whether her attire was an intentional statement or simply sloppy American style. She brought up as many art theorists as she could think of on the plane while they ordered mixers to stir with their smuggled tiny bottles. 9/11 hadn't ruined that, thank God—the little plastic vials of booze under the appropriate three ounces. They drank until they fell asleep with their necks flung like dead geese and their mouths open without any regard for keeping up appearances. Autumn had never really believed she was madly in love—it had simply seemed to be the most practical decision she had ever made. The smartest one. One she needed to make at some point in her life.

Her new home was a picturesque cottage with plants to water and windowsills for Autumn to live out domestic fantasies of baked goods, little baskets filled with homemade bread. Jorgen stuffed strange looking money into her purse, her pockets. They had unremarkable sex on a bed she made every morning. They sat in wicker chairs drinking thick, sweet coffee. Like every artistic couple, they dispersed after morning chit-chat. She wandered around with a chewed pencil and thick white paper while Jorgen developed the photographs he had taken in the states, enlarging the things most found ugly, but he thought revealed the most intriguing parts of humanity. A bony hand threaded with soft veins. A closeup of a bloodshot eye. Trash sewn into damp gutters. Wet toilet paper trailing the spiked heel of a black stiletto.

Autumn met his photographs before she met Jorgen. She'd been out for drinks in Echo Park, singing bad karaoke with co-workers twenty years younger and wandering into a dark bar nobody had heard of that was showcasing "the pretty macabre." The exhibit highlighted photos of dead bodies—not whole bodies, just little delicate slivers. A wedding ring on a rigor mortis finger. A thick red stain beneath a fan of bleached hair. A necklace of bruises. A muscular back stained black from lividity. It was horrifying but also gratifying in the same way true crime shows satiated some ugly side of desire and the urge to be repulsed.

"What makes you take these photos? Why focus on these particular parts?" Autumn had held her vodka soda in a compostable paper cup, speaking slowly so he wouldn't think she was drunk.

Jorgen asked in disjointed English if they could go somewhere quieter. On the back porch he explained the wandering nature of his lens and how everything inspired him. Between cigarettes, he said with such gusto he spat in her face: "Everything—even death—has a beauty to it."

She couldn't remember how he told her she was alluring or beautiful—or if he even did. Suddenly, they found themselves entwined, and then on a plane, and then she was forcing poetry from a lime-hued countryside.

Wasn't their life everything she had wanted since Daniel first played warped cassettes in his bedroom—or even before when she and Beth pretended to be the Runaways? Hadn't she matured into wanting the sophisticated artist's life? Here it was: bought and paid for. Here she was, submitting poems that won prizes and publishing a chapbook that garnered crumbs. The low pay shouldn't have mattered because the reviews were glowing, even if nobody remembered poets. It shouldn't have mattered because Jorgen had enough money for them both, except when he was budgeting and cutting off the WIFI. Autumn replayed their quiet coupling, still staring at the Facebook messages, still trying to find the right way to comment on old photos of her child hooked up to an IV or the black and white photos of her with a sleeping baby she would never take home.

Finally, the little circle, a warped photo of her mother and father from so many lifetimes ago, popped up and confirmed her mother had seen the message. The bubbling ellipses burbled before going blank. She sat in the office chair Jorgen had bought for her, uncomfortable on purpose so she'd still find her miserable genius. She sat, her thighs cramped, and waited for her mother to reply, to let her know they were both still alive.

Jorgen came home flush from Stockholm, invigorated by the artistic energy that had apparently been overflowing at his exhibit.

"I'll have to go back," he said, his hair wild with static and his coat dangling from his fingers like his urge to return was so urgent, there wasn't even a need to hang up his jacket.

"I want to go," Autumn said.

"Now, baby doll. You know I don't like to mix the worlds."

"But it's how we met."

"I know. I know. But it's not a date. I have to be so 'on.'"

"I don't care. I need some sort of life."

"I thought you wanted to get away."

"Not for forever!"

Jorgen finally dangled the black wool coat from the rusted hook and sighed.

"You know Ella will be there. I don't want it to be awkward for you."

Autumn willed her shoulders to look soft and shoved her fists into her pockets.

"It's fine."

"You know it's not romance time for us."

"I know. I know," Autumn swatted at the air. Jorgen chewed on the insides of his cheeks while making the arrangements.

Jorgen didn't believe in marriage. He didn't believe in children, which was fine because Autumn's child wasn't a child anymore. The first stipulation seemed fine, too, because at the time, Autumn rejected anything even tinged with what her parents had. Especially after Teddy died. She almost preferred the vituperative nights after her father whet his gullet and provoked the melodramatic tears of her mother. After Teddy, they were quiet and hollow and plastic. Her father sipped water with his head down. Her mother's face went slack while her eyes simmered. They measured their lives by errands, by yearly checkups, by Sunday grocery shopping. They went to bed at different times. They acted like Teddy was from some other dimension, his photos replaced with pricey stock photography bought at homogenous big box stores, so everyone had the same photos of rivers, and women with their hair blowing across their monochromatic faces. Jorgen's dismissal of all things American and domestic was alluring—until it wasn't.

Autumn and Jorgen developed their own cyclical existence. The same mornings with the same exotic coffee in the same chipped cups she once thought quaint. Their little warm cottage became its own version of dull. Autumn's heart still held its dry socket—the one she used to plunge with parties and drugs and one-night stands. She didn't want that life back, but she wanted something. She decided she wanted to get married. She wanted to have "the one." She wanted to be madly in love. Autumn ignored the voice in her head that said that would never happen with Jorgen. When she brought up marriage, even just a quick, pragmatic civil appointment, he reminded her of what he had said before in a matter-of-fact voice.

"I do not believe in marriage, remember?"

He also didn't believe in monogamy, something he might have alluded to early on, but hadn't fully clarified. Jorgen didn't believe in unnecessary messes. His home was sparse. He preferred wood floors so the dirt could be easily swept away. He wiped up the stove after every minimal meal of things that didn't produce crumbs. He hated baked goods for that very reason. Sometimes, when he went on his trips to Stockholm, Autumn ate crumbly muffins in the living room and waited until he was expected to come home to do a half-ass sweep that she hoped he would notice was done with the smallest amount of effort.

The monogamy conversation came up during these trips. An old life partner, Ella, lived in the guts of the city. Yes, he was there on business, but they also would get together. Sometimes he slept in her bed, sometimes the couch. Sometimes they were platonic and distant, sometimes they weren't. He relayed these details to Autumn like he was summarizing historical events, little bullet points he marked with the counting of his long fingers, which she had noticed were stained yellow at the tips from his chain-smoking that suddenly carried a lingering odor. Ella didn't mean more than someone he once cared about, but if things happened, they shouldn't bother Autumn because she was his current partner. Still, he never wanted the company on his artistic sojourns. Autumn had only come twice, and both times Ella watched from a distance, her hair stick-straight and arctic-fox white. Her eyes a bright blue that was obvious from across the room of the dimly lit gallery. Autumn knew she would be doing the same thing this time, stealing Jorgen away for a few minutes or hours—but she didn't care. Autumn needed to feel some sort of pulse, and this beautiful countryside and waiting for Facebook messages from her parents wasn't cutting it. When Jorgen still tried to change her mind, she made herself sound as dramatic as possible, slamming the slick wood of the dining table, screaming, "I'm suffocating! I need inspiration!"

He blinked and said he understood.

The city of Stockholm was beautiful, albeit a little too watercolor for Autumn's comfort level—but she could feel the vibrations of cars speeding by and a symphony of voices louder than the ones in her head. Jorgen had arrangements with the gallery, which Autumn didn't mind. She practically skipped along the water, in the shadows of tall antique buildings, gulping in the perfume of the syrupy Baltic Sea. After that, she indulged in a series of coffee and cake until she rattled from an overdose of caffeine and glucose. She lowered her high with buttery scallops and a soup she couldn't pronounce. Her dessert was a gallon of water with sunshine slices of lemon, enough to melt bloat, so that she could welcome her competition with confidence. At the hotel, Autumn slipped into her black lacey dress and messed around with her hair for the first time in months, settling on something between bedhead and aging forest nymph. She wouldn't have called herself aging, if not for the gray hairs she noticed while pulling her dark waves off her face. When had they arrived, these tiny wiry things warning her time was running out? Finally, at the age of fifty-four, she was aware of her age, her mortal limits. What a gift to have been blindly running full steam for all this time.

Jorgen had asked her to meet him at the gallery and reminded her to keep a professional wedge between them so he could perform and converse to the best of his abilities. Autumn had waved off his worries, secretly fantasizing that the moment she walked in, he would be overcome with emotion—even though that had never happened before—and would want to whisk her into the golden nightlights of the city, finding something in nature for an impromptu proposal. A soft twig or the stalk of a wildflower he could wound into an engagement ring.

When she walked into the gallery, her entrance was unnoticed by the thick crowd who stood in little clumps on the black and white checkered floor. Autumn tried to subtly scan the crowd for Jorgen but only finding rows and rows of strangers caught in laughter, taking a sip from their drink or gesturing wildly at one of Jorgen's enlarged prints. Autumn shook off her disappointment the way a dog shakes off water, sauntering into the atriums of people, owning her place as partner to the artist they were all holding in fashionable prestige. She took small, deliberate steps into the crowd's tight fist, baring her teeth in something she hoped they all took for the same fake smile they were sending to her.

Autumn sipped whatever free wine was pre-poured into the plastic cups on the shiny black tables, floating through the exhibit while still threading her eyes through the crowd looking for Jorgen—or Ella.

The beginning of the exhibit was a dimly lit corner with framed photographs of Alma Rubens, Wallace Reid, Kurt Cobain, Sid Vicious, and Philip Seymour Hoffman. The photographs were super-imposed on thick silver gelatin and doused in the faintest dust of iridescent glitter. Beside the photos were laminated newspaper and article clippings stapled to nests of white ostrich feather boas. Strung between the photographs and preserved news stories were rhinestone ropes, flickering rainbow prisms in Autumn's empty cup. She scanned behind her and found another station of pre-filled glasses, still no Jorgen. Still no Ella. Autumn took two cups this time, hiding her empty one behind the table's pointed leg.

The second part of the exhibit was a narrow hallway shrouded in amber light. Autumn held her breath, her head swimming with trapped air. She scurried down the hall, noticing the pores of tiny speakers studded into the wall. A voiceless, distorted loop of the Velvet Underground's "Heroin" gargled as Autumn walked faster down the hall's slender throat. The loop was the part of the song that always made her anxious, the fast part that sounded just like waiting for the needle felt—a feeling that made her queasy and nostalgic and thirsty all at once. The hallway seemed to squeeze around her, at its end a sheer black curtain woven with fishing wire and sequined thread, webbing out the words HEROINE CHIC. Autumn pushed aside the curtain, stumbling into the show's core—a room with four directions and clogged with the type that often frequented these sorts of openings, the kind of people Autumn could never understand. Former urchins of gritty, slimy subculture matured into some sort of high fashion. Snooty punk rockers wearing tailored leather and out-of-print pins. Asymmetrical, razored haircuts softened with Olaplex. Fishnets and tulle and jeans ripped on purpose. Autumn got the notion of places like the Scream, the Rainbow, and CBGB having "a look"—she just didn't get the pompous veneer that seemed to ferment by going to more of these elite gatherings. Autumn started to slightly regret coming, still searching the crowd and still finding not one familiar face.

She swiveled behind her to find a wallpaper of old posters washed in blinking blacklight. Posters from LA. Autumn knew the rules about touching exhibits, but she still crossed over the tiny strip of blue masking tape and felt the pimpled paper as if she could transport herself back to those places—to the carefree dancing and yelling over bad sound and finding it funny that someone noticed she had a ring of white crust around her nose. Autumn pressed harder on the posters, the wall, running her fingers down the seams before she found one that almost sent her spinning. The Scream. 1988. She only read one of the band's listed before turning sharply into the next display and telling herself it was only a coincidence.

The wall was covered with big black and white photographs of women with full lips, defined clavicles, and sleek blowouts. Typical fashion stuff. Not typical of Jorgen's work. Autumn passed by many of them with a casual glance of boredom, suddenly just wanting to push through this and go back to the hotel and realize that the city wasn't going to stuff her emptiness any more than the little sheep grazing on the neighbor's hill tried to. She passed by a photograph of a woman in a leopard print skirt and teased hair, her eyes shut. This one was slightly more interesting, so Autumn paused. The woman was propped against a damp-looking wall, half of a dirty toilet in the photo behind her. The sink looked like every other bar bathroom sink, but somehow Jorgen had given it more texture—black fur on the drain and a veiny faucet. Autumn squinted, scanning the enormous photo because it all seemed like something she'd seen before. She scanned the model's limp, lithe arms stalling on the bruises marbled on the soft underside of her elbows. It clashed with the standard fashion look but made the photograph fit more in with Jorgen's usual aesthetic and sent Autumn to check out the others. They were all alike—strange, seedy backdrops with standard cover girl models, all with bruises on their arms and their eyes either closed or halfway drawn shut. It had gotten boring when Autumn strolled into a small room painted black and lit with a few red bulbs. The Gun Club played from a turntable, slowed to a growl from hell—just like Autumn and her friends used to do to try and find the demonic messages sent by their favorite bands. On the matte walls, photographs were transformed into flimsy bedroom posters. Autumn didn't have to look hard to see Ella was the model in all of these, a fact that clenched her stomach just enough to make her wonder if she'd puke up all the delicious pastries she'd enjoyed earlier. There was Ella on a floor, posed like she was on a beach with her hair flowing and her bra a sort of bikini top, while an unknown hand tied her arm off right above her bony elbow. There was Ella smiling with glossy red lips, a bent, rusted spoon in front of her with a bright yellow flame beneath it—all in high contrast technicolor. There was Ella lying on the floor, a needle dangling from her limp satin-gloved arm. Above her was the same Scream flyer Autumn had seen earlier in the exhibit—*the* Scream flyer. Beside Ella stood a model dressed exactly like Autumn had told Jorgen she had been dressed in 1988 on the sticky, dirty floor of the Scream. A third model wore pantomimed shock—a poor, tasteless imitation of how Chrissy had looked that day.

"What do you think?" Autumn smelled the gin and pine soap Jorgen loved so much before she saw him. She heard Ella's feathery laugh and saw flashes of her snow-colored hair before she saw her face, her lipstick smeared at the edges, the fresh welts of tomorrow's hickeys swelling around her long neck.

"You are disgusting," Autumn hissed. Ella must've heard her because she winced before rolling her eyes.

"What do you mean? It took you this long to figure out the theme? The needles hanging in the front with Lou Reed didn't give it away? C'mon, Autumn, it's just art."

"This," Autumn pointed to the poster portrait, "is not art. That was my brother!"

"You mean the one you never wanted?"

Autumn played the final sequence of events in her mind so much for days after, she wasn't sure if she'd made them up. Had she actually torn the poster from the wall? Had she really asked someone who wasn't paying attention to borrow their lighter, setting the filmy paper ablaze? Had Jorgen really spat on her after she'd thrown all the drinks from another pre-poured station at him? Had she really run out before security caught her, ecstatic that she must have sensed this would all have happened when she'd transferred her money to a separate account a week before—including some money Jorgen might have thought belonged to him?

It was 2am in California when Autumn called her parents, when she left a message on their voicemail, nearly shouting that she was coming home. She stuffed everything she cared about into one suitcase and one of Jorgen's designer duffel bags, leaving everything else strewn over the floor. It wasn't until she was on the plane, watching the greener grass grow smaller and smaller, that she started to wonder how Jorgen would respond when he walked in the house, presumably with Ella on his arm, ready to confirm that they had in fact been meant for each other. Autumn was meant for something, for someone else. She was meant to be home. She was meant to be with her family.

Chapter 18

1988

It took Teddy nearly six months to get the nerve to ride four buses to the east strip of Hollywood where he waited on the sidewalk for Autumn. She was late picking him up because she'd gotten a night job. He was early because he'd left the house before their parents woke up.

"I've never snuck out before," he laughed, but Autumn knew he was nervous. His pale cheeks glowed pink. He slouched, always embarrassed by being so tall and lanky. Autumn threw her arms around him.

"I'm sorry I left," she whispered into his ear. He pulled away.

"Mom and Dad are worried.".

"I know—I just couldn't live there. It wasn't going to make me better."

"Does this?" Teddy's eyes held his unwavering devotion while still calling her out. He didn't have to say it wasn't right for her to bail on her daughter a second time. She knew that already.

"Don't you see?" Autumn knew she was talking too fast. "Don't you see how I could end up like them?"

Teddy hugged her again, and she knew she could stop making weak excuses. She took him to the apartment she shared with Chrissy and made a big deal of telling him how close to all the Hollywood landmarks it was. They'd both read *Hollywood Babylon* and loved rehashing old salacious tales. She pointed out the bus bench Lon Chaney supposedly haunted from the apartment window. Teddy squinted, and she wondered if he really knew where to look.

After several bus rides and the end of his sophomore year, Teddy decided to stay for a full weekend. He was beyond willing to risk being grounded for the trip. He was willing to lie to leave the house. The lineup was too good to pass up: Rozz William's new band Shadow Project, 45 Grave, Flesh for Lulu. Autumn knew a guy at the 7-11 who could get an ID for Teddy.

"This guy actually looks kinda like me," Teddy said, flipping the card over and inspecting it next to the window.

"He looks enough like you," Autumn said. Everything was falling into place. It was almost too easy.

Later that night, her roommate Chrissy helped Teddy with his eyeliner. They each sat on metal chairs Chrissy and Autumn had found in an alley off Wilcox. Teddy stared at Chrissy with the same adoration Autumn used to give her KISS posters. Autumn teased and sprayed her hair with Aquanet, standing in the closet so she wouldn't make anyone cough. For the millionth time that day, she got the feeling she could call her parents and tell them the whole thing was her idea, that they should come rescue Teddy and get him back to the safe bubble of nightly news, casserole dinners, and high school dances. She marched out of the closet, her hand on Chrissy's pale pink phone, when Teddy's voice cut through the worries throbbing in her head. He told Chrissy about his plans to run for office, about an ACT UP march he was organizing. No, she couldn't send him back to her parents. He was better than that. He was better than her. He wouldn't do anything stupid.

Chrissy drove them to the Scream in her gray Corolla with the pockmarked rust and a muffler dragging like a wedding train. When it idled too long, it coughed out rancid smoke. Chrissy called out shotgun for Teddy. Autumn sat in the back, not bothering to drape one of the malfunctioning seatbelts across her, clutching the seat at every red light. Teddy gawked out the window, his eyes widening every time the Hollywood sign blinked into view. He pointed out the same old Hollywood landmarks Autumn had pointed out to him on his other trips.

"Hey, Chrissy? Did you know that's where Tyrone Power had his heart attack?"

"Who?"

"Have you been to the Chinese Theater? I love stepping in the footprints. Have you done that?"

"The place with the cement blocks of hands and autographs? Yeah, your sister took me. You want a smoke?" Chrissy tossed her pack of Marlboro Lights on Teddy's lap. Autumn watched, her throat aching to remind Chrissy Teddy's ID wasn't real. Instead, she looked out the window at the Larry Edmunds bookstore she and Teddy had gone to earlier that day. He'd bought a book about Buster Keaton, and they'd eaten greasy pizza on red vinyl barstools. He'd told her he was proud that she was doing better. Now, he was lighting up a cigarette and taking dramatic pulls and blowing out smoke like he was Marlon Brando. His stiff black hair shook in the breeze. Her own hair roared in front of her face.

❧ ※ ☙

At the Scream, Teddy pranced to the bar to order vodka crans with the same ID that had allowed him at the show. Chrissy's gaze followed him the whole way.

"Listen, Chrissy. You know he's sixteen, right? My *baby* brother?"

Chrissy stared at the floor, twisting her burgundy hair between her fingers.

"I know, and I know that's too young. He's just so nice and so smart—and so genuine about being excited for this show and everything else. Plus, he says really nice things—and, like, I know he means them."

"I get it. He's a nice guy—but really, he's a nice *kid*. Just try to remember that."

Chrissy said she'd be more big sister than flattered friend the rest of the night. Autumn believed her.

They watched most of the bands together. Teddy danced and thrashed and sang along even when he didn't know the words. Autumn drank her second, third, and fourth drink. She went in the bathroom to do a couple lines off an empty Covergirl powder case. She was better about pacing herself now. A tall man with long black hair and a ripped LA Guns shirt lit her cigarette. Autumn and the man gushed about the Rainbow, both laughing at themselves for their lingering love of dying glam metal. They were still laughing when Chrissy found them at last call, her eyes wide, black makeup brindled down her face.

"I—I don't know what happened. Someone is calling 911. I didn't know. He's your brother. I thought he knew."

Chrissy kept saying the same five sentences over and over, shivering even though the room was still hot from all the breath and bodies of the night. Autumn didn't understand any of it. Chrissy yanked at her arm, pulling her through the club. Security guards yelled for everyone to leave. One of them grabbed Autumn by the arm, but Chrissy pulled her back.

"She's his sister."

The lights inside the club turned on. Murky puddles blotted the black floor. Tiny plastic straws and glass littered the floor. The entire room was dull, flat black. Chrissy tugged Autumn's arm again. The security guard walked away. Had her brother gotten in a fight? Autumn almost laughed. Her dad would finally be proud of him. Chrissy was so dramatic—she probably caused the fight.

Chrissy dragged Autumn down the black painted hallway beyond the palimpsest of band flyers. Why would Teddy be back here? This was where the bands waited to do soundcheck. This was where the bands partied. This was the room with the scratchy green carpet Autumn had scraped her own back on after a touring guitarist told her she was pretty. He'd promised European postcards. Chrissy had lain on the same floor, sometimes on the same nights as her best friend. There was nothing for Teddy back here. Why would Teddy be back here?

Chrissy stopped pulling. She dragged her hands down her temples, through her tangled hair. Autumn scanned her face. Looked at her nostrils, roamed her arms. Chrissy didn't look like she'd done anything. She was too awake. Her nose was wiped clean.

"He didn't act like he didn't know. I thought he must have done it with you before. He acted like he knew what he was doing."

Chrissy's cryptic ramblings finally started piecing together. Autumn refused to recognize anything her friend was saying.

Teddy was smart. He read a lot. He loved to know details. Autumn listed off her brother's skills and accomplishments inside her head, drowning out whatever else Chrissy was saying. She continued to tell herself how amazing and intelligent and talented Teddy was as she pushed open the door to the room she'd been in so many times before.

Somehow, she'd known—sister's intuition—exactly what she would find.

There was Teddy. Lying on his back. His face slack and blue and wet. His arm still tied off. Thick blood trickling down his arm. Autumn kneeled beside him, the coarse carpet pricking through her fishnets.

"Teddy?" she slapped his face. On the other side of him were empty water bottles, soaked bar rags, a bucket of melting ice. A siren rang outside, so loud she could feel it in every crevice of her own body. Autumn slapped her brother's face again. It was already going cold.

Part 3

Chapter 19

September 2018

Gloria paid $20 to park, so she could meet Autumn at the LAX baggage claim. Autumn hugged Gloria tighter than she ever had before, and Gloria forgot to apologize for not responding to Autumn's message. They sat in silence and traffic on the 405, with Autumn pointing her face toward the window. At the house, Gloria led Autumn around, highlighting the changes since she'd last been there. Towels had been moved to the hallway closet; toilet paper was stored in the garage, just like the separate freezer that housed the ice cream. They had a blue bin for recycling and a small bucket for compost. Gloria talked about everything except Autumn's surprising return, or her daughter leaving the Swedish man. Gloria decided against mentioning he had never made the best impression.

She was happy her daughter was back. She appreciated Autumn's enthusiasm for a party she'd almost canceled. Fiona, the event coordinator, had been more than accommodating back in June, rearranging dates and arrangements at such short notice. But since then, Gloria hadn't been able to reach out to her accommodating coordinator to finalize any of the remaining details. Fiona had been gracious and given her own ample silence. When Gloria called last week, saying her daughter was home and would help with the party, Fiona had the grace to pretend she had infinite patience. Gloria appreciated her. Fiona gave Autumn an enthusiastic tour of the antique venue Gloria and Denise had simultaneously fallen in love with. Gloria would let them figure out what needed to happen.

Autumn and Fiona circled back to where Gloria stood, Autumn probing Fiona with questions about the menu and the gilded cutlery, the chair packages. Fiona, clipboards hugged to her chest, was clearly relieved. Autumn had stepped right into Denise's fluttering excitement.

"Wait—am I understanding this correctly?" Autumn asked. "It's the same price for fifty people or one hundred fifty? Even with the food? Mom? Are you hearing this?"

Gloria stood in front of the mosaic waterfall, stepping a little to the left and then to the right to force the blanched sunlight to twist inside the smooth chunks of colored glass. The waterfall had been the big selling point for Gloria and Denise, reminding them of all the European cities they'd browsed on shared cruises.

"Mom? You're only inviting fifty people?" Autumn tugged on her mother's arm the same way she did as a child, the way she'd yank Gloria from tending to Teddy when he was a baby.

"If that. That's all there is." Which wasn't entirely true. Denise had rounded up a hundred names.

"You only know fifty people? Isn't our own family bigger than that?"

Denise had said the exact same thing, rattling off people Gloria had forgotten ever existed.

"I suppose, but we barely talk to anyone anymore."

"So? This isn't about who you talk to every day. This is supposed to be a celebration of your whole life and marriage with Dad. We need people from the whole timespan. We need old friends. Have you looked any of them up?"

Gloria shook her head. Denise had done all that. She'd shown Gloria a few internet high school databases and random genealogy searches, but Gloria hadn't really paid attention.

"Have you looked at Facebook?"

"I haven't tried yet."

Gloria hadn't looked when Denise insisted, and she hadn't done much of anything since she died. For a few days, she'd gotten up, showered, brushed her hair. She'd even put on makeup. She vacuumed the floor for Autumn's return. She'd mixed up egg salad. That was it.

Autumn spun around on the party's future dance floor. She pantomimed eating an ornate layered cake and used her hands to feather out the photo spreads she imagined fanned over the stone walls. Fiona listed off permissible adhesives, the procedures for hiring your own bartender. Autumn scrolled through Facebook on her new phone.

"Look, Mom. See how easy it is? You can find anyone now, as long as you know how to search."

Artie sensed the ambush before even stepping out of his car. He forced himself to take measured breaths as the garage door slinked into its sealed position. He closed his eyes, gulping in the stale stench of storage and coughing exhaust. It had been years since the domestic manipulation of mother and children studded the air. It had been lifetimes since he'd been on the other side of it, going over and over what they were going to say to convince Clyde to not be angry, to acquiesce to their feeble demands.

He slowed his arrival, sitting in the car with the door wide open and the key dangling from the ignition. His mind wandered back to work and the fresh-faced bosses who kept insisting he was working too hard. Morale, they pushed, with bleached white smiles. Old man, was all Artie heard, as he moseyed around the floor wishing for a disaster to fix. All he found were some spills and broken glass that he slowly shook the absorbent powder over and swept like his arms were wading through glue. That probably made the new owners think of him as even more frail and pitiful. They were probably counting the days, even if they told him it might be nice to keep him on through the chaos of Thanksgiving and Christmas. Not at this pace, Artie grumbled silently, reciprocating the same phony, toothy grin they were giving him.

This ambush had a similar tint to it. Artie knew the drill. He'd been through the presentations on why a new kitten was just what the family needed or all the bullet points of why a teenage girl's curfew could be extended for a single night. He'd heard the intricate persuasion woven by mother and the children she was vying for. It used to make him laugh a little. Why wasn't he ever asking anything of them?

Artie stood at the door that would take him from the garage into his house where he could predict his favorite foods simmering on the stove and the remote placed directly in the center of the coffee table.

But when he opened the door, he smelled must and mildew stirred into a dying Glade plug-in. Maybe his senses were wrong. Maybe he was just paranoid because of how the store had been. Maybe he *was* getting old.

"Hi, honey," Gloria said like she was noting the weather. He couldn't tell if her expression matched the flatness of her voice because he couldn't see her at first. He found her on a couch cushion on the floor surrounded by a fortress of wrinkled shoeboxes and opened cloth photo albums. Autumn sat across from her, her legs bent and out like a frog's. Her hair was looped around itself, spun like soft serve on top of her head. Gloria stared at the floor, her hands in her lap like a child about to be punished.

Something was definitely up.

"Whatcha two doing?" Artie hoped he sounded casual.

"Just going through pictures," Autumn said too quickly. Gloria nodded.

"I can see that."

"I'll get dinner in a second." Gloria's fingers twisted together, knitting something invisible between them.

Artie walked to the kitchen, each step taken as if there were tiny snails all underfoot he didn't want to crush. He poured himself some diet lemonade. On the counter was a package of linguine, a jarred Alfredo, a sweating bag of frozen broccoli. In the sink was his cereal bowl, still wearing its skin of leftover milk. Artie rinsed out the bowl. He stuck it behind his other cereal bowls in the dishwasher, sensing someone watching him. The theatrical clearing of his daughter's voice interrupted his uneasiness. European life hadn't chipped at her too much, thankfully.

"Will you come look with us?" Now that Artie had spun around, her theatrics were dissolved. Her arms were hugged around her. She wore the signature puppy dog look of the ambush he'd suspected. He was right. They were just a little rusty on their presentation. It had been too long for them, too.

"I need to go to the bathroom."

Artie took extra time sitting when he didn't need to, straining his ears to see if he could scoop up the froth of what they were plotting. All he heard was the occasional gasp of someone baited by a memory, someone he didn't want to be. Something they should know. He wasn't nostalgic. If he lingered on something that had once been fond to him, he always found the memory's thorned edge. Often, it was something he had done wrong. Somehow, his wife and daughter were able to ignore whatever ugliness brewed beneath their surface reminiscing. Or at least they were able to pretend like they could.

He washed his hands with the foaming, fruity concoction Autumn brought home from her fancy natural market. He didn't even pretend to persuade her to come visit him at work. She knew the place was rotting.

She knew it wasn't *his* anymore, even if some dated headshot hung above the public restrooms.

Artie came out to his wife and daughter and their categorized stacks of paper. Thick, matted paper of the 60s. Yellowy Kodak sheets of the 70s, the amber veneer of the 80s. Slick CVS prints. Pixelated snapshots of digital infancy printed at home. A matured digital print sent via Shutterfly or printed on Gloria's little photo printer. Stacks of professional family photos, crisp paper with the ends frayed by years of switching out frames. Were they asking his opinion on organizing? On storage?

He should be so lucky.

Gloria tugged another cushion from the couch and plopped it beside her. Artie sat down. Autumn gingerly handed him a small stack. He glanced down. Black and white slices of the brief fourteen years before he and Gloria knew each other. There was Gloria with her hair in bows. Gloria with her grandparents surrounded by thick black trees. At least they looked black in these old pictures. Beneath hers were moments of his own childhood. A crisp Boy Scout uniform, freckles he'd forgotten he ever had. There was the same family portrait everyone in the family had. Clyde and Dorothy posing with their three children, all shorter than their parents' waists. Artie felt himself smile against his will. Clyde looked like Tom Mix, his fingers and teeth pinching a hand-rolled cigarette. His lips curled like every other cinematic cowboy. His mother's anxiety dissolved in developed film.

"We talked to Fiona today," Autumn began, taking a slow, swollen breath.

"Who?"

"The woman from the Ebell," Gloria mumbled.

"Oh? She wants our old junk?"

Gloria's head shot up, and she narrowed her eyes.

"I'm kidding," Artie said dryly.

"We're figuring out food and decorations. You guys were paying for all these people and barely having anyone come."

"You didn't make it some big thing, did you, Autumn?"

"I made it a practical thing." Autumn locked her jaw, switching out the stack in Artie's hand for a new one. He looked down and saw his wedding day, an 8x10 framed with glossy oak.

"Mom has this really beautiful vision of a timeline of photos. I think it sounds amazing."

"We already went over this." Artie began to feel his pulse in the tips of his fingers. He'd already said, yes, do the stupid photo thing. He kept staring at the picture. The sallow cake in the background. The nervous smile on Gloria's face. A cramp seized in his chest. He'd forgotten how beautiful she was, how timid, how eager she was to spend the rest of her life with him. The funny thing about photographs, though, was how much they left out. At their actual wedding, everyone had noticed the sickly tint flooding Gloria's cheeks. They all called it wedding jitters. They said the same for the puddles of puke she left on the church's steps. In this preserved photo, her skin was flawless and robust.

"God, Mom. I love your wedding dress," Autumn murmured. She always gushed about the dress, and it had been the same every time she'd seen the picture. There was another wedding portrait in the hallway. Why the tepid sycophancy?

He flipped through the wedding photos quicker than he should have. It wasn't until he reached a photo he hadn't seen in years that he stopped. Autumn on her third birthday, taken with a 35mm that always stamped little starbursts of orange light on every picture. This one exploded on the window behind Autumn, bleaching out the curtains that used to hang at his parents' house, starchy white frilly things that were always freckled with dust. Not in this picture. Artie glided his fingers over the ridges of antique paper, over Autumn's tiny dimpled hands as they clapped for joy over her birthday cake and the three glowing candles. There was Artie, his mouth open in a lively rendition of "Happy Birthday." There was Gloria, her hands clasped together as she beamed at her giddy child.

For a few minutes, Artie let himself wade into moments warped and immortalized by greedy photography. For a few seconds, he allowed himself to swim in the restricted world of the lens, not letting himself glance around, only looking at what was in each picture. But he knew all the other stuff was there, creeping at the edges like a row of demons just waiting for him to look their way.

Autumn handed him the next stack.

He should have predicted the photos they would slip into his hand next. He'd let his guard down. He should have been able to look anywhere else other than the palm of his hands. A square piece of paper preserved the minutes after his second child was born. Gloria's wet hair hung over her shoulders, her pale lips kissing the baby's sticky cheek. Teddy still coated in chunky birth.

Artie couldn't stay floating in the tiny space the camera eternalized. He couldn't just see Teddy—Theodore Arthur Joyce—with his eyes closed, his lips puckered. He couldn't not see the glowing, glaring perimeter of what the photograph failed to snag. He saw the flirty midwife wiping birthing blood from her hands before motioning for him to follow her. He saw her yank his pants down and heard her breathy voice promise him the best head he'd ever had.

Artie blinked rapidly, memories splotching the present, blurring out his wife and daughter who stared at him, their mouths hanging open and ready to bombard him with questions. He wanted to chuck the pictures across the room. But he didn't. He played their game and shuffled through the stack, trying to see his son in one-dimension. A kid pointing at the pink skin that used to be a tooth. A kid singing Christmas carols for a school pageant. A kid pretending to be happy posing with a heavy baseball bat. A kid dyeing his hair black and wearing tighter pants but still holding hands with his mother whom he loved more than anything in the world.

He couldn't do it.

"Dad, I know it's hard. It's hard for all of us." Autumn slowed her words until they mimicked a tangled cassette.

"Denise was supposed to talk to you," Gloria said softly.

"Talk to me?" Had they lost their minds? Denise was dead.

"About the pictures I want up at the party. I want pictures of Teddy."

Artie shut his eyes, so he wouldn't have to look at her. They'd had an agreement. He wouldn't rattle her grief, and she wouldn't question his avoidance. That was their compromise. Silence. No questions. Swallow whatever they disagreed with. They weren't supposed to splatter the past everywhere.

"We can't just let him die." Autumn's voice quivered.

He opened his eyes.

"But he is dead." It was a logical statement, and he said it with logical precision.

"It's supposed to be a celebration of *all* the years, not just certain ones." Gloria mustered up a shaky bravery he thought long dissolved. She'd stopped making demands. She'd stopped asking or begging or pleading. But then their lives had become so safe and quiet, there wasn't anything to beg or demand. There wasn't anything outside the most placid existence that kept them sane and moving forward like little mechanical cogs in some useless machine. She was insisting they break their shared promises. He began to crack, his old self slithering out. His skin simmered.

"Not just certain ones? Come on, Gloria, do you really want *all* of our memories up there on display? Every single second of our marriage? Are you sure?"

Autumn winced for them both.

"I don't want him to be erased." Gloria locked her jaw, her eyes glaring at him, tears trickling out of the corners.

"You think a bunch of people wanting to know what happened or talking about Teddy will bring him back? It won't. It would be a bunch of people accusing Autumn of her drug past and people wanting to know how we let it happen. The people that need to know about Teddy knew him." Artie looked down. He was still holding the stack, the pictures shaking in his hands. He flung them in the middle of where they all sat. They landed, fanning out like a sunflower. All the Teddys. All the Teddys he'd failed.

"Dad. They're just pictures. They're just memories." Autumn scooped the pictures up, flushing the edges.

"Pictures. Just pictures." Artie slowly stood up, wiping the floor dust from his pants. "But they aren't just pictures. They're all part of this same phoniness. Gloria, you knew I didn't want this party. I didn't want the charade to act like our lives are worth celebrating. Why? Because we *stuck it out*? Does that symbolize love? Or does it suggest something else? Comfort, following the good rules of life? Did you ever get your happily ever after? I mean, really?"

Tears trickled from Gloria's eyes. Autumn pulled her close, patting her mother's head the way Gloria used to do for her. He remembered finding them like that when he was too embarrassed to shake them out of their mother-child reverie and would walk away quietly to the garage, the bar, another house. Other times, he'd yank Autumn out with the promise of ice cream or a drive-in movie. He'd enjoyed ripping the moment away from Gloria.

"I don't know if I did," his wife whispered to the floor.

"Then why are we even having this party? To show off? To pretend? Why isn't it enough to have it? Why bring a ghost into it?"

Autumn stood up, her hands coiled into white-capped fists.

"You need to stop," she growled. "You need to stop."

"You two ganged up on me about some pictures."

"Yes!" Autumn threw her hands into the air. "Pictures. Just a few pictures of *your son*."

"Ah, yes. Just some carefully chosen pictures to paint out this perfect life, right? Teddy's perfect life. Our perfect life. Do the pictures make it look like it's been a perfect fifty-five years? What about what's around the pictures?" Artie bent down and grabbed the stack of photographs.

"Here's this one," he waved a picture in the air. "Cute, huh? You and Teddy at an egg hunt? Cute little outfits and we finally got you both to smile. You know what we aren't seeing? We aren't seeing you push him off his bike. We aren't seeing you throw grasshoppers at him. We can't hear you say you never wanted a brother—do you remember that? How you made sure he was in earshot?"

Autumn's fists went limp. Her face paled.

"Oh, don't worry. It isn't just you. See this Little League portrait?" He flapped around the next picture in the stack. "He hated sports. We'd play catch like fathers are supposed to do with their sons, and I'd throw the ball hard enough to leave bruises, thinking that would toughen him up. I called him a sissy, thinking *that* would toughen him up. I told him he was a fag for wanting to do school plays. I was drunk or hungover when I said those things—which, oh guess what? *Isn't in the pictures*. It's around all these pictures, though, isn't it? Want to talk memories? Let's talk about every drunken mess I made because I bet you could both come up with a lot of examples." Artie's pulse crawled all over his body, and he wondered if this is how he would drop dead. Hadn't his own father just dropped dead? Wasn't he older than his dad had been? What had Clyde said before his mouth went dry, and he fell to the floor?

"Your mother is the only one who was a saint in that boy's life. I'll give her that." He couldn't stop his mouth from rolling now, speaking faster and hoping it would spark a heart attack, an aneurysm. That would stall the party for a few more months. Hell, combine it with his funeral.

"But, even her saintly motherhood has an ugly side. You know what you don't see here?" He jabbed his finger into the photo of a goth sixteen-year old Teddy cradling the family cat. "You don't see your mother warping his brain and coddling him to the point to where he couldn't fall asleep without her lying beside him until he was ten years old. I can only imagine what that does to a boy. He had no sense of right and wrong and making bad decisions because your mom wouldn't let go of his hand. Hell, he was so sheltered, how could he know shooting up one time could do him in?"

There. He could drop dead now.

He didn't die, though. He stood there very much alive while Gloria scurried her hands over all the photos, scooping them up and tossing them into the boxes. Autumn stared at him; all little girl adoration scraped away forever. Her mouth opened and closed like a puppet before she shook her head and turned away to help her mother collect the pictures strewn over the floor.

Artie's next movements were like a dream. He floated back to the garage. His disembodied hand forced the key in the ignition and turned. The car slid from the garage, gliding down the well-lit side streets and pulling into the nearly empty parking lot of a bar on 4th Street with a flickering neon sign. An apparition of himself sat on a rickety bar stool and ordered a drink. Even as a ghost, he wondered if he had the balls to take that first sip.

While her mother tried to sleep, Autumn sat on the couch with her laptop warming her lap, Safari opened to Facebook. There, she searched for the handful of names she'd collected from her mother and her own childhood. She found nearly all of them, sending out friend requests and messages. Two replied immediately, saying they were so excited to come. *It's so heartening to see a marriage last so long*, one said. Autumn was thankful they couldn't see her physically react to that message. The original plan had been to make the night fun and memorable for both of her parents. Now, Autumn just wanted to make it worth it for her mother. She hadn't always been a devoted daughter, but she wanted to rub away all her mother's pain, the way Gloria had tried to do all the times she skinned her tiny knees or fell off the monkey bars.

Autumn washed her face in the bathroom, somewhat proud of her detective work, a name on the back of her brain she hadn't looked up. It wasn't a name her mother had mentioned.

She closed the toilet seat and sat down with her phone. Her fingers shook when she typed in his name into the Facebook search bar. Daniel Perkins.

He was the third one down. The same beaming smile, two children beside him with the same beaming smiles and soft, wild curls. Autumn's heart sank a little at the thought of his life moving forward. Still, she clicked on him.

There he was. Plenty of photos with his children. None in the last two years with a wife. She scanned other details and saw one that shone the brightest. Current city: Los Angeles. Her heart skipped around until she was dizzy. She felt like she was fifteen again, believing fate over coincidence.

Just like a teenager she debated with herself for what seemed like hours but was actually less than two minutes.

She pressed the send request button with animated gusto, closing her eyes tight enough to see glitter.

Chapter 20

July 10th, 1988

Late night phone calls were always bad news. They've forever been synonymous with death and accidents and whatever other horrors worth waking someone up for. Gloria Joyce knew these facts, even before her phone rang at 1:43 in the morning. The noise lifted her from the tenuous sleep she wrestled with nightly. It was almost a relief to be fully woken by the shrill scream of the phone, until she read the glowing numbers on the alarm clock. She reached for her white wooden nightstand and considered taking another pill before picking up the phone, knowing the news would be devastating even before she scooped her fingers around the smooth handle of the beige earpiece. Bringing the phone to her ear, she sorted through all the reasons she would be getting a phone call this late. All of them circled back to Autumn and her habit of making poor decisions.

"Hello?" Her fingers dug into the curls of the phone's rubbery cord.

It was Autumn.

Her daughter coughed out the word Mom, twisting it into a single vibration.

"Mom?" Autumn cried out again.

"Yes?" Gloria whispered. She scanned the dark room, taking in a pile of dirty laundry and a bottom dresser drawer that wasn't closed all the way. She didn't want Autumn to say another word.

Autumn kept talking, the rest of the conversation a blur of incoherent buzzing, the only clear words being MOM and DEAD and HOSPITAL. Gloria tried to pray. Limp, selfish prayers that didn't make sense. She hadn't been to church since her granny was alive. She prayed again, refusing to acknowledge her son's empty bed.

Gloria couldn't tell if she answered when Autumn asked when she would be there. She didn't know how she was supposed to get there. She wasn't sure her husband was actually sitting up beside her because she couldn't remember the last time he'd actually fallen asleep in their own bed—and before three in the morning.

This mirage of her husband, his hair mussed and his eyes blinking rapidly, was real enough to take the phone's earpiece from her seismic hands and write down detailed notes on an empty envelope he found inside the top drawer of his own nightstand.

"Gloria?" This mannequin, this stranger, knew her name.

"Gloria?" She'd never noticed how many syllables were in her name. Her husband's phantom doppelgänger walked into their giant closet, his questions about her clothes echoing from inside the cavernous walk-in. He emerged with mismatched shirts and pants, tossing them her way. She was wrapped in the squishy white comforter.

"You need to get dressed." He pointed to the clashing oversized things he'd thrown to her. "Gloria?"

She stuffed herself in a pair of gray pants and a neon green sweatshirt, her cotton pajamas bunched beneath. Her arms were stiff, the muscles in her shoulders tight. The elastic waist of her pajamas dug into her abdomen.

Artie tucked his shirt in and put on pants she had ironed for him the day before. He spritzed himself with musky cologne and guided Gloria to the living room where he told her they had to wait for Joan.

"She's going to watch Veronica."

Gloria had forgotten about her granddaughter, sleeping peacefully in her My Little Pony sleeping bag on her Uncle Teddy's bed, completely oblivious to the world collapsing around her.

Joan arrived via taxi. She waltzed in wearing a pink robe, pajamas, and fresh mauve lipstick. The only woman in Artie's life Gloria was ever happy to see, even now.

"I didn't want to drive because I'd had a couple of nightcaps, but I can assure you I'll only be having water while you're gone." To prove her point, Joan marched into their kitchen and poured herself the tallest glass of water before waving Artie and Gloria out the door.

Inside the car, neither Artie nor Gloria said a word to each other. She watched the naked freeways and yellow streetlights whizz past the window. Hopefully, he kept his eyes on the road.

Gloria and Artie walked into the hospital, a safe amount of space between them. Blinding lights blared from the ceilings and walls. The waiting room's quiet clashed with the sounds of stretcher wheels and blaring announcements. Autumn slouched against the wall, one hand pressed on a vending machine and her other hand stretching the holes of her fishnet stockings. Her face was gray, slimed with tears and makeup. Red lipstick welted her lips and chin.

"Mommy!" Autumn ran to Gloria and squeezed her until she couldn't breathe. Her daughter hadn't called her mommy in almost twenty years. She also hadn't hugged her with such intensity in almost the same amount of time. Autumn reached for her hands, but Gloria yanked them back and shoved them into her pockets. Autumn's face crumpled before she looked away. Gloria couldn't feel bad. She couldn't feel anything. She didn't know why she was standing in the cold, stagnant waiting room of Cedars-Sinai in mismatched clothes over pajamas while her husband stood beside her smelling nice and looking put together, and her daughter was calling her the name she'd wanted her to call her for years. Her prayers were supposed to have made the phone call disappear. She wasn't supposed to be here.

"Teddy," Gloria said his name so quietly it was like he didn't exist. She had to say it louder.

"Teddy."

It was the loudest sound she'd made since the phone call. Artie touched her and pulled her close to him.

It wasn't loud enough.

Gloria wanted her mouth and words to be louder than the man who walked out to meet them and led them down a slippery hallway into an elevator she wished would disconnect and kill them all. She wanted her words to be louder than the man when he explained things like acute toxicity and narcotics—things that had nothing to do with her son. Teddy was planning on going to Berkley. He wanted to study arts and psychology. He was a straight-A student who never went a day without kissing his mother goodnight. He was a good boy, Gloria wanted to yell at this man in the white coat and the clipboard who thought he knew everything about her child. You have the wrong one, she wanted to yell. Autumn shivered beside her, alive and breathing and hugging herself with skinny, bruised arms.

The man droned on about mortuaries and logistics of bodies. Gloria turned away from him. A cloth wall calendar decorated with flying cardinals and leaf sprigs hung on the wall. She traced time like it were the hands on her watch, twisting it back to the day before and the day before that. Gloria placed herself into the cloth square and saw herself telling Teddy she needed him, that she had a bad feeling. She saw him cancel his plans.

But Teddy wasn't here. He was in a room covered in a sheet, just like all the other babies she couldn't hang on to, only he was too big to fit inside a shoe box. Autumn whimpered beside her, snot sliding and mixing with mascara and flakes of last night's lipstick. Autumn had always wanted to be the only one.

The calendar glowed on the wall. The man asked about funeral homes. Artie looked at her, waiting for a decision.

July was woven into the tapestry with orange thread. Their anniversary was in ten days. Twenty-five years.

The Joyces rode as one family to the cemetery, a tail of slow-moving cars behind them, their hazards blinking out of sync with each other. The sun glowed in the rows of side mirrors. Nature had it all wrong. They drove down Broadway past the Park Pantry with Teddy's favorite vegetable sandwich. Gloria noticed people staring, knowing they were witnessing a funeral procession. She placed her hand on the door, her fingers reaching for the handle to roll down the window. They should know who was being mourned. They should know her son had died.

Her hand dropped to her lap, and she continued to avoid looking at her family. She knew they all wore the same stiff expressions they'd had at the funeral. None of them really knew who they were mourning either. Yes, they knew Teddy. They'd talked with him, shared memories—but they didn't truly know him. They never acknowledged what a miracle he was, and they would never know the first sensation of him somersaulting inside of her. She'd felt him snuggle up close, night after night for all the months she'd been so careful as to ensure he would survive and enter the real world. Her heartbeat soothed him first.

If only he'd never sought love and approval from his sister. If only *her* love had been enough. When he was first born, she'd had a fantasy of running away and starting over with the bond they'd had. She'd been stupid to listen to whatever voice told her to stay.

They pulled into the Forest Lawn near the mall. She wished she could have buried him in Hollywood with the movie stars. He deserved legendary company, not just some statues of historical figures like Milton or Emerson. Those weren't even his favorite writers.

Autumn held Veronica's hand, marching them to the dirt hole. Artie scurried behind them. Denise and Bill and their children orbited at a safe distance. Gloria took her time. If she couldn't see it, it could be something happening elsewhere. The whole thing was like that. Her son didn't do drugs. His sister did. Her son was going to dabble in a slew of ambitions, succeeding at every single one. He had been born after so many had failed. Those were lost children. Not her Teddy.

Teddy arrived in the black coffin Artie had picked out, wearing the suit Artie had chosen. She hadn't been able to make those decisions. She'd already dressed him in overalls, striped shirts, brand new jeans. She'd already chosen the wicker bassinet, the first twin bed, the orange blankets he'd used until the seams split.

When they began to lower him into the dirt and everyone around her sobbed softly, Gloria remembered her children eating strawberries. Autumn only bit off the tips, throwing away the stems and the severed bits of sweet fruit. Teddy always ate his strawberries to the wick. He was never wasteful.

Autumn took Veronica out for ice cream. Gloria gave them the car keys and whatever cash was balled up in the bottom of her purse. Then she sat and tried to think about anything other than her dead son. Nothing else popped up.

She tried to watch TV, flipping through the channels but finding something that reminded her of Teddy in every show, in every silly commercial. She turned the TV off and listened to the sounds of the house—breathing vents, gargling appliances, the cat digging in the litter box. All of them so loud, she burrowed deeper inside herself. Every tangled thought led back to her replaying her son's last moments and wondering how he had gotten to any of those points. She wanted to scream.

Gloria headed for the kitchen but turned around. The door to the garage was a white slab she only touched to leave the house. Behind it was Artie's territory. She hated it in there. It stank of old beer cans and bottles, of sweat. It was where she knew he took phone calls she was supposed to pretend didn't exist, where he went to detach from the main house. Placing her hand on the doorknob was rocking the boat. Early on in their marriage, she'd rocked the boat a lot. After Teddy, and then Veronica, she found rocking the boat didn't do what it used to. She used to care. She used to want to convince him to not do the things he wouldn't stop doing. Gloria was exhausted.

But she couldn't listen to the house's cacophony anymore. So, she turned the knob. Exhaust and cigarette smoke wafted into the house. Gloria held her breath and walked in. The air stung her eyes. Artie sat on a wooden bar stool, his hand on the cassette buttons of his boom box. His finger jammed into the pause. A fence of green Heineken bottles circled his socked feet.

"What are you doing out here?" he said, his eyes tilted toward the machine and away from her.

"I don't know."

He sighed. She didn't know what to say. Gloria stepped closer. She could smell the wood shelving. She was close enough to see its frayed edges.

"You ever get splinters on that?" she gestured. He looked up.

"I'm used to it." The skin around his eyes was bloated. Red framed his irises.

"Autumn wants to leave and take Veronica." Gloria didn't know if that was the most pressing thing on her mind, but she didn't come in here to point out all the mild dangers of a room he wouldn't leave.

"Maybe she should."

Gloria opened her mouth before pinching it tightly closed. Artie looked at her, let out a gust of breath, and clicked the stop button on the boombox.

"I don't know how anyone can stay here. I don't know how you can sleep in there."

"He's my child."

"And Veronica is Autumn's. It might be nice for them to get to know each other for a while."

What about her? What was she supposed to do if the one person keeping her going left?

"Are you going to sleep in here tonight, too?"

"Thinking about it. I won't sleep in there." He waved a hand at the connected house as if a layer of drywall were a fortress. He leapt off the bar stool, walked to the garage fridge and pulled out another beer. He snapped its cap off with a lighter.

"I know, I know—it's too early, right?" Gloria stared at the gray floor, kicked the soft piles of ash with her slipper.

"Can I just sit in here with you?" She hated how small and childish her voice was. Artie pointed to the stool. She sat down.

He drank another beer and smoked two cigarettes. They sat in silence until he pressed play on the boombox, and Lefty Frizzell swarmed the walls. She pretended to hum along. Artie closed his eyes and leaned on the wooden shelf. Hanging above his shoulder were rusted tools and the shotgun his father had given to him years ago, cobwebs clogged on the trigger. He should have looked like the vision she'd imagined at the Duffy house when she was fourteen. A man, surrounded by tools and beer, leaning on a shelf he'd built himself. That was how Mr. Duffy had looked, right? The more Gloria travelled back to the house and Denise's idyllic upbringing, the more she realized she didn't really know what Mr. Duffy looked like. It was all about the kitchen counter, the fancy dishes, the fresh celery in the tuna salad, and Mrs. Duffy's rotation of domestic attire. There had never been a family image. Just a woman cloaked in her role of wife and mother.

"You want a beer?" Artie asked, knowing how much she hated beer.

"No. I'm just going to go inside."

She marched to the door, glancing over her shoulder, disgusted by what she saw. *This* was what she'd dreamt of. She almost wished he would go off with those women who called—maybe then she could be set free.

Gloria closed the door behind her and went back inside to the clanging silence. She went into her bed and hoisted the comforter over her head. She wished it were a plastic bag.

Gloria woke up to Artie standing over her. He covered her mouth with his hand. Her eyes found his in the broken glow of the moonlight.

"It's just me," he whispered. He replaced his hands with his mouth. His tongue and lips were sticky over her face, and she fought the urge to gag. She knew how to play the game of a wife wanting her husband. She let him touch her, and she pretended to like it. While he pushed hard into her, she laid her head against his collarbone, the cool skin of his shoulder. That was all she wanted.

When it was over, he stayed on top of her. His weight paralyzed her entire body, squishing her lungs. She waited to be suffocated.

Her breathing never stopped. Artie got off her and then the bed. He came back with a glass of water before walking out of the bedroom again. Even with the pillow over her head, she heard the garage door click shut and the muffled sounds of whatever warped tape he put on.

Gloria gazed out the window, at the bedspread, at the glass of water Artie left out for her a week ago, at the dust and fruit flies swimming at the top. Day and night flickered from the window. She watched the circle of sunrise and sunset, completely baffled that it could all keep happening even though her baby was dead.

She existed in a cycle of her own. Gloria cried. She slept and dreamt flimsy dreams. A sound shook her awake and for a single second she existed in ignorant silence. The ignorance was fleeting, and she was instantly slammed again with the weight that Teddy was gone. Each time she closed her eyes and thought about him, he faded a little more. She went to his room and grabbed the most potent things she could find—a black sweater in the hamper, a box of stale Chips Ahoy, his chewed pens, his notebook she had sworn never to read.

She read it.

She read and chewed the cookies until they turned to grainy slop. Chocolate drool slid down her chin and stained the margins of the pages. Her fingers traced the grooves of Teddy's words, not fully understanding them at first. They were hieroglyphics. They were braille. They were a story she had to piece together.

We were at the mall when Veronica asked Mom why she doesn't have a mommy. We were in the food court, and she kept staring at a girl who shared an Orange Julius with her mother. Every time she sees a little girl and a mom, she asks that same question.

Mom doesn't know how to hide her annoyance or how to say Autumn's name without that one tone Veronica always picks up on. I wish I knew a lie Veronica would believe, and I wish I knew how to describe my sister in a way that was worthy, and in a way where Veronica wouldn't miss her too much.

Gloria remembered the way Veronica had shoved her thumb into her mouth when she'd said Autumn was selfish, that she didn't know she was missing out on the sweetest little girl. She shouldn't have emphasized how much she wanted her granddaughter, even if the girl's own mother didn't.

I want to do so many things. I want to write books. I want to live in Paris. I want to direct movies. I want to teach poetry to kids like me—I want to see that spark when a word really connects with them. I want to go to a protest. I want to run for office.

For a moment, she forced herself to believe her son wasn't dead. She allowed herself to believe it was a mundane invasion of privacy. Gloria imagined telling Teddy she was sorry. She heard him forgive her.

Big surprise. Those asshole guys at school got away with it again. I'm so sick of being called a fag. I'm so sick of being pushed into the wall "on accident," or having my food ripped from my lunch and chewed with their disgusting open mouths, before they laugh and spit it out on my tray. I almost wish they would just kick my ass and get it over with, but I guess they know that would leave a mark and lead to questions. I don't really believe anyone would ask, though. The teachers watching lunch and the halls see them do all the other stuff and never say a word.

How could she not know this was happening? She believed him when he bounced in and said he'd had a great day at school. She should have known he was lying. They should have been that connected.

My one real friend is leaving. She told me she had a surprise for me, and led me to the park where we watched cars loop around the traffic circle. Just like the movies, she pinned me to a tree and kissed me. I know I was awkward and clumsy, and probably not the first boy she'd kissed. She never said any of that, just cried and said she hated her parents for making her leave. We smoked cigarettes. I honestly hated the way they tasted—it was hard not to keep gagging. Dee Dee looked like a movie star. She already looks European. She asked me if I was ever angry at my parents. I said no, and it wasn't exactly untrue. I'm not angry. I'm afraid. I'm afraid of my father, and I'm afraid of disappointing my mother.

Gloria choked on cookie crumbs. Her eyes burned. She couldn't stop reading, gorging on her son's final resin.

Her baby.

He hadn't disappointed her ever.

Everyone else had.

There was one more entry. The last one.

I've never run away before. I think about those teen runaways on TV and know I'm nothing like them. I'm too scared to be like them. But if I can see all the things my sister sees, it'll be worth it. For the first time, Autumn and I can be real friends. And then I can go back home. Maybe then I can fix both sides of my family.

Gloria stumbled to the living room. Autumn had an opened Cosmopolitan spread over her thighs. An overflowing ashtray balanced between her knees.

"Where is your father?"

"I don't know."

"Where is he?"

Autumn shook her head.

Gloria held the walls for balance as she marched into each room. Veronica brushed the plastic hair of her Barbies from her bed. The other rooms were bloated and empty at the same time. No Artie. No one at all.

She opened the garage door last.

"What are you doing out here again?" Artie smiled, his mouth and eyes lopsided. He turned the music up. Gordon Lightfoot this time. Gloria covered her ears.

"I need you." She didn't know how loud her voice was or wasn't. Artie fast-forwarded and hit play again.

"I need you."

"I told you—I can't be in there," he said, turning the volume up higher. He got off the stool and lumbered to the garage fridge. He pulled out another beer. Gloria watched him drink the beer in one gulp. Fluorescent lights sizzled overhead.

Gloria spun around and walked away.

"Just stay in here," she said before slamming the door as hard as she could.

Chapter 21

October 2018

It wasn't the free trip to Disneyland that convinced Veronica to come down to California a month before the party. Her mother had asked daily, selling scenarios of them making up for lost time shopping at some new vintage store, taking a small road trip to a neighboring forest or desert, or embracing childhood with sno-cones and creaking metal rides. Veronica had been too busy for all those suggestions, and, really, she was too busy for Disneyland, but the cracking in her mother's pleading voice twisted something forgotten inside her, so she found herself saying yes. She heard herself trying to sell the same trip, the same rides, the same mouse-shaped snacks to Ethan, who insisted he needed the time to himself.

"But you haven't even met my mom," she said curled up on the opposite side of the couch, holding the remote because it was her Saturday to choose a movie.

"And who's fault is that? Mine? She lived in Sweden."

Veronica tried to open her mouth and dig up her old honed persuasive skills, but she could only bubble up the kind of slobbering spit that indicated she was swallowing big, fat, ugly sobs. So, she found the goriest horror movie she could, stared past the latex wounds and CGI guts, and wondered how she ended up in this situation—something so calm and placid and moving absolutely nowhere. Ethan avoided tradition and uncomfortable expectations. Marriage. Meeting whole swaths of family. He'd said yes too many times in his life, he kept telling her. To herself she said, yeah, but those yeses were to other people. An online self-help article suggested only letting things hover for the thirty seconds an emotion was truly alive.

Her own flaming feelings lasted longer than thirty seconds. Veronica told the chomping ruminations they weren't doing her any good, something else she'd learned from a healing-themed Instagram. Her stubborn emotions continued to hover while she rolled her clothes and Edie's clothes into the same red suitcase she'd had since she was sixteen, the one she used to pack to travel with her grandparents to see vampire tours in New Orleans, Christmas lights in New York City, and soft white sand in the Caribbean. Its pockets were stretched. Its inside zippers unraveled. The handle wiggled under her grasp, the same hot pink ribbon she'd tied around it when she'd gone to Nashville to meet her dad a week after she'd turned eighteen. She'd rubbed the ribbon between her fingers when he said it was nice to meet her, but a relationship just wasn't realistic. He had other kids, a wife, a life she wasn't a part of. He hoped she could understand. Veronica was still rubbing the ribbon when he offered her a thick slab of family money to keep her distance, promising to wire even more the farther she got. Veronica pinched the ribbon now. It was slick and cold between her fingers, the frayed edges a downy feather. Some things never change.

Veronica poured thick tea tree cleanser into a 3.5-ounce plastic bottle, reciting the lines she'd been rehearsing for days.

"You are still coming in November for my grandparents' party, right?"

Ethan stopped in front of the open bathroom, a pile of dirty towels in his hands.

"Yeah, I guess. I said I was, right?" His voice was sharper than she'd hoped, but then hers had trembled more than she'd planned, too.

"I just want to be open with my feelings, so I'm going to say it. I'm hurt that you're not coming with me."

Ethan sighed.

"But even if I didn't go, why would my decision bother you? Isn't it *my* decision?" That sharpness again.

Veronica focused on the face wash slithering down the side of the plastic travel container. Under the bright bathroom lights, the cleanser shimmered. She forced herself to be fascinated by each flickering light reflection.

"Shouldn't it be our decision?" she said in a voice so small it barely existed.

"We're still individuals, Veronica. We don't need to do everything together. You're only going for a week, and you haven't seen your mom in a few years. Wouldn't it be good for you guys to have time to yourselves? I'll meet her soon."

Veronica screwed the pink cap on the bottle. She moved onto the rosewater, letting it trickle into the next tiny bottle.

"It just feels like we aren't a real family. Like really, it's just me and Edie, and sometimes my distant boyfriend makes an appearance. It feels like we aren't a real unit. Not a family, you know?" Veronica took a gulp of breath. "And I don't mean just what happened—I don't even know if you wanted to be a family then."

Ethan let out a long push of controlled breathing.

"This isn't the marriage thing again, is it? C'mon, Veronica, we've been through so much lately. Why do we need to rush into that same old tired conversation?"

"Rush?" Veronica finally looked at him. Rosewater splashed her hands. "We've been together for almost five years." She looked down again, half of her ten-dollar bottle of fancy water puddling in the sink.

"Why are you always creating a problem? You'll go and come back, and in a few weeks, we'll all go together. Let me enjoy a little time to myself, and you can enjoy your week with your mom." He didn't give her time to respond before he walked away toward the basement, toward the washer with the pile of towels that tried to spill from his grasp.

Was she trying to find a problem, or was she simply expressing how she felt? Ethan was the most secure thing she'd ever known outside of her grandparents—and, even so, she always felt like she was clinging onto him before he disappeared. Every night she lay in bed with little flashes of the ways he could hurt her blinding her dreams. She'd wake up telling herself that when he met her, she was three months pregnant, fleeing a man who swore he'd kill her—and even after finding this out, Ethan stayed. He'd gone to court to testify when Edie's dad had gotten out of hand. He'd held a cold, wet cloth to her face while she agonized quietly in forced labor. He was logical, pragmatic, never victim to emotional collapse.

Sometimes, though, she wished he was.

She wished he could collapse in the frantic feelings of love—but instead, he mowed the grass, read *The Berenstain Bears* to Edie, paid half for groceries, made the bed. He was sturdy and dependable; he just didn't want a role he couldn't live up to—whether that was husband or father. Early on, he told her neither of those things interested him. Even after Edie was born and he did all the things that made the title of dad, he shrank from anything too concrete and official. It was logical for him to pick up Edie on his way home from work because it was on the way. It was his duty to pay for half of living expenses. It made sense. However, he often warned, if it didn't make sense anymore, he wasn't tied to anything by law or name.

Becoming a biological parent would complicate things. When she found out she was pregnant with the baby they would eventually lose, he was quiet. He asked her what she wanted to do. Veronica was insulted—he knew what she wanted. He came to the appointments, he asked the right questions, he wrote budgets that included diapers. Still, she never heard commitment; she never heard him refer to the baby with pride or any of the other inflated emotions that normally came with being a parent. The baby was just another fact. Until the baby wasn't.

It was all these tugs and pulls in her brain that made her forget where she was when she tried to read *Llama Llama* to Edie. She forgot to read it the way Edie liked, with overzealous animated voices, with happy, musical cadence.

"Mommy?" Edie asked, wiping her eyes.

"Yes?"

"How come Eefan isn't coming?" Edie had never called him dad, even if he was the only one she'd ever known.

"It's just going to be a girls' trip. He'll come next time."

"Does he not want to go?" The little girl yawned, too aware with her probing questions.

"I don't know," Veronica finally answered truthfully, turning off the lamp and lying with her daughter until she fell asleep.

Artie picked Veronica and Edie up from the airport, paying for the most expensive parking, so he could help with the luggage. Veronica noticed the extra strain in his face when he lifted it.

"Grandpa, I don't mind carrying it."

"No, no. I've got it."

They waited at the crosswalk for the walking sign to pop up, and Veronica found herself still staring at the man who had raised her, who had let her ride his back like a horse even when it hurt, who would watch with genuine interest at her fifth play of the day, the man always willing to play even if it was Barbies, My Little Ponies, Sylvanian Families. He just always had to choose the manliest character, giving them the most baritone, gravelly voice. Here, under a sunshine dimmed by a curtain of brown pollutants, he looked so different from the man her brain froze in time. His hair had turned pale silver. The sides of his cheeks gone slack. There was the tiniest mound of a growing hump on his back. Where was the robust man people never believed could be anybody's grandfather?

This unfamiliar old man held the handle of her suitcase with both hands, shuffling across the crosswalk while she held onto the hand of her daughter. Here they were again: a modern splintered family driving to the home that had been her soothing backdrop since Veronica was still in utero.

Veronica was the first one at the door. She opened it carefully and stood in the doorway, holding her breath.

"I'm here. We're here," Veronica finally announced from the doorway. She held the suitcase now, having yanked it from her grandfather's quivering hands when he set it down to close the trunk.

"We're just scanning our last picture," Veronica heard her mother call out. The unfamiliar sound rattled her.

Gloria had told Veronica about this photo display, asking at the end of every phone call if she had any favorite photos she wanted to send. She'd emailed a few sullen teenager photos, where she'd sat between her smiling young grandparents wearing a spiked collar and shaved eyebrows. There was also one of her with them at Christmas as a baby, posing in front of a color-coordinated tree. It was one of the many holiday photos where her mother wasn't present. Autumn wasn't even behind the camera. The photographer was her dead Uncle Teddy, the one Ancestry plopped on her digital tree, reminding her he once existed. Veronica knew not to ask about him. Fuzzy memories resurfaced. A gangly boy with spiky hair cheering her on while she spelled three-letter words, that same boy letting her play on his floor while he did his homework from his unmade bed.

Autumn and Gloria poked their heads from the back office at the same time. Veronica stood where she was. Her mother and grandmother came toward her with similar half smiles and open arms. Gloria swooped up Edie, smacking her cheeks with wet kisses, her hand gesturing to Veronica as she asked, "Why didn't you let your grandpa get that suitcase?"

"Oh, he carried it most of the time. It's pretty heavy."

Veronica looked at her mom, holding the suitcase still as a shield. Autumn's own hands fluttered around, unsure of where to go.

"I'm so glad you're here," Autumn finally said. "I've missed you."

Veronica smiled with her lips smooshed together.

"It's been a long time," Veronica mumbled, looking at the floor.

"Too long," Autumn leaned in and whispered, "Sweden was awful, a total mistake."

Veronica nodded. Artie came in behind her, patting his jeans and trying to control his labored breathing. He plucked the suitcase from Veronica's fingers and dragged it into the room no one ever slept in anymore.

Autumn seized the opportunity of Veronica's hands being free of luggage and child to pull her into an overdue hug. Veronica squeezed her eyes shut and held her breath, one arm limp and the other one hovering over her mother's back.

⚜

Veronica hadn't intended to fly in the day before their Disneyland trip, but Wednesdays were the cheapest flights. Besides, it was easy to go through the motions of being a family sandwiched between churros and Cinderella. Especially since Autumn was in full-blown spoiling grandmother mode. Edie continued to slap Veronica's arm, tugging her own mother's ear to her sugar-speckled lips, asking, "What's her name again?"

"Grandma," Veronica whispered for the millionth time.

"She don't look like a grandma," Edie said, her eyes wide.

Autumn marched ahead of them to the Fantasyland castle. She'd scheduled one of those princess makeovers the night before, with only one slot left at 10:30. They'd barely had time to do anything other than eat too much sugar for breakfast.

"Come on," Autumn was already there, waving them over. Veronica picked up her daughter and ran as fast as carrying fifty pounds would let her.

Edie picked out a pink ponytail and a sparkly blue Elsa dress. A faux beautician who wore a contrived magic ensemble scooped Edie into a swirling pink chair and began humming "Whistle While You Work." Other Disney songs floated around them, swirling into each other and making Veronica dizzy. She sat beside her mother on the wooden bench.

"You would have loved this when you were her age," Autumn said, smiling as if she remembered Veronica at that age.

"That's hard to believe."

"Really? You loved all the most typically girly stuff. Don't you remember those poufy slips? With the bells? And you only wore dresses with ribbons. You really don't remember?"

Veronica shook her head. She watched the Disney beautician wet her daughter's hair and twist it high, sliding in the wide white hair extension. She did remember those dresses a little. One was white with a red ribbon around the waist. She didn't remember her mom being there when she wore it.

"Did you like that stuff when you were a kid?"

Autumn turned to her.

"The girly stuff?"

"Yeah."

"I guess a little. I also loved to be dirty. You hated to be dirty."

"I did?"

"Yeah, this one time—" Autumn suddenly shut her mouth and faced forward, her chin twitching in some strange way. She glanced back over at Veronica. "I should have known with us all here that was bound to come up. I can't remember the last time we were at Disneyland together."

"Didn't we used to come all the time? With the grandparents?"

"*You* came with them all the time."

Autumn faced forward, and Veronica did the same. Veronica didn't care enough to pry. The woman painted Edie's nails with pink polish and spritzed her hair with silver glitter.

Edie's patience was historic. She was captivated by the exaggerated bowing of everyone who worked at the park every time she waltzed by.

She giggled and twirled each time they called her "Queen Elsa." When they waited in the long, stagnant lines for each ride that lasted a few minutes, Edie stood with her most regal pose. Veronica was shocked.

"I can't believe she hasn't thrown a fit," Veronica nudged her mom and whispered.

Autumn waved her hands at the paintings of Mr. Toad slathered over fake rock.

"It's the magic of the place."

Veronica allowed herself to laugh, to hum while they waited for Snow White and Pinocchio and Peter Pan. She allowed herself to make a funny face when they stood with the characters, allowed herself to remember how magical it was to see your favorite princess in three-dimensional flesh. She allowed herself to link arms with her mom, noticing her mom still had the same soft arms she'd had when Veronica was four, standing on her tippy toes and trying to help her mom stir thick cookie dough. She allowed herself to remember they had once baked. Edie held her other arm, still walking with royal grace and reserve, occasionally pointing at something that piqued her interest. First, it was the Dumbo ride where Veronica and Autumn had to swallow their fear of heights, laughing at themselves for being afraid when Edie twisted the steering wheel and flung them up and down, up and down.

Then, Edie pointed to the teacups, jumping up and down.

"I can't," Veronica shook her head. Autumn stood with her arms straight at her sides.

"Yeah, I can't do that either," Autumn kneeled down to Edie, who puffed out her bottom lip and stared at the popcorn scattered on the ground. "They make us feel dizzy and icky."

"But I wanna go," Edie said, squishing a piece of popcorn beneath her light-up pink sneakers. Autumn stood back up and ran her hands over her hair.

"I can't believe I'm about to agree to this, but didn't you say she'd been so good? No fits at all?" Autumn was closing her eyes and sucking in deep breaths.

"Yeah, but I'll puke," Veronica said. Autumn opened her eyes. Little balloons of tears were at each corner of her eyes.

"So will I, but we have to."

Veronica opened her mouth to object, but Autumn was already holding Edie's hand and walking through the metal gate. Autumn closed her eyes when they sat down, resting her hands on the wheel in the middle of the pink cup Edie had chosen for them. Edie was smiling so big, her eyes squeezed shut.

"Close your eyes. It'll be easier," Autumn said, her own still pinched shut. Veronica focused on the orange underbelly of her eyelids while the cup began to twirl. She clenched until she saw darkness. Her eyes were still clamped shut when Autumn called out over Edie's squeals, "This was your Uncle Teddy's favorite ride, too!"

Chapter 22

October 2018

Artie stood in front of the blank shelves he'd now wiped down three times. He hadn't merchandised an endcap in years, and yet here he was beside two plastic carts, each one built with cardboard skyscrapers of pumpkin spice nonsense: some weird alternative "milk," pre-spiced pumpkin puree, a fall makeover of Oreos that made his tongue itch, and a jar of pumpkin butter jacked up to ten bucks because it was in a jar that screamed rustic general store.

This wasn't the stuff Allen's was known for selling.

They used to sell sturdy groceries for people with families and budgets. However, there was a new customer base, and they wanted expensive products sold in kitsch, retro packaging. They also wanted Dr. Oz's magic wand and all the things the internet swore would keep them alive an extra decade or two. Who wanted to stagnate even longer?

Artie sliced through the first box, rows of aseptic milks—the kind of plant products Veronica was always saying were good for them. She'd stopped trying to push the compassionate thing after she dragged them to a farm sanctuary, and her grandparents still wanted turkey sandwiches for the week. Health, she wouldn't let go.

Artie had to squat at a funny angle so he wouldn't feel pinches in his back or the whine of his knees. He refused to use a chair or an overturned box like the other old person still working here. He slid in the boxes, the front a glossy image of a warm cup of this pumpkin stuff and overlays of falling autumn leaves. Artie reserved one carton for Veronica. She'd been quieter than normal since she'd come, quieter than ever, really. Maybe things with her and Ethan weren't that great, maybe her shop wasn't doing so well. He'd worry about prying later. This was what he was doing now. Putting things off. Just like the image that kept flashing up in his brain, the one where he held the rifle he hadn't owned in almost thirty years. Just like the six pack he'd bought and stuffed in the garage. He'd worry about all these things later. There was work, somebody else's task to finish first.

For a little while, he was able to stack boxes and yank out difficult shelving, hammering them with a rubber mallet once he found the perfect tapered heights. He got into a flow and allowed his mind to wander, revisiting the conversation he'd had with the new child leadership. He dissected their conversation, along with their matched slicked hairstyles and faint professional stubble. They wondered, with Listerine breath, if he could stay just a little longer.

"We know we had said this would be the last month, but with the holidays coming up..."

Artie couldn't remember which of them had said it—they both seemed to share the same business casual voice. He also couldn't remember which of them had gone on about numbers and morale, saying "shoppers would love to see a face from the past—especially the ones who were having a rougher time adjusting to the new 'bells and whistles.'" They asked him in surround sound if he wouldn't mind being the holiday greeter, welcoming customers with nostalgic enthusiasm.

A greeter. Like the feeble retirees he'd seen outside a Walmart who swore they just needed to keep busy. Artie had wanted to retort that he was better than that, to remind these boys about the parts of this company he'd woven with his bare hands. Instead, he found himself nodding and letting them go on and on about their holiday marketing plan. He found himself in front of an endcap. Busy work that they passed on to justify his inflated salary, to probably justify shaving the schedules of hourly employees just enough to starve them from the benefits package. Artie and Joan had never done that.

Artie began to stack the crinkling packages of pumpkin cookies. He was three packages in before he took them all down and piled them back up, annoyed by the lopsided, sinking heap they kept forming rather than a crisp, uniform tower. He swept the packages off with one arm, not caring if all the cookies snapped in half. For the count of a single deep breath, Artie felt satisfied. Then, he started to chuckle, amused by the triviality of his anger, how he was acting like Edie when she melted at the sight of the wrong spoon. He was still laughing when he scooped the cookies back up, hoisting them onto the shelf, his eyes drifting over his hands and seeing them—*really* seeing them—for the first time in years.

They were *old*.

Each one freckled with the tan spots every aged human eventually grows. He remembered his grandfather sitting on the velvet floral couches and flipping through the *TV Guide* with those same speckled hands. He remembered the few spots his father had although he hadn't been that old when he died. Artie tried to reach back into the cart, to pick up the cookie boxes, but all he could see were his hands. The spots. The slight curl of his fingers. The quiver that wouldn't still.

It was fascinating and horrifying all at once. How had he not noticed them changing? The same hands that buttoned his shirt before work, the same hands that tried not to clutch the steering wheel too tight. These were the hands that were now being asked to vet stacks of photos nightly, to pretend he had the stamina to revisit snippets of the past. The hands that hid some of the photos behind his dress shirts in the walk-in closet, his own secret stash. The hands that held a beer at the bar before overtipping the bartender, leaving behind a full glass. The hands that held the steering wheel relieved he hadn't broken that promise. These were the old, wrinkled hands attached to a body enduring pathetic routine scans done on an annual basis now. A geriatric body about to embark on a myriad of relaxing utopias. Beaches and boats and quiet, lakeside cabins. These hands couldn't hold a vacation cocktail without consequence. He could never prove he had it all under control. Not with these withered, wrinkled hands.

There wouldn't be this lofty reveal of control and balance. He wasn't going to reinvent himself or become a caricature of what life after work looked like. He was just an old man who'd made a lot of people upset for years, a current retail novelty. He might as well be the Pillsbury Doughboy. That's the clout he had now. He would become a man everyone thought they wanted home, but whose presence would be irksome. He was supposed to make everyone else happy. He was supposed to relax on their watch. Their very own old man, rocking in his chair until he died.

He couldn't even control the steadiness of his old man hands. He tried, watching the suited baby bosses with the glossy hair and young faces, boys still climbing ladders of opportunity who contributed to their 401ks even though old age seemed so far and distant. They smiled, heading toward him, one of them holding a clipboard and the other an iPhone meant for updating inventory online. Artie bit his lip, so he wouldn't ruin their hopes and tell them it was just yesterday he was them, walking on these same floors with plans and authority. Now he was their holiday greeter, a jolly old bastard who was supposed to symbolize the innocence of a corporate monopoly swallowing one of the last mom-and-pop grocers left in the country, maybe in the world. They were opportunistic millennials hoping to sell the skin of sentiment.

"Mr. Joyce, have you given it thought? We can give you a few weeks of leave so that you can enjoy your anniversary party," the one holding the clipboard and a clicking gel pen asked.

"How did you know it was my anniversary party?"

They didn't answer.

Artie looked at the endcap, the stool he sat on, the strips of plastic unlacing themselves from the front of the shelf, the frayed sticker tags clinging to the surface. He glanced at this new dynamic duo. It wasn't their fault. It would happen to them, too.

He agreed to be the greeter. He snatched those three weeks off, which everyone would think was to plan for the party and to prepare for retired life. The two of them negotiated a last day at work, asking if New Year's Eve was too much—they just liked clean shifts of time, symbolic new beginnings. Artie told them he did, too—which wasn't a total lie. He signed the paper confirming December 31st, 2018 as his last day. Only Artie knew he wouldn't make it that long.

He smiled at them, and they smiled back. Artie beamed brighter. He was finally taking control over his own life.

It was nice having a house full of family again. Gloria was back on schedule, waking up before the coffee pot beeped three times, squirting a quarter of a lemon into her water before the sun came up. Sweeping Barbie shoes into a plastic bucket. Scooping wet towels from the floor. Listening to NPR on the lowest volume as she built Artie's lunch with folds of turkey and slices of tomato cut so thin her wedding ring glimmered behind them. She rinsed the mayonnaise-slathered knife before she could lick it.

Having Autumn around since last month made her diet easier and less lonely. She'd already lost twenty pounds after Denise's accident, a familiar shed. She'd lost close to thirty after Teddy. Five pounds after her mother. This time twenty wasn't much, just enough to loosen her skin. Gloria still couldn't squeeze into the silver dress she'd impulsively bought in January. Autumn had jumped in without her normal critical voice, filling the crisper with bags of greens and thick cucumbers, soaking grains before Gloria could say it was too late to make something diet-friendly. They swirled soups in the Vitamix, spun zucchini into noodles, and fermented cashews into pungent cheeses that Gloria admitted did taste just like chevre. They started taking evening walks together. Autumn was quiet, but Gloria's maternal wires told her she wanted to say more. She went against her parental instinct and chose not to push. They commented on people's gardens, a classic car parked on the street, a squirrel darting dangerously between speeding cars. They walked a few blocks farther to the beach, no longer condemned like they both remembered it to be. They walked past the Villa Riviera into the curves of Shoreline Village, where they tried on silly hats and posed in the photobooth.

Gloria's Fitbit celebrated another step goal. She lost ten more pounds. Autumn dragged her into an advertised gym membership deal and promised to do water aerobics with her. They bounced in the lukewarm water to clean versions of catchy new rap songs. They did bicep curls with foam weights. Gloria marveled over how her daughter was still so slender in her black one-piece. Autumn swore she had stretch marks and saggy boobs. Gloria hid herself by wearing loose black shorts and a white t-shirt from one of the apple farms that sold to Artie's work. After the class and twenty minutes in the sauna, they rewarded themselves with frozen bananas blended with a splash of unsweetened almond milk, pretending the wet mound in their bowls was ice cream.

"Nice cream," Autumn corrected.

"Nice cream," Gloria repeated, beaming.

The morning Veronica and Edie headed back to Oregon, Gloria thought of this renewed closeness in her daughter, of a bond they'd never had in Autumn's adulthood. She drank her morning coffee, smiling, gazing at the birds skipping over the concrete deck.

Artie came to the kitchen and poured his own cup of coffee. Gloria wondered if it was a sobering cup of coffee. She purposefully kept her distance, so her acute sense of smell couldn't confirm what she'd been fearing ever since finding the receipt from the bar.

Her daughter was the next to wake up, her dark hair tangled and yawning big. Her husband poured coffee for his daughter, opening the screen door and motioning for Autumn to join him. They sat in the plastic chairs, both of their feet propped on the grill. Gloria couldn't help but peek at them while she scrubbed the cutting board from last night's dinner. From where Gloria stood at the sink, craning her neck in a way that was uncomfortable, it didn't look like they were even speaking, just sipping their coffees in synchronized, genetic unison.

Veronica woke up next, Edie twirling behind her in a Barbie nightgown. Veronica dragged the suitcase she'd packed the night before.

"I almost should just leave this stuff here. I mean, we'll be back in a few weeks," Veronica kicked the suitcase closer to the door.

"You can leave it." Gloria wiped the remaining dampness from the sink on her cloth pants.

"I was just joking. I'll need this stuff at home, too."

Gloria half-winced at hearing somewhere else be called home. She had loved these last few weeks. The games after dinner. The endless marathons of everyone's favorite kids' movies that they tried to press to Edie who was still holding stiff to her devotion to *Frozen* and *Tangled*, and some silly Netflix show about some neon world of magic and a talking cat. The dinners. The visits to extended family. The restaurants they could agree on. Now, Veronica and Edie were going back to Portland where they would send photos of Edie trick or treating in a week, hoping it wasn't raining too hard for her costume's velvet slippers. They would return in three weeks for the party, and Gloria would beg them to stay for Thanksgiving. Nobody could predict if Veronica and Ethan would say yes and abandon the big annual event her bakery was always a part of. There was already talk of Christmas, and that's where Gloria had to pause because there wasn't anything to look forward to after that. The party would be over. Artie would retire, even if he never mentioned it anymore, and she would have to stuff the photographic menagerie of her life in the garage, along with everything else they'd moved past. There wouldn't be an excuse for everyone to remember her son anymore.

Gloria tried to shake those thoughts from her head, offering to help Edie get ready, eager to let a young child's voice permeate everything in the atmosphere.

"Mimi, when we are on the plane, I'm going to eat snacks, and mommy is going to drink ginger ale, but you know I can't have pop."

Gloria forgot Christmas.

"Did you know I'm going to lose my tooths one day and a fairy is going to give me a present? Did you know it will be under my pillow?"

She forgot to worry about Thanksgiving.

"I have two Halloween costumes, and I have shoes that I can't get wet!"

Gloria forgot they had a different home, her grandchild and great-grandchild.

As Edie chatted more and shook the barrettes from her hair, howling when Gloria barely brushed it with a soft-bristled brush, she forgot and forgot and forgot. It was as if there weren't this big thing to look forward to, as if there weren't still three boxes of photos to go through in the hall closet.

Chapter 23

December 28ᵗʰ, 1988

Artie didn't know his father was dead; he only knew the guys on the floor needed to decide whether to toss the broken candy canes or to see if the bakery could repurpose them. Three days after Christmas, his biggest concern was shipping the excess wrapping paper back to the supplier without crinkling the rolls.

Artie loved the opportunities in post-holiday chaos. Reconstructing displays of tinsel, cinnamon, and prickly pine into towers of overzealous goals for the New Year invigorated him. He dictated his vision of grapefruit and cabbage mountains with a skirt of popular workout tapes to his team, who leapt at the chance to take his direction. Things happened at work. Shit got done. He knew how to transform resolutions into frivolous commerce and how to anticipate failed goals, knowing he would gladly lead sheepish customers to the relocated chip and candy aisle. It was an unspoken contract between consumer and seller—and both knew what to expect. That was his sanctuary. No dead child here. No failed marriage.

He didn't want to go home. He couldn't face the dying tree or the ornaments haphazardly dangling from the brittle branches. Gloria's trees used to be stunning replicas of Dickens' Victorian. This year, she'd gone through the motions of watching Veronica open gifts, and then she'd gone back to bed. He and Autumn had heated up the pre-cooked meal from Allen's. The turkey had been cold in the middle.

Artie flipped around a few grapefruits, twisting the pinkest flesh toward the customers. A cashier announced a phone call for him over the speaker. "Mr. Joyce, Line Three." He answered the phone with the same booming, pleasant voice he'd used to answer the company line for over twenty years.

"Artie?"

He didn't need to ask to know that was his mother's voice, even if it was more vacant and shaking more than normal.

"Yeah, Mom?"

"Your father—he, uh. Do you think you can come to the house?"

"Sure, I'm off about four—"

"No, Artie. You need to come now."

Joan waved him off before he asked to leave early, like she already knew the news Artie would hear in the same living room where he'd spent his whole childhood, on the same couch, his brother and sister on each side of him. Clyde was dead. Heart attack. He held his siblings' hands and wondered when he could ask if they felt as relieved as he did. His mother stared at her hands, her eyes completely dry.

When Artie came home, he found Gloria sitting at the kitchen table. She smelled like soap and perfume. Autumn must've convinced her to shower.

"My father—"

"Yes, your mother called me."

Gloria dug her elbows into the table, her head turned to the wall.

Artie hated grief. He hated being at home.

Phones rang incessantly at Allen's and at the Joyce home. Plumbers and neighbors and strangers were all equally sorry for Artie's loss—most people on the line expressed additional sympathy: *We know how close you two were.* When he swallowed an actual chuckle, people truly believed the sound was him overcome with emotion. Both Artie and Gloria stopped answering the phone, letting calls swarm to the muted machine until the tape was full. It hadn't rang this much with Teddy because most people don't know what to say when your child dies. Everyone has a script for an elderly parent. Even if that elderly parent wasn't all that elderly, and even if his death could be traced back to a love of all things toxic to longevity.

Artie was grateful Gloria understood the grief of others. She knew how to read sympathy cards and write thank you notes for the vases of flowers clogging their living room. She knew how to drive over to his mother's and help her store the food friends brought by. Artie liked to believe they were comforting each other while eating a neighbor's casserole, but then he remembered that his mother's grief and Gloria's could never be the same. Gloria simply knew how to care for others.

At the funeral, Gloria scooted to the last pew with Veronica who quietly read her newest *Babysitter's Club*. Artie sat beside his mother. On the other side of her sat his brother and sister. Clyde lay in front of them, the side of his waxen face off-orange against the ivory satin they'd chosen to line the casket. He didn't look like himself—not that any dead person ever did. Artie was taken aback by how vulnerable and harmless his dad was, and he realized he had never seen his dad peacefully sleeping, a time when everyone looked the most innocent. He'd only seen him passed out, a sleep shell easily cracked by the noises children couldn't help but make. Artie was so engrossed in examining his father's serene face in death that he didn't notice his mother walking up to the podium to give the first eulogy.

Dorothy spoke clearly and eloquently, using words Artie didn't even know she knew, considering she hadn't had any school after about sixth grade and wasn't big on reading. She thanked the room of people for the lovely cards, the flowers, the comforting food, and the phone calls that had become anchors in her grief. She cleared her throat and began to tell a story filled with heartbreaking sentiments about a man flung from a land of shamrocks and Celtic ballads into the grinding gears of American industry. Artie could only see Charlie Chaplin weaving through cogs in *Modern Times*—he'd always believed his dad was born in New Jersey.

"Family mattered most to him. He crawled up from nothing to provide for all five of us. He taught his boys everything he knew and demonstrated to his daughter what the ideal man should look like."

Artie felt Maura and Glenn's eyes. He couldn't look at them.

"I remember when I first met him. My friends were having this lovely summer party and when I was walking up the stairs—there he was, leaning on the banister, wearing a smile my best friend said proved how wicked he was. I was both charmed and terrified—but somehow knew we were meant to be together."

Dorothy's favorite movie had always been *Gone with the Wind*. The scene she told the sobbing church sounded exactly like the moment Scarlett met Rhett. Nobody noticed.

Her eulogy continued, weaving more cinematic moments to paint a picture and a life that never existed. Clyde became George Bailey. He became Shane. He became Fredric March returning from war in *The Best*

Years of Our Lives, without any of the wartime PTSD. His drinking became akin to Nick Charles in the *Thin Man*. He was witty. He was heroic. His flaws were only temporary and used to move the plot of his fictional life along. Dorothy continued, never once mentioning Clyde's love of Hank Williams, a Christmas pull of straight whiskey, or the way he packed Lucky Strikes with gusto. This room of people mourning his father had to know these things, didn't they? They just might not have recognized the man who went beyond belting out country heartbreak or slurring the funniest, disjointed joke you'd ever heard. They couldn't really know him, not if they were buying these movie scenes as Clyde's actual life.

Dorothy motioned for her children to come up with her.

"Say something about your father," she smiled. Artie knew that Maura and Glenn would lie and say something soothing for their mother's benefit. Clyde was gone. He was nothing more than something purged into whatever unknown awaits us all. Let him have a phony legacy.

However, when it was Artie's turn to speak, he couldn't say anything at all.

Artie stayed out of the garage for a total of eight days after Clyde's funeral. He parked his car on the street and walked in the front door like all the dads did in 1950s suburban sitcoms. Unlike those fathers, though, nobody shrieked with joy and the day's news when he came in. Gloria sat in the recliner, mute.

"How was your day?" he asked, echoing the television dads.

"It was okay," she said, never looking up. Sometimes she told him about something in the house that needed repaired. Sometimes she asked what he wanted for dinner. All of it felt like she was speaking to someone else.

Eight days of that and he was back in the garage, drinking until the voices in his head went dead. Life flickered in the house, on the other side of the garage door. Occasionally, Autumn and Veronica came over from their new apartment—he heard the skid of Barbie cars and the rubber soles of Veronica's new LA Gears. That's when he would emerge. He splashed water over his face and pretended like he always came out for dinner. Gloria pretended, too. She pretended he'd never found her lying in bed wearing a quilt of old Teddy photos. They both pretended he hadn't told her it was unhealthy to not let him go. Neither mentioned the hate glowing in her eyes when he'd said that.

It didn't used to be like this. He might have drunk too much and too often for too long, but there wasn't this consumption. This inability to pretend his life was anything but normal. Was this grief, or was this how his story ended? Allen's had given him two weeks of bereavement time for Teddy and now for his dad. Both times he holed himself in the garage, drinking until his head shut up. Then he could slump in a corner of the garage, or, if he was lucky, he made it to the couch or even his bed. Usually, he woke up on the cold floor staring up at the logs of loud fluorescent lights. Immediately, the voices in his head started again—and he knew the only thing to quiet them was a beer, and another, and another, and then find whatever else he had lying around the garage. Gloria hung plastic bags on the other side of the doorknob with sandwiches he let get mushy with warming mayonnaise and mustard, tuna turned soupy. He heard her pause outside the door but knew she wouldn't come in. She'd done that before, and it hadn't gotten them anywhere.

Artie listened to the voices, the conversation in his mind, even as he poured another drink down his throat. His stomach clenched and he closed his throat to keep it all down. If he closed his eyes, the room stayed still. When he closed his eyes, his father's life unspooled in his head, competing with the lies his mother told at Clyde's funeral.

He taught his boys everything he knew.

Artie knew Dorothy meant that to be part of a paternal fable of a man teaching his sons to fish and change oil and climb onto roofs to peel off old shingles. To show a teenage boy how to woo a woman and hold the door open for her, how to scoot her chair in so it didn't screech on the dining floor. It didn't stick to Artie in the way his mother had meant it. It reminded him of his mother failing to stand up to his father. It reminded him of his own failings. It reminded him he was a shitty father himself. He had to remind himself: *Artie, you are a father.*

He'd held new babies at hospitals and next to a plastic inflatable tub; he'd carried squirming kids on his shoulders to the park and watched them lap up melting ice cream from a sugar cone. He'd been given boxes of Father's Day ties. He emptied another cardboard box of twelve glass bottles into the fridge, pulling out two and holding them both in the crook of one elbow. Was he different from his own father? Was he?

Clyde's death certificate said cardiac arrest. The family all acted like they hadn't noticed the yellowish tint seeping into Clyde's eyes, staining his skin and speckling it brown. They acted like they'd forgotten the two packs of Lucky Strikes, washed down with whiskey and sopped up with gobs of butter and crispy fried food. It was one thing inside the bubble of the 50s and 60s, but they all knew better in the 80s—just like Artie knew he was almost guaranteeing the same fate with each beer he poured down his throat. He forgot about the cold ones and tore open another cardboard box, drinking the next one warm. He wished they still had some of the holiday liquor, but Autumn had swiped the last two bottles on her last visit. Maybe she had the gene, too.

Artie opened another beer and another. He lay on the floor and shut his eyes. Everything was dark, but he was still awake.

Artie held the shotgun on his lap, flicking out the spider skeletons and weaving out the webs. Allen's expected him tomorrow, and he didn't know if he would make it. He pet the wooden handle like a cat. He wondered what would happen if Gloria was the one who found him? Even at this moment, he was thinking too much.

He'd been here before, as a young and impulsive kid not yet dented with work, family, expectations. That kid pointed the gun away, at the door, waiting for his father to walk out any minute. He was only a little boy who held his breath and whose matchstick finger wasn't strong enough to yank the trigger. Clyde laughed before he pulled out a chunk of Artie's hair with pipe-stained fingers, the inner crevices smelling like all of LA's waste.

"You little idiot. I would never leave a loaded gun around here. Some fool might do something he'd later regret."

Clyde had celebrated life and power by getting extra drunk that night and kissing their mother's hand. Artie hated that she'd giggled and followed her husband joyfully into their bedroom. He hated even more the sounds they made from there, while the kids waited for a dinner that wasn't going to come.

Artie slid the gun between his legs and leaned back into the air. He balanced his feet on the wooden rungs between the stool's quivering legs. He'd been *here* before, too. That idea inching into his head, wondering what would happen if he swallowed some of the bottles in the medicine cabinet, if he took a sharp turn off the edge of the freeway and drove smack past the guardrails. He'd always chalked them up as fantasies. He'd never really do it.

Maybe he wouldn't do it now.

He thought about his father. He thought about Teddy. The boy hadn't looked him in the eyes for years—not since they'd come back to California. He remembered the day Teddy left. Artie had been in the kitchen when Teddy walked by, twirling his keys around his finger. Teddy's backpack was fuller than normal. It was summer, so he didn't have school.

"What are you up to?" he'd asked. Teddy had stopped cold. He was a terrible liar. He turned to Artie with Frankenstein movements.

"To see some friends," he said, the keys dangling from his thumb. Artie knew he was lying, but he hoped that meant Teddy was normal. He wanted him to make all the bad choices normal men made. He'd patted Teddy on the back and told him to, "Go get 'em." Teddy had smiled at the floor.

Artie took three deep breaths, wiggling out his shoulders. He leaned forward. His lips opened and closed around the barrel of the hunting rifle. He tasted metal. He tasted his failed hunting attempts. Artie closed his eyes. He wiggled his fingers around the trigger. He'd only need to squeeze once. It didn't matter if they'd resent him more. He'd be gone.

The barrel clacked against his teeth. He almost laughed. Here he was holding the most masculine tool in the world, and he was giving it a goddamn blowjob. He slipped the gun out of his mouth and dropped his head to his hands. Teddy's face simmered back to the surface, memories lacing over the present. He shoved the barrel back in his mouth.

"Artie!"

He turned his whole body, his back still hunched over the gun straddled between his thighs. Gloria stood there, in a pink bathrobe, two glasses of water sliding from her hands and crashing to the floor. Ice spun at her feet.

He slid the gun out of his mouth and set it gently against the wall, never taking his eyes off his wife.

Chapter 24

October 31ᵗʰ, 2018

October 31ˢᵗ and beyond was always Gloria's favorite chunk of the year. When her own kids were small, she labored over crock pot soup thickened with milk, cheese, and a rainbow of root and cruciferous vegetables. She was responsible for painting the kids' faces with color pancake makeup, cutting the holes in a white sheet, for stitching up the seams in cheap plastic costumes. Artie liked to walk in the crisp night, taking a beer on the trek throughout the neighborhood. Gloria bounced from the soup to the door with a big ceramic bowl filled with tiny chocolate bars, loving the symphony of congested children's voices as they shouted: "Trick or Treat!" By the time Veronica was with them, Gloria had abandoned the soup, going with them on the walk. Artie chewed gum, sometimes brought a Coke. Gloria brought a soft sweater and backup glowsticks. Later, Autumn rejoined them and reminded them of all the Halloweens they were trying to forget.

This year, Gloria waited by the door, but only one child knocked, holding a plastic Ralph's bag. Gloria dumped the entire bowl of candy into it and turned off the porch light. She sat on the couch scrolling, waiting for Veronica to post Edie's costume to Facebook. Artie sat a foot away from her, hopping between old slasher movies.

"I'm going to give Glenn a call in the garage," Artie sat up, tossing the remote her way. Gloria nodded, watching him walk down the hallway. At least he was quiet. At least he was home. At least he was with her.

Autumn, the new Autumn, would have sat with her, but she had made ambiguous plans. Gloria figured it was a date and just hoped he had something more going for him than all the others.

Gloria sat through a few more gory scenes before turning the TV off and scooping out the last two boxes of photos that she'd let sit dormant for too long. The other ones had been sorted into stacks and slid into manila envelopes they'd labeled by year or chunks of time: 1960s, Cruises, Denise and Bill, Kids, 1980s. They had enough to scan and make larger prints, but Gloria just wanted to make sure she hadn't missed any final gems.

She opened the first box. It was serendipitous. There was Artie and his Budweiser, with Autumn dressed in a Wonder Woman costume that Gloria was just now finding to be too suggestive for her almost teenaged daughter, and Teddy with his tiny, smiling face peeking through a plastic JAWS head. His gray sweatpants and sweatshirt were two different shades, made more noticeable in 35mm. Autumn looked away from the camera. Gloria put that picture in the maybe pile.

Then there was a small stack of old Polaroids. Autumn crossing her eyes and tugging her ears to make them protrude. Artie sitting outside, smoking a Marlboro red with a sweating beer between his jeaned thighs. He never knew his picture was being taken. The next three were of Gloria, all in front of a twinkling Christmas tree. For one of the photos, she'd been directed to hold a clump of tinsel like it were a baby bird. If she closed her eyes, she could still hear Teddy's tiny little voice giving the posing cues. If she closed them tighter, she could hear before that. Teddy begging to use the camera. Artie always saying no—that he'd break it. Gloria bringing it out when it was just them. He was such a careful and cautious child; he'd never break it. He always took the most photos of his mother, arranging her poses and expressions. He loved pictures. He loved the way a memory was immortalized and snared in a piece of paper. Teddy made plans for all these photos, saying when he was big, he would look at these photos to remember his mommy. That was before he concocted a better plan, and that was to never leave.

"I know you'll miss me being a baby, but I'll still do fun stuff with you, and you can look at pictures to remember when I was a baby," he'd tell her every night after she read him a story and lay beside him, waiting for him to fall asleep. For half a beat, she thought she was still in that bed, feeling Teddy's tiny fingers in her hair, the dampness of his breath as it went deeper into sleep. Gloria squeezed her eyes tighter, her fingers clenching tighter, reminding her she wasn't in the past, she was here and holding the Polaroids her son took. Her dead son who had been dead for twenty-five years.

When she opened her eyes, Artie was looking at her, the phone still in his hand.

"I told you it was a bad idea to go looking at the past," he whispered.

"A lot of things are bad ideas," she said without looking at him and without looking at the pictures as she stuffed them back inside the box.

It had taken Autumn two months to arrange an actual meeting with Daniel. He'd responded to her friend request quickly and liked a few photos: old photos of her with Veronica, a profile picture Jorgen had taken of her against the backdrop of a sunny Sweden. She had been less obvious, slowly investigating every post, every shared meme, the dates of the pictures of him with a smiling family—all of them wearing hunter green and holding some sort of holiday prop. Autumn's heart sank until she realized the photos were nearly two years old. She scanned his main page and then the about tab and found no relationship info posted. His birth year was hidden, too. Most people their age kept that stuff private. Autumn kept hers on there just to hear the chorus of those that couldn't believe she was over fifty.

They'd been chatting through messenger for six weeks. Pithy, uncertain checks on how the other had been.

"I'm well! How are you?"

"I'm good, too. It's been a long time."

"It sure has!"

Neither of them mentioned jobs or children. Then, he posted a picture of himself in front of LACMA, posing goofily with one arm looped around one of the many famous light posts. First, Autumn wondered who had taken the picture. Then she sent him a message: Are you in LA? Did you know I moved back?

"You moved back? I never knew you left. I've been living here for ten years."

They typed for hours after that. Daniel told her about moving back to Nashville and knowing he'd hated it all along, about how he'd come to California and taken acting classes, auditioned for the Comedy Store, made budget artistic films, wrote some screenplays that almost became something. She told him about Veronica, hoping he didn't ask about how she came to be. She talked about getting her life together, moving back in with her parents, running off to Sweden, publishing poems.

"You have a chapbook? That's amazing. I knew you had such an eye for words. Does that even make sense? An eye for words? LOL."

"I don't know about that. I won a little money, though!"

"That's great! Where can I read your work?"

She sent him a list of links around midnight. Around two they typed goodnight and sent respective smiling emojis.

This went on for weeks, although the conversation shifted from catching up to books they were reading, the strength of their coffee, how the Silent Movie Theater was undergoing yet another renovation.

"Hey, why don't we go to their opening night? It's Halloween with silent horror films all day. We can pop in and out."

Autumn squealed like she were fourteen, thankful for the age of digital conversation, the ability to type a calm and measured: "Sure!"

Autumn found a parking space surprisingly quick—and even more surprising was that it didn't require a permit and wasn't plastered with street parking rules. She was thirty minutes early, more than enough time to convince herself she'd dressed appropriately for both her age and for her eternal youth. It was also enough time to keep checking her reflection in the rearview mirror, each glance producing a new wrinkle, a lipstick smear on her teeth, a sharper point to her nose. Ten minutes before their meeting time, Autumn got out of the car, locking it twice and walking away from the theater, which would get her at five minutes past six, the perfect time to look like she wasn't embarrassingly eager.

She walked down the quiet suburban streets, past the stretches with the parking restrictions and beige front doors, past the small yards with thirsty grass, past sleek cars in the driveways and onto the capitalistic stretch of famous boutiques and ritzy cafes of Melrose. Autumn inhaled secondhand smoke and heard the splash of water refills, slowing her steps so she wouldn't be winded when she turned onto Fairfax. Her smile was precise and posed, her shoulders pulled back just enough for good posture—but not too much for her to appear stiff or snooty. The warm wind danced in her hair at just the right time when she spotted Daniel, who looked just like himself in the Facebook photos, and whose smile looked just like the day he'd shown her his bluesy mixed tapes.

"Autumn!" He was the one who was too eager, walking briskly toward her and hugging her so tight, her spine popped in three places.

"I needed that," she smiled, tilting her head ever so slightly because just like high school, they were nearly the same height. Just like high school, his curls gleamed and the gold flecks in his eyes danced under the yellow streetlights.

"It is so good to see you. I'm admittedly shocked—and speechless," Daniel smiled with straight white teeth. His voice was a little lower, and he smelled like a fancier cologne. His clothes hugged him in the way only a tailor could make happen.

"You look great," Autumn half-whispered.

"I want to hear all about everything and not how it came about in Messenger, but real life. But, after Lon Chaney, of course," Daniel made a grand show of opening the door for her, and she made a bigger show of playing the woman being courted. Already their exchanges were fun and carefree, without the menacing high of tight Southern cliques looking for the appropriate insults to land on their heads.

They sat through three movies and greased their fingers with a shared bucket of popcorn. They drank Cherry Coke before realizing the theater sold wine and beer, and then they drank two glasses of Chardonnay. The fourth movie was getting ready to start when Daniel leaned over and stage-whispered, "Let's get out of here." They mashed their slippery fingers together, nearly running down the street, peering inside every window until they found a bar with burgundy walls and indie rock lowered to a muffled swirl of distorted stringed instruments. They ordered shots and mixed drinks, sheepishly acknowledging that wasn't the best choice.

"It just doesn't feel like we could make any wrong decisions," Daniel said, laying his hand on hers and looking directly into her eyes. Autumn felt a carousel in her stomach she hadn't felt in forty years. When she closed her eyes, they were in the dimly lit room at his grandmother's, the handheld tape player with loud buttons held between both of their hands. There was Daniel, skinny and awkward with a woman in the living room he had barely introduced, reminding Autumn that the old woman was senile and couldn't hear when he laid her on the rough, stained carpet.

"Autumn?" Daniel was in the present, pushing a damp glass filled with vodka and seltzer water. When she squeezed the lime into the glass, it stung her cuticles.

"I was just remembering your grandmother's house." Autumn's hand flew to her mouth as she hadn't meant to be so honest. Daniel grinned into his own cocktail.

"That house was my favorite place," he murmured.

"Do you ever go back to visit? Nashville is the place to live now, you know."

Daniel looked up, his eyes sagging slightly.

"No. That place never had anything for me. It still doesn't. It's still the same good ole boy rednecks."

Autumn wanted to tell him she'd been a couple of times, that it was actually super cute with lots of cool restaurants and renovated Victorian houses, but something instinctively made her shut up. Daniel ordered them two more drinks. These came thick and dark with a heavy pour. Autumn felt her mouth moving and heard a marshmallow of stories: Veronica and her parents and her shit jobs and an impulsive trip to get a passport and flee for Sweden. She wasn't sure she was telling it right. Daniel's own mouth was moving, and Autumn had to lean forward and breathe slowly to wrangle some of what he was saying. There had been a marriage to an actress who had hoped to star in Daniel's first big film. He was still hoping for a first film. They had two little boys who hated him now because he'd broken their mother's heart. He had writer's block. He was running out of savings. His apartment in Koreatown didn't have parking, and the whole building's water was turned off on Monday mornings, but it was cheap. Soon, though, nothing would be cheap.

"Do you want to go there?" His voice floated around her, the bar swaying like it were a waterbed mattress.

"There?" She tried to say with precise enunciation.

"To my house," he was saying, and she was nodding, and then she was doing everything in her power not to puke inside the Lyft Daniel paid for with the last of his savings. Then he was showing her his trinkets: a chip of paint from the gates of Falcon Lair, a picture he'd taken of Cielo Drive, and a strip of ruined film he'd found at an estate sale and swore it belonged to Buster Keaton. Autumn held each one, thinking how much Teddy would have loved each of these warped souvenirs.

Daniel whispered into her ear that he'd hoped she'd be in California, that all this time he'd been looking for her, that it was like a fairy tale. She was in the process of pulling the bell-sleeved dress over her head when she had to run to the bathroom, curdled vomit spilling from her mouth and sinking into his stained toilet bowl. She hadn't puked in some guy's toilet in a long time. Looking at the antique rings inside the murky water only made her hurl more. She closed her eyes and concentrated on how cold the tile felt beneath her knees. Eventually, she was able to go back to where they left off, ignoring the anticlimactic way Daniel lived, plastic bags on the cupboard handles like he were twenty-five. She was able to slide out of her underwear and lie in a way that deceived her age.

They were both too wasted to take it further.

"We're so old now," he murmured into her hair. It was comforting to feel too old with someone else. So soothing that she drifted into the heaviest avalanche of sleep she'd felt in ten years or more, Daniel's arm wound around her waist.

Part 4

Chapter 25

The party wouldn't start for hours, and Gloria was already disappointed. Everything was exactly where it was supposed to be, but nothing looked the way she'd imagined. Gloria and Autumn had meticulously examined the doodled seating charts and buffet trays from a bird's eye view for weeks, double-checking that the smallest of details would be executed to perfection. Standing in the room with everything just so, she couldn't decide if they had scrutinized to a fault, or if her new medication fogged her judgement. Those damned pills made her groggier than the doctor had warned and were giving her the worst reoccurring nightmares. She'd woken up several times that past week, convinced the dead were still alive.

Gloria strolled between the circular tables, straightening a few cloth napkins, flicking a speck of invisible dust off a gleaming silver plate. She searched for the positives. It was obvious the decorating team had been dedicated, from the floral centerpieces of ivy and fresh peonies to the exact range of silvers and whites and appropriate bluish grays. Lighting was arranged as requested, the brightest bulbs shining on the fanned photo spread. For weeks, they had painted frames of all shapes and sizes a bright silver, coating the wet paint in fine, flaked glitter. The rest of the room was subtle, softer—weaving forgiving watts and beams meant to simulate candlelight.

If Gloria could turn off her inner critic, she would see how impressive the décor truly was. The party planners had done all the classy design tasks high on Gloria's priority list, and they'd found a tasteful way to stitch in some of Autumn's ridiculous ideas. Autumn had sworn the party needed a dose of kitsch—a gaudy buffet of classic family recipes but also bags of Fritos, Oreos, and Raspberry Fig Newtons, each of which held its own secret fond spot in the Joyce family narrative.

Gloria had allowed it, and she had to give credit: it didn't look too hokey—plastic packaging nestled in a bed of fluffed, eye-pleasing tinsel.

"""

She'd allowed Veronica's flamboyant zines, too. Veronica designed anti-establishment mini-manifestos splattered with heavily Xeroxed photos of snarling punk bands and angrier anarchist-feminists. She'd taken the same aesthetic to family photos and anecdotes of the Joyce marriage, framing each page with midcentury clip art. Because Gloria loved her granddaughter, she not only permitted the hideous booklets—she placed them front and center with the parchment paper guest book and a pen that looked like an ancient quill. Gloria stepped back and gave herself full permission to lash out at the haphazard design scheme of the party's entrance, to find something to blame for her unwavering dissatisfaction. She couldn't. The food, the decorations—they weren't the problem. Something else was off.

It wasn't her appearance. Her dress not only fit, but it was almost too big. Gloria had been hesitant to buy a dress three sizes too small, not having the best history with sticking to diets. Grief strengthened her willpower. She owed it to her beautiful dead best friend to keep the snacks out of the cupboard, and she owed it to herself to keep secretly drinking and buying diet teas and laxatives. Artie had to get his snacks elsewhere. Gloria knew when he stopped on his way home for chips and Oreos, the crumbs and grease streaked down his pant legs when he walked through the door. Gloria was relieved that's all he stopped for.

She marched around the room, imagining the room bulging with music and laughter and people talking loudly about the past. She pumped the silence with the anticipated embarrassing and heartwarming stories, with the expected smells of French bread and garlic butter warming over an open flame. She smeared the pockets of vacant space with the future of the party she'd been planning for years.

She never told Artie her suspicions. He didn't need to know she'd found the beer in the garage, or that she'd opened the outside trashcan every morning, surprised to have found nothing but the household trash. She hadn't been able to find the smell, the one she could still taste. It was carved into her being, just like the scavenger hunt for counting serrated caps. She never found anything beside the cans hidden in the garage fridge. He came home. There weren't any suspicious phone calls. They slept beside each other. In her silent conversation with herself, she wondered if he could simply have just one or even simply want one.

Gloria shut and opened her eyes. She hadn't counted any bottles or caps. The garage fridge was filled with food, and her husband only smelled like cologne and mouthwash. She hadn't pried. His only transgression in the past two weeks were chocolate chip cookies and a king-sized bag of gummy bears. He made jokes at the dinner table. He scooted closer to her in sleep. Maybe marriage did evolve.

She shut and opened her eyes again.

The room was still a muted version of what she'd hoped for.

The whole room was dull, as if lying under a sheet of thin parchment paper. The sparkles, the colors, the shapes—all of it clouded, none of it looking like she had envisioned for the past five years, when she decided a party would atone the past.

This invisible fog had been here before. It had dimmed themed Christmas trees and packages she'd wrapped with the same precision used in holiday storefront windows. Clouds crowded Thanksgiving spreads although each dish looked like it lived in a glossy cookbook or in the later years, on a popular cooking show. The fog ruined her daughter's first steps, first loose tooth, first day of school, prom night. Her son saying mama for the first time. The day she became a grandmother.

Her wedding.

Gloria twirled around the room, knowing she couldn't simply waltz the truth away but choosing to do just that. She chose to scrutinize the room through someone else's eyes. Was everything where it should be? Was everything finished? Had all the Ts been crossed and the Is dotted? Each of these questions were answered swiftly with a quiet and comforting "Yes."

It would have to do.

A smile waxed over Gloria's face, squeezing her cheeks until they ached. For a moment, the blurry parchment began to dissolve. The room looked exactly as it was—colorful, glittering, and every tiny piece exactly in its place.

The heavy front doors swung open, ushering in a gush of salty air. Artie and Ethan followed, both looking uncomfortable in their crisp gray suits, their gleaming shoes clomping over the shiny floor. Artie's eyes met Gloria's. He had to be as happy as she was, excited and ready for whatever would come next.

Artie had timed his arrival perfectly. He had enough time to congratulate Gloria on a perfectly pieced together party, enough time to agree with her that Veronica's tiny magazines were tacky, cheap looking, but also the most endearing souvenir they'd ever had. There were a few spare minutes to flip through the programs, to find the charm in the photocopied photographs, in the fun vintage font of her well-crafted blurbs.

"I always wished she'd gone into journalism. Or advertising. She has such a way with words—she should've come to Allen's with me," Artie said.

Gloria squeezed the pamphlet between her hands.

"She sells these magazine in her shop. I'm sure she writes cute slogans over the desserts," Gloria responded.

"I know, but it would've been nice to have one kid come with me."

Gloria offered a sagging half-smile.

"Life is full of sacrifices," she said, rearranging the papers, the vase of flowers, fluffing the fake quill's feather. Artie restrained himself from vivisecting her words. Old Artie would have overreacted. New Artie let the comment roll off his back. He wasn't going to be impulsive. He wasn't going to waste time on unnecessary arguments.

Artie had transformed, even if no one knew it. His first transformation could be labeled a mistake—barging into a bar and ordering a drink. He knew about relapses and the necessity of abstinence; the phrase "you can't have just one" had been branded into his brain. Even when he went to the bar, he believed that crap. His hands had trembled around the slippery glass. He had been terrified to take that first sip, and so he left, still sober. He bought a six-pack and hid them in the very same garage he'd made his broken promise. Artie waited for whatever terrible thing was supposed to happen to alcoholics who fell off the wagon, even if he only bought the beer and never touched them. Nothing happened. Gloria didn't say anything, and he didn't slide into unhinged debauchery. He became a man who sat in a garage with beers he never drank. He mulled over his thoughts and still made it to bed before 1am. He made plans. He was in control. He transformed again. He bought snacks and candy instead. He spent time with his wife, letting her pick out the night's movie and eating the healthy smaller portions she swore were good for them. He drove home from his decaying career and drove past the bar without giving it a glance. For the past two weeks, Artie went to bed at the same time as his wife and never got the urge to sneak a few beers. He was a new man.

New Artie ignored his wife's passive-aggressive comment, wrapping an arm around her waist. Today, he wasn't merely a husband celebrating a long marriage. He was a changed man shaking off absolutes and stringencies. He could embrace nuance and complicated decisions. Gloria smiled at him, oblivious to all his latest epiphanies.

The venue's heavy doors whined open, a delta of people pouring in. Artie stepped into another transformation—that of a man celebrating a long, happy marriage. He became a man telling light-hearted jokes, licking cocktail sauce from the tip of his finger, swallowing stuffed mushrooms whole. Between columns of familiar faces—family members only seen once a year, a few old colleagues, and a couple unknowns—Artie was able to avoid the photos on the wall and the conversations he didn't want to have. He walked past the open bar and refused three offers for drinks, finding the virgin section of classic Coke bottles and bottled spring water. It wasn't an effort watching frothy beers and glasses of white wine slosh beside him. He told a few more jokes and answered questions about retirement. Nobody could believe he was finally doing it.

"But then again, those stores just aren't the same," several said to him.

"You mean *the* store," he responded to everyone.

"I mean, old-fashioned stores in general."

He repeated the same banter with a string of cousins, his sister, then a plumber who had retired last year and found it necessary to bring up Clyde. Artie wondered how old Hank made it to the guest list and wondered if he was part of that frantic Autumn sweep—where she had to find any and all lost faces to fill her personalized guest list quota.

"Your dad sure was hoping you'd be like him. He didn't think selling groceries was man's work, you know. Too much groveling to the customer." Hank blinked his watery old man eyes.

"I wasn't anything like him, though," Artie said out loud to someone for the first time in years.

"Oh, he knew that, too. Talked about how the apples do fall very far from the tree."

Artie tried to forgive this old man's rambling senility. Hank had to be about twenty years older, making him nearly a centenarian.

"Hank, when you worked with my dad, how old was I?"

"Oh, I started young—right about eighteen. You were about ten, maybe eleven. Pimple-faced with a funny teen boy voice."

Artie crunched the numbers in his head. There wasn't a magical formula to place this man years ahead of him. By every calculation, they were less than ten measly years apart. This shriveled man was his peer.

"Excuse me." Artie was already a few feet away from Hank when he blurted his exit. He was at the buffet, slathering toast with bruschetta, dragging carrots through a trio of flavored hummuses. He examined his warped reflection in the serving spoons. Was he an old man? Was he going to start rambling like that, losing the necessary filters to function socially? Artie glanced over his shoulder. Hank still stood where he'd left him, blinking his same watery eyes. Artie had to look away. He swung his head to the opposite side of the room. There was Bill.

Bill. He hadn't seen him since the funeral. His old friend was dressed in sleek tailored black with his hands buried in his pockets. His face looked as heartbroken as it had in June. Artie instinctively didn't want to talk to him, didn't want to be reminded that people die and never come back. But this was his best friend. This was Bill. Besides, he reminded himself, the new Artie wasn't operating on impulse anymore.

Artie marched with big strides, so he wouldn't convince himself to stop. He was in the middle of his last wide step when he noticed Bill wasn't alone.

On impulse, Artie spun around and walked away from his friend.

Daniel slipped in without anyone recognizing him, including Autumn. She was painting a Ritz cracker with a smoked cheese spread, the same cracker she caught when it fell off her plate after Daniel startled her by seemingly appearing out of thin air.

"Ta da," he said, opening his arms wide and wiggling jazz hands.

"Did they see you yet?"

"Who?"

"My parents."

"I doubt they'd recognize me, or even know I exist."

"Funny, because I figured my mom wouldn't stop scanning the crowd until she found you. I told her you were coming."

"And your dad?"

Autumn stuffed the entire cracker into her mouth and shrugged—knowing her dad didn't know Daniel was coming. His old wrong advice echoed in her head: *Find someone who can give you a good future. Find someone good for you.*

Daniel wouldn't give her a good future. He was exactly like her—full of ambitions that went nowhere, full of long lists of how they would improve themselves and failing at each step of the way, both parents of children who hated them.

"If you could have a regular job, what would it be?" Autumn asked out loud.

"What? Aren't we supposed to talk about love and the institution of marriage and how it failed us, but look at your parents?" Daniel shoved a stack of cucumbers into his own mouth.

"I wasn't ever married, actually," Autumn said.

"Why do you sound so sad about it? Consider yourself lucky." Daniel smiled too wide.

"Am I lucky? I feel like I failed, honestly. Look at them." She gestured to the dance floor, to her parents and other rare couples who had survived. They all danced the same, gliding to the left and the right, all of them knowing every word to "Unchained Melody." Autumn hummed, waiting for Daniel to say something.

"They're just people dancing," Daniel said finally, scooting closer. Up close, she noticed the red webs on the whites of his eyes, an eyelash that had freed itself. She could see a few coarse grays peeking out from under a flat black dye. She hadn't realized he dyed his hair. Her own grays laid under a blanket of ashy blonde balayage, freshly woven in last week at a salon her mother paid for.

"They're people who did everything right, aren't they?"

"I thought you said your parents used to fight all the time. At least that's what I remember. I also remember you said he was a drunk, a cheater."

Autumn couldn't take her eyes off the dance floor. The next song slid out of the speakers, the Supremes. The same people who had made it, who had a cushion of retirement and a completed checklist of smart choices, shook their hips and pantomimed every line of the song. They were having a blast.

Autumn smiled. Mascara stung her eyes.

"You're crying?" Daniel sounded genuinely concerned, dabbing her eyes with one of the decorative napkins.

"I didn't do what I was supposed to do." Autumn spoke extra slowly, forcing herself not to cry. "I made such stupid decisions."

"Did you? They brought us here, to right now—back to each other if you want to hang on to this whole 'marriage is a good thing.'"

"I made so many bad choices," Autumn held the napkin to her eyes, which were now wet and smeared with black. *And I made others make bad choices, too*. Her chest trembled with stifled sobbing.

"I think you might have had too many cocktails and too many thoughts. Let's go dance and have a good time." Daniel gripped the backs of her arms and forced her into the crowd.

✦

Ethan was charm personified, threading around the room and finding something in common with Veronica's entire extended family—and the strangers. He carried Edie around the room, fixing her a plate and setting her up at one of the cloth tables with the coloring books he'd insisted on bringing. He'd also been the only one to think about bringing blankets and the iPad they never really used. Edie would have a quiet station upstairs to go to once the party became cocktails and the trays of little French desserts. Ethan would be the one to carry up an assortment to Edie, knowing Veronica's daughter loved sweets and became overwhelmed easily. He was the same way.

Veronica knew he would probably eat them up there with her. Both zoning out on some Pixar short or vintage cartoon. Wasn't that what Veronica had always wanted? Wasn't that worlds beyond the world she would've had if she'd stuck around Edie's biological father?

Veronica imagined this party if she had done exactly that. She'd probably have concealer caked over bruises, terrified to talk to any male relatives, staring at the floor waiting for it to open and dump her into any warm abyss. Edie would probably be forced to entertain, an arm dislocated like Veronica's had once been, or maybe she'd have the whiplash Veronica had told everyone was from a car accident that never happened. Veronica wouldn't have a booming vegan bakery waiting for her at home or stacks of avant-garde punk rock zines adored by an entire community. She wouldn't have Ethan.

Veronica walked beside her charming boyfriend, listening to him deconstruct the aesthetics of the party and half-ignoring everything he was saying.

"The lights. Look at how they're arranged. That was intentional," he mused, craning his neck to better examine the glow of each bulb.

"Of course it was. Didn't you hear my grandma talking about it?"

But he hadn't. That was on her last visit. The one he hadn't gone to. Suddenly, all the nice things he'd done for Edie dissolved, and that was all she could focus on: another lack of commitment.

"I've never noticed such detail at some family party. My family would never have this kind of party, though."

Veronica stopped walking. Ethan did, too.

"My grandma has always been about these tiny little details. You guys could collaborate," Veronica said.

"What?" Ethan was visibly annoyed. She spun away from him, nose to nose with the photographs splayed across the stone wall. Her eyes locked in on her own image.

She was about three, wearing a rainbow shirt that rode up over her protruding toddler belly. Her hands clutched a pink balloon. Her whole family stood behind her. Her grandparents, their hair still dark, their faces smooth and barely middle-aged. Her mother, whose eyes looked away, probably looking for the next place to run to. A scrawny teenaged boy with teased black hair and a bleached-stained Bauhaus shirt stood next to her mother, his gangly arm around her waist.

"That's my Uncle Teddy." Veronica ran a finger down the glass, trying to connect with the mummified memory, her uncle's ghost.

"The uncle you just remembered existed? It's so strange nobody wants to talk about him." Ethan leaned forward, resting his chin on her shoulder.

Veronica peered farther into the picture, trying to remember that off-white paint, the floral couch. She noticed one of Teddy's hands was holding her own. Even in the faded image, she could see how tight her tiny finger wrapped around his was. She had loved him.

"Veronica?"

She turned around. Her mom and a new strange man were linked arm and arm. The man smiled.

"I've heard so much about you," he said. He had a gap between his front teeth. Stubble bristled his cheeks.

"I've heard that a lot today," Veronica said.

"I've heard a little about you, too," the man said to Ethan, whose charm was fizzled out.

"You probably haven't heard about me?" The man winked to her mother, who giggled. Another Johan, maybe. Some other wannabee artist promising her mother they would be rich and famous one day.

"That depends. Who are you?"

"This is Daniel!" Autumn said.

Veronica *had* heard of Daniel. A long-lost love from before she was born. A Tennessee boy obsessed with history, books, and blues. A boy who wrote poetry like John Berryman and knew how to develop photographs the real way. A boy who kept his head down around football players. Veronica wondered if her mom remembered telling her all those little details.

"Look at Bill," Autumn said, her voice weighted. Their gaze shadowed hers, landing on the old man walking with Artie. Veronica barely recognized him. Denise and Bill weren't a huge part of her life; they'd lived far away for most of it. But Veronica knew all about the era when her family was linked with theirs and how happy her grandma was to be reunited with her best friend for a few months before she died.

"He looks so sad," Autumn said.

"He probably is," Veronica said.

"Who's Bill?" Ethan asked.

"Bill and Denise were my grandparents' best friends. Denise is the one who died in the car accident."

Autumn stared at her daughter long enough to make Veronica feel uncomfortable.

"They were all of our best friends. They've been around for forever."

Bill walked alongside Artie, a noticeable slowness to his gait. His hair was thin and pasted to his head. Artie looked robust beside him, his own elderly characteristics dimmed by the rapid aging of his best friend.

"Oh my God." Autumn's hands flew to her open mouth. "Oh my God. Dee Dee is with him. Keith, too!"

Autumn ran to them. Daniel, Ethan, and Veronica watched her dash through a crowded dance floor before swallowing all these people Veronica barely knew with a single embrace.

Gloria's head spun. She'd been a ping-pong ball the entire party. She hadn't had time to pause at the photo montage, to taste most of the snacks. She'd only danced to a few songs, sweat glittering through her make-up like dew. Faces and hands swarmed her every second. Hugs suffocated her. Kisses left a dampness she couldn't wipe off. Her tongue tired of thrashing about with constant thank yous and her ears ached from the cacophony of congratulations. Gloria needed Artie. They needed more dances. They had only posed for one photo. This was supposed to be *their* day.

She couldn't find Artie because she was forced to listen to every single memory oozing out of her family's mouth—and not her nestled family, but cousins, nieces, nephews, random people looped by the tiniest string of genealogy. They remembered Gloria as Artie's teenaged girlfriend, her lankiness, and the way she stood pigeon-toed.

"Oh, and remember when I caught you two in the den? I couldn't believe a mute girl who stared at the floor all the time and wore dumpy clothes was so fast!" Maura, Artie's sister, laughed, her mouth full of half-chewed crackers. Her lips Barbie doll pink.

"You're lucky I never told my mom. She would've killed you!" Maura smiled, her clip-on beaded earrings flapping like wings. She looked so much like Dorothy now.

Gloria excused herself, allowing Maura to discover the mini fruit tarts. She walked to the seam of the crowded dance floor, tablecloths grazing her hands—which she hoped rested at her sides naturally and not in the gnarled fists she sometimes noticed in photos later.

The dance floor and buffet were packed. Autumn had excavated a lot of forgotten shadows from the past. Girls from high school who were now old ladies, some with their white hair short and curled the same way Gloria's own grandmother's had been. These women who had once been vivacious, smoking pastel cigarettes, and bleaching their hair a la Jayne Mansfield. These women cornered Gloria into another unwanted trip down memory lane.

"Remember homecoming? All the girls were so jealous of you coming with Artie."

"They wanted to know if you stuffed your bra."

The old women cackled. They couldn't be her peers.

"I didn't, but I do remember the looks you all gave me." Her voice was smooth and steady, young and sturdy. She pushed out a laugh. It was hearty and nothing like theirs.

"We all wanted to go with Artie. Lucky you, you got him."

One woman stared at Gloria through bruised pupils, caked-on mascara. Her face too taut to be real. Her hair dyed a glossy golden blonde. Gloria stared back.

Cheryl Anne Brown. The most popular girl in school who laughed at everything Artie said, who was sent home daily for scooting her skirt too high above the knee. A girl who glowered at Gloria every chance she got. A girl who unbuttoned her sweater one extra button when Artie came around. Gloria had caught him looking, too. Back then, she just stared at her shoes, waiting for him to know what he was doing was wrong. One time, Gloria went to see Artie, and his mother had pondered out loud whether he was Cheryl Anne's. Gloria never found out if that was a joke. Gloria trembled in old uncertainties. How alive they could still be.

"What about Denise? How is she? Is she here?"

Denise. Denise hated Cheryl Anne even more than Gloria did—and she wasn't quiet or demure about it. Cheryl Anne didn't just chase after Artie. Everyone's boyfriend was game. Denise plunged a steak knife into Cheryl Anne's car tires the summer after their sophomore year. She smeared glue over Cheryl Anne's brand-new pillbox hat three weeks before graduation. Gloria had forgotten the deliciousness of Denise's revenge, how unhinged it was. Maybe it was Denise's spirit swelling into her, looking this decaying version of Cheryl Anne straight in the eye.

"Denise passed away in June, but I'm sure you knew that."

Cheryl Anne smiled, and she suddenly didn't look that old. Her eyes weren't melting with degenerative disease, they were just like her own—a little worn for the wear. Pinched with crow's feet and moist with expensive moisturizer. She could still swoop in on someone's husband. She could still lay out a question and pretend it was innocent.

"Oh, yes. I had forgotten. I don't know how; it was so tragic."

Gloria didn't wait for her to ask any more questions because she knew Cheryl Anne would go for the jugular next—either alluding to whatever transposed between her and Artie fifty-something years ago, or she'd remember they had once had two children. Hopefully, Cheryl Anne hadn't found Artie. She knew he would avoid her—or any women like her. He'd mastered avoidance after making his promise in the garage knowing her trust was slow to return. Merely standing in line behind a woman at the grocery store made her uncomfortable. His hand grazing a bottle at a holiday whirled her nerves. His abstinence almost made her more anxious. He became quieter. They shut out the world. Even when they'd gone to visit Denise and Bill, he fastened his eyes on Bill and only talked about profit margins and touchdowns. Gloria hadn't known she'd noticed that tiny detail until now.

Gloria flung herself back into the party, giving guests elaborate narrations of the photos hanging from the wall. They needed to hear from her how great her life had been.

"Here we are at Pompei. You should go. All these people still frozen in ash, doing exactly what they were doing when they died. It's incredible!"

"Oh, here is Autumn when we moved to Nashville. Look at her sullen face. She hated everything back then."

"This is Veronica's first time at Disneyland. She's so happy to meet the princesses. I wish we had a picture of her during the fireworks. I'll never forget the terrified look on her face!"

Gloria had a caption, an elegy for each framed photograph. She'd crafted these stories for weeks, curating the best nostalgic experience. What she hadn't expected was how she would gloss over Teddy. She wanted his face there. She wanted to see him smiling, his arms noodled around her neck. She wanted to remember what his hugs felt like.

She wanted *him* here.

She didn't know how to talk about her child in the past tense.

"Oh, look at Artie and I here! Truth be told, we were both so stinking drunk that day. We were in Vegas and had just seen Sammy Davis Jr. I think it was amazing—I honestly can't remember. What I can say is, wow, look at us. We never took a bad picture."

Everyone agreed with her.

Artie survived the first hour of the party. He ate the snacks. He accepted the congratulations. He stopped at some of the framed photographs, the safe ones. A montage projected on the wall opposite the gallery of pictures, a woven blend of still moments and snippets of home videos. He had to congratulate Gloria on preserving their entire fifty-five years and then some. Watching her move across the room, truly in her element as hostess, did make him happy. It had been a long time since he'd watched her from across any room—it was usually only a cushion or two apart on the couch now, both tousled and wearing their dingiest. Here, she shone. She mingled with effervescence. She was able to touch upon each guest and he knew she was showering them each with personalized compliments. This was her special day. And like the photos, he let himself admire the moment as a spectator. A sober spectator holding a bottle of Mexican Coke because it was the fanciest celebratory drink he allowed himself to have. He stood at a distance from the party, finding his family in various tableaus of pure happiness. Veronica danced with Edie, Ethan bopping awkwardly beside them but smiling. Autumn threw her arms about wildly on the dance floor, her hair thrashing like flames. She danced with some guy who looked slightly familiar, but who wasn't familiar in some way at this party?

Where had Autumn found all these people? Old coworkers and friends from his car club in high school. A few musicians who had been devout fans of his failed music repair shop. They were still session players; they were still collecting enough money to survive. They still played guitars he'd built forty years ago. They were old like him but vibrant. They had stylish haircuts and suits by Manuel. They smiled, revealing teeth too white to be their originals. Artie talked to them at length, trying to soak up their gusto for life. He almost wondered if the shop could've kept him going. Another impulsive choice that might have been a mistake.

"Your old shop is some flashy new bar. We don't even go. Why go to that when we can just go to Tootsies or Robert's!"

"You gotta come out and see it, Artie. Now that you're retired, you can!"

He could. He could live. He could approach Gloria and see if this first year they couldn't just rent some overpriced RV with all the same trimmings as a new house. They could stop at all the cheesy sites—giant balls of yarn, dinosaur statues, whatever else popped up in the middle of nowhere. There were things he'd never seen in his own country. He heard Gloria talking about their cruise to the Mediterranean, but he had never been to Mt. Rushmore or the Grand Canyon, not from anywhere but a plane, and it just looked like some big brown puzzle piece from up there. He wanted to find her right now, while she glowed and gleamed, and get her to agree to this second, third, or fourth chance. This party was fine, but it wasn't real. Tomorrow was real. Dancing to Johnny Cash and Reba at some bar on Broadway in Nashville could be real. Seeing all the stretches of quiet nature between destinations could be real. Eating roasted chilis in New Mexico could be real. They could take the most unflattering pictures of these aged versions of themselves, and he would like them more than whatever glamour shot from 1967 twinkled on the walls of this overpriced party hall.

Artie patted his old friends on their polyester shoulders, his empty Coke bottle choked in his hand. He excused himself to the knitted clusters of people, smiling and nodding and agreeing with rushed fervency to their congratulations. Had anyone seen his wife, he asked the blur of familiar faces.

He found her standing at the edge of the dance floor, facing three women he didn't recognize from behind. What he did recognize was the tense expression on Gloria's face. He hadn't seen her look like that in years. One of the women turned slightly, and he immediately recognized a withered version of a girl who should never have been invited. Artie's first reaction was to find Autumn and chastise her for digging up too many faces and not running the list by both her parents. His next reflex was a rattling chuckle. It was just like when she was little, declaring the events she witnessed through the lens of a naïve child. Nice ladies and fancy perfume and how nice they were to her daddy. How angry he'd become at her and then at himself for believing she was too young to understand. Maybe at fifty-four, she was still too young to understand—and maybe Artie at seventy-three was too old to blame everyone else.

Artie couldn't go over to Gloria, not now. He pretended to dance, peering through shoulders and stone pillars toward his wife. Gloria and the former it-crowd of Lakewood, California continued their painful-looking chat, projected home videos laced over them. Gloria's cheeks and silver dress glimmered with the tinsel of their Christmas tree from 1980. They burned with Teddy's red sweater he'd received that year. Artie's half-ass dance faltered, and he bent his ankle in a way he knew would be sore tomorrow.

A sharp finger jabbed him beneath his shoulder blade. Artie swung around, startled. Another ghost.

A woman with glossy platinum hair styled like Veronica Lake beamed at him with bright red lips, a strong jawline, and a set of white veneers he hadn't noticed since Denise first smiled at him from her backyard when they were twelve. He batted away this memory of Denise, or tried to, because Denise kept tumbling back into his mind. This woman was almost identical—only a tad sleeker and slightly less petrified with fillers and collagen.

"Uncle Artie? Why are you looking at me like that!"

Uncle? The blurred space behind the woman sharpened, bringing Bill and his own younger twin into focus.

"Oh God, Dee Dee," Artie said to the woman, to his unofficial niece, "I didn't recognize you. You changed your hair."

"About a million times since I last saw you," Dee Dee wrapped her arms around Artie's neck and squeezed. Her arms were soft around his throat and smelled like amber.

Dee Dee's younger brother Keith came up and shook Artie's hand. Their father followed. Bill's handshake was papery, thin, flimsy. He looked terrible. His eyes were dark sockets. Tremors Artie didn't remember. Bones stretched under thin skin. Grief had devoured him alive.

"Bill, you must be so happy to see them!" Artie gestured haphazardly to Dee Dee and Keith. Both smiled at their father.

Neither Dee Dee nor Keith had been at their mother's funeral. Gloria hadn't understood it. Artie had told her everyone grieves differently.

"I know we both should have been there," Dee Dee said, reading his mind. She sounded so much like her mother. "I couldn't handle it, and I would have had to have made so many intricate arrangements. I couldn't handle those either. And, Keith, he didn't want anyone to see him cry. Dad said me and Keith are like Mom, and she wouldn't want us to waste our time at her funeral when we could be living. And that did sound like something she would say." Dee Dee smiled again, fanning her eyes dry.

Bill's mouth flopped into something resembling a limp grin.

"Denise did hate funerals."

Artie nodded. She hated reality just as much as he did. There was an instant kinship to Dee Dee, too. She was so far removed from the little girl digging in his backyard. Artie couldn't stop gawking at her, consumed by how every gesture and expression mimicked her mother to a tee.

"Show us around." Denise's birthed doppelganger waved her arms. It was uncanny—she was Denise incarnate. The dramatic performance in the simplest movements. The striking beauty. The way she casually convinced Artie to lead them to the photos he'd been avoiding all night. Artie found himself proudly narrating each piece of the exhibit as if it were the most profound capsule of time. There was a significant pause at the third photo in the set, a snapshot of the Joyces poised in front of their moving truck.

"I remember this day," Dee Dee leaned forward. Her breath fogged the glass. "I was so sad Teddy was leaving. He was my best friend." Her voice was so quiet it almost didn't exist.

Somehow, Artie had forgotten the friendship between Dee Dee and his son. They were destined for connection the moment they were born days apart. Their conceptions synchronized. The infamous cruise ship that Bill and Gloria were unaware was so iconic. Neither of them knew how he recalled Denise's coconut breath. The soft insides of her cheeks.

Artie's mind coughed up more cobwebs. Dee Dee walking first, holding Teddy's hand so he could walk with her. The two of them racing on bikes. Dee Dee purposely pedaled slow enough for them to both win. She was more compassionate than her mother.

"On to the next one," Artie said, guiding them farther down the gallery, his throat dry and itchy.

The next framed visions were innocuous nothings. Then, they landed at Christmas 1987. Autumn's big white hair and fishnets. Veronica's giant red bow. Teddy emulating his sister in whatever vampire look he was wearing back then. Artie remembered telling him men don't dye their hair, and they certainly weren't supposed to be wearing makeup. Teddy's eyes were lined with black. His face powdered ghostly white.

"I love this!" Dee Dee said, running her fingers down Teddy's tight black pants. "He sent me a picture of this look. I didn't believe it was real. His letters were just oozing with all this art and music he'd discovered. All the stuff Autumn loved, of course. He loved her even more than me." Dee Dee boasted just like Denise had boasted before her about every boy in California, and later, the world. She spun around, this time poking the corners of her eyes and pressing to hold the tears in. Some leaked under her fingers, dragging inky mascara down Dee Dee's smooth cheeks.

"I should have been there, too. Teddy would have wanted me there. He was so fragile, always wondering if anyone loved him." Dee Dee's beautiful face twisted into something ugly and slobbery.

"We shouldn't have moved away," she started speaking faster, louder. "I blamed my parents for years. Who moves their child right before their last year of high school? The Teddy I knew would never have touched any drug. I would have taken him to prom and applied to all the same colleges. I would have married him if he wanted to." Dee Dee puckered her lips and dropped her head. Artie tasted her regret. He could taste his own, too. He had made Teddy fragile. He had made his son question love and decision making, just like Clyde had done to him.

"Excuse me." Artie marched away from Dee Dee. He peered over her shoulder and found her brother and father actively consoling her. Men who knew how to love.

Artie was safer at a distance. He messed things up when he got too close. Even now, with him being farther from Dee Dee, she laughed again. Gloria laughed, too, no longer surrounded by her old nemesis and mingling with the neutral guests. Autumn sat with that same familiar man, talking with their heads touching. Veronica and Ethan carried separate plates of food to Edie, who scribbled furiously into a coloring book. They didn't miss him. They didn't need him. His presence was the same as Teddy's in the pictures, quietly hanging in the background. Teddy should be here smiling with them. They wanted him close.

Teddy. Teddy. Teddy. He didn't know if he was only thinking his name or chanting it out loud.

Artie headed for the bar with his head straight down, not wanting to catch the gaze of someone who wondered what would happen next. He ordered two Greyhounds and sucked each one down through their tiny stirring straws. It was just a science experiment, to see if he could cultivate numbness on cue. That's all he wanted. He only dug around through the buckets of melting ice and pulled out a Dos Equis as an additional safety measure. He held it with both hands, covered the label and hoped if Gloria looked over here, she wouldn't notice. He tried to stay invisible.

He slid behind a pillar and continued to observe. It was almost a reflex, the way he tore the cap from the bottle. To survive, he had to drink this one, and another, and another after that.

They'd either understand or forget he was even here.

The party dwindled down. Gloria couldn't believe the event she'd anticipated for so long was almost over. The trays once piled with food were now smeared slabs of silver littered with shriveled clumps of decorative kale. Empty flutes were Xs on bunched tablecloths; the catering staff rushed to scoop up lipstick-stained forks and plates pimpled with hardened cubes of cheese.

It wasn't over. The crowd was simply done eating. They were dancing and laughing and shoving themselves into the photo booth that spat out damp strips of funny faces, sloppy kisses, children sticking out their tongues. Gloria swished between the tables, drinking it all in, trying to remember what the room had looked like hours ago when she'd made sure everything was in its proper place. She wanted to stuff that moment into eternal memory, the way she stuffed boxes with photographs and arranged them like Jenga cubes into her closet. Before planning this party, she'd been terrified to slide out a box on its own—afraid every moment she'd worked to store with precision would immediately unravel. They hadn't. She'd yanked out multiple memories, and everyone had survived.

The music was loud now. Poppy and funky with a healthy pulse of sound throbbing through the walls and the polished floor. Music purred under her heels, which ached as badly as the rest of her legs and feet. That would be one good thing about the party ending, ripping off these shoes and constricting hose. But for now, Gloria would dance until her ankles turned gelatinous and every varicose vein burst. At seventy-three, she remained a pro at walking in painful shoes and pretending everything was fine.

The crowd of glittering dresses and smooth suit legs swallowed her once more. Heat and humidity radiated from the center of the dance floor. Hot mist spritzed Gloria's face while she shut her eyes and tried to find a dancing style to mesh with whatever this music called itself. Autumn was there, still with that boy Daniel. What a strange thing that she'd found him. How happy they both seemed, thrusting their arms up in synchronized uncoordinated dance moves. Gloria had to laugh to herself.

Veronica and Ethan were there too, lazily swaying and looking in opposite directions. Gloria knew that look well. She'd worn it at many a party. It didn't mean they were doomed—look at her and Artie—just that things weren't going all that well in the now. She liked Ethan but also hoped her Veronica didn't make the classic mistake of settling. Sometimes, that nagging fear scraped into her—telling her she'd made that mistake herself. It was a dark curiosity, the possibility she was celebrating fifty-five years of settling. Gloria pushed the worries out of her head, choosing to decide her granddaughter was simply tired but still happy. She swirled away from whatever was bothering them, webbing herself deeper into the dancing strangers. Dancing made her think of Artie, whom she hadn't seen for at least an hour. She wanted to dance with him.

"Aunt Gloria!"

A voice played in the space between her and the others like an old Walkman, muffled with squishy headphones and a tape left too long in the sun.

"Aunt Gloria!"

There it was again. So strangely familiar and yet a voice she'd never heard before. Gloria opened her eyes, never realizing she'd shut them, and blinked through thick mascara.

It was Denise.

It couldn't be Denise. This woman wore more black than Denise would ever wear at once, her hair a bright platinum Denise had stopped wearing when she became convinced it accentuated the wrinkles nobody else could see. But it was Denise. Gloria teetered, the floor tilting slightly beneath her.

"Hey, too much champagne." Bill held her up with one trembling arm. He was the same Bill she'd last seen at the funeral.

Slack jowls. Thin, damp hair. Rail-thin.

"Bill?"

"You know me?" Bill said in a Jimmy Stewart impersonation Gloria had forgotten he could do.

"Don't you remember me, Gloria?" the ghost woman asked. Her voice was even syrupy like Denise's but with more bounce. She sounded like a teenager. A teenager who was always hungry and always full of effervescent energy the second she walked in the door. A teenager who loved the way Gloria made grilled cheese.

Deirdre. Dee Dee. Gloria had almost forgotten the girl existed. She didn't really exist now, not as Gloria remembered her: Denise's first child, wearing a chic white bonnet around her porcelain doll face. Blinking her long, thick lashes and drool like pearls on her open cherub mouth. She was as pristine and camera ready as her mother but never acknowledged the fact. Dee Dee watched her feet every time she took a step, all the way until she was five. She divvied up Skittles with Teddy, giving him all the red ones. She always let him go first. Dee Dee and Teddy had been inseparable since they were born mere days apart. They were latched together from the time they were babies propped beside each other on couches and pillows.

"I'm so glad we get to be parents at the same time," Gloria remembered saying to Denise. It had been lonely with Autumn. Artie out nearly every night or working long shifts. Denise and Bill still lived it up on a social scene Gloria had to find an overpriced babysitter to be a part of. Even then, she was yawning before the night was even truly starting.

"Oh, honey, I could never forget you." Gloria pulled the girl who was now a middle-aged woman close to her, shutting her eyes and trying to smell the past. The plastic toys Dee Dee and Teddy carried with gummy fingers. The bubble gum dancing in Dee Dee's mouth. The salty dust of potato chips scattered over the kitchen counter.

"You're crying." Dee Dee pulled away, gingerly touching Gloria's cheek.

"It's just been such a long time." Gloria hoped her smile looked happy.

"That's what Artie said." Dee Dee tucked her hair behind her ears, her eyes on the floor just like when she was two.

"You saw Artie already?"

"For a second. I don't think he wanted to talk about Teddy. I'm sorry—I can't imagine any of us can ever accept that he's gone." Dee Dee's chin shuddered, her lips contorting even as she tried hard to push them back together. "I miss him, too."

No, Artie wouldn't want to talk about Teddy. He barely allowed these pictures, and he was probably avoiding them like the plague. Artie couldn't handle raw emotion. Not when Teddy died, and not when he'd lost his father. He'd actually put a gun in his mouth. Gloria remembered walking in and the promises bubbling out of him, promises he upheld for so long. She was wrong to plaster Teddy all over this room, but she couldn't keep burying her child forever. He'd loved her too much to deserve that.

"We can talk about something else." Dee Dee's eyes were wide, a fake smile stretched across her face.

"I—I have to go to the bathroom. I'll be right back," Gloria lied.

Gloria darted over the party's remnants. The whittled crowd, the pile of painful shoes at the lip of a dance floor peppered with dropped napkins and glasses. The naked tables. The empty photo booth. The paper programs made by Veronica trampled around the room, ripped, wrinkled, dirty. That muscle memory resurfaced, dragging her across the room. It told her what she would find, how she would react. She'd been here before.

Artie stood behind a pillar sucking from a beer bottle like it were his mother's teat. From over here, it could just be him having a beer. It could just be him having a few too many, a few wobbly steps to the car, a headache in the morning. It could be someone making a rare ass of themselves.

Not to Gloria.

When she saw him now, and all the other times before, it wasn't just her husband drinking a beer. It was her mother. The strange men. The vituperative things spat from bright red lips. The way big costume jewelry felt as it smacked the side of her face. It was a husband changed by marriage, a mouthful of overnight beer. It was the way he smelled after leaving another woman's house. It was the drinks he and these women probably toasted to each other from a small apartment balcony, while Gloria changed diapers and tried to hold another baby inside of her.

No, it wasn't just a beer, not even here and after all they had been through. It wasn't just a failed marriage. It was the lies she'd gobbled up because she'd failed herself. She'd told herself it would be different. She told herself he wasn't lying when the shotgun hit the cold garage floor, a quiet thud nobody else heard but them. It was this party. The biggest lie of all. This was what she wanted when she shoved her fingers in her ears to drown out the sounds of whatever men her mother brought home. She hated the smell of alcohol in her mother's mouth, too.

Gloria's shoes glued to the floor. Artie held a fresh bottle to his mouth. The orchestrated lighting of the party twinkled in the green glass, like the Emerald City in the Wizard of Oz—the magical place where that big scary man was a sniveling nothing behind a curtain.

But Gloria wasn't Dorothy or Judy Garland or any other movie metaphor. She was a woman who had made a lifetime of choices she couldn't take back. She was another wife, another mother, another woman who threw a party people would talk about for years.

A party they'd never forget.

Chapter 26

November 22th, 2018

By 4 o'clock, Thanksgiving dinner decorated the dusted mahogany table. Gloria didn't recall pinching cheese shreds over buds of cauliflower and broccoli or mashing clumps of oily margarine into steaming potatoes—but there they were, the garnished dishes swirled inside vintage casserole pans. She'd gone through the motions as she did every year, suddenly finding herself holding a bouquet of serving spoons with two fresh burns branded into the soft underbelly of each arm.

Autumn arranged the steaming mound of seitan she'd made the night before, skirting its smooth sides with orange slices and anointing it with some thick amber glaze. Gloria had agreed to a revised holiday menu. Healthy-ish, if only to keep her newer clothes from getting too snug. Artie didn't argue or even politely ask for the traditional foods he looked forward to all year—but then again, he hadn't said much since the party. She snuck out to the garage at night to open the fridge—finding nothing but a box of Honest juices she had bought when Veronica was there with Edie. The smooth floor of the garage was slick and cold. The open space only invaded by their cars and overstuffed storage containers. It was quiet. Gloria didn't trust quiet.

There was a pattern Gloria could trace. After the quiet was destruction. The universe wouldn't give her another dead child or a husband with his head blown off, but Gloria didn't want to even predict what was going to come next. She didn't want to know—although not knowing was almost worse.

This Thanksgiving, Artie roamed the dining room, a small Dasani water bottle stuffed into his back pocket. Every time he sat down, it fell to the floor with a thud. It crinkled when he shoved it back in his pocket and wandered around the house. Gloria had forgotten the wandering. What was he thinking when he fiddled with the hallway cabinets or refolded a hand towel? After fifty-five years, she still didn't know. He remained a stranger.

"Mom? Mom? The oven." Autumn carried her heavy roast to the table. The oven bleated, coughing out pumpkin spice. Gloria couldn't believe she was about to eat a pumpkin pie made from a block of squishy tofu. She couldn't believe she'd never heard the oven and the timer she'd always found so loud and annoying.

Artie forgot how much weight a look could carry. His fingers compressed under the hard stares of his wife and daughter. When he reached for his fork, it was like walking through mud. He had already noticed what they thought were stealth little sniffs over his cup the past couple weeks. That's why he'd bought the big pack of water bottles. Just to get a little space.

Carrying more weight than the stares were the eyes that wouldn't meet his. They scraped over his fingers, over his water, over the door to the garage—but they wouldn't dare meet his own eyes. They didn't ask if he was sorry, if he cared, if he wanted to live or die. He wasn't a person to them. He wasn't the child with the skinned knee. He was the man of the house. The person who climbed ladders and fixed appliances that wouldn't turn on. He was Dad. He was Mr. Joyce, the other half of the Joyces on a checking account he hadn't directly accessed in thirty years. His name stamped on Christmas cards he never saw. His identity linked to a vested retirement, a nest egg, the funds needed to revive expensive annual vacations. They couldn't afford his failure. He needed to remain in place and not mess up their plans.

Don't worry, Artie thought to himself, spooning slippery roasted vegetables onto his plate. *There will still be a retirement. Take the girls. Tell the world whatever you want about me.*

Next, he sliced an end from Autumn's roast. He glanced over, ready to compliment how good it looked, but she was twisting her napkin between her hands and wouldn't look up from the strangulation of the cloth. She hated him, too. He knew seeing him drink stirred up old worry in her— he'd felt the same way about his own dad. He knew how to make himself invisible and meek, too. Artie remembered how relieved he'd felt standing over his dad in the coffin. His waxy face sealed shut, Artie letting out an exhale he'd swallowed for forty-five years. That didn't make him an ungrateful son, and he wouldn't blame Autumn for feeling that same relief. He just hoped she would cling to a few more positive moments—because, surely, they'd had more than he and Clyde had. If Teddy were still alive, it'd be different. If Teddy found him, his son would have to prepare a face of shock and grief—he'd have to disguise his relief. He wished it were Teddy who would find him. That was one detail he was agonizing over. Not the last day of work, not how to show up for Christmas, not how to pretend everything was fine for just one more month.

He only worried about who was going to find him.

Autumn sliced sharp triangles into the tofu pumpkin pie. She scooped a dollop of TruWhip on each one and sprinkled cinnamon over that. The lighting in the kitchen was big and bright, so she snapped a photo, saving them to post later and maybe to send one to Daniel who was having his daughters over. Autumn had wanted to invite them all here although now she couldn't imagine them sitting at that quiet table, probably scared to ask for salt and shatter the smoldering silence. Autumn was afraid to ask about a boardgame or even Crazy 8s. That was what she had missed most while living thousands of miles away. Family games.

Instead, she tried to be animated without being agitating. She slid plates silently over the cloth placemats and hoped both her parents could hear her internal thoughts. *Hope you like that splash of cinnamon! Can you even taste the tofu? Do you think we could all smile and play a little Yahtzee?*

They didn't appear to hear any of them. Her dad chewed with his mouth open. Her mother stabbed her own slice of pie until it began to sag, the TruWhip slipping to the side. The crust crumbled.

Autumn sat at the table with them. Swallowing soft pieces of pie without chewing. Her glass of Chardonnay was hidden behind the coffee pot. She'd been sipping all day. She couldn't wait to swallow the entire glass. Gloria used her fork to shave off the edge before smashing it to the plate. Artie ate a second slice without whipped cream. Autumn measured the length of the table with her eyes. It was so long for just the three of them. Big brackets of emptiness, giant swaths of autumnal decor on the same tablecloth her mother had been using for years. It used to be threaded with flecks of gold. Autumn could see Daniel and his daughters sitting here in a different time. He had said it was all too fresh for his daughters. They pledged allegiance to their mother, to the way of life she had wanted them all to head toward. Autumn fought an urge to call, maybe even Facetime to show him that this was the life his two girls wanted. It was fancy dishes that only came out four times a year and vintage serving ware in pristine condition, a traditional tablecloth, a miserable marriage lasting for decades. She wanted to show them the American Dream lived here in all its unblemished ugliness.

Instead, Autumn picked up as many plates and glasses as she could without dropping them, carefully setting them into the bare chrome sink. There used to be a white enamel sink. That wasn't at this house, though. That sink lived in the Lakewood house before Teddy was born. Another Thanksgiving where Artie's transgressions were the elephant in the room. Autumn was too young to understand why her mother locked herself in the bathroom to cry. She thought all dads drank the bottle beside their bed in the morning before swishing their mouths with black coffee.

Rinsing the plates with the spray nozzle, Autumn recalled another Thanksgiving. The one when they'd first moved back to California. Autumn had lain in her bed, terrified of her changing body and the thing thrashing about inside her. Everyone said the baby moving was magical. She thought it was creepy. The baby made her pee all night long. It was on her fourth or fifth trip to the bathroom she saw her mother walking down the hall toward the kitchen, tying the frayed belt of her robe so tight Autumn wondered how the woman could breathe. She watched from the open door, squeezing it all out of her, so she could get a little stretch of uninterrupted sleep. From the toilet, she heard her mother.

"You are worthless."

Something thumped against the wall.

"Who is it this time? Huh? What is wrong with you? Why don't you just leave us alone?"

She remembered her mother's voice grew louder. She remembered hoping the urine trickling out of her was muffled enough. The rest was blurry. Did her mother throw a ceramic casserole dish at her father? Were there really dusty shards stuck to the carpet? Her mother wasn't the type to throw things. She simmered in her anger. Only one remaining swath of the night's memory was entirely accurate—the moment she crawled into bed beside her snoring brother. He, the same thumb-sucking, bed-hogging, sleep-kicking urchin she was always pushing out of her own bed and sending back to his room. Teddy didn't send her back. He looped an arm around her and yanked her close. She didn't even mind the suckling sound of him nursing his own fingers, even though he was too old to be doing that.

What would Teddy think of them now? Would he believe their father had stopped drinking? Would he believe there'd be fifty-five years of marriage to celebrate? Autumn didn't know how to answer these for her brother. She hadn't even been able to squeeze the poison from his arm after dousing him in ice cold water, while their father sat in a garage drinking his tenth beer of the night. She didn't know Teddy well enough to warn him against the things she flung herself into. She never believed he would be as stupid as she'd been.

Autumn poured the last of the wine into her glass. She finished the whole glass, hoping that would be enough to wipe the memories clean.

"Hope everyone had a great Thanksgiving," Autumn said when she came back to get more dishes. Her parents nodded, taking synchronized sips of their waters.

Chapter 27

December 2nd, 2018

Veronica positioned the glowing tree behind her before accepting the Facetime from her grandparents. The crumpled pillow and mess of blankets on the couch where Ethan had decided to sleep was cut from the frame. Ethan hadn't spoken to her since he'd said he didn't want to hear her cry, and that's why he was sleeping on the couch. Edie found him in the morning, plucking his eyeballs open, blinding him with the marmalade sunrise.

"Why are you sleeping here?"

He'd lied and said he'd been too hot.

Veronica shook the morning from her face, poising her happiest smile toward the camera, saying hi to both her grandparents and her mother. Their awkward angles and frozen computer glitch expressions squeezed Veronica's heart. She almost broke character. Veronica noticed her grandpa not making his usual jokes, her grandma looking like she hadn't slept, her mother forcing a smile identical to her own. She wished she was superimposed in their misery, just to forget her own.

Edie squeezed under Veronica's arm, making faces at herself while the family all said hello to her.

"Ethan slept on the couch," the little girl said through fish lips. Veronica wasn't prepared for that. Luckily, her family excelled at pretending things never happened, so they said nothing and talked about the Christmas tree, Edie's Christmas list, and how long the three of them would be staying. Except Veronica didn't know if Ethan was coming. She avoided the question, and they followed her lead.

Except her grandpa. He didn't do the usual family dance. His head hung and his eyes drooped to the side.

"Grandpa? When is your last day of work?"

He came to and made eye contact with the lens.

"Next week. I'll have a big chunk of time before Christmas. Can't you and Edie come early? Ethan can always come after. We'll send him a ticket."

Veronica knew the bakery would be insanely, unbearably busy. She knew they would run out of flour and powdered sugar and giant tubs of Earth Balance. Customers expected her fondant snowmen, the iced cookies conjuring faded childhoods. Ethan would rot from stress if he had to handle it all.

But there was something urgent in her grandfather's voice. He needed her there.

Against rational judgment, Veronica said yes. She would gladly accept an extra two weeks with her family and whatever misery they were enduring without her.

Artie revered the symbolism of beginnings and endings. He'd always given special attention to finality. He celebrated the most banal ends with individual, personal ceremony. After he'd lost his first tooth as a child, yanking it out with gray thread and a brass doorknob, he'd stared in the mirror for hours trying to recall what a full mouth of miniature milk teeth looked like. He'd wedged his clean pinky into the soft gum, tasting lye and whispering prayers to the tooth fairy and her stashed collection of baby teeth. It wasn't too many years after that he found the personal stash of his teeth, along with Maura's and Glenn's, buried in his mother's white jewelry box.

Driving through thick morning traffic on the 605, Artie tried to remember what had happened to that jewelry box, to the teeth, to the rope pearls, screw on earrings, and rhinestone brooches. He squinted his eyes nearly shut and tracked the box from the family's storage unit to the donations they'd given the Salvation Army. The bronze ballerina pirouetting on a spring was gone. The tinkling music Artie had loved as a child would never be heard again. Everything came to an end.

Even his job.

This wasn't his final trip to Allen's, but it was one of the last. His eyes lapped up the parade of cars, the concrete walls built to block out the noise for these little suburban pockets he'd grown up in. That wall wasn't always there.

There had been the first and last day in his first home with Gloria. The Lakewood shopping center had an opening day, and one day it would close. There was an opening of the Pike, a closing, and a resurrection with a tiny replica of the rollercoaster none of them would see again. He'd left his childhood home. He and Gloria abandoned the apartment they blamed for those earliest marital problems. They believed the beach and a view of Catalina would solve everything. He missed that sense of new beginnings, of hope. They'd left that home. And left the ranch house in Nashville. And began again in a Carroll Park house Gloria had wanted to live in since she lived a few blocks away in an earthquake damaged apartment with her mother. They renovated and gave the house new life through Gloria's vision: a kitchen island, pink tile in the bathroom, a laundry chute they rarely used. She hadn't wanted to change everything—they salvaged the crown molding, the built ins, the tiny copper knobs Gloria found charm in. This would be his last home. It would probably be Gloria's last home. Artie hoped Autumn stayed with her mother, kept their nightly walks, and continued to make all those weird things Autumn called food. Inching along the middle lane of the freeway, he painted scenes of the afterward. Autumn pushing her mother to those counseling groups to mingle, and his wife finding a lonely old widower who had a few things in common with her. The thought made him sick, but it wouldn't really happen. Gloria was loyal. He would be the one searching for someone as lonely as he would be without her.

This was aging. This was dying. Imagining how everyone would live without you. He could go on for hours, all the way to a world where Edie was an adult trying to remember her great-grandfather. She might get the details wrong—he hoped she got some of them wrong, and he hoped nobody corrected her. Edie didn't even know he was a man. He was grandpa. He was separate from men. Artie wanted to keep it that way.

Artie turned slowly onto the exit, remembering the day before Veronica got her license. They'd practiced on the 605 because it was a little less cutthroat than the 405 and the 101. He'd been listing off driving tips for months. Veronica's hands high on the steering wheel, her seat pushed as far forward as it would go. Her cheeks ballooned with breath she wouldn't let out until they parked, and Artie took the wheel.

"Now, sometimes these ramps have a speed limit, and they don't mean anything. It can say twenty and you can go forty-five. Not on this one. Go slow."

Veronica's eyes were wide, and her fingers curved and white like nooses around the pleather wheel. Her bottom lip slid into her mouth, her teeth out like when she was a little girl.

"Like this?" she'd asked.

"Just like that," Artie had told her. That was twenty years ago. That was the last time she'd really needed him. It was only days later that she bounced out to her own car, cranking her music loud enough to hear through her rolled up windows. She sang on mute with her seat pushed back as far as it would go.

Artie walked through the automatic front doors of Allen's twice, pretending to forget something just so he could walk through them again. There would be a last day for walking through these doors, just like there had been a first. The doors had to be pushed open back then, bells connected so someone could hear you walk in. Produce was crammed into wooden crates, their prices advertised with big red plastic numbers. The registers clanged. The bags were paper sacks that tore at the seams. Meat was packaged in thin cellophane that was always smeared with blood. Allen's abandoned cellophane years ago, dressing its meat in compostable green wrap to change with the times. The produce section changed, too. Local farm products showcased on signs with chalk paint. Plastic transformed into biodegradable boxes. Fruits and vegetables shrank and wilted. They dimmed without the glow of pesticides and waxes. Everything dimmed.

He couldn't pinpoint the greatest era of Allen's. Artie was trained to sell media res. The current zeitgeist sold via phones and internet, a click of a button and bags dropped off at your door—no human interaction necessary. Allen's couldn't survive in that—they weren't surviving. At least, they weren't surviving before the superpower monopoly swept them under their wing.

They couldn't fool Artie, not in a million years. They could change the face of the store. Rip out the linoleum and replace it with glossy wood, too, simulate a bygone age of rustic community. It was all contrived nostalgia, meant to balloon somebody's pocket—even Artie's pocket benefitted from the suits and their daily tasks. Today, they wanted him to deconstruct and rebuild holiday endcaps. People needed to see something new and dazzling when they thought they only came in for their usual staples.

"Let's do a baking theme today," they suggested. They gave him the endcap positioned at the epicenter of all eight main aisles. They encouraged him to greet everyone, to name drop his own name to every customer. To remind them of who he was as if it mattered.

"Mr. Joyce, you're a celebrity to all generations of Allen's shoppers. Old customers love the security of seeing your face, and it makes the new ones feel we haven't completely erased history," they said, after showing him the boxes of allergen-friendly chocolate chips and five types of flour.

"Should I start telling them I'm leaving?" Artie asked, sliding in a row of coconut flour first. Dry white flakes dusted his dark blue jeans.

"Sure. I suppose now would be good. You only have a couple weeks left. But maybe say *retiring*. Leaving has such a somber tone to it. Besides, you'll probably still pop in?" The child in the designer suit smiled. Even if Artie suddenly got cold feet—and he wouldn't—why would he drive over here to buy groceries when there was a Ralph's, a Vons, a Sprouts, and a Trader Joe's all within a five-mile radius? Why would he just pop in to visit strangers? To check and make sure they still had his photo hanging up? And Joan's?

"I may pop in every once in a while," Artie lied. He wouldn't even haunt the place. Not even for a last time.

Autumn's eyes burned from the sugar high she'd been riding through a marathon of holiday baking. She handed the spatula to her granddaughter. Edie loved licking spoons and turning on all the kitchen gadgets. Autumn couldn't remember if her own daughter had been the same way, or if they had ever baked together. Now the three of them were at their designated spots on the dining table, each of them with a flour-dusted cutting board and a wad of sticky dough in their hands. Gloria swept their debris.

Veronica flattened the dough with precise choreography. She made a pastry lasagna between slices of wax paper, calling the design laminated dough. Autumn knew all about Toll House recipes on the bag of chocolate chips but nothing about baking procedures such as folding cold butter into envelopes made of dough.

"It'll be worth it for Christmas pastries, right? I make these for our shop all the time. People know how to make vegan chili and cupcakes but not croissants or danishes. That's what sets our bakery apart—we have the fancy desserts. That's probably why we're still open." Veronica coughed out an attempt at a laugh. Autumn heard something there, something she knew mattered. Her maternal sense was faulty, though, and she couldn't go beyond the initial sensation of knowing something was wrong.

"Are you worried about the bakery?"

"Why would I be worried?"

"Because you're here and it's December—I'm guessing that's a really busy time for you, isn't it?"

Veronica folded the dough again and pressed its seam, carrying it across her open tabletop palms. Autumn went to the fridge and opened it, moving several containers together to make an even surface for the dough to rest.

"Yeah, it's busy. But Ethan can handle it. So can all the other people that work there." Again, there was that something in her daughter's voice.

"Are you worried about Ethan?"

Veronica shook her head, but the corners of her eyes bulged with fresh tears.

"What are you worried about?" Autumn whispered so quietly, she wondered if Veronica even heard her. Her daughter looked at her and shook her head again.

"It's really nothing." Veronica's eyes swallowed the tears, and she put on the same happy face she always had, especially for those she kept at a safe distance. Autumn had to press harder, to try harder at this maternal thing. It didn't have to be too late.

At the table, Edie pounded her chocolate chip dough with the sides of her fists, interrupting Autumn's opportunity.

"That dough is so ready to become cookies," Veronica said, wiping her hands with the tea towel she'd flung over the back of her chair.

Autumn pushed her rolling pin over her own gingerbread slab. She rolled it to an even inch, watching Veronica teach Edie to use an ice cream scoop for cookie dough. One by one, wet balls dropped onto a sheet of parchment paper with a slight smack.

Gloria wiped the edges of the dining table with a wet paper towel. "Everything looks wonderful," she said, never looking up.

It was an unspoken rule all the Joyces had to watch *It's a Wonderful Life* the week of December 20th. Autumn had always preferred Christmas Eve, nibbling on cookies and drinking something hot out of a vintage mug. She told them how last year she sat alone on one of Jorgen's itchy wicker chairs drinking warm white wine and watching the movie in augmented Swedish. She hadn't minded the dubbing because she knew the entire script by heart. Even as the Swedish George Bailey went on and on at all the wrong times, she heard Jimmy Stewart's timbre, the voice every generation knew by heart.

Last December, Veronica had gone to her favorite theater dressed like it was 1946, and Ethan played along. It was the one Christmas tradition he went along with eagerly. He tolerated shortbread cookies, the excess food thrown away five days after the holiday, the sharp pine needles littering the floor and sticking to his socks. Veronica missed how much he hated Christmas. It was the perfect juxtaposition to her fervent excitement, to the Bing Crosby songs she hummed around the house and her obsession with Rankin-Bass. It wasn't evidence of incompatibility; it was proof they balanced each other out. She thought he'd had the same epiphany last year and couldn't help digging through the spiny branches while Ethan had crumpled the shredded wrapping paper, stuffing it into three different Hefty bags. Veronica hadn't expected anything extravagant—she didn't necessarily even care about diamonds. It could have been made from tin or pewter or a hammered spoon. It could have come from one of those quarter machines at the grocery store. She just wanted to see something tangible and real, a physical piece of commitment.

"I guess nothing matters if it's not a ring," he'd said, knowing exactly what she was searching for.

"I was just checking to see how dry the branches were." She'd watched her fingers freckle with tiny red welts from the pine bristles instead of looking at him.

Sitting beside her mother now, she wondered if Ethan was reveling in the freedom to hate Christmas. Was there even time for freedom with the number of orders probably coming into the bakery? On her grandparents' mounted wide screen TV, the angels blinked to each other in crystalline high definition. Autumn was already sniffling, her chin trembling. Veronica touched her own dry cheeks.

Gloria technically watched the movie with them. She sat in her cushioned reclining chair wearing sparkling readers and playing her internet games. Artie had sat with them for *Miracle on 34th Street*, holding Edie's dancing fingers in his own hand and answering her often repeated questions. Surprisingly, he hadn't wanted to stick around for the second movie.

"But, Dad," Autumn had said, "it's our tradition!"

"I just want to read Edie her bedtime story," he'd responded. Edie skipped to the room, a stack of Berenstain Bears books fanned under her arm.

"It's so weird that your grandpa didn't want to watch this with us. It's his favorite one," Autumn said right after George saved his brother from the frigid water and lost the hearing in one ear.

"We'll probably watch it again. Maybe when Ethan gets here," Veronica said.

"When does he come? Aren't flights going to be insane the closer it gets to Christmas?"

Veronica opened her mouth, but she'd run out of excuses for him. Ethan hadn't really given her a set date, which probably meant he hadn't gotten a ticket. She couldn't use Christmas as an excuse because he didn't care—and she didn't want to use her child as bait either. Although, that would get him to get a flight.

"Is he coming?" Autumn asked quietly. Veronica glanced at her mother. She'd wanted her mother to be sitting right beside her for so long. She'd wanted her close when the nurses told her she was pushing too hard—both with Edie and this last time.

"I—I don't know," Veronica admitted.

"Are you two okay?"

"I don't know that either," Veronica snuck a look at her grandma, who was pushing on her touchscreen with rapid little taps. She didn't hear a thing.

"We've been fighting a lot more lately. Well, arguing. Not actually fighting." Veronica stared at her lap, at the grease stains on her loose gray shirt.

"Because you've been gone so much?"

"No, not that. We did argue about him not coming. I just feel that he's a little distant—since...everything. I just feel a little worried about the future and I keep saying how worried I am and it's stressing him out."

"I don't understand." Autumn scooted closer so they could keep the conversation wedged between them.

"I want to move on from what happened. I want to get married. I was even hoping that stupid party would make him realize that it could be forever. Fifty-five years! Isn't that proof of success?"

"Did he see your grandpa at the end?"

"We left way before that. Edie fell asleep at the table."

"I wouldn't look to them for marriage examples." Autumn gently tilted her head toward the soft reclining chair. Gloria remained immersed in the neon bubbles bouncing across her glass screen.

"I know that now. Or maybe I always knew it. I didn't know about Grandpa, though—I mean, I didn't believe it, anyway."

"The drinking?"

"Any of it." Veronica didn't want to repeat the conversations she'd heard when everyone thought she was as sound asleep as her child.

"By the time you came, it was different. Or at least by the time you would remember. I don't think you and Ethan would be like them. It's different times and you guys aren't teenagers rushing to get married because you've broken moral code, you know what I mean?"

"You think—?"

Autumn placed a finger over her lips.

"I understand that urge to want to do it. I tried to get Jorgen to get married, but he was a different situation. He hated the idea of commitment. Turns out, he was committed everywhere." Autumn pushed out a weak laugh. "And everything happens for a reason, right? I've reconnected with the person I've been in love with since I was fourteen. It couldn't have worked then."

"But it will now?"

"I guess I don't really know. It seems like it could, though?"

"Isn't he fresh from a divorce and doesn't want his kids to meet you because they'll automatically resent you?" Veronica couldn't help feeling a little empowered knowing her words stung.

"I hate to put it in those exact terms, but I guess things are different when you're looking from the outside," Autumn stared ahead. George Bailey was an adult now, finding out Mr. Gower had given him a free suitcase for all the traveling that would never happen. This was the worst time to criticize her mother. She didn't need to be bold now. Veronica considered closing the conversation by suggesting they eat the rest of the Christmas fudge and top off their sugar coma with hot chocolate from scratch, that they pause the movie and just talk about anything for a few minutes without judgement. These were the conversations Veronica had wanted for years. She didn't suggest anything, though, not with the way her mother's face was twisting and with the reverberations of barely audible beeping coming from her grandmother's phone. Neon bubbles exploded quietly.

"Maybe you're right," Autumn said. "Sometimes I think I'm living in how I felt at fourteen and forgetting that forty years changes a person. Marriage and children and things not turning out how you want are their own sort of cocoon, like here." She motioned to the screen, to the restored reel of Jimmy Stewart and Donna Reed doing the best Charleston over a floor spreading open above a pool. Veronica had always wanted to go to a party like that. No party had ever been that fun, and the more she lived, the more she realized there weren't parties like that in real life. Her mom was right. Life and time wrung the dreams and plans right out of you. All these things you're supposed to want, none of them play out the way you imagined as a child.

"It's a lot easier when you're Edie, huh?" Veronica inched closer to her mom and spread a family heirloom afghan over them both. The great-grandmother who'd crocheted the pink and green thick yard had been dead for over a decade. Veronica realized she barely knew Grandma Dorothy. All she knew was the woman only served canned fruits and vegetables and had shag carpet and a room dedicated to smoking, even though nicotine glossed every wall in the house. There were games in the hallway closet that smelled like old people, and there was a permanent brown stain in the toilet, which had a squishy seat and metal bars on each side. The before was a mystery. She could ask her grandfather, but he wouldn't know anything outside of what he remembered. He wouldn't be able to go back to the Depression and see her childhood of oranges in her

Christmas stocking and standing in ration lines. He wouldn't be able to see his mother as she prepared for her own wedding day. They'd all seen the photograph on the mantle every Thanksgiving and Christmas Eve. Her great-grandmother had been beaming, her lips a dark gray in colorless gelatin. Nobody could ask her if she'd been truly happy that day.

"Yeah, Edie has it easy." Autumn laughed, slipping her hands under the blanket, poking her fingers through the holes in the design.

"She wanted to be a doctor last week. Today it was a princess, a mom of ten babies, and a chef who only makes pizza. I hope she does do everything she wants to do—except the ten babies." Veronica laughed.

"I hope she never stops wanting to do everything."

"I hope she never grows up."

"I hope she never wants to get married."

They giggled together, just as George Bailey told Mary he never wanted to get married. He wanted to do what he wanted to do.

They cried as Mr. and Mrs. Bailey burst from the church, pelted with tiny grains of white rice from all the hands of Bedford Falls.

Chapter 28

December 25th, 2018

Artie's final Christmas trotted along like all the others before him. He sat at his usual spot on the couch, holding the same roll of Hefty drawstring trash bags he held every year, wearing the same threadbare robe he'd had for at least two decades. A carbon copy of every Christmas before, where only the couch and Gloria's elaborate Christmas trees changed.

But this Christmas wasn't like the others. Artie would be dead in less than forty-eight hours.

He was the only one privy to the invisible, dark undercurrent slithering beneath the day. Nobody would suspect it in the living room mirroring the living rooms of every other middle-class suburb. He wasn't an anomaly. He was a boring, traditional man, born after the country's favorite war, a homogenous baby boom. All those babies grew up to live in duplicated domestic domains. Artie was destined for dull normalcy—unless he embraced the power to change that.

His entire life had been normal and predictable—holidays were no exception. Even the four measured sips of coffee he took before taking his spot as the robe-clad facilitator of Christmas day trash. Those coffee sips were a strange custom he had, and maybe an even stranger one to notice—he only kept its routine and observation because his own father had taken three gulps of his own coffee before plopping himself on the couch and scratching dandruff from his thinning hair. His dad's coffee had been accented with dark whiskey and was immediately refilled by his mother who took on the role of handing out the presents and maintaining the cleanliness of the floor while he and his siblings ripped through the traditional three gifts they were given each year. That was two more than most kids, they were reminded—as well as three more than the most unfortunate. Their stockings didn't merely have oranges but usually new socks and fancy candies they only saw on this holiday. Clyde's own stocking always bulged with a fresh bottle. It was the one part of the holiday he took real interest in. Artie avoided that tradition, even if he wore so many of the other hats his dad wore before him. Even in his drunkest years, he sobered up on Christmas.

2018's Christmas echoed the others before it, but Artie had worked hard to make this one stand out—and not only because of what would happen after. He hoped this day lingered longer than the day after. That their shared Christmas blotted out his actions, maybe even erased them and the questions his family would have. He hoped they would remember the Christmas Eve where they all sat down and watched *It's a Wonderful Life* together, where they all signed the note to Santa Edie wrote in misspelled hieroglyphics, where all the adults had to take turns eating more cookies after the little girl went to sleep and divvied out who filled the stockings and who wrapped the presents set to magically appear by the next morning. When they woke up, it was a chorus of sleepy laughter and feigned surprise, except for Edie. She squealed, genuinely believing Santa had materialized. Artie had joined in, acting as though he had never seen those stick-on earrings or the Rudolph PEZ before. The whole spectacle was heartbreaking, and he was thankful he would never watch that mirage shatter for Edie. Watching her hug each of her presents, eating chocolate before breakfast, was what he hoped would flicker in his brain before everything went dark. Artie shook his head. He had promised himself to be present and make this Christmas the best one yet. He not only wanted to curate a day that made his family forgive him but one that eclipsed the ones that didn't hold up as well as others. This day would trump the Kodak perfect moments. He would out-do every picture the family had ever framed. Crafting the best day of his family's life was supposed to be the scope of his focus, not fast-forwarding to the finish line.

After Edie worked through the first layer of gifts, the adults began handing out theirs. Veronica and Ethan were smooshed together beside Artie, both of their hands at their sides. Ethan had flown in on the 23rd and was set to fly out the 26th. A quick, dutiful trip. Artie knew it bothered Veronica. Obviously, she wasn't going to confide to her grandpa about relationship problems, but he knew her better than he knew his own children. She'd been distracted over the last few weeks, barely competitive during their board game tournaments, wearing a strange, sticky smile. She wore it now while opening one of the gifts from him and Gloria. Artie watched her open it. He hadn't helped choose gifts in years although this was one he had come up with. Gloria had only clicked the bubble for expedited shipping.

"These are so cute! Grandma, where did you find these?" Veronica held out cake pans shaped like the Aristocats, Little Foot, and Cheer Bear—all of whom had been her favorites within her first five years of life.

"I didn't find them. Your grandfather did," Gloria said from her recliner.

"Grandpa?" Veronica laughed, but Artie noticed tears twinkling in her eyes. Her smile was big and trying so hard not to crumple and bawl.

"Where did you find them?" she asked.

"There's this place that'll make anything. I found it on the computer." Artie glowed with how well he had done. He'd never been skilled at giving presents. He nailed it this time.

Gloria unwrapped hers next. She picked at the paper around the tiny box like it were chipped paint. It was excruciating to watch, especially since Artie was finding himself swooped in the holiday excitement of reading the reactions of his gifts. Finally, Gloria scratched off the paper and opened the tiny velvet box. She probably expecting the normal and predictable jewelry he bought every year. Every October, they visited the same jeweler, and Gloria would gush over some piece of jewelry, and that's what she typically received on Christmas.

"Oh!" Gloria held a dramatic hand to her heart and clinched her eyes shut. This was her usual reaction. He imagined she cultivated the reaction she'd always wanted to have with a real proposal. Only he and Gloria shared the experience of their engagement. A quiet conversation inside of his car preceded by, "Remember when we did...you know...a month ago?" Gloria had cried and left tiny puddles on his white shirt. He had looked stoic and strong and suggested a marriage they could achieve in just a couple months. Artie hadn't thought that far until that moment, but he did love Gloria, and he was supposed to take responsibility. They probably were going to get married after school, anyway. Isn't that what all the high school sweethearts were talking about? The ones who weren't going to college, and even they were planning an engagement after they received whatever fancy degree they were getting. Because Artie hadn't been planning it, he didn't have a ring and didn't have any money. He'd found a plain gold band at a pawn shop on Long Beach Boulevard. Since then, Gloria had received several upgrades—but back in 1963, she was married wearing a gold band with a diamond chip that she had to fit with a plastic piece on the underside of her finger, so it would stay on. Today, he added a ring with the biggest diamond yet.

"You were due for an upgrade," Artie winked, like he did every year.

"You remembered," Gloria whispered, not to Artie but to the ring on her finger.

"That's pretty, Mom," Autumn stood on her knees and craned her neck to look at it. "It's flashier than Dad normally goes.

"This one is special," Artie said. Gloria locked eyes with him, and for a moment, the room melted, and he was giving her that ring in 1963, and everything that followed for years and years was just as cinematic, everything she had hoped for when she agreed to marry him. Of course, that was silly, and he was giving it now on this perfect day he had been planning for weeks.

"There's something else," Artie said, digging under the tree to get the wrapped cube. The bigger box was ripped through quicker, the light catching in Gloria's new ring.

"A coffee cup," Gloria smiled. They all laughed. A cup paled next to glittering gems.

"Don't you see what's on it?" Artie asked. This was the real gift. Gloria spun the cup around and gasped. She dropped it into her lap, catching it before it fell to the hardwood floor.

"Artie," she couldn't speak. The cup passed around to Autumn and Veronica and then back to Artie.

He hadn't seen the cup in real life, just on the screen at work when he pulled away from contrived morale to sign up for Shutterfly and slowly scan in the family photos he'd been collecting. They were smaller on the cup, but Artie knew the impact they had. Family portraits, holiday snapshots, park picnics—all of them with Teddy smiling and alive, holding tight to Gloria's arm. Artie handed the cup back to Gloria. She held it to her face, twisting it around and pausing at each picture.

"Artie, you're cut out," Gloria said. Artie got up from the floor and peered over her shoulder. She was right. In every photo, he was sliced in half or removed completely.

"But *he's* there," Artie pointed to his son's small, pixelated face. "I'll email them tomorrow."

Gloria hugged the cup, not really worried about his presence in the photos.

Autumn was next. His poet whom he had tried for years to steer in any other lucrative position or into a lucrative marriage, neither of which had worked. He'd done the same with Teddy. Her gift was a stack of books tied with a fancy golden thread: a crisp thesaurus, an original edition of *Rebecca*, and a blank journal of a thousand pages.

"You've always been such a talented writer," Artie said, as Autumn loosened the string. That would be the lingering gift. Acceptance from her father. Authentic acceptance. Something he hadn't given to her before, and something he'd never been able to give to his son.

"I will," she said.

"There's something else under there, too." Artie pointed at the tree, whose branches were shaking off brittle needles every time they reached for another package. Autumn dug under the tree, finding the wrapped stick. She unpeeled the paper and held her new ballpoint pen with both hands.

"Thanks, Dad." She bounced over to him and gave him a strangling hug. He hugged back as hard as he could.

Artie missed Edie opening her gift—a framed photo of the two of them feeding ducks at the pond. He was almost glad he hadn't watched her open it. It wasn't meant to be the same as the others. It was meant for Edie to look at every time her memories blurred or smeared. If she saw the picture, maybe she'd remember the day she was held in his arms while they dug into a bag of romaine and grapes for a cacophonous group of ravenous ducks and geese. He wanted her to look at them years later and remember the slick mud and the way they held hands even when there wasn't a single car around, the way he protected her from the most brazen of geese. The picture frame was wooden and pink and had silver lettering on the top and bottom that read: *Grandpa's Girl*.

"So few kids in her generation will probably even have framed photographs," Gloria said, still clutching her coffee cup.

Artie and Gloria chose Ethan's gift together, a restored version of *Nosferatu* and a book on Boris Karloff Veronica said he wanted. He hugged them both and said thank you.

Artie's cultivated Christmas continued. The brunch, charcuterie snack, and dinner were filled with laughter, and everyone changed from pajamas into their holiday best. They propped up their phones and took family photos with the timer feature, facing the window with the best light. They snacked and gorged and changed into loose clothing before clearing the dining room table and making it a space for Clue, Life, Monopoly, and a side game of Guess Who and Connect Four with Edie. They each ate a piece of pecan and apple pie and sucked on melting fudge. Autumn, Veronica, and Ethan made peppermint martinis, and Artie drank black coffee. Gloria squirted lemon into seltzer water. Edie drank sparkling cider from an antique champagne flute and pretended to be a glamorous woman who drank a lot of "spicy drinks" and called everyone *dahling*.

When Artie went to bed after he watched *Christmas Vacation* and mused with his family over how much Chevy Chase had aged and laughed over Clark's comic eruption, he went to bed with a smile on his face, and right before he drifted off to sleep, he remembered his plan for the next day.

He couldn't go through with it.

Chapter 29

December 26th, 2018

Ever since Artie was a kid, December 26th had been somber and heavy. There was nothing to look forward to. The sky went black before dinner. Stomachs thrashed in pain from the gluttony of the night before. Serotonin bled dry.

Artie glanced at the wide space under the tree, the naked tree skirt. The siphoned stockings flung over the back of the couch. Everything was deflated. Even so, that wasn't enough reason to push him back in his original direction. The family's beaming smiles were freshly branded into his brain as was the way they cheered every time he solved the mystery in Clue, retired with the most money in Life, or when Edie beat him for the fourth time at Guess Who. They didn't deserve to find him dead. They didn't deserve everything that came before. This Christmas was his atonement, and he wasn't going to shatter what he had built in a single day.

"You ready?" Artie asked Ethan, who stood in the living room with his black bag flung over his shoulder.

"Yup," Ethan said with a little too much enthusiasm.

"Let's go." Artie led the way, letting Ethan out before he closed and locked the door. That's when he saw Veronica standing near the couch, holding one of the lifeless stockings with her face wrinkled, stifling a sob.

⁕

Headed for LAX, Artie couldn't shake the look on his granddaughter's face, piecing it with the withdrawn ways he'd noticed since she arrived.

"Were you all not able to get a flight together?" Artie asked, turning on his turn signal and waving at the line of slow-moving cars beside them.

"Oh, we didn't try. Veronica and Edie were already planning to stay until New Years, and I had to get back to the shop," Ethan said while staring out the side window.

"So everything is fine with you two?"

Ethan laughed nervously. A twang of sympathy prevented Artie from asking any more questions. He would've felt awkward being grilled by his girlfriend's dad, if he'd known him, and even more so by her grandfather. Plus, he liked Ethan and admired how he'd claimed Edie even before she was born and never saw the situation as baggage. Whatever was going on with them, it would work out.

"Actually, it's been a little rough lately. And I don't really know why. We've had arguments before, but these are little nitpicky things that explode out of nowhere." Ethan looked away from the window to the gear shift. "It's even worse now, though. We aren't saying anything at all." Ethan sighed.

"Out of nowhere?"

"It's not all out of nowhere, exactly. Just the timing is strange."

Artie clamped his tongue. He had to let Ethan talk at his own pace.

"Veronica's always wanted to get married, but she's been extra persistent—especially after we lost the baby. Because of that, she's doubting my commitment, I guess." His laugh was bitter this time.

Artie wanted to laugh but happily. That's all? She wanted to get married? No other problem had such a simple solution.

"Well, do you? Want to get married?"

Artie could hear the smack of saliva in Ethan's mouth each time he opened it to say something and then changed his mind.

"Marriage just hasn't ever been my thing, you know?"

No, Artie didn't know. It wasn't really anyone's "thing;" it was just what you did.

"But it's Veronica's thing?" Artie said slowly.

"I guess. I mean, aren't we basically married? We own a bakery together. I've been in Edie's life the whole time. We own a house. How much more married can you get? What, bring God or courts into it? That doesn't sound like love, does it?"

Artie tightened his fingers around the steering wheel. Not when you put it like that.

"Oh, Artie, I don't mean there's anything wrong with it. Times are different. You don't need marriage like you did before."

Artie smiled. "I don't know if we really needed it then, either. It didn't do anything for us that it doesn't do now. It's a ritual, a step, a rung in life. If you feel like you're already married and it would make Veronica happy, why not?"

Ethan stared at his hands this time.

"I just feel like we would lose ourselves and become what the world expects of us, you know?"

"I do," Artie responded because he did understand that.

When Artie came back from the airport, Veronica, Autumn, and Gloria were sitting at the table eating matching salads. Edie was dressed up like a mermaid, thrashing her fabric flipper around the floor.

"I already ate!" she announced before Artie could think to ask.

"I was showing them the Alaskan cruise," Gloria called to him. Artie sat in an empty chair and listened to the conversation as it resumed. Autumn and Veronica were talking a million miles a minute about all the things they would do on that boat, and Gloria narrated an involved schedule for each of the seven days.

"Did you book it?" Artie asked, surprised.

"No, not yet. But I already know what we're going to do—I've been thinking about it for years. I could list an itinerary for every day," Gloria laughed. So did Veronica and Autumn. Artie smirked. Yes, here it was. The retirement she had been waiting for. They didn't notice when he stepped away to pretend to be a shark in Edie's water.

"Grandpa, there aren't any sharks in this water." Edie sat up, her arms crossed, waiting for him to lower his hand-fin.

Just like that, he was irrelevant again.

He tried to find a movie or show or game on TV, but he couldn't focus on any of it. He tried a book next but read the same sentence twenty times, immediately forgetting each word. All he heard was a play-by-play of how his life was going to go. Repeat all the things he had done before but as an old man. Walk in Paris and hope his sciatica or sore hips didn't kick in. Go to a beach and leave his shirt on. Wear so much sunscreen he would look like a ghost. Relax. A lot of relax. Like today. Do all this sober because otherwise he would ruin it for everyone. Don't eat too much sugar or fat. Exercise as much as was comfortable for an aging body.

Artie tried to play Sudoku, but he kept messing up and his booklet only had two pages left. His former plan hadn't included things to keep him busy. He was supposed to be dead in twelve hours. Instead, he was walking around and trying to live without making too much of a ruckus or disturbing anybody else.

He scooped up his gifts from the day before, still in a neat little pile on the floor, topped with Edie's drawing. She had chosen to make a disjointed comic strip of them playing mini golf, building Legos, and feeding ducks. Artie carried these gifts to the big closet in his and Gloria's bedroom. He had a little space on the shoe rack. Fancy shoes he never wore lined the top shelf. The lower shelves were filled with a stack of photos he had collected, a notebook, and the tie Autumn had given him for Father's Day in 1991. How sick did he have to be to think using that tie would've been a good idea? As if Autumn wouldn't remember she gave it to him—she would know she had chosen the pattern of famous movie cowboys interlaced with the Marlboro Man's doppelganger. Now that he had decided to live, he sat on the carpeted floor with the tie on his lap and remembered the high-pitched cackle Autumn had let out when he'd opened it twenty-seven years ago.

"A Father's Day tie like no other!" she had laughed, holding her stomach muscles. They had all laughed because it was so ridiculous. Gloria laughed until she cried. Artie laughed until he choked. None of them dared to break the spell and acknowledge it was the first time they'd really laughed since Teddy was gone. Veronica had stopped asking where her uncle was. The photographs were replaced. A flat veneer where Teddy had been. Artie maintained the better life choices he promised, and in return, nobody mentioned Teddy.

Until this year.

Artie knew it would hurt to unearth his son again—he just hadn't known how much. When Gloria and Autumn had taken all the boxes and albums out, he'd grabbed a stash. Scanned them without looking for the coffee cup. He knew he couldn't face them until the very end. There wouldn't be another opportunity.

Now, there was. Artie held the pictures in his hands, ready to have that crucial conversation.

He told the little boy in the Tee-ball uniform it was okay to be afraid of the ball. Hell, it was okay to be afraid. He told him his dad didn't let him be afraid either. He told the little boy to run away if he wanted to, go pick the flowers or ride the swings, or do whatever you want to do. He told the boy on stage in his first performance that he was sorry he hadn't been there, that he'd failed as a father and a husband that night. He told the boy with his arm tightly around his mother, his cheek pressed to her hip, that it was okay that his mom babied him—maybe he was jealous because she didn't need him anymore, and the love Gloria had for their son was so unadulterated and genuine. Maybe he regretted destroying the last embers of love from his own wife and hated watching them rekindle for another. The list went on. He apologized to all the versions of his son and said all the things he couldn't say when the boy was alive. Everything he said was said too late. Artie pushed the pictures back to their place on the shoe rack and stuffed the tie far into a pile of forgotten clothes in case he started to change his mind.

He went back downstairs and found reruns of *Cheers* while Edie pushed around a Baby Alive in a toy stroller and pretended to find an adventure. From the kitchen, he heard the belching and purring of the dishwasher. Laced behind that was the steady discussion planning out the rest of his life.

Artie read a magazine. He made a sandwich. He ate half a bag of chips. He walked outside and picked up stray leaves. He went back inside and waited for dinner. He flipped through the channels. He tried to play with Edie. He waited for Gloria to tell him what to do. He said goodnight to everyone in his family. He shoved his fingers into his ears and told the voices in his head to shut the fuck up.

After everyone was asleep, Artie found himself in the garage opening a beer and staring at it. This was not how he was supposed to retire. He was supposed to be free from the shackles of work but not relaxed enough to forget the shackles of his habits. He just wanted one, really this time. He knew how it was to get carried away. What if he could just have one? Then he could just soften the edges, ease tension, avoid anger. One drink was safe and normal. He was normal and boring—he could have just one.

He set it on the counter next to his opened box of tools. There was no one drink, ever. He knew it. And if that was going to be how he was going to get through this last stretch of his life, then why wasn't he going through with his other plan? If he was committing to this family and to his marriage, then he shouldn't need the beer to survive.

He left it on the counter, left it to go flat and attract bugs and dust. He walked away, forcing his mind to conjure up the looks on everyone's faces when they opened their gifts. He was still thinking about that when he lay beside his wife, she clenched her body into a fist and turned away from him. He placed a hand on her shoulder, and she stiffened, not wanting to be touched.

Artie rolled away, too, squeezing his eyes shut and willing the next several hundred or thousand or however many days he had left to live to fly by and be as painless as possible.

Artie woke on December 27th with an epiphany. He'd been wrong about his plan the whole time. This wasn't a fear of failure or giving into demons.

He was merely speeding things up.

Everything has a cycle. Seasons spin on repeat for eternity. Holidays and birthdays multiply. Babies are born and people die. He was once afraid of death and always faltered when asked to clarify what really happened *afterward*. A cat, a grandparent, a brother, a son, a father died, and everyone wanted to know why. It was just life. It happens to each and every one of us. But what was life, really?

It starts before a person even knows they exist. It's parents and friends and a wedding day not planned for. A baby born, one you have to pretend is premature. Furniture made from cardboard boxes. A wife who burns toast because she's human, and a husband who flirts because he's human, too. A girl at work who seems fun and the antithesis of all things domestic, and so you let her blow you in the backseat of your car, the same backseat where you conceived your first child. When she says, "Fuck me," you oblige. She knows you're married but so do you. You bring your heartbroken wife flowers and promises you can't keep. She accuses you of not feeling anything. You believe you're the strong, supportive husband. You thought you proved that when you got her pregnant again and moved into a house with real furniture. She loses that baby, and you lose yourself in so many arms and legs you lose count. You don't even remember all their names. There is a little girl, who cried and shit as a baby, but now she wants to ride your shoulders and touch the ceiling. She has a big mouth, blabbing the things she didn't know she was supposed to keep secret. Your wife loses more babies. One of them stillborn on the kitchen floor. You drink more than you ever have before. More than the night your father said he was proud of you for holding down twelve beers without falling over. Your daughter's first word was beer. You told her they were drinks that daddies had after a long day at work. You told your wife they were to blame for the affairs. Your bosses ignore you coming to work blitzed because you're still more competent than the younger guys they hire—and you don't do it that often. The worst drunken offense happens on the cruise with your wife's best friend—at least you can say you didn't have sex with her but with your wife with whom you finally conceived a second viable child. You can't believe it was *that* child who overdosed. He was straight and narrow and liked to draw and paint and read stories. You wanted him to play basketball. You wanted to share a beer with him like your dad did with you, but when you tried, he cried and ran to his mother, and you made fun of him for that. You know he died thinking you didn't want him. He died thinking you believed him to be a sniveling mama's boy. You wished you had the courage to be a mama's boy. You drank more and more and more—and you forgot the side story where you tried to do something meaningful and different and it failed miserably, and you came back home with a pregnant teenage daughter who screamed "rape" in your face, and you still thought she had gone on a date with that boy and didn't think he was a rapist because his dad was famous, and he was a star quarterback. You sure didn't like the boy with the curly hair and the hazel eyes who gave your daughter records and political books. No, he wasn't right for her, and when you saw him at your anniversary, you didn't have the guts to admit you were wrong. Maybe you're wrong about Ethan. Maybe he's not such a nice guy. Or maybe you're wrong about marriage. Maybe you're wrong about growing old. Maybe you're supposed to wither and wonder every night when you go to bed if it'll be the last time. You still get yearly checkups and colonoscopies to keep yourself alive as long as possible. There must be enough streaming TV to keep you busy. Oh, and don't forget the scattered cruises, trips to rainy Portland, and dinners at chain restaurants. That's the cycle. That's life. Repeating each day wondering if when you close your eyes, you're closing them for the last time. Wondering if everything will go dark.

He was going to die, anyway. He could shrivel. He could rot while alive from a slow-burning terminal illness. He could grow so feeble an adult would have to change his diaper and wash him. He could forget who he was and think he was somewhere else in time. That was the most terrifying because then he might ramble out all the secrets and observations he'd kept bottled for seventy-three years. Or he could have a say-so, a choice. He could decide that December 27th, 2018, was it. He had a beautiful holiday with his family and was choosing to go out on a high note; he wasn't going to waste away. Artie sat up in bed, energized, his brain on fire before he'd even had coffee. Everything had a last day. He'd write notes. They'd understand.

His heart raced, but he still brewed coffee. It was his last, after all. He wasn't meant to find himself in his later years and start attending groups for bereaved fathers or emotionally deficient men, where they all sat in a circle and found the voice of their feelings. He wasn't meant to work on himself. If he were, he would've started earlier. It was too late, he told the small voice in his head that argued growth was still possible.

"Nope," he told himself. "Old dog, new tricks. Never happens."

He was so immersed in his new plan that he missed the periphery. He didn't hear the girls ask if he could watch Edie while they ran out, but he must've nodded because they left her there. He didn't hear her ask for lunch. He was too busy scribbling goodbye letters to all of them.

"Grandpa? Why won't you answer me? I'm hungry still."

He stuffed the last one in an envelope.

"Grandpa? Don't you hear me?"

He microwaved a corn dog, covering his ears when it beeped. Why was it so loud? He couldn't focus with all the racket. Luckily, Gloria, Autumn, and Veronica came back then because he had to figure out how he would do it. The tie was still a bad choice, and the thought of strangling to death was terrifying. That was something impulsive people did—he was executing a refined plan.

"Artie? Are you okay?" Gloria asked. He could hear the judgment in her voice and saw it on the face of his daughter and granddaughter. He remembered the beer. Did they find the beer?

"I'm fine," he snapped with authority.

"I'm hungry!" Edie was now screaming, and all four were staring at him. The microwave bleated for a single beat at a time. He knew exactly how many pauses there were between each beep. That was something consistent, something he could control. Counting the beats in a stretch of silence.

Veronica squeezed ketchup onto a pink plate, and he knew they could handle everything. He had been here all this time and couldn't get Edie a simple corn dog. He hadn't even considered ketchup.

Artie tried to feign his high note for the rest of the day. He poured Edie a glass of chocolate milk and asked Autumn about her poetry. He asked Veronica which cake she would bake first. He asked Gloria if she wanted to take a walk. To his surprise, she said, "Yes."

They only went around the block, but that was enough time for Artie to paint the last scene with his wife.

"Do you remember the first day we met?" he asked, holding her hand, the new ring digging into his palm. Gloria smiled.

"The day Denise dressed me all up, and you had the bloody nose?"

"That's the day."

"Of course." Gloria squeezed his hand tighter. The diamonds dug deeper.

"Did you ever think we would be here, all these years later?" Artie slowed his pace. His wife laughed.

"Not at all. Right before I found you, I was dreaming of becoming Denise's mother. I thought she was the most perfect human ever created. Did you know she spiked all her drinks? The coffee, the lemonade. I never smelled it on her."

Artie had been their neighbor his whole life. Gloria didn't know evenings at the Duffy house. Both Duffy parents were sauced by nighttime. Just like his own dad. Just like all the other dads on the street. He remembered the empty bottles of mouthwash blooming from everyone's trash cans.

"I'm glad we got here. There's been a lot of life between that day and today, hasn't there?"

Gloria slapped him playfully.

"This is the kind of thing you should've said at the party!"

"Oh, you mean instead of drinking too much?"

He shouldn't have mentioned it. Gloria's mouth snared mid-smile, while her eyes flashed.

"Yes, instead of that."

Artie let go of Gloria's hand and wrapped his arm around her waist.

"You were the perfect wife," he whispered in what he hoped came out as romantic and young lover-like. He hoped she heard him over the roar of traffic and choir of horns on Ocean Blvd. He hoped she'd remember the sound of the Pacific.

While Gloria and Autumn spiraled zucchini noodles and turned cashews into cream, Artie pillaged the medicine cabinet. Behind *Frozen* Band-Aids and half-empty bottles of over-the-counter pain relievers was the exact bottle he was looking for. He held it up to the bright vanity bulbs framing the mirror—one of Gloria's decorating choices. The bottle glowed amber, the shiny capsules like exotic bugs trying to get out. Gloria hadn't found a prescription that ever knocked her out. She hadn't taken a single pill since Autumn arrived in August, substituting them with some herbal concoction their daughter recommended. Gloria swore the herbs were better, that they gave her a good night's rest. He knew that was a lie. She was always half-awake, even with her eyes closed. Sometimes, she stared at the ceiling not knowing he could make out her face in the diluted moonlight. If luck could be on his side tonight, it would cause those herbs to work authentically and give his wife a sound sleep—that way she wouldn't later blame herself for ignoring the strange rustling in the closet.

Artie waited until they were all in bed, swallowing two of the pills with tap water he lapped from his hands. Ten minutes later, he took two more. His nerves hummed while he waited. His arms were slightly heavier. His legs were sacks of heavy cement when he walked into the garage and saw the flat opened beer right where he left it. It was fitting. He shouldn't get to enjoy his last drink. The beer was warm and thick, washing down two more pills. His stomach clenched, and he held his mouth closed with both hands. Then, he drank two more, and two after that, finishing the stale beer.

The cold garage floor, the slick wood inside the house—both became jelly. He struggled to stay upright, hoping he wouldn't bump into anything that would cause a commotion. Artie only had to make it to the closet, and when he did, he just had to sit on the carpeted floor and wait. He took out two more pills and chewed them raw. His hands fumbled in the dark for his stack of photographs, not that he could see them. Still, he put them on his lap and tried to sketch out Teddy's face in the rotating shadows.

He'd always been afraid of death. Hated open casket funerals. Couldn't drive fast enough past a fresh car accident. Hospitals reeked of it, even when he was only there for a baby being born. He was still a little afraid. He was freezing, and he knew that meant he was close. He had to calm those little bursts of regret, pet them like nervous dogs, stifle them like a leak from a busted faucet. Artie needed the end to be like he promised, with a loved one waiting to take you to the other side. It couldn't just be black nothingness. It couldn't.

He willed his eyes to see his son waiting for him, ready to hear his apologies in the afterlife. He stared at the hanging hems of dresses he didn't remember seeing his wife ever wear.

Chapter 30

2018

On December 28th, 2018, Gloria awoke refreshed. She hadn't slept that hard in years. She'd even forgotten to take those vitamins Autumn had suggested—the ones she had to pretend worked. She would forever feel guilty for sleeping so soundly.

She was the one who found Artie slumped in the corner of their closet with a pile of photographs spread across his lap. A circle of wet spread beneath him. She didn't need to look at the pictures to know what they were of. She needed to get her daughter and granddaughters out of the house, so she could figure out what she was supposed to do next. Then, she could cry.

They came back from getting the doughnuts Gloria insisted were necessary and found their father and grandfather zipped in a body bag, carried out by men of various styles of emergency uniform.

"Heart attack," Gloria heard herself explain, one she could later give to extended family, friends, and the online obituary she would ask Veronica to write.

Heart attack made sense. It was better than trying to relay how she actually found him. Eyes open. Flesh-colored foam oozing from his open mouth. Artie always slept with his mouth closed. Her own failed prescription bottle tipped over at his hip. An empty beer can in the garage. She couldn't admit suicide because she didn't want people to think her husband had chosen that instead of waiting out the rest of his life with her. A heart attack could just happen—even if seventy-three was slightly younger-than-average life expectancy. It was a side effect of aging, and everyone would take solace in it happening in the middle of the night.

He went peacefully, she and everyone else would lie.

If everything went as it should, Gloria's own mortality was supposed to be shaved to the nub. Everyone would expect her to follow the love of her life.

But she wasn't ready to die yet.

She revised the Alaskan cruise, trading in Artie's ticket for three new ones. A girls' trip where they could celebrate and mourn at the same time. She thought about the trip dangling on the horizon while she navigated this new role of widow. This was the only marital phase she'd ignored as a child mapping out her future life. Autumn and Veronica helped her plan the funeral and dissect the altered logistics of Social Security, estates, and retirement funds for one. At the funeral, she dabbed her eyes dry. She sniffed during the chorus of heartfelt eulogies. Gloria snuffed out the worry dancing in her head—how had she lost two of the men in her life to the same acute toxicity stamped on their separate death certificates? She had to hope her family wouldn't ever want to dig Artie's up—and if they did, she hoped it was after she was dead and absolved of responsibility.

After the funeral, guests gathered at their home. Autumn and Veronica laid out the family albums on the coffee table.

"Wow, look at this one." Someone she didn't recognize pointed to a picture of her and Artie at a Vegas blackjack table. She didn't tell them how he'd disappeared into the Golden Nugget after they'd posed holding hands.

"We saw Frank Sinatra on that trip. Or was it Dean Martin that time?" Gloria pondered, with a finger to her head. "I honestly can't remember. We saw them both so many times."

Everyone was impressed.

The guests marveled over their family's preserved lives, with Gloria presiding over them, giving exaggerated details to each exhibit. With Autumn and Veronica in the other room, she could paint scenes that never happened, moments that insinuated Artie and Teddy were inseparable. She molded moments where Artie cheered the loudest, where Teddy asked his father for advice. To her audience, she shaped stories she fantasized were happening to the unknown place her husband and son had ended up. In front of her curated albums, Gloria granted herself full poetic license to tell whatever story she wanted people to remember.

Gloria never told a soul about their pact. She avoided admitting their broken promises to anyone but herself. Although, she found herself often trying to piece together why Artie broke his. TV wasn't distracting enough, and Autumn couldn't always be there—not when she was chasing after some old boyfriend who was chasing after divorce lawyers who were chasing cash.

In 1988, months after Teddy died, she'd discovered her husband seconds before he was about to blow his brains out with a hunting rifle that had been nothing but a prop of masculinity prior. He'd never been able to actually kill anything, thank God. Gloria had never been able to forget the look in his eyes when he lowered the gun from his mouth. She never asked what she had looked like. Angry? Disappointed? Horrified? Whatever expression she'd worn, it'd been enough for him to burst into ugly tears, mucus sliding down his face like the first day they'd met.

"What are you doing?" she had asked. It had been such a strange and normal thing to ask—like he were placing the pickles on the wrong refrigerator shelf. Inside, her body spun hot and cold all at once. Pulses pounded in every internal cavity. A tiny voice she'd thought she'd swallowed years ago—asked over and over, *how could he do this if he loves me? How could he want to leave me like this?* Gloria had forgotten that clingy little girl who wanted nothing more than someone to love her the most.

"I'm sorry. I'm sorry." The words gushed out with thick spit. He spewed foamy bile on the garage floor. Gloria gagged on the stench of stomach acid and old beer. She held her breath when he held her in his arms and swore it was done. He was done disappointing her. Gloria believed him and made her own fatal promise. She stuffed Teddy's photos farthest back in the closet. Artie came home with bouquets of the reddest roses and pinkest peonies.

They watched movies on the couch.

They kissed goodnight.

They ate dessert.

They went for walks.

They drank unsweetened iced tea.

They watched bad TV.

They carved out a shared placid existence. It was safe and dull. Gloria insisted that's what she wanted, but she was the one who first shook it. She resurrected the dead without permission.

Six months after Artie died, she marveled over the extended daylight and Northern Lights with three generations of her own descendants. She held Edie's gloved hand as they slid over melting glaciers. Gloria shared binoculars with Autumn, neither sure if they'd seen an actual whale, or they'd both needed that memory to exist.

On the last night, Gloria wandered into the cruise's deck bar alone, wishing she had Denise to doll her up for the night. Why had they never taken a trip with just the two of them? They would've had a blast as old ladies flirting with the bartenders.

Gloria sat on the plush stool before asking the handsome bartender to whip up the most lavish drink from the menu. He shook her drink with the grandiose gestures he knew she expected, pouring her drink into a frosted pink glass and swirling in a paper umbrella.

"Ta da," he sang, plopping her drink in front of her and meeting her eyes for longer than was comfortable. He winked and then walked away.

For the duration of her drink, Gloria drifted into a crafted daydream. This bartender was the same one from 1971. Florin. He remembered how she liked her drinks and knew not to ask about Denise. He asked her how life on land was going. Gloria closed her eyes and imagined her life ending on a high note.

Acknowledgements

The first thank you goes to April Gloaming. They are giving space to some of the best voices out there, I'm honored that they gave my book a place in their literary family.

The second chorus of thanks goes to the encouragement of mentors and educators over the years. Thank you to Mrs. Barnett who called me an author in 1990 and to Mrs. Powell who said my writing made her cry. Thank you to Christine Guillen for remembering the imagery of the ring on the mother's hand and to Frank X Gaspar for instilling the importance of a writer's "place," as well as the importance of feline companions. Thank you to Dr. Marilyn Elkins, for not only inspiring me in the classroom, but in real life as well.

When I moved to Nashville in 2012, I claimed it was for the pursuit of a literary life—even if I was partially chasing a cheaper cost of living. The latter has changed considerably since, but the city's writerly landscape remains as full and vibrant as ever. Thank you to the Porch for making that possible, as well as the AMAZING indie bookstores that call Nashville home (Parnassus, Novelette, Howlin' Books, and the Bookshop to name drop). Thank you to East Side Storytellin' and the Nashville Poetry Fest and every other reading series I've enjoyed as a reader and a listener. Finally, thank you, Nashville, for giving me the crit group of my dreams— I'm a proud Critter.

And, last, but definitely not least, thank you to my family. To my Mima and Grandpa for always wanting to go to Crown Books. Grandpa remains my number one fan. Thank you to Grandpa George for preserving our family's ancestral story. Thank you to Grandma Sue for modeling a vibrant life that balances beauty, brains, exercise, and cats. Thank you to my mom, for showing me what it means to dream and to always believe in a creative life. To my dad, demonstrating that commitment to one's art wasn't always glamorous. To my brother and sister-in-law, to my sister, to my in-laws, to the bookshelves of my aunts, to the nights of Star Search, to the family stories made immortal via photographs and camcorders.

Thank you to my husband and favorite reader, Justin Dale Gordon. You are a true partner of all facets, and I'm beyond fortunate to share the creative and domestic with you. To my daughter, Tallulah: you taught me the true meaning of inspiration. Your baby era sleep schedule taught me the true meaning of discipline and the benefit of writing bursts. Thank you.

Ashley N. Roth is a Nashville-based writer, educator, and performer. Her writing has appeared in *Moonsick Magazine, Literary Orphans, Crack the Spine, Jersey Devil Press,* and elsewhere, with her short story "Adolescent" earning a Pushcart nomination. Her multimedia work has also appeared in various exhibits including the Flying Toaster Video: An Art Exhibit Dedicated to the 1990s, Bowiescapes, and Art All Night in Trenton, New Jersey. When not writing, she can be found revamping www.ashleynroth.com, starring in campy music videos alongside her husband, or perfecting vegan pastries with her ten-year-old daughter.